EVA HNÍZDO is a Jewish Czech, born in Prague in 1953. She is the granddaughter of a man who lost his life by deciding not to emigrate in 1938, and a daughter of parents who, after surviving the Holocaust, spent most of their adult lives under an oppressive communist regime. Eva studied medicine at Charles University in Prague and became a doctor. She escaped to the West in 1986 and obtained political asylum in the UK in 1987 with her husband and two sons. She worked as a full time GP partner at the same surgery in Watford for twenty-three years. Now retired, she spends her time writing.

Why Didn't They Leave?

EVA HNÍZDO

The Book Guild Ltd

First published in Great Britain in 2021 by
The Book Guild Ltd
9 Priory Business Park
Wistow Road, Kibworth
Leicestershire, LE8 0RX
Freephone: 0800 999 2982
www.bookguild.co.uk
Email: info@bookguild.co.uk
Twitter: @bookguild

Typeset in 11pt Adobe Jenson Pro

Printed and bound in the UK by TJ Books LTD, Padstow, Cornwall

ISBN 978 1913913 366

British Library Cataloguing in Publication Data.
A catalogue record for this book is available from the British Library.

I would like to dedicate this novel to my many relatives whom I never met because they were killed by the Nazis.

Acknowledgements

I WOULD LIKE TO THANK:

Stephanie Karfelt and Cecelia Griffith for their help and inspiration. Also Jana Šumicová at Theresienstadt, The National Holocaust Centre and Museum, and Petr Brod, for their help with Czechoslovak history.

I would also like to thank Julie Maloney from WRA Women reading aloud for making me believe that I am a writer.

Thank you!

Eva Hnízdo

Contents

PART TWO
Zuzana

PART THREE
Life without Magda

Main Characters

Magda nee Stein b.1928 mother of Zuzana

Zuzana Williams nee Novotna b.1953 daughter of Magda, married to Harry Williams

OTHER FAMILY CHARACTERS IN ALPHABETICAL ORDER

Aaron Garcia b.2000 son of Magda's niece Joan Aron and Juan Garcia

Angela Williams nee Gordon b.1933 Zuzana's mother-in-law, married to Richard Williams

Adam Williams b.1987 Zuzana's son

Amy Smith b.1999 granddaughter of Magda's aunt Judita

Ann Mai Chang b.1922 mother-in-law of Magda's nephew Nathan

Becky Smith nee Fisher b.1967 daughter of Magda's nephew Nathan and Jiu

Ben Smith b.1967 Becky Smith's husband

Bertha Goldman nee Grün b.1900 wife of the brother of Magda's uncle Samuel Goldman, mother of Miriam Goldman

Bruno Stein b.1888 Magda's father, married to Franzi

Dagmar Novotna b.1944 stepmother of Zuzana, second wife of Mirek Novotny

Dana Katz b.1920 ex-wife of Magda's uncle Ferdi

Eva Weiss b.1934 daughter of Magda's aunt Gerta and Victor Weiss

Ferdi Katz b.1898 Magda's uncle, brother of Franzi, Hilda and Gerta

Franzi Stein nee Katz b.1900 Magda's mother and Zuzana's grandmother

Gerd Goldman b.1928 Magda's cousin, brother of Irma

Gerta Weiss nee Katz b.1908 Magda's aunt married to Victor Weiss

Hana Stein b.1918 Magda's cousin, daughter of Karel and Tereza Stein

Hans Goldman b.1895 Magda's uncle, brother of Samuel, husband of Helena, father of Irma and Gerd

Harry Williams b.1953 Zuzana's husband, father of Adam

Heda Katz nee Abeles b.1880 Franzi's mother and Magda's grandmother

Helena Goldman nee Stein b.1902 Magda's aunt, married to Hans Goldman

Hilda Weber nee Katz b.1910 Magda's aunt, married to Jűrgen

Irma Aron nee Goldman b.1926 a cousin of Magda married to Petr Aron

Jack and Tony Kelly b.1987 twin sons of Magda's cousin Lucy

Jiu Fisher nee Chang b.1944 married to Magda's cousin Nathan

Joan Aron b.1969 a daughter of Magda's cousin Irma, mother of Aaron Garcia

Juan Garcia b.1965 partner of Joan, father of Aaron

Judita Fisher nee Stein b.1919 Magda's aunt, married to Simon Fisher, mother of Nathan

Jürgen Weber b.1908 married to Magda's aunt Hilda

Karel Stein b.1900 Magda's uncle, married to Tereza, brother of Otto, Bruno, Helena and Judita, father of Hana

Lucy Kelly nee Weber b.1948 Magda's cousin, daughter of Hilda and Jűrgen

Marie Stein nee Hanakova b.1913 Magda's aunt married to Otto

Mirek Novotny b.1924 Zuzana's father

Miriam Goldman b.1925 Magda's distant cousin, daughter of Samuel and Bertha Goldman

Nathan Fisher b.1939 Magda's cousin, son of Judita and Simon

Olga Stein nee Lustig b.1880 Magda's grandmother

Oskar Stein b.1924 Magda's brother

Otto Stein b.1908 Magda's uncle, married to Marie

Petr Aron b.1920 husband of Magda's cousin Irma

Richard Williams b.1933 Zuzana's father-in-law

Ross Kelly b.1970 son of Lucy and brother to the twins Jack and Tony

Ruben Stein b.1870 Magda's grandfather

Samuel Goldman b.1893 brother of Magda's uncle Hans, father of Miriam

Sean Kelly b.1944 Lucy's ex-husband

Simon Fisher b.1910 husband to Magda's aunt Judita and father to Nathan

Tereza Stein b.1894 Magda's aunt, married to Karel

Tomas Sedlak b.1923 second husband of Magda

Victor Weiss b.1897 husband of Magda's aunt Gerta

Other important characters not family

Bob b.1948 brother of Zuzana's friend Roxanne

Debara b.1930 mother of Zuzana's friends Bob and Roxanne

Roxanne b.1952 Zuzana's best friend married to **Derek**, mother of **Susan**

Siobhan b.1987 a temporary girlfriend of Zuzana's son Adam

Stein branch of the family

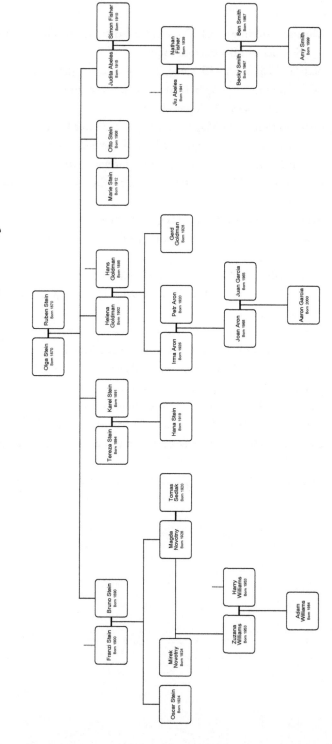

Katz branch of the family

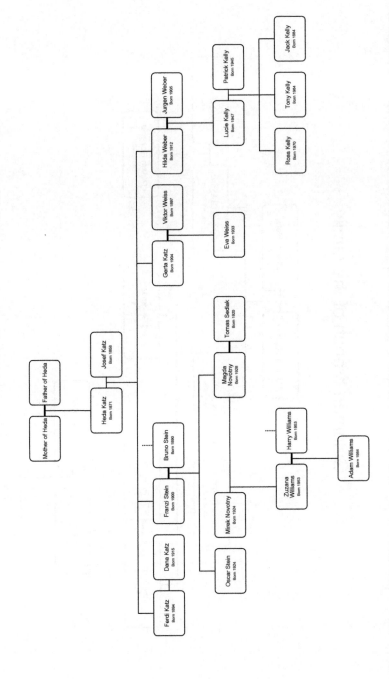

Goldman branch of the family

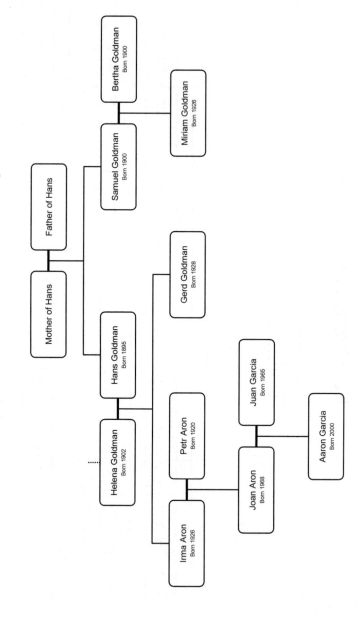

Williams branch of the family

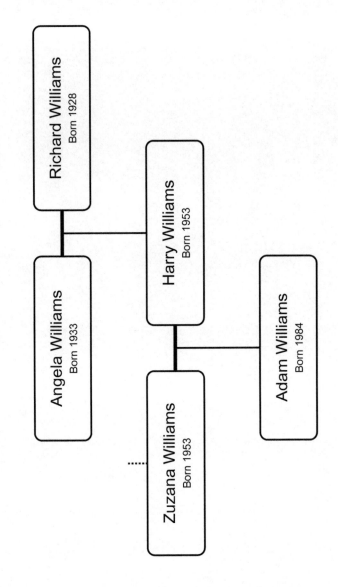

Richard Williams
Born 1928

Angela Williams
Born 1933

Harry Williams
Born 1953

Zuzana Williams
Born 1953

Adam Williams
Born 1984

PART ONE
Magda

CHAPTER ONE

Magda Prague 1940

THIS IS THE WORST DAY EVER — MAGDA CAN'T GO TO SCHOOL ANYMORE

This is the worst day ever, Magda Stein sobbed as she walked home. She walked past the renaissance palaces of Mala Strana, and across the bridge over the River Vltava. Normally she would look at the beautiful view of the Prague castle from the bridge. Today, she didn't notice where she was going. It started raining, and the raindrops were mixing with Magda's tears. People were looking at her, but 12-year-old girls cry easily, those strangers on the street probably thought she had an argument with her friends or lost something. This was much worse. Today, Magda had been told she couldn't go to school anymore.

The teacher asked all Jewish children to go to the school gym after lessons. The headmaster was waiting for them. He was pacing up and down on the small, elevated platform that was sometimes used for children's concerts and theatre performances, his shoes made a squeaky sound. He was pale and talked very quietly.

"We have been told that we are no longer allowed to have Jewish pupils. I am very sorry."

His eyes were looking on his feet. Magda did that when she was lying. *What will we do?* she thought.

Magda loved going to school. She always had good marks, and she liked to hold her hand up first when the teachers asked questions. Sometimes, she didn't know the answer when she put the hand up, but by the time the teacher called her up, she was ready to say something, and she was often right. It didn't always work. The week before, she didn't know the answer.

"So, what is it, Magda?" the teacher asked.

"Oh, I forgot! Sorry."

Everybody laughed at her. Usually, Magda was part of the popular group of girls who laughed at the ones they singled out as weird. Girls like bespectacled Ela, who wore ugly shabby clothes and read books in the interval instead of playing or talking with the other girls. Sometimes Ela was so engrossed in her book that she didn't notice the school bell marking the beginning of the next lesson.

"Four-eyed Ela, wake up, the teacher's coming!"

Ela dropped the book, rushing to her desk. Or the fat shy Jana, always eating something her mother baked in their bakery shop. The girls called her Stuffed Face. But when the girls laughed at Magda last week, she didn't like it.

Now, she couldn't go to school anymore. *My brother Oskar doesn't like school; he'll be happy. The only thing he likes is football.* Magda thought.

In the physical exercise lessons, Magda couldn't do the things other children could, jump over the vault, climb the pole or the rope. She always got the giggles and got stuck in the middle of the climbing rope.

"Come on, Stein, climb up or down."

The teacher hated it, but she had to help Magda to climb down. PE was the only subject where Magda never got the top mark. *Who cares?* Magda's brother Oskar was in his school football team, and he ran, too. He kept teasing Magda that she was fat and clumsy. *Well, he is stupid. I am far cleverer than he is. Even Daddy says that. It's better to be clever and clumsy than stupid and good at moving, like a monkey.* The image of her brother turning into a monkey made Magda stop crying.

Magda's father Bruno told her she was his little princess. When he was at home, Magda often sat on his lap and he told her stories.

Daddy loves me. Magda was not so sure about her mother. *Of course, Mummy loves me, too, but she prefers Oskar. Mummy can be nasty to me sometimes.* Last week, Magda ate half of the chocolate cake their cook Anna was preparing for dinner. There was plenty of it left for everybody, but Anna got angry. Magda's mother Franzi got very cross, too — she sent Magda to her room without any supper. The punishment didn't last long. Magda had a secret weapon whenever her mummy punished her. She cried, loudly, sometimes for hours, like an actress. Eventually, her father couldn't bear it and came to her rescue. When Magda couldn't cry any more, she started thinking about something very sad, like cute little puppies dying. Then she could cry again. It worked. Her daddy didn't want his little Princess to be unhappy.

When she cried like that after the cake punishment, Bruno took his daughter back to the dining room after exactly 10 minutes, she checked on her nice Longines Swiss watch that she got for her birthday. She was still allowed to eat her dinner. Not the cake, her mother didn't allow it. But Magda had enough of that cake anyway.

The cook Anna didn't seem to like Magda; she kept chasing her from the kitchen. It didn't occur to Magda that it might have something to do with her always eating sultanas and looking into the pots to find out what was Anna cooking. Once, Magda dropped the pot of soup she was tasting and Anna had to make the soup again from scratch. Fortunately, Magda didn't get scalded, but the soup went everywhere, on the hob and on the floor.

Anna used to be a cook for one of Franzi's Czech friends, who was moving from Prague to Brno. "She's a wonderful cook, but moody, I hope you can cope with that, Franzi," the friend said.

The friend was right, Anna had a temper. Almost every month, she gave Magda's parents her notice about something silly, only for Bruno and Franzi to beg her to stay. Yet, she always stayed and soon became almost part of the family.

Magda remembered when the Nazis arrived in Prague. It was 15 March 1939. They were standing on the pavement, Franzi was holding Magda's and Oskar's hands, Bruno was standing behind them. It was very cold for March, and sleet was blowing in their faces. Magda was watching those cars and tanks, driving on the other side of the road. Their steering wheels were on the left, not on the right like her daddy's car. The cars used to drive on the left, but the Nazis changed that in one day. They just kept driving on the right when they crossed the border.

The pavements in Prague were full of people, watching the invasion. That was the first time Magda saw her daddy cry, although he told her that it was the sleet hurting his eyes when she asked him. He was not the only one, many of the adults on the pavement seemed to cry. Now the Nazis were in power. What used to be Czechoslovakia was now called Böhmen und Mähren. The country was much smaller now. After the Nazis invaded Poland, too, the war started.

Magda used not to care if she was Jewish. Sometimes she felt it was great to be both Czech and Jewish. In December, Hanukkah brought the candles, the dreidel game — the dice with Hebrew letters. She liked the little gifts of chocolate coins and other sweets that she and Oskar got every one of the eight days of Hanukkah, and the festive meals. Sometimes, Franzi let her light the candles. But unlike many other Jewish families, for Magda's family, the celebrations did not end on the eights day. The family celebrated Christmas, too, in the house of her uncle Otto, who was married to a non-Jew.

Otto and his wife Marie didn't have any children, but they always had a Christmas tree and Aunt Marie baked ten sorts of Christmas cookies. She had a cook, like Magda's family, but she said that she preferred cooking the Christmas meal herself. All the family went there for dinner every Christmas Eve, and they always had fried carp with potato salad. Magda didn't like carp, you had to watch for bones.

"Don't talk, Magda, you will get a fish bone stuck in your throat and it would have to be cut out!" she remembered her father saying.

Bruno probably just wanted to scare her, but why not have meat instead of fish, and be able to talk at dinner? The Czech Christmas cookies were yummy, especially the little moon shaped vanilla rolls, made with ground almonds. Aunt Marie and Uncle Otto always left lots of presents for the children — Magda and her brother

Oskar, cousins Irma and Gerd — under the Christmas tree. Cousin Hana wasn't a child anymore, so she didn't get any toys, but they always gave her books. The other adults never got any presents. Aunt Marie said the presents were from Baby Jesus, but Magda knew very well that Uncle Otto was buying them. Aunt Marie was a Roman Catholic like the Stein's cook Anna. They both wore a cross on their neck. But otherwise they were very different. Aunt Marie was beautiful, whereas the cook Anna was fat and ugly, with a wart on her big nose.

"Anna's nose is more Jewish than mine!" joked Bruno.

The religion classes in school were once a week, always the last lessons in the day, so that Catholic, Protestant and Jewish children could all go to a different class. Magda used to go to the Jewish religion class. The rabbi was old and couldn't manage the children. There was such noise! The children talked, threw the wet sponge for washing the blackboard at each other and didn't listen to the lessons. Magda only managed to learn some Hebrew letters. The letters were also used as numbers, strange.

"You sounded like a class of monkeys, not children." Franzi once said when she was picking Magda up.

Later Magda went to the Protestant classes. The whole family was baptised shortly before.

"It might help us with the Nazis", said Bruno.

The Protestant pastor Mr. Homola was nice. The way he told those biblical stories was a bit like theatre, he changed his voice, made faces. He also made Oskar, Magda, and the other Jewish children feel special. When they joined the class, he said: "We must all respect and be nice to these children, they come from an ancient tribe that founded our religion. They are our brothers and sisters, and they are living through hard times."

It was nice, but it also made Magda giggle. *Tribe? Like the American Red Indians from the books Oskar reads? I am not Jewish anymore; I am a Czech Protestant.*

But the Nazis didn't believe that. *And now I can't go to school, I will never see Pastor Homola again.*

When Magda got home, Anna opened the door for her.

"Oh Anna, where is Mummy? Those stupid Nazis decided that Jewish children can't go to school."

Magda cried, and this time it was real. Anna embraced her, which was weird, but it was nice to be pulled to Anna's large breasts, warm and soft, like lying on a pillow. Then she started baking a chocolate cake. That cheered Magda up and she stopped crying.

"Big chocolate cake, really?"

"Yes Magda, and it will be all just for you," Anna said. "I will make something else for your brother."

"Oskar hates school, he'll be pleased!"

But she was wrong, he wasn't. He tried to hide it, but Magda was pretty sure he was crying, too.

CHAPTER TWO

Magda 1941

KING DAVID AND HIS STAR

Franzi was sewing and sobbing. It was strange because she never cried. She was stitching yellow stars on all their coats and jackets. Magda thought the stars were pretty.

"Why are you doing this, Mummy?"

"The damned Nazis!"

Magda giggled. *Mummy is swearing, and she never swears.*

Bruno came in and explained that the Nazis ordered all the Jews to wear the yellow stars to be recognised on the streets and started telling Magda it was the David's star, after King David from ancient history. Magda remembered the rabbi mentioning King David and how he killed the giant Goliath and became an important king. *He was little and clever, like me,* Magda thought.

"We should wear David's star with pride; we are a civilised, ancient, educated nation," said Bruno, but Franzi was still weeping.

Next day, Magda went out wearing the yellow star. People were staring. She saw Marcela and Dana, two girls from her school. Magda started running to them, waving, but they didn't look at her or talk to her; they crossed the street. Magda felt different, as if she didn't belong to Prague anymore. She tried to cover the star with her hand, but it was uncomfortable. A big older German girl in the ugly uniform of the Nazi girls' organisation – Bund Deutscher

Mädel — passed her on the pavement. She bumped into Magda, hard. *Was it an accident?* Magda wasn't sure. *I should have gone out on my bicycle,* she thought. But then she remembered that Jews must not own bicycles. Magda loved her beautiful new red French bike Hirondelle. It meant 'swallow'. When she was told she must give it to the Germans, she had deliberately let it go downhill, where it crashed into a wall. The front wheel and the handlebars were now bent, and the frame had been scratched. Magda had kicked it, too, very hard. That way the Germans wouldn't be able to ride it. She still had to give the bike away. The man collecting the bicycles had given her a funny look. "I had an accident two weeks ago," Magda had lied. "You should have seen my bruises!"

She passed the shop of the parents of a girl from her school, Jana. Magda and the other girls used to tease the fat, shy Jana, who was always eating something her mother baked in her bakery.

Jana's mother saw Magda with the yellow star and ran out of the bakery. "Here you go, little darling!" She gave the surprised Magda a large piece of chocolate. Magda didn't even manage to say thank you. She was never nice to Jana, calling her Stuffed Face. Did Jana's mum not know that?

Magda walked past the cinema. They were showing Vlasta Burian's new comedy. But Jewish people were not allowed to go to the cinema. Suddenly Magda just wanted to go home. Anna used the chocolate given to her by Jana's mother to make Magda a hot drink. It was nice. At dinner, Magda told her parents about the girls crossing the street.

"They used to be my friends and now they're not. They are horrible!"

Bruno looked at her and pulled her on his lap. *I am a bit too old for that,* thought Magda, but it was comforting.

"It is probably more complicated than that, Magdicko."

He used to call her that when she was little.

"They just don't know what to say. They see the yellow star, they know you can't go to school, their mothers are probably telling them that it is dangerous to speak to the Jews. You are all only 12; it is confusing and hard even for grown-ups."

"I'm nearly 13," Magda said.

He smiled and gave her a kiss. "Of course, you are almost a grown-up."

CHAPTER THREE

Magda 1941-1942

Magda still couldn't go to school, but she was getting at least some education. A group of Jewish children started going to Franzi's friend Mrs Klein, who was a teacher. They had lessons for six hours a day in her flat. Magda liked mathematics, physics, chemistry and geography, but she didn't think Mrs Klein was very good at those. She had textbooks to help her to teach those subjects, but she preferred history and French. It was not like real school; Mrs Klein didn't give them marks. Magda didn't like that.

"I would be top of the class if we got marks from Mrs Klein," she said at dinner.

"Stop bragging, you silly bighead!" said Oskar.

But Bruno said, "No, Magda is a good pupil. I am proud of her."

Oskar, who was two years older than Magda, couldn't go to Mrs Klein's lessons. It was winter now, and Bruno and Oskar had to shovel snow in the streets. It was hard work. The Nazis ordered all the Jewish men and older boys to do it. *Daddy is so strong.*

"I like working in the fresh air and my muscles are getting stronger – look, Magda!"

Oskar showed her his muscles, too. "Look at my biceps, I could be a boxer!"

But Magda told him that he couldn't box with a mouse and he started chasing her round the room, until Bruno stopped him.

Bruno Stein used to be a lawyer, but he didn't have his office anymore. The Nazis didn't allow Jewish lawyers to practise. The only thing that remained from his office was the golden door plate with his name JUDr Bruno Stein. JUDr meant Doctor of Law in Latin, Bruno told Magda once.

Uncle Otto came for coffee, without his wife Marie. He was upset, telling Bruno that a little town in the north of the country was being changed into a ghetto for Jews. Some Jewish men recruited by the Jewish community office were ordered by the Nazis to prepare the town. The inhabitants of the town were moved out. The old fortress town was changed to a ghetto, the adjacent Small Fortress into a Gestapo prison. Magda asked what a ghetto was, but both her father and Otto ignored her.

"Hitler has given the whole town of Theresienstadt to the Jews – how generous!" said Uncle Otto to his brother in that funny voice he used when he was teasing Magda. Otto was always joking. He sometimes pretended he couldn't see Magda because she was too little.

"Yes, damn Nazis. But it could be worse, my friend Hugo who works at the Council of Elders told me that it will be a place for older Jews and for the Great War veterans. He thought it would be better than living in Prague and that the Jews will be able to look after themselves in Theresienstadt. And we won't have to go," said Bruno.

"Oh Bruno, you and your optimism; if you were thrown in the river with your arms and legs tied, you'd be saying that things will get better until you drowned. Remember how you used to talk about the Germans, that they were a civilised nation, this mad antisemitism would stop? Do you see it stopping? It was obvious after they took over Austria. You were talking about the Germans living here for 600 years and that they are German Czechs, really. What nonsense!"

"Yes, I remember, I was stupid," Bruno said. "I didn't realise the Sudeten Germans would be so influenced by Hitler. You told me that you would be willing to give me a million for every German living in Czechoslovakia who would be happy being called a German Czech, remember? I can't see me becoming a millionaire that way! We should have left, like Judita and Simon."

Otto embraced his brother. "No, Bruno, we couldn't have left Mother here and she wouldn't want to come with us. We'll manage somehow."

Judita, the youngest sister of Bruno and Otto, and her husband Simon Fischer left in 1938. Magda remembered overhearing the argument. Everybody wanted to emigrate, but Grandma Olga stopped them.

"Family must stay together," Magda remembered her saying. They all stayed, apart from Judita and Simon. Judita whispered something to Grandma Olga after that lunch and Magda heard Grandma saying, "It's a mistake, but go if you must!"

Aunt Judita and Uncle Simon lived in California now; they used to send postcards with palm trees and the sea and photographs of their baby boy, Nathan. He was born about six months after they left. But then the letters stopped coming. The Germans were at war with America. They were at war with everybody, and they seemed to be winning.

Magda became an exceptionally good packer. She had learnt to pack so well that Mummy said she could do it as a job. It seemed as though almost everyone was being told to leave for Terezin, which the Germans called *Theresienstadt*, the town the Nazis made into a ghetto.

Franzi said they must help their friends with packing. Everybody was allowed 50 kilograms of luggage, so they squeezed in as much as possible. Magda wondered how people would carry it. Her family had their own cases packed, too, but had only been called once and in the end did not have to go. Bruno had taken Magda's mother's diamond necklace and returned without it, saying the transport cards were cancelled.

One of Franzi's two sisters Gerta and her husband Victor left last month, with Eva, their little daughter. Eva was cute, with curly blonde hair and blue eyes. Once, a German woman on the street said to her friend, "Look at that perfect Aryan child."

Aunt Gerta, who was also blonde, had covered her yellow star with her clutch purse and walked faster. She was laughing about it when she was talking to Magda's mother later. "That just shows how stupid those Germans are, with their Aryan race."

"They are too scary to be laughable," said Franzi.

Magda disliked it when her mummy was scared, because Franzi, unlike other mothers, was rarely afraid of anything.

Those in the family who had been sent to Theresienstadt sent postcards with very similar messages: *We are well and healthy. Please send us some biscuits and warm clothes.*

Nothing else. It was written in German, too. Many of Magda's relatives spoke German and Czech, but not everyone. A postcard in German came even from Auntie Gerta.

"Why does Auntie Gerta write in German, Daddy?"

Gerta's German was poor. Bruno always used to tease her about it but neither Bruno nor Franzi were laughing today. They looked anxious.

The teacher Mrs Klein went to Theresienstadt, too, but no card came from her, which was strange, because she used to be a good friend of Franzi.

"Mummy, what will happen to us?" said Magda, touching her mother's arm. "Will we all have to go to Theresienstadt, too? And who will teach me now?"

Franzi didn't reply; she went to the kitchen, started rearranging the drawers. She was banging the pots and cutlery, almost throwing them around.

"We'll be fine, Magdicko, don't worry," said Bruno, but Magda thought he looked worried, too.

Money was tight. They used to own a leather goods factory, but the Nazis had confiscated it. Bruno told Magda there was a name for this: Aryanisation. All Jewish property being taken over by non-Jews.

"It is usually Germans, but some Czech people are more than happy to steal Jewish property! The crooks!" said Bruno.

Otto used to run the factory, dividing the profits between his mother Olga and his brothers and sisters, Magda's father Bruno,

Karel, Helena and Judita. Now the money was taken by the Germans. Magda overheard her parents talking about not having enough money to pay Anna, but when Bruno went to talk to her, Anna shouted:

"I am staying – whatever those Nazis do, I am going to look after you, don't you worry!"

Anna's rations were better than the family because she was not Jewish. The Steins' ration cards had a big J on them for *Jude* and there were lots of things they couldn't get. Fruit, sweets, jam, fish – the list kept getting longer. But Anna was resourceful, and she shared her rations with the family. When she went home to her village, she always returned with food. It was illegal and she could be shot. Bruno kept telling her not to do it.

"You will get arrested at the checks on the railway station, it is not worth the risk."

Anna didn't seem to be afraid of the Nazis. Sometimes she brought meat, eggs and potatoes. She knew Magda liked jam and sometimes called her and gave her a spoonful. Magda used to think Anna didn't like her, but she had been ever so nice to her lately.

"Anna, what will you do when they send us to Theresienstadt like other people?"

Anna gave her a big hug. Her apron was full of flour; Magda got dirty from it, too, but she liked resting her head on Anna.

Magda did not have a teacher now that Mrs Klein had left for Theresienstadt. She still hadn't written, not even to her sister Herta, who was married to a non-Jew, a Czech man called Milos. Magda heard her parents talking about that. Being married to an Aryan saved Herta from being sent to Theresienstadt like her sister.

"Hilda won't go either; Jürgen will protect her." Hilda was Franzi's other sister, married to a German.

"What does Aryan mean, Daddy?" Magda asked.

"It's a lot of nonsense!" he said.

Herta came for coffee. "I haven't had a letter from my sister since she left. She might be ill, or dead!"

Franzi tried to calm her down, but she didn't sound cheerful either.

The Steins had recently received another card, the call to go to Theresienstadt. People were ordered to go with their luggage to a place on Veletrzni trida. Sometimes, they stayed there for days before going to the railway station.

"Don't worry, Franzi, I'll sort it out again," said Bruno, leaving with Magda's mother's diamond earrings. He came back without them, but the cards had been cancelled again.

"What will happen when I run out of jewellery?" asked Franzi.

"We will start giving him our crystal and other things – your fur coat, for example," said Bruno.

Magda didn't understand it. "Him? Who? Who are you giving my mummy's jewellery to?"

Bruno smiled but didn't answer. Later, Magda overheard him speaking to her uncle Otto. "The official I have been bribing had managed to cancel the calling cards so far; let's hope the Germans won't find out and arrest him."

"Oh, that man is clever like a fox; they won't catch him," Otto said, trying to sound more convinced than he was.

Instead of Mrs Klein, Magda started going to Mrs Abeles. Not to learn physics, chemistry or any other school subjects; she was learning how to make embroidered belts.

Mrs Abeles used to have a shop with belts and handbags. The Nazis had Aryanised it like everything else. When Magda learnt the word and used it, her uncle Karel said she had a very mature vocabulary. She felt proud of herself. Six girls, all Jewish, were now going to Mrs Abeles' flat twice a week. Magda liked embroidering the belts, mainly because she would get to keep one. Magda's belts were not as good as the ones the other girls made; she was never good at sewing. But she was learning. Mrs Abeles gave her a simpler pattern and it still looked nice. Magda liked Mrs Abeles. When the girls were making the belts, Mrs Abeles was singing. She taught them the songs, too.

"Karel Hasler, the man who wrote these songs, was arrested by the Nazis."

"Why did they arrest him? Is he Jewish?" Magda asked.

"No, Karel Hasler is not Jewish, he is a Czech patriot; this is why the Germans hate him," said Mrs Abeles, wiping her eyes. Magda wondered if they sent him to the same place they were sending the Jews.

CHAPTER FOUR

Magda 1942

MAGDA WORKS FOR THE JEWISH COMMUNITY OFFICE, BUT NOT VERY WELL

On the days when she didn't go to Mrs Abeles, Magda worked at the Jewish town hall community office. They were very busy, organising the transports and other things for the Nazis and work assignments and help for people. Otto and Bruno had an argument about them.

"Those cowardly brownnosers, they are almost as bad as the Nazis."

Bruno disagreed. "They do what they can, Otto, and they are trying to help. They are forced to do the things for the Nazis."

"Always so damn fair, you are like a fairy," said Otto in a jokey tone of voice.

But he wasn't smiling, and neither was Bruno.

Magda was worried that working in the Jewish town hall made her a brownnoser. She was supposed to file papers, but she was not good at it and found it boring. She spent her time on an empty balcony, sunbathing when the weather was nice and reading when it wasn't. She liked reading books about the adventures of schoolgirls. Magda couldn't go to school, but she could read about it. Her older cousin Hana said the books were rubbish and that Magda should read proper literature. She recommended *The War with Newts* by Karel Capek, which Magda found long-winded. *And newts, yuck!* she thought.

As Magda was either sunbathing or reading, the files kept piling up. The clerk, Mr Kohn, noticed. "Magda, have you done any work? There seem to be more papers to be filed here now than when you started!"

"Sorry, Mr Kohn," Magda said, blushing, and started filing.

But then she had a brilliant idea. She took the files home in a bag and burnt them. Magda did it secretly when nobody was home, so no one would be asking why she was lighting the fire in the summer. She knew her parents would be cross about that. In the town hall, nobody noticed anything. In fact, Magda was praised for doing the filing so quickly and nobody seemed to miss those files anyway. *And if the clerks are brownnosers, as Uncle Otto called them, maybe he would approve.*

CHAPTER FIVE

Magda 1942

UNCLE KAREL'S HISTORY LESSONS ARE EVEN MORE BORING THAN SPORT

Oskar didn't work in the Jewish community office; he worked in the parks, collecting rubbish. It was strange because Jews were not allowed to go to the parks otherwise. They could only go to a place called Hagibor, close to the Jewish cemetery. It was quite far to walk; Oskar often used to go there by tram to play football. He wanted to be a member of Maccabi Hacair, but his parents didn't want him to play for a Zionist club.

"We are assimilated, more Czech than Jewish," said his father.

Oskar had joined the school football team instead. He was dropped from the team when he was thrown out of school. A couple of times Oskar walked with Magda to Hagibor to play volleyball with the Jewish girls, but Magda wasn't any good. Tall Ida, playing on the other team was teasing her: "You're playing for us, Magda, aren't you?"

All the other players laughed. Magda didn't like Ida, who was sporty like Oskar. Magda thought she was stupid; they used to be in the same class and Ida's grades were never better than three. Magda's grades were always one, apart from PE. Ida was a member of the basketball team, volleyball team and a few others too.

"Who cares about your stupid ball games? You can't be a member of any team now anyway and sport is the only thing you are good at, you stupid Ida!"

Magda thought Ida might start fighting but she didn't. They were all laughing at Magda, so she went home. Oskar didn't like it when Magda said Ida was stupid. Oskar liked Ida.

They would be a good match with their stupid sporty brains, thought Magda.

The long walk home through the streets in the heat made Magda decide that the whole thing was not worth it. She was never going to go to Hagibor again.

Bruno's older brother Karel suggested that he could give the children some history lessons. Uncle Karel used to be a university professor, teaching history, but even if the Nazis had not closed the universities, they would not let him work. Karel, his wife Tereza and their daughter, Magda's favourite cousin Hana, had a flat full of books. Books were everywhere, on the tables, chairs, sometimes even on the floor. Magda's father called Hana the family intellectual. Grandma Olga thought that at 24 years old, Hana should get married soon. She called Hana an old maid and said something about blue stockings. Magda didn't think Hana wanted to get married. She always wore trousers, not blue stockings, and never wore lipstick. Her black hair was short, almost like a man's. She had studied medicine before the Nazis closed the universities.

Magda never liked history at school, but Uncle Karel's lessons were even worse. All those dates and countries fighting wars. Magda got into trouble. When she yawned, he asked, "Am I boring you, Magda?"

"Yes. History is boring anyway. Who cares about what happened so many years ago?"

Karel got offended and shouted. He was red in the face. "You will learn the hard way. Everything that happens now will be history one day. And similar situations keep repeating themselves in history. We should learn. Almost everything that is happening now has happened before."

Magda didn't ask what she would learn. She had enough of history.

However, Oskar asked again about the yellow stars. Didn't he remember they were the Star of David, symbol of the Jews, and how

Daddy said they should wear them with pride? That was, of course, stupid – nobody in the family liked wearing them; Mummy was always holding her handbag to cover it. But Oskar asked and there was some more tedious explanation coming.

"Surely, the Nazis invented those, Uncle Karel?"

"Now you see, Oskar, Jews were forced to wear some markings throughout European history. Even in the Islamic world before."

Oskar found it interesting, but Magda just could not listen to all those stories about medieval Italy or Spain and about people doing nasty things to Jews anymore. The Nazis were bad enough. She got up and walked out of the room.

"Magda, the lesson is not over!" Uncle Karel shouted after her.

Magda walked out anyway, but Bruno caught her in the door. Her parents had heard Karel's shouting and they were now very cross with Magda; Bruno even tried to spank her. *At my age!* Magda was offended, but Bruno stopped when she started crying.

After that, Magda's history lessons stopped. Uncle Karel said there was no point unless she took an interest. Oskar liked history and he was always reading something. That was funny because he was never any good at school. Hana asked him once why his school results were not better, when he read so much.

"School books are not as interesting," he said.

Now Magda and Oskar were learning French from Hana. Hana's lessons were fun. She told them stories in French, about a little girl who knew how to time travel and who travelled back several centuries. Hana called the stories *Les Voyages de Dominique.* Last week, Dominique went back to the French Revolution and narrowly escaped guillotine. *If Hana taught history instead of Uncle Karel, I might like it,* Magda thought.

For Oskar, Hana talked about *le football.* "*J'aime jouer au football.*"

Hana also taught them mathematics, physics, biology and chemistry. Magda liked that, too. Uncle Karel was teaching Oskar history for a short time after Magda's rebellion, but then he stopped. Instead, he gave Hana books about history for Oskar to read.

He told his daughter: "But Hana, don't let Magda read those history books even if she begs you. Magda is a creature of the present and future."

Magda wasn't sure if she should be cross, but not having to learn history anymore was good.

"Why are you not teaching us history, Hana? Could we add it?" asked Oskar.

"I don't know enough, not like my father. Just read these books he sent you."

Oskar read them all. Magda thought he was turning into a bookworm, a reading maniac like Ela from her school.

One day, Grandma Olga came to dinner and spoke about Hana. "She is a communist. I don't understand how Karel could allow that! And a Zionist, too. That organisation is full of Polish Jews."

Magda knew who Polish Jews were. They wore black coats and hats, and their hair was long with weird locks in front of their ears. Her family didn't like them.

"They are a disgrace, so backward. They just create antisemitism," Bruno said once.

"So, did they make the Nazis hate Jews?" Oskar asked.

"I don't know," said Bruno. "But why be so obviously different? And all that religion, eating kosher, praying all the time – it is stupid. This is the 20th century!"

Magda's family ate pork and only went to the synagogue on Yom Kippur. Bruno used to fast, but Franzi couldn't bear not eating till sundown, so Anna and Magda used to take her some food. Franzi would meet them in front of the synagogue and quickly eat the sandwiches, laughing while she did. Bruno would keep up the fasting until he was allowed to eat, but one day, when they all had roast pork with dumplings and sauerkraut for Yom Kippur dinner, Uncle Otto said, smiling, "It's kosher pork."

CHAPTER SIX

Magda 1942-1943

MAGDA LOVES HER COUSIN HANA

Magda asked Hana about communism and – what was it called? – Zionism.

"I have joined an organisation called Hashomer Hatzair," Hana said. "It's a Jewish socialist organisation; they want to move to Palestine and become farmers and workers, not just stick to the traditional Jewish jobs like shop-keeping. Jews will live outdoors, do sport and work manually. And eventually, we will have our own state."

One day Hana told Oskar and Magda about her trip to Russia, which she called the Soviet Union.

"Children, it is so wonderful: everybody is equal, nobody is poor or rich, the workers made life better for everybody. And women are free, equal to men." She started reciting some poems about the land where everybody is free, but Bruno, who walked in, interrupted her.

"Hana, please! Don't mess up their heads. Stalin is killing so many Russian people. And did you hear about Trotsky? The main reason why he had to go into exile was because he was Jewish. Stalin still had him killed in Mexico. Russia has always been antisemitic. If you must be involved in any of those movements, maybe Zionism is better. Although the Hashomer Hatzair are no better than communists."

"I should have gone to Palestine in 1938," said Hana. "I wanted to, but my parents stopped me."

Franzi joined in. "Who would want to follow the Zionists and move to live in the desert with camels? Are we Bedouins or what? I'm glad we stayed in Europe."

Hana laughed and kissed her aunt. "I'm sure you would be a splendid camel rider, Auntie Franzi."

Franzi kissed her back, but then Hana looked serious and asked Franzi, "But are you glad we stayed here even now, Aunt Franzi? With the Nazis in power?"

Franzi stopped laughing, too. "Who would have thought there was going to be another war? And about the hate the Nazis have for Jews."

Oskar, who had been quiet up until then, asked Hana to bring him some books about communism and Zionism.

"I will, Oskar – you are a clever boy."

"I always had better marks at school than Oskar," Magda reminded them.

"Magdicko, Magdicko!" said Bruno, and gave her a hug.

When her parents and Oskar left the room and Hana was going to go home, Magda switched to more important topics. "Hana, do you have a boyfriend?"

Hana blushed. "Yes, he came to the Soviet Union with me in 1936. His name is Vladimir, like Lenin."

Magda didn't ask who Lenin was; she was much more interested in the boyfriend. "Is he Jewish?"

"Yes, he is, and his family is very religious – that might be a problem. His mother wears a wig, and his father is a rabbi. They came from Poland, Lodz. They would never let him marry me."

Hana seemed sad, but Magda remembered something. "You once said that marriage is old-fashioned, that men and women should just live together." Magda remembered this statement because it created a big argument.

"You are from a good family," Hana's mother, Auntie Tereza, had shouted. "You have to marry if you want to have a man and children."

"Yes," said Hana, smiling. "Maybe we should have eloped and gone on living in sin in Palestine while it was still easy. With the camels, as your mummy says. The British don't let many people in now."

Just a few days later, Magda woke up in the night, hearing voices of her aunt Tereza and Uncle Karel. She crawled quietly in the hall and listened. Tereza was crying.

"Hana's gone," she said.

"Transport?" asked Bruno.

"No, her friend Pavla, the communist, came about an hour ago. She whispered and said she couldn't stay for long. She said we shouldn't worry; she was not followed. Pavla told us Hana and her boyfriend Vladimir crossed the border to Slovakia and wanted to go to Russia, but it's so dangerous! Half of the western part is occupied by the Nazis. What if the Nazis catch them?" cried Tereza.

Magda couldn't stand it, she loved Hana, so she burst in on them in her pyjamas with the pattern of little red roses. "What will happen to Hana?" Magda started crying, too.

The adults were so upset they didn't even tell her off for eavesdropping. Tereza hugged her. Karel said Pavla would keep them posted.

"She is in the resistance," he said, and then looked at Magda and frowned.

"Will the child keep quiet about all this?"

"I am not a child anymore, I'm even working, and I will not tell anybody, I can keep a secret!"

They let her stay. She listened to them talking and she held Aunt Tereza's hand. Aunt Tereza pulled her closer, stroking Magda's hair.

Pavla kept her promise. After about a month, she told Hana's parents that Vladimir and Hana got through to the Soviet Union.

"Maybe they will go to Palestine," Magda said.

"No," said Uncle Karel. "Apparently, they are trying to go to Shanghai, China."

Tereza started crying. "The Chinese, a cruel race – poor Hana. And the food, and they eat with wooden sticks!"

Karel told her off. "The Chinese civilisation is older than ours, and being Jewish, you should know better than to talk badly about another race."

Magda wondered when they would see Hana again. They didn't get any more news. Then another friend of Hana came to say that Pavla had been arrested by the Gestapo. People were disappearing. Most of the family and their friends had already left for Theresienstadt.

The Steins remained, but all Franzi's jewels and the mink coat were gone. *How long will Daddy manage to keep cancelling our calling cards for transports?*

CHAPTER SEVEN

Magda 1943

THE CALLING CARDS ARRIVE, AND THIS TIME THEY CAN'T BE CANCELLED

They were still getting postcards from Theresienstadt, but not everybody wrote. Magda overheard Otto saying they seemed like the postcards he used to send to his mother from being a soldier in the war. He called it the Great War, but when Magda asked if that war was greater than the one now, he said, "No, I hope not, Magda. I hope everybody will join and beat Germany."

"Those postcards were all lies, and the ones from Theresienstadt are, too."

Bruno and Otto usually argued. But this time Bruno did not say anything. He pulled those old postcards from a drawer. Some of them didn't have anything handwritten on them apart from the address. The rest of the postcards, both sides, were printed with *I am well and healthy* in various languages from the Austro-Hungarian empire: German, Croatian, Italian, Slovak, Czech, Hungarian, Slovenian...

Oskar asked Bruno why the postcards looked like that.

"So that the soldiers couldn't write the truth about what was happening," Bruno said.

He started telling them something more about the war, and this time Magda listened.

The calling cards came again and this time they couldn't be cancelled. Magda's family started to pack. Large suitcases with warm clothes, crackers that Anna baked, some books. Oskar wanted to take his football. At first, Franzi didn't want to let him, but in the end, she did. Magda didn't like the crackers, baked mainly from water and flour; they didn't have any taste.

Anna was crying. "I will save my rations and send you food to Theresienstadt, don't worry."

"Will you find another job?"

"I will work in a factory, they are recruiting," said Anna.

The cards told them to go to Schwerin Street in three days' time. It also said that they must hand over their house keys and that they could only take 50 kilograms each. Neither Magda nor Franzi could carry 50 kilograms, so they were going to take less.

Uncle Otto came with jam and some other food. He also brought two young men carrying ugly old furniture. They put it down and started picking up the Steins' furniture and taking it away. Oskar almost cried when they took away his beautiful American roll-top writing desk. Franzi and Aunt Marie were packing glasses, china, silver and even books into boxes. They took the paintings from the walls and replaced them with some prints Otto and the young men brought over. The men took all the nice furniture, paintings and all the boxes away. Otto was now working for the Jewish community office – Judenrath – as an office clerk, sorting confiscated Jewish furniture. His team put everything in storage, systematically dividing it. The storage was in empty flats whose Jewish inhabitants were deported. One flat full of armchairs, another flat full of beds, sofas, pianos. They also had paintings and carpets. One of the Judenrath employees decided which furniture was not good enough for the SS and those pieces were sold in auction. The better pieces were saved for a special auction for German SS, Gestapo and army officers. They were coming with their wives to pick what they wanted.

"Fortunately, I don't meet the people whose possessions are confiscated, but a week ago we took the furniture from my friend Aron. Do you remember that beautiful bookcase and desk inlaid with different types of wood and all his paintings? The Aron family were deported a month ago. I wonder where they are?" Otto seemed upset.

He told Bruno that one of the storages was full of grand pianos. The Germans were picking which piano they wanted. Some of them sat and played very well.

"If they are good musicians, they can't be such bad people." Bruno was always optimistic.

"They can't all play – one SS officer came yesterday, went over all the keys with one finger, producing a rrrrrrrrrrrr sound, and said he would take this one because the sound was very good. I doubt that he could play."

"I know you didn't want to work in the Jewish community, Otto," said Bruno, "but you are doing a good job helping people to hide things. Just be careful – the Germans would shoot you if they knew."

"How are you helping them, Uncle?" asked Oskar, but Otto said he didn't have time to talk now.

Magda looked at the men and asked, "What are you doing? Why are you taking our nice things and replacing them with ugly ones? And where are you taking our furniture and china?"

"Some kind Czech friends will hide it for us. We will get it back when the Nazis lose the war," said Bruno.

"The Krejci family and two of your former lawyer colleagues will hide those things for you, Bruno. I have sorted it all out. Mind you, who knows if you ever get it back from that miser Krejci even if the Nazis lose? Just wait and see, they will get used to your nice crystal and china, paintings and furniture. They won't want to give it back."

"You have to leave something so that it doesn't look suspicious," said Aunt Marie.

Magda noticed she was wearing her mother's last pair of earrings, red garnet ones. "Those are Mummy's earrings!" she said.

"Yes, and I will keep them for her till you all come back once the Nazis lose the war."

Franzi and Marie embraced.

"Are the Nazis losing?" Magda asked.

It was her brother who replied to her question. "Of course they are, you should listen to the BBC."

Oskar and his parents listened to British radio. It was prohibited, punishable by death. They always made sure the windows were closed.

"Daddy, what if they catch you and arrest you for listening to British radio?" asked Magda, who was scared to listen; she preferred music anyway. The newsreader was very serious, some Czech man living in London. Oskar was always listening. He spoke about Stalingrad, a town in Russia where the Nazis lost. Oskar was so excited! Now he was replying to Magda's question.

"They are losing in Russia – they will lose everywhere, won't they? They will lose like Napoleon, right, Daddy?"

The adults were quiet.

Uncle Otto looked at Bruno. "Bruno, your son is asking you a question. Will Hitler lose like Napoleon?"

But Bruno just smiled, put his hand around Oskar and Magda, and said, "We must all be brave and hold together where we are going; if we do that, it will all pass."

He and Uncle Otto helped the young men move the paintings, chandeliers, carpets and furniture.

In the evening, Grandma Olga came to say goodbye. She was crying.

"Don't worry, Mother, Otto and Marie will look after you and we will be alright," said Bruno.

"Grandma, the Germans are going to lose the war soon and then we will be home again!" said Magda. She didn't understand why that made her grandmother even more upset.

Next day, the Steins took the heavy luggage and went to the assembly place where their cards told them to go. There was a long queue of people. At the door, Bruno had to give the SS the house keys and his watch. Magda had to give up her nice new watch, too. The SS asked if they had any gold, money, valuable things. Magda was glad Uncle Otto arranged for the things to be hidden. The SS took Bruno's Masonic ring; he had forgotten to take it off.

There were a lot of people in the assembly place, and the room was crowded and smelly.

They all sat together on the floor. Everybody had a pallet with a number. They were given the same number and told to remember it.

"Don't we have names anymore?" asked Bruno.

The SS officer hit him with the back of his hand and told him to move. The SS officer had a large ring and it cut Bruno's cheek, making it bleed.

"Stop it, you nasty man!" Magda screamed, but Franzi put her hand over Magda's mouth.

"Maul halten, Kind," said the SS officer quietly. It meant shut up.

It was frightening to see her strong father being hit like this. Magda thought Bruno might hit the German back, but he didn't – he just looked angry. Franzi was holding Magda with her face to her chest; she was afraid the SS might strike Magda, too. He didn't; he walked away. Bruno put a white cotton handkerchief to his bleeding cheek.

Magda saw her cousins Irma and Gerd Goldman sitting with their parents Hans and Helena. Irma was older than Magda, but she was quiet and shy, and when they used to play together, she always did what Magda wanted. They used to play pretend games: school, where Magda was always the strict teacher, and sometimes she used to be a princess and Irma was her servant. The Steins moved closer to them; Irma's mother, Helena, was sobbing, holding her children, while Uncle Hans looked angry. Aunt Helena was a pianist, but her Steinway piano must have been somewhere in the storage Uncle Otto was talking about. She used to give concerts but stopped when Cousin Irma was born. Irma played piano, too and her brother Gerd played the tuba. It didn't sound like music – more like an elephant's roar. Gerd made a face at Magda, sticking out his tongue. Magda didn't like Gerd.

Aunt Helena said they and some other people had been there for two days now.

"Where did you sleep?" asked Franzi.

"Here, on the pallet on the floor," answered Aunt Helena, and started crying again. Magda didn't like seeing adults cry, so she and Irma moved away and started playing a game of cards. They were too old for childish pretend games now. The boys, Oskar and Gerd, started kicking a ball.

Magda couldn't sleep that night. It was hot and noisy; the SS were shouting; people were crying, adults and children alike. The smell was getting worse. People were sweating and there was no place to wash. Most of the toilets were blocked. A pregnant woman was sick in the corner and didn't wipe her face properly after.

The next morning, the SS started calling numbers and people walked away with their luggage. Someone said they were going to the railway station. Oskar was kicking his football up on his foot, counting. An SS officer stopped and said in German, "You are good – pity you are a smelly Jew." Oskar stopped and put the ball back into his backpack. Irma's mother was crying again, while Uncle Hans was pacing around, murmuring something about America. "We could have gone!" or something like that. His hands were shaking. Uncle Hans was a heavy smoker and he always somehow got black market cigarettes, but he couldn't smoke here.

Irma, Gerd, Oskar and Magda were playing cards when they called their numbers: Magda's family and Aunt Helena, but not the others. Uncle Hans went to speak to the SS officer to explain they were a family, and it must be some mistake, but the officer hit him, several times, until Uncle Hans fell on the floor. He got a nosebleed and tried to wipe it off with his sleeve, but he just smudged the blood. He tried to get up, but then he saw the SS was holding a gun. It was the same SS man who had hit Bruno the day before. Another soldier called him Holger. Aunt Helena was hugging Gerd and Irma, but Holger pulled her up and told her to walk with Magda's family to the station. Irma and Gerd stayed with their father, Uncle Hans. He was holding their hands and the blood from his nose was dripping everywhere. He tried to argue with the SS again, he wanted to join the Steins and his wife, but the Nazi kicked him.

"Stop it, Hans, I will look after your wife and we will see you soon," said Bruno. Franzi and Aunt Helena were holding hands when they all walked slowly to the Bubny railway station.

They were walking in the middle of the street, all those tired Jewish people with luggage, rucksacks, sometimes little carts. Jews were not allowed to walk on the pavement.

Pavements were full of Czech people. Nobody tried to help or talk to the tired mass of people approaching the railway station. The people on the pavement were just staring.

Magda saw a woman with a red hat. The hat was like the one Aunt Marie was wearing.

"Aunt Marie!" she shouted.

But the woman turned and gave her a cold stare. Same hat, different person.

CHAPTER EIGHT

Magda 1943–1945

THERESIENSTADT

The stench on the train was dreadful. Hundreds were jammed in carriages. The woman next to Magda was carrying a baby, and it screamed and screamed. Magda tried to make funny faces, but the baby had its eyes closed and couldn't see her. Magda was hungry because she hadn't eaten anything for hours. She wanted to eat the crackers Anna made but Franzi told her to wait as they might need them later.

When they arrived, they had to walk a long way from Bohusovice railway station to Theresienstadt. It was hard with the heavy luggage. An old woman with a scarf collapsed. Her husband stopped to help her. "Stop, my wife had a heart attack – help me!" he shouted. The SS shot them both. Magda screamed and stopped, but her father pulled her and told her to be quiet and walk with him. Magda had never seen anybody dead before.

In Theresienstadt, the SS started checking their luggage and took away anything they wanted and all their money. Theresienstadt was an 18th century walled old military town full of barracks and that was where they were going to live. Bruno said it was like being in the army again. Magda had seen Daddy's photos from the war – he had been in the cavalry. Bruno loved horses; before the Nazis came, he had one stabled in Prague and used to ride it in Stromovka Park. He rode in competitions, too, jumping fences.

Franzi never liked it. "One day, you will break your neck, Bruno!" she said. Bruno said cavalry in the war was much safer for him – fewer people got killed. But Magda suspected he just liked the horses.

Bruno knew what barracks looked like, but they were all upset when they realised how many people would share the rooms. The five of them were placed in a small room with two bunk beds and a dirty mattress on the floor. Magda, as the youngest, got the mattress. At least they were together. They were lucky. Normally, men and women were separated on arrival, but the same people who helped Magda's father postpone their transport in the past were now also in Theresienstadt and they still had power. Not the power to save themselves but to get an easier life. The Judenrath were organising life in the ghetto. Magda's father became a Ghettowache – a Jewish policeman. At first, he didn't want to do it, saying it meant working with the Nazis, but Franzi told him to try, as it would be safer for them all. Privileged people like that could stay together with their families.

The day after their arrival to Theresienstadt, everybody was divided into groups and told what to do. Franzi worked in the kitchens. Oskar did various cleaning jobs. Magda was told to go to work in the vegetable fields with a group of girls of a similar age. She didn't do much work; it was almost like in Prague when she was sunbathing instead of filing. But this time, it was not Magda's fault. She didn't have a clue how to look after fields; nobody in her family ever did. They were town people. Sarka, a tall blonde girl who spoke with a strong Moravian accent, said her family had a big farm. Sarka has blue eyes and a thick plait of dark blonde curly hair. Nobody would think she was Jewish, but she was.

Magda asked her about it. "Yes, but I look like some Nazi, it's so annoying. I'd like to look like you. But I wouldn't want your clumsy hands. You are doing more damage to the patch than pests. You will get us into trouble. Go and lie behind the bush – we will call you when it's time to go."

That was what Magda did. She tried to repeat her times tables and remember other things from school – if the Nazis lost the war, as Oskar said, she was going to go back to school. The girls called her before the woman guard came to escort them back. Magda was wearing tracksuit bottoms with rubber bands at the end of the leg; she could use them like bags. She usually stuffed some potatoes, tomatoes or beets into them. She needed to walk slowly so that it didn't show. There were the Berusky, the German women from Litomerice, a town close to Theresienstadt on the other side of the river, working in the ghetto. *Beruska* meant ladybird in Czech, but her mother told Magda that it was from the word *bere*, meaning to take in Czech, because they were stealing from the prisoners. They searched the girls, but for some reason they never searched Magda. The potatoes and other vegetables that Magda was smuggling in her trousers showed, but perhaps the women felt sorry for her, so they ignored it. Maybe it was because she was the youngest. Magda always brought the vegetables to Franzi, who cooked them a special soup. Magda felt proud.

"I am feeding our family, Oskar!"

Oskar didn't even tell her not to brag. He was tired and he had been coughing badly for a long time. Daddy always told Magda off for bringing the vegetables; he said it was too dangerous.

Ever since Sarka told Magda she would like to look like her, Magda felt much better in the company of boys and she started dating. Magda only enjoyed the beginning of the relationships. But after a while, they tried it on, touching her breasts and kissing her, so she dumped them. The most fun was stealing other girls' boyfriends. The girls resented that, but Magda didn't care.

Hans, Irma and Gerd never joined Helena. They had arrived in Theresienstadt on a train, but another train took them away again, to Poland. Aunt Helena begged the tall, freckled SS officer with red hair to send her to Poland too, to join her husband and children.

The SS officer smiled: "So you want to join them? Very well."

"You're such a joker, Bernt!" another SS officer said. Aunt Helena kissed Bernt's boots. She was on a train east the next day; they all came to say goodbye. The train consisted of cattle wagons. People were crammed inside and stuck their hands through the railings.

"One day, we will all be together again," said Bruno.

After Aunt Helena's departure, the ghetto was made to look better. There was more food, and the Nazis gave people paint and ordered them to clean the streets. They even got some of the special money – Ghetto Geld – and could buy some extra food. Oskar was sweeping the streets and collecting rubbish. Then one day the Swiss Red Cross came to inspect the ghetto and to make a film. At least that was what the others said. Magda didn't see any of it. The guards took many people to the fields behind the town and made them stand there all day without water and food. Bruno said it was to avoid showing how overcrowded the ghetto was. They got parcels from the cook Anna and from Aunt Marie and Uncle Otto. They wrote them postcards in German.

We are all well, Franzi wrote.

Magda walked through the town with the boys she dated; they sat in a coffee shop serving weak tea and bread spread with mustard. They paid for it with the Ghetto money. They were all tired and hungry, but it felt almost like a normal life.

Bruno kept telling everybody to be careful, but in the end, it was him who got them into trouble, for trying to smuggle a letter and some drawings out of the town.

Franzi saw the drawings, done by an artist whose family was later arrested. The drawings showed the town as it was, the dirt, the suffering, the beatings. "Bruno, please don't try to smuggle it, it's dangerous."

"Someone has to do something to fight the Nazis, Franzi. Somebody might smuggle those drawings abroad, for the English, Soviet or American army to know. The Swiss Red cross people thought this town was a spa for Jews."

"What if the Czech policeman who promised to post the letter gets caught or betrays us, Bruno?" worried Franzi.

No one knew how the Nazis discovered the letters and drawings, but the SS came and the red-haired Bernt beat Bruno with his fists. Magda and Oskar watched their brave father being beaten and not fighting back. He was just trying to cover his face. Blood was pouring from his eyebrows and nose, and his face started to be covered by black bruises. The SS arrested the whole family and took them all to the Small Fortress, which was a separate part of the town, also walled, connected to the main town by a walkway. It was not part of the ghetto, but a prison for Gestapo. Not all the prisoners were Jewish.

The Nazis beat and kicked them on the walk there. Bernt had his pistol out and Franzi was terrified that he would shoot her husband or son. He didn't, but just before they arrived in the Small Fortress, Bernt suddenly hit Bruno's face with the pistol, several times.

"Don't look, Magda!" whispered Franzi, covering Magda's eyes.

The Small Fortress was much worse than Theresienstadt. It was a prison where they couldn't go out; they were locked in cells, men separated from women.

The cell where the SS put Magda and Franzi was so full they couldn't lie down, so Magda slept sitting up, leaning on Franzi. There were so many women in the cell, all dirty, as there was nowhere to wash. Everybody had lice. Every morning, Appel happened – the women were ordered out of the cell and stood there for hours while some of the other prisoners cleaned the cell and carried the dead bodies out. Almost every night somebody died. On the Appelplatz, the women who didn't stand straight were beaten by the SS with leather whips. Magda spent the days in the cell next to her mother, mostly finding and killing lice. She never saw lice before; they were disgusting. They crunched when she crushed them, though, and Magda liked that. It was satisfying. The Nazi female guard, Brigitte Schaschek, was making disgusted faces. She had a Czech surname with a German spelling – it meant clown in Czech. At first, Magda found it funny. Not for long.

"Those Jews stink, they are like vermin," said Schaschek to another guard Inge, a pretty blonde with cold grey eyes.

"It's because you don't let us wash!" Magda shouted, also in German.

"Stop it, you'll get into trouble," Franzi shushed her.

It was too late; the woman came and whipped Magda in the face with her leather whip.

"I am her mother – let me punish her, please," said Franzi in a stern voice.

"Let me see it," Schaschek said; she seemed amused. Franzi beat Magda up with her hands, making slapping noises, but it didn't hurt half as much as the whip.

"That'll teach her." The guards left; it was time for their lunch.

Franzi embraced Magda as soon as the guard left. She wiped the blood off Magda's face gently, kissing her. "My darling, I am so sorry, I just needed to protect you."

They both cried, holding tight. Magda never spoke to the guards again.

Sometimes they still got parcels from Anna, but recently the SS commandant Heinrich Jöckel came up with what he thought was a good joke. He told the cooks to put all the parcels including the paper into boiling water and make a soup out of it. It was disgusting, but the prisoners, always hungry, still ate it. The soup had sausages, biscuits, sugar, salt, but also safety pins, hair clips, and some soggy paper and string floating in thin, watery liquid. Franzi almost choked on one of the hair clips. She was sick. But she took the hair clip out of her vomit, wiped it and gave it to Magda. So now Magda had a hair clip.

Franzi tried her best to shelter Magda from the worst. She gave her some of her food portions, she cuddled her, and she was always with her. In the winter, Magda got sick with diphtheria; she was burning with a temperature and breathing heavily. She couldn't swallow. It looked as if she was going to die. Franzi begged the young blonde German guard Inge on her knees to bring a doctor.

"Please, my daughter is so young!"

In the end, the German doctor came and gave Magda the diphtheria antitoxin injection. That was very unusual, as the doctors didn't attend Jews. "Take her to a single cell, otherwise everybody, even you, will get this." The doctor told the male SS guard Gruber.

Gruber was angry that the doctor came to see a Jewish prisoner, he was arguing with Inge about it earlier, but he took Magda from the large cell and pushed her to move to a single isolation cell. Magda had a high temperature and was very weak. She was only shuffling.

On the courtyard, slippery with ice and snow, Gruber pushed her even harder, shouting, "*Schneller, schneller!*"

Another guard sprayed her with cold water from a hosepipe. "That will make the dirty little Jewess move faster!"

Magda didn't remember how long she was in the single cell, a cold, small, cave-like dwelling with a wooden door. She was too sick. She lived, but the 15 women she infected all died. Franzi had had diphtheria as a child and so she survived. It was spring when Gruber unlocked her single cell and pushed her back to the large cell. Franzi was waiting for her with a warm embrace. She also had some food saved for Magda. Magda greeted the other women she remembered, but some of them didn't reply.

"You are alive and all the women you have infected are dead!" Mrs Reuben said.

"It's not my fault!" Magda tried to defend herself, but Franzi shook her head and pulled Magda towards her chest to stop her from talking.

They didn't know where Bruno and Oskar were; there was a Jewish cell for men, and Franzi wondered if they were there. She was trying to look for them when the prisoners were walking through the yard. Once she thought she had a glimpse of Oskar, but she wasn't sure. The man she saw was very skinny and had orange skin, as though he had jaundice. That couldn't have been her son…

Franzi and Magda were in the Small Fortress for eight months. Spring 1945 came. The Germans seemed to be nervous and there were fewer beatings. Was the war coming to an end? Due to a typhoid epidemic, the Nazis took everybody from the Small Fortress to Theresienstadt. On the way, the group passed some Czechs working in the field.

"When will the war end?" whispered Franzi, addressing the rumours they had heard.

"In about two months," the man whispered.

"We won't survive that long," Franzi sighed. Fortunately, the Czech farmer was wrong. The war ended for Magda 2 May 1945. On that day, the Red Cross took over the running of the town, and 8 May, Theresienstadt was liberated by the Soviet army.

Magda and Franzi were hungry, thin, with their skin full of scratches and boils, but they no longer had to worry about being beaten or shot. They couldn't wait to go home, but they were only allowed to leave quarantine in July 1945. Many people died of typhoid even after the liberation. Fortunately, neither Magda nor Franzi became ill again. They were lucky; they remained healthy. They were reunited with Mrs Katz, a tall woman who used to work in the ghetto kitchen with Franzi. She was fat when Magda saw her last, before they were arrested and moved to the Small Fortress. She was thin now. Mrs Katz always used to laugh at Magda bringing the stolen vegetables in the legs of her tracksuit bottoms.

"I am so glad you are here; I was looking after your mother-in-law Olga Stein – she walks very badly, but she is alive. She was looking for you in Theresienstadt when she came, but you were already arrested and put in the Small Fortress. Let me lead you to her. She spent all the time in the room in the barracks and the Nazis didn't deport her. We were worried they might shoot her, but I think they must've forgotten about her being there. I have been bringing her food."

"That is so wonderful, thank you so much, let us see her now. Oh, thank you, Mrs Katz, you are an angel. What about your family, where are they?"

Franzi wanted to ask more questions, but Mrs Katz shook her head and covered her eyes. "They were all deported east."

"We are looking for my husband Bruno and son Oskar, and, of course, the others. They will come back. Let's pray for it." Franzi started to pray lately; she never used to.

"I am not sure miracles happen," said Mrs Katz, and took them to Olga.

Magda couldn't recognise her grandmother Olga. She was thin and quiet. She embraced Magda and Franzi, and just held them, repeating, "You are alive, you are alive."

Magda used to think Grandma Olga was great. So elegant, dignified and powerful. Coming for tea to her house was like dining with a queen. She had, and demanded, impeccable manners. The cake and tea were served on fine china; so were the sandwiches with the crusts cut off. The maid used to bring it all on a fancy tray. One of Olga's friends had married into a wealthy English family with a grand house. Ever since Olga visited England, she started serving a 'five o'clock tea' instead of a coffee and cake like other families. Magda remembered how her mother used to dress them for those visits, washing their necks and ears, making sure the clothes were ironed and clean. When Oskar came in dirty from playing football, Franzi panicked.

"I can't take you to your grandmother Olga like this, and if you wash and change, we will be late! We mustn't be late!" Franzi feared her mother-in-law.

This frail old woman was not at all like Grandma Olga before the war. She even seemed smaller. Franzi and Magda looked for Bruno, Oskar and their other relatives, but they and Olga were the only three of the family there.

CHAPTER NINE

Magda 1945

THE WAR IS OVER, BUT IT'S NOT EASY TO GO BACK TO NORMAL LIFE

When they were finally allowed to leave Theresienstadt, they took a train to Prague using the rail connection the Nazis had built and rang the bell at Uncle Otto's apartment. Otto, normally so calm, full of wit, was shaking. He embraced Magda and wouldn't let go. He lifted Grandma Olga as if she was a child and carried her to the most comfortable big armchair, and although it was July, he covered her with a blanket. Olga closed her eyes and soon fell asleep in the chair, and when they tried to wake her up for dinner, she told them to let her sleep.

Aunt Marie made a wonderful dinner, but both Magda and Franzi were sick. Irma, who was also staying with Otto and Marie, told them to be careful. "At first, I was sick, too."

Irma escaped from the camp and she hid till Prague was liberated 9 May 1945, when she came to Otto and Marie. Irma changed; she was still quiet but seemed stronger, tougher.

"How did you get back to Prague, Irma, and when?" Magda asked.

"I escaped and pretended to be German. I was lucky."

Magda became curious, but Irma told her she didn't want to talk about it. In the end, it was Aunt Marie who told Magda. They were sitting in a coffee house. They sat so that Magda could see the view at the river and Prague castle; she still needed to be reminded she was really back in Prague. Magda was eating her second cake and had half of Aunt Marie's cake, too. The cakes were more like biscuits. The rationing system didn't allow for much, but Marie used a lot of her rations to treat her favourite niece. Aunt Marie, always slim, was watching her figure, while Magda was constantly ravenous.

"Irma was so brave, Magda, I wouldn't have believed she could have done this. It's an incredible story."

Magda felt jealous. Suddenly, she felt Irma was an adult, whereas Magda, now aged 18, was not.

"You remember you told me how Helena begged the SS officer in Theresienstadt to help her join her husband and Gerd? She went on a transport a day later. I know Irma is still hoping Hans, Helena and Gerd are going to come back, but they went east. It is quite likely they all died in the gas chambers. Irma saw Gerd in Auschwitz at a distance, but she couldn't talk to him." Marie had tears in her eyes.

Magda grabbed her hand. "You think they are all dead, don't you? But they will come back, Aunt Marie, it just takes time. They must come back, at least some of them." Magda didn't realise she was shouting till she saw that the people in the coffee shop were staring at them. One woman, sitting next to them wanted to say something but didn't.

"Shhhh, of course they will, Magda, but let me tell you about Irma. Irma told us how bad Auschwitz was. Lice, dirt, hunger. But you know all this."

"Yes, we spent whole days in the cell crushing headlice. Quite a satisfying crunch. How long was Irma in Auschwitz? What else did she tell you? She didn't want to talk about it with me. Aunt Marie, Irma seems different – we don't seem to have much in common anymore."

"I am not surprised. She told us about the beatings, the work. One female guard called Greta Bauer was apparently especially scary. She used to beat them with a leather whip. Irma told me that the woman enjoyed it and often laughed when she was whipping them. Magda, oh, poor Magda, did they beat you, too?"

"No, only once, we were just locked up in that horrible stinky cell. They left us alone otherwise."

"Irma told us she was not beaten as much, because she was always trying to move and work fast and making herself unremarkable, not noticed. But once Bauer whipped her badly because she thought she was not working hard enough. Irma was tired and felt faint; she told us she would have died if she hadn't met Rosa, a girl who worked in the kitchens. Irma told us that Rosa spoke with a soft Viennese accent and often sang. Rosa was good for Irma. She brought her some food from the kitchen and they became friends. When they were put on a march to another camp, this girl Rosa persuaded Irma to run away."

The shy, meek Irma? thought Magda.

"Imagine the courage, Magda. They burnt their forearms to destroy the numbers and pretended to be Germans escaping from the Russians. Some local Germans gave them money for train tickets. Irma got back to Liberec and then to Prague and worked as a servant for a German family. She was here and we didn't know. She only came to us when Prague was liberated. Otto opened the door for her, he called me and the three of us just hugged for a long time."

They were interrupted by a plump young woman sitting at the neighbouring table. "I couldn't help hearing you – what an incredible story. You should sell it to a newspaper. My brother is a journalist, I could help."

Marie blushed.

"Story? The whole family suffered so much; this is not for entertainment!" Aunt Marie sounded angry, and when the woman carried on talking to her, Magda couldn't believe her ears when Marie swore at her, told her to go to hell. The polite and ladylike Aunt Marie? What was happening?

When they got home, Irma was there, reading a newspaper, but when Magda wanted to talk to her, ask her questions, Irma got quite unpleasant. "I told you I don't want to talk about it. I survived, you survived, let's hope the others did, too. Nothing else to talk about, Magda."

They were all waiting for Hans, Helena, Gerd, and Bruno and Oskar to come back, but they didn't. Not yet anyway. Hana and her parents Karel and Tereza were also still missing; so was Franzi's sister Gerta and her family. Magda remembered the cute blonde little Eva.

"The Red Cross will find them," said Franzi.

But Otto got up and left the room. He kicked the door on the way out.

It was crowded in Otto and Marie's apartment, with six adults living in three rooms, but it seemed spacious after the ghetto. After all the prisoners were released from quarantine in Theresienstadt in August, Magda went back for a small case of her things that she left in the Magdeburg barracks where they lived before they were arrested and taken to the Small Fortress. One of the girls found it, and when she heard from Mrs Katz that Magda was alive, she asked her to write to Magda. Magda took a train back; she was so happy to find the case. There were some family photographs, clothes and even her diary. On the way back, she got a ride on a lorry with Russian soldiers.

"Hey, devotchka, pojdi s nami."

Magda understood some of their Russian, as it was similar to Czech. A blond soldier with wide cheekbones and a cigarette in the corner of his mouth helped her up to the front cabin of the lorry. They offered her food and chocolate, and they sang songs. She liked the song 'Kalinka'. She was sitting between one of the soldiers and the driver in the front. Her case was at the back. On the outskirts of Prague, they told her to get out, threw the case to the ground and drove off. When she looked, the bottom of the case and all her things were missing.

"You were lucky. You could have been raped," said Aunt Marie when she got home.

Olga moved to a small apartment with a lift. She was walking slowly with a stick, but she was getting stronger. She had changed, though. Her old confidence was gone, and once she embraced Otto and repeated, "My poor children, this is all my fault!"

Otto kissed her but didn't say anything. Magda suddenly remembered how Grandma Olga didn't want any members of her family to emigrate when they still could.

Irma didn't move in with her grandmother Olga but visited every day and looked after her.

Hana came back to Prague in August, but only stayed for three weeks, then she moved with a friend to Brno. She found a job working as a secretary for the Brno communist party. Hana already knew that her parents were both dead. She got a reply from the Red Cross, with the dates of Tereza and Karel's death in the gas chambers of Treblinka. *Karel, the historian. How come that he didn't predict what was going to happen?* thought Magda.

Hana was still a communist. "We will build a new society, with everybody equal."

Otto was going to say something sarcastic but stopped when Marie gave him a look. "You are smart – you will find out what is right, Hana!" he said instead.

Magda and Franzi moved out from Otto and Marie's apartment after two months. They were allocated a nice apartment by the repatriation organisation. It was on the embankment, with the view of the river and Prague Castle. They were waiting and waiting. They were reading about Nazis being lynched or executed. The commandant from the Small Fortress, Heinrich Jöckel, was executed, but neither Magda nor Franzi celebrated. They were still waiting for Bruno and Oskar to come back.

The new apartment on the embankment was much smaller than the one they had before they were deported to Theresienstadt, but it was in a nice building with little damage from the war. It had three large rooms and a kitchen, high ceilings, and nice doors with decorated glass inlays. Life resumed to a sense of normality, with Uncle Otto and Aunt Marie helping. Both Franzi and Magda got some money from the government and they were also all getting money from Uncle Otto, because the factory, confiscated by the Nazis and returned to them by the state in 1945, was doing well. Hana refused her share.

"I don't want your capitalist money; we will confiscate factories once we come to power, just you wait and see."

Magda hoped that Hana was wrong. It was nice to be wealthy again.

Otto's cynical belief that they would never again see the things hidden by Czech acquaintances during the war proved wrong: Franzi and Magda got back all their paintings, furniture, jewellery, silver that was hidden. It seemed that Otto picked the right people to hide their belongings. It was strange, seeing the furniture, paintings, crystal glass, Persian rugs again. Magda had been a child the last time she had seen them. Now she was 18.

The only things that were damaged were the family photo albums and a cookbook diary of Franzi with handwritten recipes. The family who took it to keep during the war got frightened in the time after the assassination of the Reinhard Heydrich in Prague in 1942 and buried the albums and cookbook in their garden. When they dug it out, the covers of the albums, but especially the cookbook, were partially eaten by mice. Magda looked at the cookbook. It was funny – Franzi often started writing the recipes in German, then switched to Czech. All her friends and family were bilingual, and Franzi told Magda the conversation used to be neither Czech nor German; it was both. The cookbook was a mess, but Magda wanted to keep it, as she remembered the different cakes and she was looking forward to the time when food rations stopped and Franzi could bake like she used to.

"I could only bake the cakes when Anna let me into the kitchen. Now I can cook all the time."

Their cook Anna came to see them; she cried and cried, blowing her nose loudly. She called Magda her poor little darling. *That's silly, I'm a head taller than Anna.* Anna looked fat compared to Magda and Franzi, but Magda had been putting on weight. The problem was, when she saw food, she couldn't stop eating. Jam out of jars with a tablespoon, bread rolls, potatoes. People were complaining about the rationing, but people coming from concentration camps felt they had almost too much food. Franzi told Anna she couldn't employ her again.

"Magda and I are just two women now; we can look after ourselves."

"What about when Doctor Bruno and Oskar come back?" asked Anna.

Franzi did not reply. Her eyes were wet. *She told me they might come back, so why is she crying?* Magda wanted to ask. Did Franzi not believe Bruno and Oskar were alive? Magda opened and closed her mouth again – no, she was not ready to talk about it either.

Not everybody was so lucky with getting their property back. Irma lost all her family's valuables; the friends of her parents claimed the Germans had confiscated them. Magda thought they were lying. Irma knew they were.

"When I got to the flat of the Novaks, I could see through the open doors our crystal chandelier and the painting of a red-haired half-naked woman by Bukovac. My father used to love that painting. But Mrs Novak quickly closed the door, embraced me, and offered me coffee and cake. She took me to the kitchen and asked lots of questions. When I asked when I could get the things that they were hiding for us, she said there was a raid by Germans and they took everything, even some of their things."

"Why didn't you say anything?" asked Magda.

"What's the point? They are just things."

This was the new Irma; it wasn't important for her. She probably lost her parents and brother; she didn't care about china and crystal.

"Can you tell me about your escape? Whose idea was it?"

"My friend Rosa."

Magda was not surprised. It wasn't like Irma to be brave like that. Magda wanted to hear more, but Irma got up. "I have to help Marie in the kitchen, and I think you should go home, Magda."

Magda was offended, but Irma was already leaving through the door to the kitchen.

They were all waiting. Waiting for Magda's daddy and brother, for Irma's parents and brother. Franzi was also waiting for her mother Heda, Magda's other grandmother, and her brother and sisters. Franzi had two sisters and a brother. Blonde Gerta had a Jewish husband Victor and the Aryan-looking daughter, little Eva; Franzi's other sister Hilda and her brother Ferdi married non-Jews – Hilda a German called Jürgen and Ferdi a Czech called Dana, who divorced him as soon as the Nazis came. Hilda and Jürgen survived but moved to America after the war. In the beginning, there was hope, but after several months and finding out the full truth about the concentration camps and the gas chambers, Magda was convinced most of them were dead. Yet, she was still hoping, especially for her father and brother. They were not deported to the east so surely they would come back. In the end, the family just tried not to talk about them.

Everything looked the same, but everything had changed. Franzi had changed. She used to be strict; now she carried on being how she was in Theresienstadt: kind, loving, and looking after her daughter. Magda knew she wouldn't have survived the war without her darling mother. Irma was different, too. She showed Magda her burnt tattoo number; it was an ugly, bulky scar. She was still quiet, but she seemed tough. They didn't have anything to talk about anymore. It was a pity; she was Magda's cousin, and they didn't have many relatives left.

Then one day, Otto phoned Franzi to say that he had received information about Irma's parents and brother. They had all been killed. He didn't know where Irma was, and he was phoning around to find her. "I phoned Mother, but Irma wasn't there either – where can she be?" Otto was worried.

That was lunchtime. Magda went to visit Grandmother Olga that afternoon, but just as she was going to ring the bell, she heard shouting. It was Irma. "You killed my parents and my brother – they will now never come back, I hate you!"

Irma's voice was shrill. Magda waited before she rang the bell. She thought Irma would open the door, but she heard the shuffling of Grandma's feet. They were both behind the door; Irma had her hand round Olga's shoulders and they both had red eyes from crying. Irma kissed her grandmother and whispered something in her ear. Then she left. Magda remembered that shrill, angry voice of her cousin all her life.

Irma was now dating Petr Aron, a distant relative who spent the war in America. He came back as an American soldier. Petr asked Magda for a date first, but Magda didn't like him. He was good-looking, but loud and bossy. 'Mr Know-it-all', she called him. Petr gave Magda and Irma nylon stockings and cigarettes, Camels. They both smoked now. Magda had never seen stockings as thin as this before.

"They are made in the USA. Everything is better in America; Europe is so lame," said Petr.

"Why don't you go back there then? The war is over, we don't need you here."

But Irma told her not to be rude and thanked him for the stockings. Magda didn't. He was annoying, but she kept them anyway.

"What do you see in him? He's an idiot!" Magda said later.

"I have nobody, and Petr will look after me," Irma replied.

Magda understood this; she was lucky to have her mummy.

Petr and Irma married just two months after they met. Magda was wondering if it was so early because Irma was pregnant, but she wasn't. It was a modest wedding and it made Magda feel sad to see such a small gathering. They used to have such a large family.

Hana often came to visit from Brno where she still worked for the communist party, but she told Otto that she was planning to go to Palestine. Otto opened a bank account in Hana's name and put in it her share of the profits from the factory. He was hoping she would take it one day.

"I don't want to stay in Europe. Eventually the British will let the Jews have their own state in Palestine and it will be a new beginning. Jews will have a home."

Otto and Hana argued about it; he didn't think it would be that easy.

"The British keep turning the ships back from Palestine. I read they now have camps for the Jews in Cyprus. They will never give the Jews a state! Move back to Prague, Hana, I will find you a proper job, not at the communist party. Haven't you heard about Stalin and the unspeakable things he's done?"

"He liberated us from the Nazis. How can you forget that, Otto?"

"Yes, but Stalin first had a pact with Hitler, don't you remember? He only fought the Nazis because they attacked him. Hana, Stalin killed millions, do you remember the Ukraine famine? It was his doing."

Otto and Hana could never agree on anything.

Magda then heard Hana talking to Franzi in the kitchen: "Aunt Franzi, I will now finally live among camels in Palestine, like you predicted."

It was nice to see Franzi and Hana laugh.

Franzi and Magda waited for a whole year. Then a Mr Weiss, a man who had been also imprisoned in the Small Fortress, phoned – he got their number from a friend. He said he had some information, so Magda's mother invited him for coffee. Magda wished she hadn't. Mr Weiss was about 60, thin and bald, with shaking hands. He had been in the Small Fortress in the Jewish male cell, like Magda's father and her brother Oskar.

"We had to work in an underground factory. It took an hour to walk there, and if we didn't walk fast enough, they beat us. The worst was a young man called Heinrich Braun, a tall man with a broken nose. He was a real sadist. Even the other SS seemed to be afraid of him. Food was even worse than in the Small Fortress, often consisting of rotten potatoes and cabbage boiled with slugs. They must have done it on purpose. We were being worked to death; not many survived."

Mr Weiss shook more, and he spoke in a monotonous, quiet voice. The cup made loud clunking noises on the saucer.

He is going to break this nice Rosenthal cup we only just got back! thought Magda.

He told them that Oskar was beaten to death by two of the SS officers.

"They were kicking him when he was on the ground; his face was covered in blood and we heard his screaming and his bones crushing. They forced us to watch. Heinrich Braun hit my face with a whip when he saw my eyes were closed. 'Do you want us to start on you, too, Jew?' he said. So I watched your Oskar being killed – I am sorry!"

Oskar was only 20 years old.

Magda got angry with the man. "You shouldn't have told us that! Why? What's the point? Why did you come? Just shut up and leave, get out of here!"

He put the cup down, spilling some of the tea. He quickly picked up his coat and left. He was mumbling something, probably an apology. Franzi started shaking and had to sit down. Magda didn't know what to do, so she just held her.

After an hour, Magda knew that her mother was better, because she told Magda off for being rude to Mr Weiss. She wanted her to phone him and apologise, but Magda didn't. When her mother asked, she told her she lost his telephone number, but Franzi knew she was lying. Uncle Otto made some more enquiries, to be sure. Mr Weiss was right: both Bruno and Oskar died in 1944, soon after the family's arrest in the Small Fortress. Magda wondered what happened to that evil SS Heinrich Braun; she hoped to find his name in the newspaper among Nazis who were arrested and sometimes executed, but his name was not there. She hoped he was dead.

One afternoon, Franzi came back from shopping, angry. "I met that murderess, Dana. She could have saved my brother Ferdi if she hadn't divorced him when the Nazis came. She started talking to me. I crossed the road."

"Ferdi might still come back, Mummy."

He didn't. They got a message that he died in Majdanek.

Many other relatives were killed, and friends, too. Ms Klein, the teacher, died in Auschwitz. Mrs Abeles survived; she met Magda in the street and told her she was going to be opening a new shop soon.

Magda tried never to think of the war. *If I ignore the memories, I might forget it all and life will be normal*, she thought. Prague was a fun place. She went dancing in various Prague bars and met new people her age. Magda preferred people who were not in the camps, people who were not Jewish. Boys and men always liked her. It was easy to date a different one every week. Magda still didn't like it when they touched her, but now she let them kiss her.

She stopped dating other men when she fell in love with Mirek, a medical student. He was handsome and they had fun when they were together. He was not Jewish, and that was important. She didn't want to be Jewish, or at least she didn't want people to know she was. Mirek met her at the swimming pool. Magda was diving from the highest diving board – ten metres into the water. She was not good at it and it hurt, hitting the water with a big splash, but it attracted attention to her and her beautiful new swimsuit. It was navy blue with a little skirt and white border.

"Are you Magda Stein?" a tall man with curly hair asked. "My name is Mirek Novotny, I used to go to school with your brother Oskar, we played football together."

"Oskar is dead," Magda said. Mirek embraced her and started kissing off her tears. It felt good, although it was wrong from a stranger. Now, Mirek was no longer a stranger. Magda loved him and he loved her. Other girls were envious that she had such a good-looking boyfriend, a future doctor. She could get married like Irma. Unlike her, Magda wanted to have a big wedding, with everybody telling her how beautiful she looked.

Magda dreamt about the future. *Mummy would live with us and do the household chores. She is good at it. It's funny, she seems happier not having servants around.*

Everybody changed. Grandma Olga came back from Theresienstadt with tuberculosis but got better with a new drug, streptomycin. She had survived only because of kind people like Mrs Katz looking after her, bringing her food. Franzi gave Mrs Katz a golden bracelet, one piece of jewellery that was hidden with Czech friends during the war. Magda thought she would rather have the bracelet herself. Grandma Olga, who used to be so strong, now seemed fragile. After the filth and deprivation, she seemed to have become a lady again, never biting into an apple but cutting it carefully with a special fruit knife on a plate. She didn't shove food in her mouth like Magda. The hunger Olga had felt for two years did not go away so easily, but her ladylike manners were still there. However, she no longer told her family what to do. She was quiet now and often cried. She couldn't walk well. Magda heard her mother talking to Aunt Marie.

"My mother-in-law never liked me, but she seems to be much nicer now."

"She doesn't have anybody but you and us now," said Marie.

When Magda was a child, everybody did what Olga told them to do. As children, they used to behave much better in her house than at home. They ate slowly, with her watching and correcting their table manners. Even when Magda asked, she never got another portion of cake. "A girl should not be greedy, Magda."

Olga was very different from Magda's other grandmother, Mum's mother Heda. They never saw grandma Heda a lot, as she lived in a little town quite far away. But when they did come to visit her, Magda could have as much cake as she wanted.

Grandma Heda was gassed in Auschwitz. Magda and Franzi last saw her leaving Theresienstadt on a cattle train. She was so old and frail. Her eyes were scared; she didn't even look at them. *I mustn't think about it*, thought Magda, so she stopped.

CHAPTER TEN

Magda 1945-1948

MAGDA FINISHES SCHOOL AND GETS MARRIED

Now that Magda was 18, she had not thought about going back to school, but then she met some girls from her old class. "We are all waiting for you! Are you coming back?"

Yes, and when I was kicked out of school, you used to cross the road so that you didn't have to talk to me, Magda thought. She didn't say anything aloud. Her father had told her years ago that it was also hard for them and they wouldn't know what to say. So now she didn't say anything because she wanted them to be her friends again. She went to see her old headmaster. The school years had Latin names: prima at age 11, then secunda, tercie, quarta, quinta, sexta, septima and the last, octava. He offered her a place in quarta with the view that she would jump two classes if she passed the exams from all the subjects. When the Nazis stopped Jewish children going to school, she had only finished secunda. But Magda was 18 and didn't want to go to school with 14-year-olds.

"No, I'd like to graduate next year with my class!"

"You would have to pass exams from all the 12 subjects for the past five years; you will never make it. And if you fail, I won't let you jump any classes. You'll have to start with the 12-year-olds!"

That's a challenge – I'll show you! Magda thought. She started studying. She worked hard and she was helped by her photographic memory and determination to prove everybody wrong. *Irma couldn't do this!* she thought.

She was still jealous of Cousin Irma. She was fed up with everybody talking about how brave Irma was. Instead of learning the subjects grade by grade, she studied subject by subject. Five years of subjects. Her first exam was mathematics. The headmaster was present at the exam. Magda passed.

Physics, chemistry and biology followed. German was a piece of cake; she got grade one, the best mark. Czech language and literature were harder. She only got a grade three. Magda was not used to mediocre marks, so she studied even harder, even studying geography and history. *Uncle Karel would be surprised*, she thought.

Magda finished with the exams just in time to join her class in their last year before graduation. The headmaster told her he had never heard of anybody else doing this. At the graduation ceremony in 1946, in his speech, he talked about Magda for over five minutes. It was an impressive achievement.

After her graduation, just like she wanted, Magda had her big wedding with Mirek. Like she planned, everybody told her how beautiful she looked. Mirek moved into the apartment with Magda and his mother-in-law. *We are going to be so happy!* thought Magda. Her mother looked after the household, while Magda didn't do much housework; she only occasionally washed the dishes. It was her mother's household, not hers. That suited Magda just fine. *I will never leave my mummy; we will always live with her.* Living with parents was not uncommon, as there were not enough flats in Prague, but even if Mirek and Magda could live alone, Magda wouldn't have it. Mirek didn't mind. Franzi was a good mother-in-law.

They had income from the factory, and Mirek's parents, wealthy owners of a department store, supported them financially, too. Mirek and Magda went out a lot; life was good.

Magda and Franzi didn't talk about the war, what they went through, who died. It was as if things you didn't talk about didn't really exist. Yet, Magda slept badly and had nightmares full of SS officers with nasty, threatening faces.

Her mother seemed all right, but she started praying. Magda first saw that worn little red velvet-bound prayer book on her mother's bedside table. She looked inside. The writing was in Hebrew on one side and in German on the other side, written in the old-fashioned curly German writing. Magda couldn't read either of them. Franzi couldn't read Hebrew, but funnily enough, that was the part of the book she had opened. She was just sitting in the armchair, holding the little velvet-bound book, opening and moving pages from right to left, back to front. Sometimes, her eyes were full of tears. Magda didn't like it.

"You can't read Hebrew, Mummy, can you?"

"No, but it calms me down, looking at this old book, and it brings me closer to my mother and to your father and brother. Looking at the pages, I feel like I am praying to the Jewish God, praying for them to rest in peace."

"Mummy, it makes you sad – put it away. What's the point?"

Franzi put the book away and went to make a cup of coffee, but Magda often saw her sitting and turning those incomprehensible pages. They still didn't talk about the war.

"They didn't come back," they would say, not: "They were murdered."

After two years of waiting, the hope disappeared. Only Franzi's sister Hilda and her German husband Jürgen survived, but they moved to America.

Otto and Franzi had the names put on the family tomb in the Prague New Jewish cemetery, but the exact day and month of death was missing with most of them.

Magda's father Bruno and brother Oskar	The Small Fortress, Theresienstadt, 1944
Franzi's brother Ferdi	Majdanek, 1943
Franzi's sister Gerta, her husband Victor and their daughter Eva	Majdanek, 1943

| Irma's parents, Hans and Helena, and her brother Gerd | Auschwitz, 1944 |

| Franzi's mother, Magda's grandma Heda | Auschwitz, 1944 |

| Hana's parents, Karel and Aunt Tereza | Auschwitz, 1944 |

Franzi told Magda it might be better if she didn't tell people they were Jewish.

"Why not?"

Franzi told her about a conversation she had in the lift. She introduced herself to one of the neighbours, a blonde 50-year-old woman living on the floor below them. She asked Franzi where they moved from. She was friendly, but not for long.

"We just came back from a Nazi prison, the Small Fortress in Terezin."

Franzi didn't expect the answer. "Well, everybody suffered during the occupation, not just you."

Yes, but how many of our relatives did the Germans kill? Franzi didn't say it; she kept quiet. She overheard conversations like this in the shops. People said that the returning Jews were making too much fuss and abusing the situation. *I am not religious, and if I stop telling people that we are Jewish, they won't know.*

Funny, Franzi never thought the Czechs were antisemitic. Maybe she was just over-sensitive.

Still, Jew seemed to be a swear word. "Don't be such a Jew!" she heard a boy say to a friend who didn't want to share his sweets. Czechs talked about 'your people' when they talked to her.

Franzi, always a Czech patriot, no longer felt she belonged there. She was an orphan, widow and bereaved mother. Still, Franzi had a task: Magda. She must make Magda as happy as possible. *Magda mustn't ever see my tears.* She needed to look after her daughter, like she had in the prison.

Looking after Magda is the reason why I survived. I must stop thinking about Bruno and Oskar; they are dead, while Magda is alive.

CHAPTER ELEVEN

Magda 1946–1953

THE COMMUNISTS TAKE OVER – A NEW REASON TO EMIGRATE

In the Czechoslovak elections in 1946, the communist party won the most votes and formed a coalition government. Although the government was democratic and President Edvard Benes, who spent the war in exile in London, kept his position, the communists held most of the important posts.

Uncle Otto was worried. "Stalin is going to turn us into another Soviet state, just you wait!"

"No," Marie argued, "we have a long history of democracy, and President Benes and Prime Minister Masaryk are good people, and they were in England during the war – the West will be on our side."

"I heard enough optimistic talk in 1938 before the Munich conference, remember? This is similar, Marie, can't you see it? They are going to confiscate our factory again, maybe this time we should emigrate while we can."

Otto was right. In February 1948, communists staged a coup d'état and took over. The new president, Klement Gottwald, soon started nationalising all private businesses, even small shops, and there was gradual closing of the borders.

Everybody was talking about emigration again. Magda remembered those arguments she'd overheard as a child in the large family gatherings in Olga's house. So many of them were killed by the Nazis.

It was different this time. Irma and Petr already left for America. Hana and Uncle Otto and Aunt Marie seemed restless.

One day, when they were all visiting grandmother Olga and talking about it, Magda remembered that lunch before the war, the day Aunt Judita and Uncle Simon had decided to emigrate to America. She had been watching the adults arguing; Grandma Olga had wanted the whole family to stay together. This time, Olga wanted them to leave. Mirek didn't want to emigrate, as he had a good medical job, and his parents and brothers were all in Prague. Magda didn't want to leave either. *We only just came back from the war!* she thought.

"Franzi, you, Magda and Mirek should go, while it is still time. Otto and Marie, you too," said Grandma Olga. "We should have all left in 1938, and it was my fault we stayed. Otto, the communists have taken power, so you will lose the factory – they talk about nationalising everything. A nice name for theft. These are hard times and people always turn on the Jews in hard times. We mustn't repeat the same mistake. In 1938, I stopped you all from going. Hans and Helena, Karel and Tereza, Gerd, Bruno, Oskar – they would all be alive if they left like Judita and Simon. I cannot bear it. Go, please go!"

"I can't go," said Franzi. "What would I do? I don't know anything, just how to knit and cook, and I only speak Czech and German. I am old; I will stay. But Magda and Mirek, you should leave. Everybody needs doctors. I will be fine; I will move in with Olga."

Darling Mum, always the selfless one.

Magda lost it. "No, I am not leaving you here, Mummy, I cannot live without you. Daddy and Oskar are dead – no, no, no, I will not leave you!" she sobbed, and became so worked up that she fainted.

"Hyperventilation," Mirek snapped, annoyed. "I know it is hard, Magda, but stop those hysterical scenes!"

In the end, Otto and Marie left, just in time, for France. They had friends there. In 1949, Hana went for a week's communist conference in Berlin and didn't come back. Later, she wrote from the newly formed state of Israel. She no longer called it Palestine. By 1952, it became impossible to travel to the West. Mirek and Magda stayed; so did Franzi. She looked after Olga, the mother-in-law who never liked her.

Mum is the best woman I have ever known. She is a saint. A Jewish saint thought Magda.

Grandma Olga died soon after Otto and Marie left. They didn't come to her funeral because they would have been arrested. Leaving the country was a crime punishable by five years in prison.

Everybody had to go to political meetings. The speakers praised Stalin and the Soviet Union, explaining the dictatorship of the proletariat and the class struggle. Magda was not only not interested in the least, but it all sounded like lies. The workers from the family factory, nationalised like all the others, kept writing Franzi and Magda letters; they even sometimes popped in and brought them home-grown vegetables or eggs. If all the workers hated the capitalists, how come they didn't hate Magda's family? They even held a memorial service for Magda's father and brother. *Class struggle indeed, they are not fighting with us*, thought Magda, and stopped paying attention. Those political meetings reminded her of Hana. Magda didn't tell anybody she had a relative in Israel. 'The Zionists', together with 'the Imperialists', were the enemies. She stopped writing Hana letters; it was dangerous. She didn't write to her other relatives abroad either.

Magda and Mirek learnt to go to the cinema late to miss the newsreel, which was always shown before the main feature film. Those newsreels were full of optimistic praising of workers and farmers – now in collective farmers' groups – living happy productive lives. Most people knew some farmers who were forced to join the groups and give up their land, like the Steins had to give up their factory. Anna, the former cook, came one day and cried. Her brother Franta, a farmer, refused to join the farmers' cooperative group and was arrested by the police and sentenced as an 'enemy of socialism' to four years in prison. Two of Franzi's husband's friends who spent the war in exile in Britain and flew with the RAF came back only to be arrested as 'imperialist spies'. Then Franzi met Mrs Katz from Theresienstadt, who told her in a whisper that her husband who survived Buchenwald was arrested and sent to Jachymov uranium mines for forced labour.

"Mrs Katz said her husband could never watch his mouth and he hated communists, claiming they are like the Nazis. I heard from someone this Jachymov is a terrible place, like a concentration camp. Poor Mrs Katz!" sighed Franzi.

The situation got worse; more people Franzi knew were being arrested just a couple of years after being liberated from a Nazi concentration camp. For some people, like one of Otto's school friends, it was only four years between being imprisoned and tortured by the Nazis and their new imprisonment in the communist Czechoslovakia. Most people didn't believe that the Czech police would behave like the Nazis. Yet they often did, and the forced labour in Jachymov uranium mines exposed the prisoners, who were all political, to radiation and no one seemed to care.

"You and Mirek should have emigrated. I would have coped, Magda." But Magda would never leave her mother.

Then came the political trials. Top communist functionaries were arrested and accused of treason. All those arrested were Jewish. The newspapers denounced "Zionist imperialists." By December 1952, most of those arrested were executed.

Franzi was scared. "The antisemitism, it is here again."

CHAPTER TWELVE

Magda 1953

MAGDA HAS A BABY, BUT LIFE IS HARD

In 1953, Magda got pregnant. Magda and Franzi were so happy. Magda wanted to have many children and make her family large again. She was sick a lot in the pregnancy, but having a baby was worth it. Her baby, little Zuzana, was born in the winter of 1953. She had lots of dark hair from the beginning and looked like Irma. She cried a lot. Magda was tired and she cried too. She was so pleased Franzi lived with them. Her mother did almost everything: cooking, shopping with those long queues in the shops, as well as cleaning the apartment.

Magda looked after the baby, who seemed such a selfish little thing, wanting attention all the time. Magda loved her, of course, very much, but she found it hard. She liked baby Zuzana best when she was asleep: the tiny hands in fists, the lovely head with dark hair – she was so beautiful. Magda could watch her sleeping for hours, but then Zuzana would wake up and cry. Suddenly, wanting more children seemed stupid. Magda did not want to do that again. Mirek said she was making too much of a fuss. When Magda cried, Mirek just left, banging the door behind him.

It got better when Zuzana grew older, but Magda's marriage was not going well. Mirek had one affair after another, and they argued a lot. People kept telling Magda they saw him with other women.

Sometimes he said that he was going to be on call for the weekend, but when she phoned the hospital, he wasn't there. Magda made jealous scenes and shouted, but Mirek never argued; he just left the room. He told Magda she was superficial. He had a cold voice. When they went to the theatre or concerts, she often fell asleep and Mirek hated that. Magda preferred to go dancing; her mother was always willing to babysit. *I get bored by Mirek's books, opera, galleries*, she thought. They used to go out often, but now Mirek seemed to prefer to go out with other women. There was a lot of shouting. Magda's mother didn't like it. She never shouted at Bruno.

The politics became a problem, too. Magda wanted to go to university. Her mother could look after Zuzana, but the clerk in the university admission department told her they couldn't enrol her, because of her 'bourgeois' background. She got a job as a secretary at a record company. She enjoyed it, gossiping with the other secretaries and always knowing which records were coming out. She could always get the records as soon as they were produced and at a discount. She flirted with her boss. Who said that she had to be faithful to Mirek? He wasn't faithful to her. However, Magda didn't go past flirting; she wanted to make her marriage better.

If I stay faithful, maybe Mirek will stop seeing other women and love me again, she thought.

But no, she didn't think Mirek loved her anymore.

They decided never to tell Zuzana they were Jewish.

"That way, other people won't know either. It is better," said Franzi.

"She's only half Jewish anyway, and hopefully she won't look Jewish either."

"Don't be silly, Jewish women are beautiful, you are." Magda was surprised. *Mirek is nice today…pity it can't be like that all the time.*

Baptism never helped the family to escape Nazi persecution, but Magda still wanted Zuzana baptised even though religion was frowned upon by the regime.

"Where do you want to baptise her?" asked Mirek. "The Roman Catholic church is the most influential one. If she is in any church, let's pick the most powerful one." It was pure opportunism.

The priest in the little baroque Catholic church was worried. Neither Magda nor Mirek had a clue what to do.

"Who is going to supervise this baby's religious development?" the priest asked.

They needed four godparents.

"My father is a Catholic," said Mirek, but when he spoke to his dad, he found out that he had left the church.

Mirek's father thought the baptism was a stupid idea, especially now the communists were in power. The cook Anna, who came over for the Christening, was the only Catholic among the godparents. The other three were Mirek's parents, he a lapsed Catholic and she an atheist, and Franzi, who was baptised in 1938 but into a Protestant church.

The priest no longer cared. They all lied, answering the questions which were part of the baptism.

Do you believe and trust in God, the Father, who made Heaven and Earth?

Do you believe and trust in his Son, Jesus Christ, who redeemed mankind?

Do you believe and trust in his Holy Spirit, who gives life to the people of God?

They were told to answer each of these with: "I believe and trust in Him."

They all said it, but none of them believed in God, not after the war.

Baby Zuzana was now a Roman Catholic. Magda hid the paper in the safe and they never mentioned it again. They celebrated Christmas and Easter, not Hanukkah or Passover.

When she grew a little older, Zuzana loved Easter. Magda and Mirek spread chocolate eggs round the apartment and let her look for them.

It started with Magda shouting, "Wow, I think I saw a bunny running and he dropped something!"

So, they looked if the Easter Bunny dropped something. He always dropped chocolate eggs or little chocolate rabbits and chicks.

At Christmas, they had a Christmas tree and sang carols about Baby Jesus, but Magda wasn't even sure if Zuzana knew who Jesus was.

At about the same time, Magda started pushing Mirek to join the communist party. "They are in power and everything will be easier for us. We'll be safer."

"What would my parents say?" said Mirek. He wasn't close to his parents, but he respected his father's integrity. The relationship between Magda and her in-laws was cold. They saw them for Christmas and birthdays, and there were gaps in the conversation. Franzi, normally so tolerant, told Magda that the Novotny were antisemites.

She said, "Mirek's mother was telling me that at first, she didn't want him to marry you, but he is not that clever with money, so it is good that he married you, because Jews are crafty with money. 'And Magda is Jewish, but nice.' But Magda, that was not the worst thing! She said, 'So many of you came back from the camps!' as if that was a bad thing! I don't want to see that woman again if I can help it."

Magda didn't see her in-laws often. She always felt they didn't approve of her. Now she had a reason to avoid them.

Often, when Mirek looked after Zuzana, he left her at his parents and picked her up after three or four hours. He was meeting other women and Zuzana was serving as an alibi. Mirek's parents probably knew, but they never mentioned anything to Magda.

Mirek's party membership was useful. He got a promotion. He could travel abroad. But while the communist party membership helped his career, it did not save their marriage.

When Zuzana was nine, Mirek left Magda for another woman. *Good riddance*, Magda thought, but then she started crying.

Her mum embraced her. "Don't worry, Magda, we'll be fine. We lived through worse."

Magda didn't tell Zuzana about the divorce that followed. "Your father had to go away for a while," she said.

The habit of not discussing a painful past was hard to break. Eventually, people found out, but Magda still didn't talk about it. The war, her Jewishness, her marital breakdown. It was as if those things didn't exist if she didn't talk about them.

CHAPTER THIRTEEN

Magda 1964–1967

MAGDA AND ZUZANA TRAVEL TO THE WEST – THOU SHALT NOT STEAL

When Stalin died, the political situation in Czechoslovakia improved. In 1963, Magda could study again. She couldn't have done it without her mother looking after the household and Zuzana. Magda became a pharmacist. Before her graduation, she changed her name back to her maiden name. She was Magda Stein once more, like when she was a child. She liked it better that way.

It was no longer dangerous to be in touch with people in the West and it was possible to travel there, so Magda re-started corresponding with Uncle Otto and Aunt Marie in France and her relatives in America – her cousin Irma and her husband Petr. Irma also gave her addresses of her aunt Hilda and her uncle Jürgen, and Aunt Judita and Uncle Simon. Magda even wrote to Hana in Israel. They all invited Magda to come to visit and Zuzana pushed for it, but Magda felt America was too far. Instead, they wrote letters. Magda didn't speak English; they wrote in Czech.

Magda kept writing to Otto and Marie but slowly, the only correspondence with the other relatives was the exchange of Christmas wishes. The fact they were all Jewish made no difference in that. They all just followed what everybody else did.

In Czechoslovakia, people visit the graves of relatives on All Souls' Day, 2 November. For many, it is the only time they visit their family graves. The previous year, 1962, 2 November was Friday. Magda was annoyed to arrive at the Jewish cemetery only to find it was closed. It was Sabbath. She came home and complained to her mother.

"Of course, I completely forgot!" Franzi laughed, smacking her forehead with her palm.

Fridays were not special for either of them. They were trying to forget they were Jewish. Magda remembered it when one of the letters from Irma mentioned Hanukkah. She last celebrated Hanukkah before the war. Zuzana didn't even know the word.

Otto and Marie kept inviting them, and France was not that far. Magda wanted Franzi to go too, but Franzi said she was too old.

"Go with Zuzana, Magda! I will stay at home."

Otto drove to meet them in Austria and then took them to Bavaria. It was the first time Magda had seen Otto since 1948. Marie didn't come with him, and Otto showed them the beautiful old towns and took them to expensive restaurants. Compared to Bavaria, Prague, with its peeling paint on the walls and old palaces in bad repair, was shabby. Zuzana, who grew up in the communist Czechoslovakia, was much more surprised than Magda. It seemed that Zuzana's large brown eyes doubled in size. She was staring at the shops, the choice of fruit, the cars. Everything looked so much better.

Zuzana's parents were always careful not to talk to her about politics, as she could have said something at school and cause trouble. As a little girl, Zuzana was extremely excited by communism; she even wrote poetry about Lenin and workers and capitalists. This communist fervour stopped after her first trip to the West. The first thing that changed Zuzana's political opinions were the colourful plastic straws. They only had real straw ones in Prague. The German waiters thought Zuzana was cute, collecting the straws and getting excited about every new colour. Often, instead of just giving her one straw for her drink, they gave her the whole box. She brought the straws back as gifts to her friends.

The West was wonderful: the food, the shops. Magda loved it. Otto was very generous, buying them clothes, ski boots for Zuzana and gifts to bring for Franzi. However, Magda always felt she deserved those gifts without having to be too grateful. *Who knows if Otto didn't take some of the money from the factory when he emigrated, money that should have rightfully been divided?*

Otto and Marie seemed to be so wealthy! Otto worked as a director of a leather goods company on the outskirts of Paris, using his previous experience. Marie had worked for a while in a fashion boutique, but she had stopped working some time ago. They had done well, and Otto had made some good investments on the stock market.

In the beginning, Otto went shopping with them, but Magda spoke German, so he just gave her money and left, meeting them later in a restaurant. The shops were so much better than in the communist Czechoslovakia. One day, looking at handbags in Kaufhaus – a large, beautiful department store – Magda suddenly became furious. The shop had so much variety, hangers with skirts, dresses in all colours and sizes. It almost made her dizzy. In Czech shops, the choice was limited, and even then, they might not have what she wanted in her size. She found a nice red suede handbag she wanted, but the German shop assistants were ignoring her, talking to each other.

Those evil Germans caused the war and killed my daddy and Oskar, Grandma Heda, and all the others, and they are so rich now – it is so unfair! These older people were probably all Nazis and the younger ones are the brats of Nazis. I hate them!

"You bastards, you murdered my grandma and my daddy and brother and now you live in this luxury! I am not going to pay for this handbag!"

Magda didn't realise she was saying it aloud, in Czech. Zuzana stared at her. Magda walked out of the shop with the handbag without paying. Nobody stopped her. Zuzana followed her with eyes wide like plates. She wanted to say something, but Magda told her to keep quiet about it.

"Those bloody Germans don't deserve to be so wealthy."

That was when Magda's criminal behaviour began. It was simple. She took several items to the changing room, then sent Zuzana to return one to the shelves while she was trying the clothes on. Alone in the changing room, Magda stuffed one thing quickly in her bag and carried on trying on the other clothes. Sometimes she bought something; sometimes she didn't. Did Zuzana notice? If she did, she didn't say anything. Zuzana was not that observant; she usually sat in an armchair outside the changing room and read a book. It was a funny picture: the serious looking girl sitting among the bored husbands whose wives were trying on clothes. Zuzana wasn't interested in clothes, which Magda found annoying. Even when Magda stole some clothes for Zuzana, there were no questions. Zuzana wasn't interested enough to remember what they bought. Of course, the shoplifting was very dangerous — the possibility of a scandal if Otto and Marie found out, and the German government might deport them and not let them travel to West Germany again! She knew all that, but the danger made it thrilling and it felt like sweet revenge.

Daddy and Mummy would be shocked. Magda suddenly remembered the fairground when she was six. She went to a fair and there was a stall selling nice rings with colourful glass that looked like precious stones. The shopkeeper was not looking. Magda took the green ring and put it in her pocket. When she came home and showed her parents, they asked her how much it cost. They had given her some money for the fairground rides. Magda was not fast enough to lie. Bruno was so angry. He made her come with him back to the fair, apologise to the stall keeper, a gypsy woman with large hoop earrings, and return the ring. He also gave the woman some money. Little Magda was embarrassed and cried, but this time, Bruno didn't soften. He spanked her – quite hard, too. Magda couldn't remember being spanked like that ever, before or after.

"Don't ever do that again, Magda. I am not having you grow up as a thief!"

Yes, but Daddy was killed by the German Nazis. Magda had seen enough people looking just after themselves in Theresienstadt in order to survive.

Life is tough and you can't trust anybody.

Eventually, the shoplifting stopped. The risk was not worth it, and Magda didn't need to do it; Otto gave her enough money anyway and she worried that Zuzana might notice something.

From then on, every summer, Magda and Zuzana travelled to Paris and stayed with Otto and Marie in their beautiful flat in Trocadero, an expensive part of Paris. Zuzana was now learning French as well as English and Russian; she was good at languages.

CHAPTER FOURTEEN

Zuzana's memories of 1964-1966

IN 2000, ZUZANA REMEMBERS HER CHILDHOOD TRIPS TO THE WEST

Now I live in what we used to call the West, in England, I am thinking about the past and how different everything was, living in communist Czechoslovakia. On our visits, Prague is different from London, but the difference is not as huge as the one I witnessed on my first visit to the West in 1964. That visit was a shock.

When I was a child, I believed everything I heard at school. My parents, worried that I would say something which would incriminate them, didn't talk to me about politics. I believed Lenin and Stalin were the best people in the world, my protectors, and that communism was the best way of life. I imagined the West as being nasty, divided into oppressors and oppressed, cities full of starving beggars being ignored by fat capitalists smoking thick cigars.

Then my mother took me on my first trip to the West, visiting my Great-Uncle Otto. My communist beliefs vanished quickly. I loved our trips to the West. Everything sparkled; people were better dressed; the shops were all different, not like the uniform shops in Czechoslovakia, where all butcher's shops had the same front sign saying 'Meat and Sausages' in standard pink and all vegetable stores had signs saying 'Fruit and Vegetables' in green and yellow. In the West, every shop looked different. Of course, what was even more different was what they were selling. Unseasonal fruit, a big choice of meat and the clothes shops! Whole rows of dresses, skirts, blouses. And the neon lights! In comparison, Prague seemed grey.

Everything was different. When my mother stole the handbag, I stood there, staring at her, while she walked out of the shop, gesticulating for me to follow.

"Don't stare at me and don't tell anybody, Zuzana. It serves the German bastards right!"

We stayed in Munich for three days. We did more shopping. I was curious if my mother was now a permanent shoplifter. But if she ever stole anything again, I never knew.

Next time, we flew directly to Paris. I loved visiting Otto and Marie, Paris was beautiful, and my mother was nicer to me in their company. Once, she wanted me to go shopping but I wanted to stay at home. She was shouting at me, with her usual, "You are so selfish; like your father, you never do anything I want you to do!" drama.

But then she went further: "No wonder you have no friends – you are such a bookworm, and you are not interested in the things normal girls are, like fashion or dancing. You are ugly, not like the other girls, and nobody will ever marry you!"

"Stop it, Magda." Otto was suddenly stern, serious. "That is no way to talk to your daughter, stop it."

To my surprise, Mother stopped, and compared to our time in Prague, those times in Paris were like islands of peace.

CHAPTER FIFTEEN

Magda 1964–1968

WHY CAN'T MY DAUGHTER BE MY BEST FRIEND?

L ife felt good. Zuzana was clever, she was doing well at school and she seemed mature for her age, more like a friend rather than daughter. Friend? Not really. Magda loved her so much, but Zuzana seemed distant. When Magda took her shopping for clothes or shoes, Zuzana complained.

"Can't you buy it without me? I don't care what I am wearing. Shopping is boring."

Magda couldn't understand that. *What is better than shopping trips together, trying clothes on, talking about fashion? That is what mothers and daughters do!*

The arguments often came unexpectedly. *Like Irma's letter the other day.* Magda was showing Zuzana a letter from Irma. She thought they could laugh about Irma's bad grammar.

"Irma is a bit stupid," she joked. Zuzana hardly ever agreed with her mother's judgement of people. *She is so contrary!* Magda thought.

"Mother, Irma went to German schools, didn't she? She has been living in the USA since 1948, so it's a miracle she can write in Czech at all." Zuzana made one of her disapproving faces.

Magda hated being called Mother. So cold and impersonal. "Why don't you call me Mummy? And why are you always arguing with me? You don't know anything about Irma, you have never met her."

Zuzana used one of her weapons. Silence.

Magda's letters to her relatives didn't have grammatical errors, but they were short. Even at school, she always used to struggle with essays. "What do you write about?" she kept asking her classmates. In the letters to her relatives, she just described her week, including what they had for dinners, wrote that Zuzana was doing well at school and what was the weather like.

Zuzana always wrote long letters to her father and mother from school summer camps; she liked writing. Her letters were witty, with long descriptions, quoting conversations. She inherited her interest in writing from her father. Mirek always talked about wanting to be a writer. Zuzana was a lot like Mirek. Magda found it annoying.

Zuzana taught herself to read when she was four. When she was little, books were always the best presents, but when Magda chose books for her now, they were never the ones Zuzana wanted. Zuzana didn't like romantic novels or stories about schoolchildren or crime stories; she soon started reading adult literature: Pushkin, Tolstoy, Stendhal, Hemingway, Capek, Kafka and many others. In the beginning, Zuzana enthusiastically recommended books to her mother or grandmother, but neither of them liked reading, and even when Magda tried, she never finished the books.

There were now many new books criticising the communist government of the 1950s and Zuzana gobbled them with passion. Now the censorship had stopped, she became a fervent anti-communist. Magda was afraid it might still lead to trouble.

She wanted a daughter who would be her best friend. Instead, she had a critical intellectual who seemed as bored by their conversations as Mirek used to be.

"You are just like your father, so cold and detached."

They argued and it usually ended up with Zuzana crying. Yet, Magda didn't want to make her daughter cry; she wanted her to change.

Mirek saw Zuzana once a week. He took her to theatres, galleries; he read books Zuzana was interested in and talked to her about history and politics. Zuzana loved him. She came from the meetings with her father happy, talking about what they had done and seen. Sometimes, she went to have dinner with him and his new, much younger wife. Zuzana was describing the food and the interesting, modern recipes, French or Italian. She liked Mirek's new wife Dagmar. Magda got insanely angry and jealous. Her daughter should be loyal to her, not to that bastard Mirek who'd abandoned them both. It was easy for him, being a father; he was the fun parent. It was Magda who looked after Zuzana, went to school parents' evenings and had to bear Zuzana's moods. Yet, Mirek often disappointed Zuzana. He promised he'd come and then cancelled at the last minute. Mirek went on holiday to the West, skiing in the Alps in the winter, beaches in Italy in the summer, but he never offered to take Zuzana with him. Magda tried to make Zuzana ask him to take her on holiday. She also asked Zuzana to tell Mirek they need more money for Zuzana's sport and other hobbies. She didn't talk to him directly. When Zuzana asked him, he said, "Let me talk to your mother about it." He never did.

Zuzana got upset. "Don't tell me to ask Dad about things. Ask him yourself!"

They had an argument again. *She can't count on Mirek – why can't Zuzana see it?* It hurt Magda to think Zuzana loved her father more than she loved her.

Magda was still happy, though, living with her mother and Zuzana. Franzi usually managed to keep the peace. Zuzana was different with her grandmother Franzi, and she often laughed. Whenever Zuzana was in trouble with Magda, Franzi found excuses for her. Zuzana was rather absentminded and was constantly losing things: plimsolls, exercise books, gloves. She lost a golden chain with a small ruby pendant that Magda used to wear as a child. Magda was so furious, she shouted at Zuzana, a long tirade of lists of the things Zuzana had lost since the beginning of school year and how careless and selfish Zuzana was.

"As if we haven't lost more, Magda. They are just things. It isn't important, leave Zuzana alone." Franzi kissed Zuzana but pulled Magda towards her, too, hugging them both at the same time.

They are the only ones I have left, Franzi thought.

Magda always looked forward to her daughter's ballroom dancing lessons. All 15-year-old girls looked forward to those, as it was an entrance to the adult world. All except Zuzana. The girls and the mothers, who were acting as chaperones, got new dresses; the girls learnt how to dance and meet boys, who dressed up in sharp suits. Magda had several beautiful lacy dresses made for her daughter, but Zuzana said she preferred trousers. None of the clothes Zuzana had from Paris were dressy enough for dancing classes, so Magda took her to a dressmaker. Zuzana was making faces, standing there while the dress was pinned on her by the dressmaker. It was a beautiful pale baby blue lace, baby doll shape, very short. Magda was glad miniskirts were not fashionable when she was young; her fat legs were the only bad thing about her figure, but Zuzana had nice long legs, so it suited her. Zuzana looked beautiful, but she complained that she felt faint standing so long while the dressmaker was pinning the dress on her and that she hated pastel colours. Then Zuzana found Franzi's old dress, wrapped in a plastic cover in the wardrobe. She asked what it was.

"Oh, Mummy, do we still have this old thing? I remember when you brought it back from the Krejci family after the war. Why do we still have it?" asked Magda.

"It is a memory, although I will never fit in the dress again, and where would I wear it, anyway?" Franzi felt the beautiful thin silk of the dress and the lacy inserts. She saw herself, slim, wearing it at a party, dancing with her beloved Bruno.

Zuzana thought the dress was amazing. She tried it on – it fitted her beautifully, but it was black. Zuzana wanted to have it for her dancing lessons.

"I don't think so, Zuzana. It is old, it might fall apart, and you can't wear a black dress – it would be as if you were going to a funeral!"

Franzi agreed: young girls did not wear black. "Why don't we give it to her, Magda? She can wear it later."

Magda said no, wrapped the dress up again and put it on the back of her wardrobe. She could see that Zuzana wanted the dress badly, and not giving her what she wanted gave Magda power.

In the dancing lessons, Magda sat with the other mothers, watching. She saw their daughters dancing, smiling at their mothers and chatting to them during the break. But Zuzana was not paying enough attention, so she was dancing badly, bumping into people. In the break, instead of talking to Magda or the boys, she read a book she smuggled in her handbag, sitting on the stairs. With the skirts being so short, Magda kept making faces at Zuzana.

"Your panties are showing," Magda whispered, coming to Zuzana and pulling her up. Next time, Zuzana sat on the stairs even further from her mother.

What was worse, she kept disappearing to the loo. Magda was sure Zuzana just sat there and read. They had a big argument on the tram on the way home.

"You are so ungrateful. Any other girl would be happy to have such a beautiful, expensive dress, but you were embarrassing there!"

Zuzana looked at her mother with the cold, emotionless face she wore most of the time and said, "Let's take the dress back or give it to somebody. Maybe we could get the money for the dancing classes back if you said I was ill. I really hate it and there is this weekly TV series we are both missing."

It was *The Forsyte Saga*, the British TV series, and yes, it was good, but they were repeating it on Sunday morning.

"Dancing classes are the best time in a young girl's life or should be. I would have loved to do that, but I was too old after the war. You never do anything the normal way – every other girl there was enjoying it."

"Well, I don't like those classes and I will never learn how to dance. Who does ballroom dancing anyway? That's not how we dance at parties."

They were in the tram, so Magda was trying to keep her voice down, but she was furious. Sometimes Zuzana was like a stranger.

I was sitting in the prison scratching myself and picking lice when I was her age. She is so lucky!

But of course, Zuzana was never told about the family imprisonments, about being Jewish, about her grandfather and uncle being killed by the Nazis – none of it. She knew they died in the war, but she probably thought they were soldiers.

Maybe we should tell her. But no, if Zuzana doesn't know she is Jewish, she's safe.

When they got home and Magda really started shouting at Zuzana, Franzi stopped her. "Magda, just leave her alone. The dancing is not important and she's a good girl."

Zuzana, who adored her grandmother, kissed her and said, "Maybe you can teach me how to dance, Grandma!"

"Charleston, ha?" Franzi winked. At that time, there was a Czech pop song on the television: A young singer asked a grey-haired old woman to stop knitting and teach her how to dance Charleston, promising she would do all the chores later. The old woman (probably not as old as she seemed) put her knitting down, got up and danced the Charleston with the young singer.

Franzi and Zuzana started to dance the Charleston together like in that video clip, with Zuzana singing the song.

"You are both impossible." But they made Magda laugh, too.

The crisis was over; she started dancing Charleston with them and Zuzana kissed them both, laughing.

Why can't it always be like this? Magda thought.

PART TWO

Zuzana

CHAPTER ONE

Zuzana remembers
1966-1967 in 2000

SKIING SAVED ME FROM BULLYING IN THE NEW SCHOOL

I changed schools in the autumn of 1966. The new school specialised in languages, and we were taught English as well as the compulsory Russian. I already knew German, French and English, too, but not very well. It was hard to get a place in the language school unless you 'knew somebody'. When I told my husband Harry in 2000 that I got into my school via the black market, he thought I was kidding.

"It's not like that anymore, Harry, but my mother misses it. She was a master of the system of favours; she always 'knew somebody'. I think one of the teachers in the new school was my father's patient. My parents never thought it was immoral, as everybody did it. The whole of society was based on contacts, exchanges of favours. A pharmacist got a rare drug for the butcher; the butcher brought her meat not normally available. My father fitted an extra patient in; the patient, a car mechanic repaired his car where normally there was a waiting list."

"Nepotism and corruption are everywhere," said Harry.

But not like this, you don't have a clue, I thought.

My 13-year-old son Adam entered the room and listened to me talking about the new school.

My parents were divorced and rarely agreed on anything. But they did agree the language school was good for me. I liked languages but I didn't want to change school.

"I don't want to lose my friends," I said.

"You will get new friends and it's a very nice school." Once my mother's mind was set on it, I didn't have a chance.

I tried to persuade my father, but he just said, "You'll be fine, Zuzana. The other children will come from similar families, so you'll have more in common."

That was the first time I experienced my parents being snobby.

"You mean class? I thought that stupid prejudice was long gone. We are all equal under socialism, aren't we?" I was being sarcastic, of course. Class differences had never gone away. I suddenly remembered my friend Ludmila Fried, who lived in one of those ugly early 20th-century working-class tenements with the entrance to the flats on the balcony and with a communal bathroom. Ludmila's father was a printer at the communist party newspaper *Rude Pravo* and he was a Stalinist, even after Khrushchev criticised the cult of Stalin. Mr Fried was a party member with a very early membership number, and the fact that they lived like this, with a tiny one-bedroom flat and only running water on the balcony, showed a naïve idealism.

Most old communist party members had well-paid government jobs and nice flats or houses; they even had special shops. When Ludmila first came to our flat on the embankment, full of old furniture, paintings and chandeliers, she stopped, staring, and said, "This is a real bourgeois flat!" I thought it was funny; my mother didn't. My bourgeois background could have prevented me from going to university.

In political questionnaires, when asked about her father's profession, my mother would put *office clerk, died in the war*. Nobody discovered that her father was a wealthy lawyer and a factory owner, so yes, we had a bourgeois flat. I liked Ludmila; she was smart and nice. She also read even more than I did, but with a systematic determination. She picked authors from different periods, and her reading was more like a research. She kept notes and divided the books by country, time and genre. She believed in her father's politics, so I should have been a class enemy, but Ludmila liked me, and she also liked coming to our flat. Then one day she asked if she could have a bath, and that became a habit; she did it every week. Now I was changing schools, would our friendship last? In the end, Ludmila's family moved to Ostrava.

The new school was about 30 minutes' walk away. The tram connection took longer. I preferred it. I could read on trams. My attempts to read while walking ended with a big bump on my forehead. There were lampposts on the pavement. I still remember all those people laughing.

Father was right. My new schoolmates were all from privileged backgrounds – their parents were often communist party members, some were diplomats, people with connections. The girls wore makeup, listened to Radio Luxemburg and knew all the hits. Their fathers brought them records from their trips to the West. I was not interested in pop music. I liked reading. But they thought my talking about Franz Kafka, Simone de Beauvoir and Alberto Moravia was weird. For my part, I thought their interest in pop charts was childish.

Maybe they had a reason to hate me. I even looked different, wearing those expensive but old-fashioned elegant clothes bought for me by Marie in Paris.

The first day in my new school, the teacher introduced me to the other pupils and sat me next to Jitka, a pretty blonde girl with a small, upturned nose and large blue eyes. Those eyes seemed cold as they assessed me. Jitka's skirts were short, and her hair was long.

With my short, straight black hair, I looked at odds with everyone else. Mother said short hair was more practical.

In the breaks between lessons, nobody talked to me. I suppose it was partly my fault because I read a book at every opportunity. In my old school, everybody was used to me sitting in the corner, reading. Eventually, the teacher put me in charge of the library, and other children used to ask me about the books. I was also useful for providing them with summaries of the books we were supposed to read. Some of them let me copy their maths and physics homework in return. Science was never my forte.

In the new school, the bullying started slowly. The boy who stuck his leg out 'accidentally' so that I tripped over it; the girl who spilled her drink on my exercise book. I was quite clumsy, so I didn't think much of it. But then I noticed the sudden silence when I came into the girls' changing room. They did not talk to me, but all their eyes seemed to be on me.

I was always good at sport, but in the new school, PE was painful. There was always someone who bumped into me or elbowed me, the little aggressive gestures common in ball games. It happened too often for it to be a coincidence. Sometimes it was hard not to cry, but I didn't want to give them the satisfaction.

My mother kept asking me why I didn't invite one of the girl's home. I was evasive. She would not understand. She always told me how popular she used to be at school. I could imagine her well as one of those gossiping girls that were torturing me.

That year was a tough year, but it changed in February, on our school skiing trip. It started badly. We arrived by coach at the mountain hotel, and the teacher divided us into rooms. Three at a time. There were 18 girls, so it should have been easy, but nobody wanted to share a room with me. In the end, I was allocated to Jitka and Monika. Monika, a tall, sporty, freckled girl with green eyes and a perfect figure, started making gagging noises. Jitka wrinkled her nose and stared at me with those cold, icy, stabbing eyes. "Get on with it, girls," the teacher said, ignoring their hostility.

We unpacked our large backpacks in the room. Monika and Jitka ignored me. They took most of the space in the wardrobe, and when I put some things in the drawers, they took them out and put them in the smallest compartment close to the bottom of the wardrobe. They did not talk to me. Fortunately, I had my book. I always had a book.

I took my book to dinner, too. The teacher noticed I was reading and wanted to say something but changed her mind. I suppose she did feel sorry for me after all.

Everything changed the next day. The teachers asked us to ski down, one after another, so that they could divide us into groups. I had been skiing with my parents from the age of three. With skis or skates attached to my feet, I was graceful. I skied down: fast, elegant turns. The male PE teacher clapped and said, "First group, obviously." Soon we were divided into three groups, but nobody in the first group skied as well or fast as I did, not even the boys.

At lunch, when I was carrying my tray to the empty table in the corner, four girls and two boys asked me to sit with them. Monika got up and said, "We're in the same room – we should eat together, too."

Then she asked me how I learned to ski so well and what I was reading now. It was as if the old hostility had never happened. The rest of the week was fun. I was the centre of attention; everybody wanted to talk to me about skiing. One evening, Jitka put her makeup on my face and combed my hair differently. I looked better; it was as if I changed into a pretty, popular girl. But it was not me who changed. Suddenly I was a member of the club.

My son had listened to me talking, without interrupting, but now he kissed me and said, "So when they found out what a good skier you were, they realised that maybe you are good at other things too, Mum."

Adam obviously wanted a happy ending, but it wasn't so simple.

On the way home, I started thinking about it. I was still the same bookish girl with short hair, the girl nobody wanted to talk to. *How come that one ski run made me suddenly popular? Will they go back to their hostility when we come back to Prague?* They didn't. But suddenly I didn't care. I didn't become friends with Jitka or Monika. I still read in the breaks. I sometimes joined the others in the cinema or talked to them in the school canteen. But otherwise, I kept my distance. If the difference between being hated or popular could be based just on a single skill, I could live without it. Still, it was nice not to be bullied.

CHAPTER TWO

Zuzana 1967

WHAT, I AM JEWISH?

My parents never told me I was Jewish. As a child, I knew my grandfather and other relatives died in the war, but not why. I am not sure why I never asked. I think I understood that my parents didn't want to talk about it. Or maybe, like many teenagers, I was too self-centred to be interested.

My ignorance was made easier by the fact that nobody talked about the Jews. Yes, we learnt at school about concentration camps for people who were fighting the Nazis, but the Holocaust was never mentioned. In our textbooks, it was mainly the communists that were persecuted by the Nazis. There were some nonspecific references to 'antifascists but no details. The Holocaust of the Roma gypsies was never mentioned either. Even when censorship lifted and I read novels with Jewish characters, I never thought that those characters had anything to do with me.

I remember once when I was nine years old, a girl told me that her parents thought I was Jewish. I told her it wasn't true and that I didn't know any Jewish people. When I came home, I asked my mother.

"You shouldn't really be friends with people like this," she said.

In 1967, Otto and Marie came to visit from Paris. It was their first visit. When I asked Uncle Otto why they didn't come before, he told me about their illegal emigration in 1948 and that he was afraid the police would not let them leave again if they came to Czechoslovakia. Now it was no longer dangerous for them. The government was much less oppressive.

When I was a teenager, I read a lot, and lots of those newly published books contradicted my history textbooks. Later, when foreigners talked to me about Prague Spring, I always told them the spring lasted for at least four years. The year 1967 felt free.

That day in 1967, we were all walking with Uncle Otto and Aunt Marie in the Old town, and we came to the old Jewish cemetery. I liked that cemetery, with its haphazard tombstones. It was a solemn place. We went to the Pinkas synagogue. On the walls inside, in alphabetical order, there were names of the 78,000 Czech Jews killed in the war. I have been there once before, so I wasn't taking much notice.

But then, the shock came. Mum and Uncle Otto were looking for names, and there they were, my grandfather Bruno and his son Oskar, Mum's cousin Irma's parents, and many other relatives I had heard about. Otto, Marie, my grandma Franzi and my mum spent a long time finding all the names. When we left the museum, my grandmother was crying, and my mother was holding her hand.

"Mum, I am confused. I thought the names on the walls were all Jewish?" I said.

One would think my mother would tell me the truth then, but she changed the subject.

That was how I found out I was Jewish. Later, I met many people of my generation with similar experiences. One of my friends came home complaining that a boy at school called her a Jew. She thought he was swearing at her.

"I beat him up," she said.

"Do you want to see a Jew?" asked her father.

"Yes, where?" asked my friend, then aged 13.

"Look in the mirror!" her father said.

The stories were all different, but similar. So were the reactions. I was angry. Why did they not tell me? Slowly, my mother and grandma started telling me things about the war. It was mostly funny things like the one about my mum burning the files in the Jewish community centre; Grandma only found out when my mum told me and playfully pretended she was going to spank her for it. They both told me about the vegetable fields in Theresienstadt, and the headlice. They didn't talk about the dead ones – my grandfather and Oskar.

In the political thaw, the Holocaust was now mentioned in news and textbooks. It was no longer just communist antifascists who were victims of the Nazis.

In 1967, we also all went to Theresienstadt. It was a mistake. It was alright when we were in the main town; they were telling me about the kitchen Grandma used to work in and what the crowded accommodation was like. We saw the room where Great-Grandmother Olga survived the war. They told me about Helena, the sister of my grandfather who had kissed an SS officer's boots when he told her she could go to a transport to join her family in the east. They had all died, apart from my mother's cousin Irma, who now lived in New York. Then we walked to the Small Fortress; it was a guided tour. They showed us the cells; my mother showed me the tiny cave-like cell she was quarantined in when she had diphtheria. They showed me the Jewish female cell, and I couldn't imagine that such a small place could hold almost a hundred women.

My mum and grandma were alright up to the point when the guide showed us the small male cells. The guide told us about the slave labour in the underground factory and the starvation. The SS officers sometimes just came and shot randomly through the window at the men, cramped together in the concrete cell. Almost nobody survived.

Grandma Franzi started crying and couldn't stop. My mother was sobbing, too. The other tourists were staring; I didn't know what to do.

"Let's go," said Grandma. "We shouldn't have come. No point opening these wounds." She stopped crying and passed my mum a handkerchief. "Come on, Magda, darling."

We went back home; they were both quiet on the train, and

when I asked questions, they both told me they didn't want to talk about it. I wanted to find out more.

Later, somebody told me about the youth group in the Jewish community centre. I told my mother. She made a big scene. "You will not go there. It is not safe for people to know you are Jewish."

I would have probably gone but for Grandma Franzi, who agreed with Mother, and I didn't want to upset her. I didn't mind upsetting my mother. She was cross with me all the time anyway.

Much later, I stopped being angry. They wanted to protect me. Maybe I didn't have many friends because I was Jewish? But I never really encountered antisemitism. In fact, sometimes it was the opposite. People somehow thought I was more intelligent and sophisticated, being Jewish. That is, of course, a prejudice. Pinkas synagogue, the place where I found out that I was Jewish, was closed soon after the Soviet invasion in 1968. It re-opened in 1995. I took Harry and Adam there; it is impressive, those rows of names on the walls.

CHAPTER THREE

Zuzana 1967-1968

By the time I was ten years old, I had decided that although she looked after me and loved me, I did not trust my mother's judgement. She would say things deliberately to hurt me or manipulate me into doing what she wanted. Her 'everything is possible if you try' attitude made her incredibly determined and successful, but it meant she just bulldozed over obstacles. I was an obstacle sometimes.

My mother would often seek my advice, but it was only so that she could blame me if things didn't go well. She treated me like an older sister she never had. She asked me what to wear and where to go on holiday. I did not have a clue, so I made it up as I went along. Soon, though, I concluded that a simple, "I don't know, Mum," was safer. I couldn't win. She blamed me anyway, for not being helpful.

And her advice to me just wasn't safe. I remember telling her about some playground arguments. "Tell her…" It was always something hurtful. I lost friends by telling them what my mother advised me to say. I soon stopped telling her about my problems.

My father had moved out when I was nine and soon got married to Dagmar, an exceptionally beautiful former model. She looked after my father as if he was a child. Dagmar was a good cook, but she also did all the shopping and housework. She was nice to me, but I thought she was rather stupid. Dagmar was different from my mother. Neither shared my father's interests, but whereas my mother was smart and never pretentious, Dagmar pretended to be a sophisticated, cultured woman, although all I ever heard were clichés. Once, my father saw me making a face when Dagmar confused Debussy with Stravinsky, talking about their music as if she was an expert. Later, when he drove me home, he gave me a useful lesson.

"You know, Zuzana, one needs to decide what is important. You can't have everything. I have a beautiful young wife who looks after the household and me and makes my life very comfortable. If I married an intellectual, she wouldn't do that for me. There is always give and take."

At that time, his advice didn't sink in. Only later, as an adult, I realised my father was, despite his weaknesses, a wise man. He never criticised or humiliated Dagmar, no matter what stupid things came out of her mouth.

I saw Dad every week, and it was always fun, but I knew I couldn't count on him. He loved me, but I only had a small place in his life. He never took me on those holidays abroad, although I knew that his other friends took their children. He often cancelled our meetings at the last minute, and when I phoned him, wanting to tell him about some problem, he often didn't find time for me. My father was great, but not in a crisis. My mum was reliable, and she would have loved it if I confided in her, but I feared she would make hurtful remarks, so I kept my distance.

I envied my mother the unconditional love she had from her mum. I thought Grandma Franzi was wonderful. She used to knit pullovers and baby clothes for a state-owned company; it did not pay much, but she could keep some of the wool. She used to knit me stripy, multicoloured jumpers. Once, she made me a skirt with a teddy-bear pattern. I loved that skirt. She looked after me and my mum, and she protected me from my mother's hurtful behaviour. Once, when I was about six, my mother was told off by Grandma for making bubbles with chewing gum and teasing me because I couldn't do it.

"Ha! You are useless, Zuzana, look at my bubbles!"

I had started crying but Grandma Franzi had saved the day. "Magda, stop it! Are you an idiot, laughing at your daughter?! And stop that disgusting behaviour with the chewing gum. You are like a child!"

I always loved watching my mother being scolded by Grandma.

CHAPTER FOUR

Zuzana 1968

Even though I now knew we were Jewish, neither my grandma nor my mother told me much about our relatives. I was interested, but they both avoided the subject.

There was only one story Grandma told me and it was about her sister Hilda. I thought it was the most romantic family story I knew. The story of Hilda and her German husband.

One day I came back from school after learning in history about the expulsion of Germans from Czechoslovakia in 1946. Almost 14 million Germans were expelled from Poland, Czechoslovakia, Hungary and other countries, and sent to Germany in the postwar years. We were told it was a good thing, but to my surprise, Grandma disagreed.

"Not all Germans were Nazis," she said. "My sister Hilda married a Sudeten German called Jürgen and he was one of the nicest men I have ever met."

Grandma made us a cup of lemon tea and started telling me the story of a poor, handsome German and his young, wealthy Jewish bride — Grandma's sister Hilda.

"Hilda was always beautiful, elegant – everybody liked the way she looked. Even my mother-in-law Olga. I was never good enough for Olga. Hilda and I always joked about it. I told her that she would make my mother-in-law much happier than I could, but she replied that I made Bruno much happier than she ever could. Hilda did not need a job, or indeed a husband. My parents gave her her dowry money when she told them she didn't want to get married. She painted pictures, made pottery and lived in an elegant apartment in Prague. Hilda was a real artist."

"Have we got any of her paintings, Grandma?" I asked.

Grandma showed me some watercolours of flowers and birds, and they were beautiful. I liked the bold colours and the flowers looked alive. The flowers were never in vases but thrown haphazardly on a kitchen table or in a sink, as if somebody was going to put them away. I loved them.

"I used to leave your mother and Oskar with Hilda every Sunday afternoon, and they all painted with watercolours. They enjoyed it, and Hilda was generous with her praise."

"Yes, my mum told me neither her nor her brother were very good, and they made a mess with the watercolours, but they loved it. I wish I could have had an aunt like that; I can't draw anything. But Grandma, you said Hilda did get married eventually!"

"Yes, Hilda was 23 when she met Jürgen in the Krkonose – Riesengebirge in German – mountains. I have their pictures, hold on."

Grandma showed me a photo of them in skiing clothes. They both looked like film stars.

Grandma carried on. "Jürgen Weber was a skiing instructor. He was divorced – his wife left him. He had a daughter, Gertrude; she was only two years older than Magda."

"Really, was she a friend of Mummy?" I had never heard of Gertrude.

"No, and you will understand why. Gertrude was German and her mother would never have allowed her to be friends with a Jewish girl. I never met her mother, but Jürgen said she was a Nazi. 'She is in love with Hitler,' he said. 'She is always cutting his pictures out from the newspapers. If she didn't leave me, I would have left her. But Gertrude is not like that; she is my lovely girl.' Jürgen was right – Gertrude was lovely."

Grandma told me that Jürgen and Hilda immediately fell in love, but they were the only ones who believed it.

"Even I thought he only married her for her money, but my parents didn't try to stop the marriage. Even if they had tried, Hilda generally did what she wanted to do anyway.

"Jürgen was older and extremely good-looking in the blond German Aryan way. He was a good dancer and was not only a ski instructor but also a gigolo. Being divorced, with a young daughter, he was not a good match for Hilda."

"Gigolo? Really?" That was exciting!

"Hilda and Jürgen married in 1934. Of course, when the Nazis came five years later, everything changed. There was a lot of pressure on Germans not to be married to Jews. It was already illegal in Germany."

"What pressure? What happened, Grandma?"

"Imagine, Zuzana, the German newspapers were writing about Jürgen being one of the few Germans in Prague still married to a Jew. Jürgen thought the newspaper got his name from his first wife. When Hilda read the article, she came to see me and cried. Hilda loved him, so she asked him to divorce her. Jürgen did not want to hear about it. Hilda meant it; she didn't want him to suffer. She was repeatedly begging him to divorce her. He said: 'No.'"

"What happened? Did they stay together?" I loved the story; it was so romantic.

"Being married to an Aryan meant Hilda was not deported. However, in 1944 Jürgen was sent to Poland to a labour camp."

"Was it a concentration camp like Auschwitz?" I asked.

"No, not quite – there were no gas chambers, but it was bad enough."

Much later, when I was researching family history, I found out the camp was Klein Stein in Poland, a camp for forced labour. Most of the prisoners were men married to Jews or 'die Mischlinge', as the Germans called people who were only partly Jewish.

I kept asking Grandma for details. "What happened to Hilda?"

"She was sent to Theresienstadt soon after, at the end of 1944. We didn't know it; we were already locked up in the Small Fortress."

Grandma told me that Gertrude occasionally came to the family lunches at Olga's. She did it behind her mother's back. A plump blonde girl, she had nothing of her father's angular beauty. Gertrude was, of course, a member of the Nazi girls' organisation. It was compulsory. She used the Heil Hitler salute like anybody else… but she also later sent food parcels to her father's Jewish relatives in the concentration camps.

"She was only 17 when she sent parcels to us, Hilda, and also to other relatives, some of whom she didn't even know."

I liked Gertrude, and I imagined that she didn't like her Nazi mother.

Grandma carried on. "After the war, when we were waiting for everybody to come back, Hilda and Jürgen didn't return to Prague; they moved to the mountains where they met. Some of Jürgen's relatives were Nazis, so he stopped seeing them after he married Hilda. In 1945, speaking German was dangerous. The Germans were mobbed, sometimes even lynched. Then the expulsion of all German inhabitants of Czechoslovakia happened. Gertrude, now 19 years old, and her mother were among those dispossessed Germans."

"Even the nice Gertrude?"

"Nobody cared. She was German, so obviously a Nazi, wasn't she? Soon after, Jürgen and Hilda emigrated."

"Where did they go?"

"Jürgen could have stayed, because of his Czech Jewish wife, but he had to hide his nationality. His Czech was heavily accented, and they spoke German at home. They couldn't stay in the mountains. Their Czech neighbours hated them because of Jürgen; their German neighbours that were not deported hated them because of Hilda.

"They came to visit us in Prague, but in December 1945 they emigrated first to Guyana and then to the USA. I haven't seen my sister since then, but we used to write."

"In Czech or German?" I asked.

"German, but we stopped – you know how it is, correspondence with relatives in the West, it is not safe."

"How about Gertrude?" I asked.

"Nobody ever heard from her again."

Grandma was sad. I wasn't. I loved their story. It was so romantic! Gertrude and Jürgen were both heroes.

I thought that it ended well for Jürgen and Hilda. They did not have to live through the communist regime, and they were happy in America, where they settled. Grandma told me they had a daughter, Lucy.

I always remembered their story. I imagined they were Americans now, not German, Czech or Jewish.

CHAPTER FIVE

Zuzana 1968

SOVIET INVASION

2 1 August 1968, the Soviet Bloc armies invaded Czechoslovakia. Thirty years later, I talked about it with my son Adam. He was 11 then.

"So, what did the Czech army do? Did many people die?"

"No, Adam, there was no fighting. The radio was asking everybody to keep calm. People were demonstrating, shouting in Russian at the soldiers on tanks to go home. There was a pop song we were all singing, telling the Soviet soldiers to go home, that our girls don't love them."

"Did you sing it? And demonstrate?"

"I remember approaching the tanks in our street. I wore a tiny miniskirt; I was 15. The soldiers flirted, but I just made a face and said, '*Idite domoj*.'"

"Go home." Adam repeated the Russian. He was electrified; he got up from his chair and started pacing the room. "Were you scared, Mum?"

"No, the soldiers seemed confused. They were told the Czechoslovak people and government were asking for help against counterrevolutionaries. They expected to be welcomed. In Prague, they randomly shot bullets at highly decorated 19th-century buildings. Maybe they thought these were palaces? One was the

National Museum on Wenceslas Square. You know you said once that Grandma's house looks like a little castle? They shot at it, too."

I remembered that growing up, I didn't used to like the house we lived in. It had 19th-century architecture with little gargoyles and gothic arches; I learnt to like it later. I suppose it is now aged enough to be beautiful.

I told Adam that we had been on holiday in the mountains at the time of the invasion. My grandmother Franzi was with us. I remember hearing about the invasion on the radio. I cried.

"When we came back to Prague three days later, the window in my room was broken by the shots. The glass-fronted small bookcase above my bed had bullet damage, the glass shattered all over my bed, and I retrieved a bullet embedded in my Czech copy of *Alice in Wonderland*. I still have that book."

Adam was listening, open-mouthed. "You could have been shot, Mum!"

"Everything was changing – censorship and propaganda in schools were reintroduced and the Soviet army left some of the soldiers behind 'temporarily'. To us nothing was more permanent. 'Temporary like the Russian army' meant forever. The invasion was now described as 'Brotherly help aimed to prevent an invasion by NATO'. I was 15. After the Soviet invasion, I pestered my mother to emigrate. But she told me she was too old and that she couldn't abandon her mother."

"Why didn't you all go?" asked Adam.

"We could, but Grandma was quite frail, and your Grandma Magda wouldn't leave without her."

"But you emigrated later, Mum, on your own, right?"

I didn't tell Adam that my main reason for emigrating four years later was to not be with my mother.

"Grandma Magda was only 40 when the invasion happened. I could have grown up in the West. France, USA, Canada, even Israel. Our relatives abroad would have helped us."

I blamed my mother for it for years, for not being brave. But I did not understand the bond she had with her mother. They had already lost too many people.

I told Adam about the two students, Palach and Zajic, who burned themselves in a protest against the invasion. We all went to Palach's funeral. It was one of the last demonstrations to be allowed. We walked slowly; most of us were crying. Mother tried to stop me going, as she was afraid I might get into trouble. But I got used to not obeying my mother.

Then Adam suddenly came closer, hugged me and said, "If you emigrated then, and not later, you would have never met Dad, and I would never exist."

I kissed him and said, "I am glad you exist, my darling."

"Oh, may I have a hug, too?" asked my husband Harry, walking to the room.

"I was just telling Adam about 1968 and the invasion."

"Mum could have been shot, but instead, the Russians shot *Alice in Wonderland*, Daddy."

I had never told Harry about it, so I had to start again. Adam kept interrupting, telling the story for me, but when he kept asking about 1968, Harry said, "Come on, Adam, it was 30 years ago."

CHAPTER SIX

Magda 1968

FRANZI DIES

The year 1968 was an unhappy year for Magda. Never mind the Russian invasion: Magda's mother died. Magda and Zuzana came from a skiing holiday, and Franzi looked pale and was complaining of pain in her left arm. Franzi had had a heart attack. She had another one in the hospital and died.

Magda had never felt so alone. She didn't know how to tell Zuzana, so she didn't. For now, she told Zuzana that Franzi was still in hospital and was too weak for visitors. Magda felt the funeral would be too traumatic for Zuzana, so she didn't tell her about Franzi's death until after the funeral. There were not many people in the cemetery. Otto and Marie came from Paris. Magda kept that from Zuzana, too. Franzi's name was going to be engraved under the name of her beloved husband Bruno; unlike him and Oskar, her exact date of death was going to be there.

Otto tried to make Magda tell Zuzana and take her to the funeral.

"No, she is so young, I don't want her to go to funerals. I will tell her about my mummy later."

Otto thought it was a bad mistake, but Magda just couldn't face telling Zuzana, not yet. On the day of the funeral, Zuzana went to school, not knowing. Magda only told her about it a week after the funeral, when Otto and Marie were already back in Paris.

"I have bad news, Zuzana. Your grandma died."

"What? When?"

When Zuzana found out that Magda had kept it all from her until after the funeral, she cried and left the room, slamming the door behind her. When Magda followed her, she tried to embrace Zuzana, but Zuzana pushed her away.

"Leave me alone, why did you not tell me about Grandma? I will never forgive you!"

"Zuzana, you are the only person I have now, can't you be nice to me?"

"You make everything about yourself, leave me alone."

Zuzana's voice was cold, and her now dry eyes were angry. Magda cried and tried to kiss her, but Zuzana pushed her away again.

Alone, I am so alone. "You have your lovely daughter, Zuzana," people said to comfort her.

It was not the same. Fifteen-year-old Zuzana was annoying, opinionated and not at all friendly. She reminded Magda of her husband Mirek, and sometimes, when she was angry, she told her so.

"You are so selfish, just like your father!"

It made Zuzana cry, but Magda feared the coldness in Zuzana's eyes. Of course, they loved each other, but it wasn't the same as Magda and her mother. She had no one now.

Magda found life without her mother hard. She had to learn how to cook and do the shopping. Zuzana never offered to help, and Magda found herself losing patience. They had both been spoiled by Franzi, who had managed the household without complaint. They only found a practical routine slowly. Magda managed to do the shopping during her lunch break. As the chief pharmacist, she would not get told off for disappearing for a few hours. Zuzana would do the washing up, dusting and vacuuming when asked, although Magda wished she wouldn't be so sour about it.

They didn't seem to have anything in common. Zuzana made

nasty comments about Magda's favourite TV programmes and she was always contradicting Magda's opinions about anything: politics, fashion, people.

Oh, I miss Mother so much. And Daddy and all of them, thought Magda, crying herself to sleep.

CHAPTER SEVEN

Magda 1969

THE BREAD

Franzi dying made Magda think about the war again. She had nightmares, seeing the Nazis beating and kicking her brother and father, the crunching of their boots hitting Bruno's and Oskar's bloodied faces. Magda had a way of dealing with those nightmares. Waking up, crying, she would wave her hands in a certain way and scream, "*Aaaaahhhh!*" That chased those memories away, but the nightmares kept coming back.

That was when she started carrying the bread with her. The small quarter of the loaf of bread, rye with hard crust, was wrapped in a plastic bag. In the bag, she had a pocketknife, too. It was always in her handbag wherever she went. It was sitting at her desk at work; a smaller piece went with her to theatre, concerts, 'just in case'. She never ate the bread. After couple of days, when the bread became mouldy or too hard, she put it in a big bag in her kitchen, and later gave it to her friend Marcela, who kept chickens and rabbits.

There was a delicatessen shop close to Magda's work, so for lunch, she usually bought some open sandwiches, often with Hungarian salami and gherkins. Still, the bread was always in her handbag, too. Sometimes, she took the bread out of the plastic bag and looked at it.

If somebody had asked Magda why she carried with her bread that she never ate, she would probably not tell them. The answer was simple. She didn't ever want to go hungry again. If she told people she had spent three years locked up by the Nazis, they would understand it. She never talked about the hunger either. She remembered the soup with the hairpins, needles, string, paper; all the rare, tiny parcels the prisoners were allowed to get were put together to boil. She remembers Franzi choking on a hair clip from the soup. Magda still had the hair clip, but she didn't have her mother. She didn't have to be afraid anymore. The war had finished more than 20 years ago, and so did the suffering. If any of it came back, she would be prepared. The bread would help her.

CHAPTER EIGHT

Magda 1969

PARIS

On their visits to Otto and Marie in France, Otto often spoke about other relatives living abroad. Zuzana was curious and started to write the names down. Magda didn't want to talk about them.

Zuzana enjoyed going to France. Otto was funny, in a self-deprecating way. Magda and Zuzana loved visiting their beautiful flat in Paris: it had five rooms and balcony. Otto and Marie kept buying them things, especially clothes.

"You must be the best dressed among your friends, Zuzana."

"I am not interested in fashion, and I don't have any friends." Zuzana was hard to please.

The things Otto bought were usually expensive; Magda would have preferred if he had given her money, as she could buy much more with that.

"I am not rich enough to buy cheap things," said Otto.

Marie took them to expensive boutiques, talking in perfect French to the shop assistants and making decisions about what Magda and Zuzana should wear. Marie was still beautiful, although she was in her 60s: blonde, tall, with a perfect hairstyle and makeup, long legs, always wearing high heels. Ever since she was a child, Magda wondered why Marie had married Uncle Otto, who was much shorter than his wife, and his face, full of wrinkles, looked like rubber. He really was an ugly man, but he had kind, smiling eyes, and his dark humour was irresistible. Zuzana claimed he was the most fun person she'd ever met. She loved Uncle Otto and so did his wife. Magda loved him, too, of course, but she found his jokes sometimes irritating, because he almost never took anything seriously.

Like that conversation about Greece. Although Magda and Zuzana always got permission to go to the West once a year, it was only with a written invitation from Otto, who undertook to cover all their expenses. But travelling was still a dream for Magda. Otto and Marie didn't travel a lot, but this time they were talking about going to Greece.

"That must be wonderful," Magda said.

"Yes, all that history!" said Zuzana, who even as a child loved reading about Greek mythology. She knew all the names of the Greek gods.

"Wonderful?" Otto said. "What's wonderful about it? I don't have to go to Greece to wet my ankles, I can do that in my bathtub at home, and apart from the sea, Greece is just full of ruins."

Magda did not feel the need to be grateful for Otto and Marie's generosity. She felt they owed it to her for leaving her, her mother Franzi and Otto's mother Olga behind. Magda also still suspected that Otto took some money that belonged to them all when he emigrated. She never said anything about it, though.

Life with Zuzana did not become any easier. The arguments continued and Magda did not want to be alone with a daughter who didn't approve of her.

A year after Franzi died, Magda put an advert in the paper. She wanted to have a man in her life again.

CHAPTER NINE

Zuzana 1969

MY MOTHER'S MARRIAGE GIVES ME MORE FREEDOM

My mother was upset when Grandma died, but so was I, and on top of that, I missed her funeral, because my mother didn't tell me. I didn't think I would ever forgive her. Grandma Franzi left an empty space. I was never close to my father's parents and didn't see them much after my parents' divorce, but Grandma Franzi was much closer to me than my mother or my father.

For some time afterwards our flat was quiet. In the morning, I had breakfast in my room then went to school. After school, I often went to read in a park or to a library. I came home for dinner, but I would have preferred to read a book at the dinner table or eat my dinner, like breakfast, in my room. Mother did not allow it, so I just stared at the wall, not talking to her. She usually shot some poisoned sentences at me, and after the arguments, we often both cried. Life at home was very tense, but one day, Mum surprised me; she told me she put an advert in a paper, she was looking for a man. She asked me if I minded.

"No, of course not. You shouldn't be alone, Mum."

I was thinking about the man being a welcome alternative victim for my mother's tantrums and manipulations. The problem was, Mum couldn't write letters. She had no imagination. Her replies were very boring. When I read one, saying it was too short, she said, "Write one yourself for me if you are so clever!"

I did, and in those months, Mum and I spent lots of time together, reading the letters, replying. She met many men and told me about the dates. Soon, there was only one man. Tomas started coming to our apartment, usually fixing things.

"He is so useful around the house! Your father couldn't fix anything!"

"Yes, Mum." I wondered if being a handyman was Tomas's main attraction.

When mother married Tomas, my friends asked me if I minded getting a stepfather. I didn't; I was hoping he would keep my mother out of my life. I didn't want another parent. They married – a small wedding, the only guests were Tomas's sisters and Otto and Marie. Otto gave my mum a new car as a wedding present. It was just the cheapest car there was, a Trabant, and my mother would have preferred a Skoda.

"But Mum, a car is a great wedding present."

"They could afford to buy me a better one."

Of course, she gushed with gratitude when she thanked Uncle Otto. Mum passed her driving test, but I thought the examiner was probably somebody who went to her pharmacy. As a driver she was scary. She let Tomas drive most of the time yet was constantly declaring what a good driver she was.

My mother was always proud of skills she thought she had but didn't. On the other hand, she never talked about her amazing achievement of passing all those exams to graduate with her class from secondary school, or her success of becoming a pharmacist. That was impressive, but she thought it was normal.

Tomas didn't interfere with my life, and we didn't talk much. We just exchanged amicable snippets. Tomas's opinion on almost anything was rather superficial, sometimes racist, always very right-wing.

He said things like: "Mussolini introduced order in Italy; they need someone like that."

His jokes about black people and Roma gypsies were terrible; in his eyes, they were all stupid and lazy. He knew my mum was Jewish but talked about how cunning the Jews were and that they ran everything. I couldn't understand why my mother put up with it.

Of course, we were all right-wing at that time, as a rebellion against the government. It was the case of 'Enemies of my enemies are my friends'. Still, my arrogant teenage brain couldn't take Tomas seriously. I kept discussions about politics or books for my father. *It is curious that both my parents' spouses, Dagmar and Tomas, are so stupid*, I thought.

CHAPTER TEN

Magda 1970

The dating advert had an unexpected effect. Zuzana became interested, and helped Magda write the replies to the men. Zuzana was good at writing and she was suddenly very friendly. It was as if Magda's dream of having a daughter who was her best friend became true. However, now that Magda had a husband, her daughter went back to being the distant, cold stranger who often made Magda angry.

Zuzana went out a lot. Magda suspected she had a boyfriend. She asked.

"I have several," Zuzana said.

Was she serious? Magda asked her if she was on the pill.

"Of course, Mum."

Zuzana was thinking about university. She wanted to study English and Czech, not something practical like law, pharmacy or medicine. *She is so stubborn and distant.*

Magda tried to start conversations, asked her about her friends, but Zuzana's evasive answers usually closed the conversation down.

"Zuzana doesn't love me; how can I change that?" she asked Tomas.

"Of course she loves you, Magda, but she is a teenager – they are all a pain in the neck."

Magda liked Tomas's practical attitude to everything. He did a lot of housework; he even cooked.

He liked sex – that was a problem. Magda never did. She liked flirting, but somehow, a man kissing and touching her never did anything for her. She could usually see it coming. Tomas had a different look in his eyes, touched her hand when he talked, and he was suddenly keen to go to bed. He didn't mean sleeping.

I really can't see why people like sex, but once a week is all right, I suppose, Magda thought.

It was part of the marriage, so on the weekends, she let Tomas kiss and touch her, and have sex with her at least once. Weekdays were different. Magda made excuses. She was tired, busy, Zuzana might hear them…

"Mum, we could all emigrate!" Zuzana was constantly pestering her about emigration. Magda, who was never interested in politics, was happy. She could see absolutely no reason to emigrate.

The housing situation in Czechoslovakia was bad: people lived in small, often multigenerational flats, but they could have weekend houses, either modern cabins or old farmhouses, not suitable for permanent living. Tomas and Magda bought a weekend house, a small country cottage, and started growing things.

Magda remembered being in Theresienstadt and lying behind a bush instead of working. Sarka would be proud of her now; Magda became quite a gardener.

Zuzana avoided going with them to the weekend house. At first, Magda forced her to come and help in the garden, but Zuzana hated it and made the atmosphere unpleasant with her grumpy face and loud sighs. Tomas, however, performed miracles: planting fruit bushes, trees and flowers, and repairing the old cottage, even the roof. Magda loved the weekend house, and the weekends were nicer with just the two of them.

Zuzana and Tomas never argued, but that was mainly because they almost never talked. They didn't have any common interests apart from skiing. Zuzana was still skiing a lot but didn't do any other sport. Magda wanted her to play tennis and even bought her a beautiful white tennis dress. Zuzana never wore it.

In 1970, life under the communists became more oppressive again. Even Magda with her connections couldn't get permission to travel to the West. Magda and Zuzana both missed their trips to Paris.

CHAPTER ELEVEN

Zuzana 1970

I EXPLORE MY JEWISH IDENTITY

I was in a different school now, and everybody was friendly. I wasn't. After the bullying, it took me many years to trust other pupils again. Being distant, cool and not interested in the others worked like a magnet. Suddenly, it was other people being keener on my company than I was on theirs. I still didn't have any close friends, and I liked it that way. I felt free.

I met Milada in the library. We were reaching for the same book, a collection of stories by Jewish authors, some translated from Yiddish – authors like Sholem Aleichem, JJ Singer, Isaac Babel and other authors I didn't know. The book was called *Raisins and Almonds*. Fortunately, they had two copies, so we could both borrow it. We started talking about why we wanted to read it. It was great to find someone with similar taste. We were both Jewish, but only Milada was Jewish from the time she was a baby. Of course, that is silly – I was Jewish from the beginning, too, I just didn't know it.

Milada was tall and rather domineering.

"You must come to the Jewish community town hall. At least, come with me to the kosher canteen for lunch – the food is so much better than in the school canteen, and it's cheap."

Kosher food? I thought. *My mother would have a fit.* Nobody in my family had kept kosher since before the First World War. I remember my Grandma Franzi telling me how upset she was as a five-year-old on Christmas Eve. It was 1905 and her grandmother came to visit unexpectedly. Franzi's parents had to get rid of the Christmas tree quickly and broke most of the decorations.

This grandmother of my grandmother was probably the last religious member of our family.

My mother's disapproval made the Jewish centre even more tempting for me. That week, when we did not have any afternoon classes, I went with Milada. In the kosher canteen in the Old Town, Milada knew everybody. She introduced me, and they were friendly. One of them, a girl named Alena, started talking to me about a book she was reading, *The Skin* by Curzio Malaparte. I had read that book recently, but when I lent it to one of the girls at school, she said it was disgusting. Alena liked the book as much as I did. We started talking.

Milada was smiling like the cat who got the cream when we were leaving.

"See, I told you you'd like it here." It was as if I joined an exclusive club where everybody was Jewish.

Milada told me there were lectures, too. I didn't tell my mother about it.

"What kind of Jew are you? Your father is not Jewish anyway. People do not like Jews – the less they know about it, the safer," she would say.

I joined a Jewish youth group, much later called The Children of Maiselova Street. I started going to the various activities. I didn't care about Mum's disapproval. I felt accepted for the first time in my life. Most of the young people originally attending the lectures emigrated, Milada's older sister Vera among them, but somehow, the new generation, people who were too young before 1968, found out about the lectures and started coming. We were in a minority and belonging together felt good.

Not all the people were like Milada, with a strong Jewish identity. Most of us were from families celebrating Christmas and eating pork like any other Czech family. Daniel, a good-looking, serious boy, told me how he found out about being Jewish. He was only five years old when his mother told him:

"I have some bad news for you – you were born Jewish, and it will always give you troubles. It is better you know; forewarned is forearmed."

I told them I never experienced antisemitism and felt that it was not a problem in Czechoslovakia, or at least not in Prague. Milada and Daniel both disagreed.

"The reason you never experienced antisemitism was that nobody, not even you, knew you were Jewish. Try telling people – you'll see. Why do you think your mother didn't tell you? To protect you from antisemitism," said Milada angrily. She felt she was my mentor in all things Jewish and was always looking to educate me. In fact, I found Milada's constant advice tedious.

Daniel was on Milada's side. "You also didn't have a father with a tattoo from Auschwitz on his forearm, wearing short sleeves in the summer. On one of the parents' evenings in the summer, both of my parents showed the tattoo. After that, some of my friends stopped talking to me. It confirmed my mother's warning."

"Did you tell your parents, Daniel?"

"No, there was no point; they expected antisemitism everywhere. For them, every non-Jew is an antisemite unless proven otherwise."

Daniel told me his mother survived Auschwitz, but all her other relatives were killed. She married a man she met in the camp. Daniel became my main source of information about what it was to be Jewish. Still, I thought that his parents almost made him grow up in a concentration camp by constantly talking about it. *Would I listen to him for hours if he wasn't so good-looking?* I wondered.

This discussion with Milada and Daniel made me think. Like me, my mother was very dark: olive skin, black hair, large brown eyes. People found us exotic-looking. Later, when I was an adult, people abroad often asked me if I was Mediterranean, Greek or Italian. Nobody ever asked in Prague. Did they know I was Jewish? There were other things I never noticed before. The sayings: 'noise like in a Jewish school', Tomas talking to my mum about 'her people', meaning Jews, even expressions like 'unchristian prices', meaning unreasonably expensive. Sometimes people said things like, "He is Jewish but very nice." I had never noticed these things before.

Daniel and I became quite close, but then he stopped coming to the centre. Somebody told me later that his family emigrated to Israel.

I wondered: *Will Daniel tell his child the same thing about being Jewish, or would it be different, living in a Jewish state?*

Bizarrely, the only Jewish activity allowed by the communist state was the religious, orthodox organisation. They wanted to show that there was religious freedom. Churches were allowed, too, but regularly attending any religious ceremony earned people a black mark. None of us took religion seriously, yet those communal celebrations of Chanukah, Purim and Passover at the Prague Jewish town hall were enjoyable. Previously, I only knew the holidays from novels. Purim especially. It was a bit like a carnival: everybody dressed in silly costumes, masks with funny noses and in the various readings, everybody was making noise whenever they heard the name of the evil Haman, who wanted to kill all the Jews in Persia. The noise was usually made using a wooden rattle normally used in Czech Easter celebrations. Then I found out that it was also a celebration of murdering 75,000 enemies of the Jews and somehow it seemed less fun.

One day, my mother was walking in the Old Town and saw me coming out of the Jewish town hall with other people. As expected, I came home to a big scene.

"You are so stupid," my mother shouted the moment I got home. "You will not be able to go to university; how can you be so selfish and careless?! Your grandmother would be so upset!"

We had a row. Tomas was quiet, so then Mother had a row with him, too, for not supporting her.

"Zuzana is *your* daughter," he said.

I didn't argue any more, but I was determined to carry on. I loved those lectures. They were held on the third floor of the Jewish town hall. I later found out that the reason they were allowed even in the time after the Soviet invasion was that the youth club organiser told the secret police that if we couldn't go to his lectures, we might get influenced by imperialist Zionists from abroad.

I never forgot the lecture about the uprising in the Warsaw ghetto. Our history textbook only talked about left-wing anti-Nazi fighters, never about the Jews. The bravery of fighters who held the SS and Nazi army off for 63 days amazed me. We were shown pictures of the detonation of the synagogue by Nazis which marked the SS victory. We were all moved.

The lectures were mainly about Jewish history, but once also about the position of women in Jewish religion. That lecture was good, too, showing various powerful women in the Old Testament, and talking positively about equality and respect. The lecturer was not religious, though, and her lecture was more literary. I was surprised later when I found out more about the Jewish Orthodox attitude to women. *Blessed are you, Lord, our God, ruler of the universe, who has not created me a woman,* was a prayer the men said in the morning. I didn't like the way Jewish women had to cover their heads when they were married, and then there was the mikvah – the way to cleanse women after their period.

So I stopped going to the religious celebrations. Pesach seemed to be based on: *We are the chosen people; everybody hates us, and God will punish them.* I didn't like that either.

On the weekends, we often went to someone's flat to have a party – lots of wine, kisses, long discussions about politics, books, the Russian invasion and of course, the perennial Jewish question: emigration.

CHAPTER TWELVE

Zuzana 1971

I would find any excuse not to go to the weekend house with Mother and Tomas.

"I have to study," was the main one. I just wanted to be alone, not constantly in the company of my mother and Tomas. Besides, now I could have parties in our flat, too, without her knowledge.

My enthusiasm for my new friends did not last long. I did not feel particularly Jewish, and I didn't approve of religion of any kind. Milada gave me lots of unsolicited advice on what I should or shouldn't wear, the colour of my eyeshadow ("Green, definitely green") and what I should study ("Medicine or pharmacy – that is always useful"). I'm sure she meant well, but she was reminding me of my mother. I didn't really like the other girls either. The reason why I stayed was simple. The boys. Suddenly, they started being interesting.

They were all fledgling intellectuals like me, so all our communications started with books. We all pretended to be much more sophisticated and educated than we were. Kafka, Dostoyevsky, Camus, James Joyce. When I read detective stories or romantic novels, I kept it a secret. In fact, I found James Joyce and Camus rather tedious.

I developed a mask of slight boredom. People became interested in me when it looked as if I was not interested in them. I kissed many boys that year. We went on long walks, or to the cinema or galleries. Sometimes we sat in the Old Jewish Cemetery, between those old stones knocked over at different angles, newer stones piled on the older ones, no flowers, just stones with Hebrew inscriptions, the date often showing the Jewish calendar more than 3,000 years ahead. That made it stranger. It was a quiet, mysterious place, behind a wall in the centre of old Prague.

I wasn't having sex, not yet. I let the boys touch me, semi-undress me and then I always stopped them. I almost had sex in the old Jewish cemetery once. It would have been my first time. Jirka, an older philosophy student, touched my breasts and kissed me while we sat on one of the graves one night. He got more forceful, putting his tongue in my mouth, and I tried to push him away. Then we saw somebody with a torch, and we fled. I didn't like French kissing, but I wanted to lose my virginity, get it over with. Much later, an American friend told me that he always believed that the only freedom we had in the communist countries was sexual freedom.

"Especially in the blessed period after the pill and before AIDS," he joked.

He might have been right; there were not many virgins among the girls I knew. I took precautions – no, not condoms. I went to a gynaecologist and got the pill.

My first-time having sex was with Jirka. It was so unremarkable that I don't remember it very well. There was no pain, no bleeding, I don't think he realised it was the first time I had ever had sex. It didn't last long, and I didn't find his moving inside me exciting. What was the hype about? I did not enjoy it, but that was soon going to change. Rather typically, it was a book that changed my attitude. It was *The Wonder of Love* by Oswalt Kolle. Milada found it in her parents' bookcase. I remember the afternoon: we were lying on the floor, reading it. I got curious. If I was going to have sex, I might as well become good at it. Now thinking about it, it was interesting that neither of us was shocked nor embarrassed. I was keen to try all those things, and I did.

I had many boyfriends that year. I remembered my mother telling me how she used to change boyfriends in Theresienstadt.

Now I understood. Doing this felt good. I had all the power. I still saw Jirka more often than the others. Now I knew what I was doing, it got more exciting. Jirka was more experienced, but I was a fast learner. He was not exclusive. Jirka probably had other girlfriends, too. I consulted that book of Milada's parents frequently. Then I didn't need it anymore.

My mother was worried about me. Not about sex, about politics. Every year in May, during the celebrations of the 1 May (The International Workers' Day) and 9 May (the liberation of Prague by the Soviet army), all the houses were decorated with Czechoslovak and Soviet flags. Every tenant was given a supply of small Czechoslovak and Soviet flags for all the street-facing windows and there were large flags on the main doors. I didn't know then that celebrating the 9 May instead of the 8 May as the end of the war was another communist lie. The Soviet army entered Prague a day after the end of the war. That's not what I'd call a liberation.

I detested the Soviet flags anyway; it was only two years after the 1968 invasion. On the way home from school, I managed to remove five large Soviet flags from the buildings in our street and put them into a dustbin. My mother saw me. My parents never beat me, but this time, she slapped my cheeks several times.

"Are you crazy? Do you want to be thrown out of school?"

"We should have emigrated – I hate it here," I cried, my cheeks burning.

Mother tried to make me hang the flags back up, but they were dirty from the dustbins.

In 1971, I graduated from secondary school and went to university after big arguments with my mother. She wanted me to study medicine or pharmacy, being dead against the subject I picked – Czech and English.

"Do you want to become a teacher? That's all you will be able to do with the degree in Czech and English."

"Maybe I will become a writer," I said, but I quickly went out before the argument got worse. I kept to my plan. I passed the entrance exams with good results. Studying English and Czech was easy, as I had already read most of the books on our lists.

The political situation got worse. They were forcing us to join the SSM – the Union of Socialist Youth (Svaz Socialisticke Mladeze).

With my friends, we still talked about emigration. A lot of people I knew disappeared. They went on holiday abroad and did not come back. Jirka, my main boyfriend, went to Denmark. He sent me a postcard that said, *I decided to become Hamlet's friend.* I didn't love Jirka, but I was upset.

I compensated for the loss of Jirka by having more sex with several boys. I liked surprising my boyfriends with new skills, so I read more sex books. Before my first oral sex, I practised with a carrot. I was getting quite a reputation. Of course, not an entirely good reputation. The girls called me a slut, and some of the boys did, too. But even those boys would go out with me and have sex if I wanted. Milada tried to talk to me.

"Why do you change boyfriends so often? People talk."

"I don't care, let them talk. It's nobody's business who I am having sex with, Milada. You don't have to defend me if they gossip about me – you can even agree with them. I really couldn't care less, as long as you remain my friend."

I thought she was going to be annoyed, but she found it funny. We all heard about the hippies in the West and their 'free love'. To my surprise, unlike others, Milada did not judge me. She had a steady boyfriend, Martin, and she liked sex, too. Sometimes, we had a party of four in our flat when my mother and Tomas left for the weekend house. We listened to music, French kissed and then we had sex in the dark, hearing the other couple breathing.

I didn't want a steady boyfriend. When they got possessive, I let them go. Sometimes I would have sex with two boys on the same day. I liked the freedom which I didn't have in other aspects of my life. I used sarcasm against the people who dared to judge me. Looking back, I was much less witty than I thought. My confidence now seems more like arrogance. But I needed that pretence of toughness.

My mother thought her marriage was happy, but I doubt Tomas did. He always did exactly what my mother wanted. I often wondered why. Maybe he loved her, but loving my mother was hard. Did they have sex? I once overheard an argument between them.

"Are you not interested in me anymore, Magda? You always make excuses. Why?"

"I am tired, Tomas. Don't you think about anything other than sex?"

One day, when I was about 16, Tomas embraced me from behind and held me tight. He had an erection; I could feel it on my back. I pushed him away and gave him a hostile look. He never tried again. I was not afraid of Tomas; in fact, I think he was afraid of me. Of course, I should have told someone, and I would have if he'd carried on. It just made me like him even less.

I kept going to the Jewish community circle. We all somehow managed to get hold of prohibited books: smuggled copies of novels printed by 68 Publishers in Toronto, sometimes books typed in samizdat. Years later, when I was telling my son Adam about it in England, I had to explain to him that samizdat is a Russian word for self-printing, and that it was producing copies of prohibited books for people to read. Adam thought it was cool.

I remember reading the Czech translation of Orwell's *Animal Farm*. It was typed on thin copy paper, and each of the readers had to type 20 pages with ten carbon copies. The next reader typed the next 20 pages. I typed it on an old typewriter from before the war. I had to retype it several times, because it was full of mistakes; my two-finger typing was neither fast nor accurate. I made sure my mother didn't find out, as she would have been furious. Good job she was never interested in what books I was reading.

CHAPTER THIRTEEN

Zuzana 1972

I MAKE A MOVE

O ne day, a miracle happened: my mother and I got permission to travel to France to visit her Uncle Otto and Aunt Marie again. Officially, the permission depended on the availability of hard currency in our banks. In fact, it was the police deciding who could and who couldn't travel. We had been trying to see Otto and Marie in Paris for a long time, but after 1969, it seemed impossible. But then my mother had an idea. She remembered a woman who regularly came to the pharmacy. They used to talk, so my mum knew the woman worked in a bank. The woman needed medication, which was hard to get, even on prescription. My mum arranged for the woman to get us permission with a quota of hard currency, in exchange for the drug. The fact that Tomas didn't come with us made things easier. He was a hostage, a guarantee that my mother would come back.

I had a secret plan. This was the last time I would be using the barter system of favours in a communist country because I was not going to live in that system anymore. I persuaded my mum that this was such a unique opportunity that I would not go just to France but to England, too.

"I only have two weeks' leave, and I want to go to France. Stop making selfish, silly plans. We will go to visit Otto and Marie."

I resisted the temptation to get into an argument about selfishness, because this time she was right. I was ready. I met Karel, a friend of Jirka's. I knew he had worked on a farm in England in the summer three years before, when travelling was still possible, and asked him for the address.

"Are you planning to escape, Zuzana?" asked Karel.

"Are you?" I was careful.

Then we both decided we could trust each other. Karel gave me the address of the farm. He was also planning to leave. Karel had permission to go to visit an old aunt in Germany, but he wanted to go to Australia or the USA. It was a relief, being able to talk about emigration with Karel. He had good advice about rules of political asylum and other practicalities. Then he started kissing me. *Karel is the last man I will have sex with in Prague*, I thought.

I told Karel about my family, that whenever they didn't emigrate, it was a mistake. I was determined not to repeat it. I was planning to make England my new home.

Of course, that was not what I told Mother.

"I will go alone from France, I can hitchhike, and I always wanted to see England. I will be able to work and earn some money; they are hiring students in England to go strawberry-picking – I have the address. I will work in the strawberry fields, and then go to London. I have such a long holiday, almost three months. It will be good for my English. Please, let me do it, Mum!"

Eventually, she gave up arguing. This was indeed one of my rare victories. I stayed for ten days with my mother in Paris, but I was restless; I couldn't sleep, thinking that I might never see my mother or my Czech friends again. Mother made it easier for me with her constant complaints.

"Zuzana never does anything I ask her to," was her most common one.

One day, Otto took me to the Louvre, while my mother and Marie went shopping.

"You and Magda seem to have a hard time, but your mother loves you, Zuzana – try to be a bit nicer to her."

"It's hard, but OK. I will when I come back."

I was careful; Otto was sharp, and I didn't want him to suspect anything. Otto refused to hear anything about hitchhiking and bought me a train ticket. I kissed them all and left, dragging my heavy luggage.

When I got to England on the ferry, I took a bus to the village in Kent with the farm Karel told me about. Fortunately, they were still hiring. It was July, and in the end, I spent the whole summer first picking strawberries, then working on an apple farm, thinning the apple branches and then harvesting. I got tanned, and my English improved. I talked to the other workers, and I joined a village library and re-read Steinbeck's *Grapes of Wrath*, this time in English, now I was a fruit picker, too.

The work was hard, but the farmers were friendly, and I had enough money, especially as Uncle Otto gave me £100. That was a lot of money for me.

I only applied for political asylum at the end of August. I finished my job and hitchhiked to London. It took me a while to stand on the correct side of the road – the English driving on the left was confusing. Once or twice, I stood on the wrong side, and the cars that stopped to pick me up were travelling in the opposite direction. Then a young man in a weird car with an oddly sloped rear window – a Ford Anglia – took me all the way to London. He flirted with me, and I flirted back. He bought me lunch and then asked if I would let him fuck me. At first, I was not quite sure if I understood. I thought, *Why not?* But then I decided I had too much else on my mind.

"No, thank you," I said.

He smiled. "Don't worry, I am not going to force you. I just thought I'd ask. Where would you like me to drop you off?"

I got out of the car at the nearest suitable place, at one of the underground stations in London. He took my luggage from the boot, and suddenly I had the image of my mum and the Russian soldiers who stole her things in 1945. Was I doing the right thing? Should I go back to Prague? I still had my railway ticket. I took a deep breath and took the underground – or tube, as the English called it – to an address Milada had written for me in Prague. It was that of her sister Vera. She had emigrated in 1968. She planned to go to Israel after she improved her English in London, where they had relatives, the Blumenthals. Milada and Vera's aunt's opinion about Israel was similar to my grandma's. Desert and camels, and the PLO – why would anybody want to live there? Vera stayed in London with the relatives. Her sister Milada did not tell many people that her sister emigrated, as it was not a good idea to do so. The police knew, of course, but they did not necessarily use that information.

Unlike Milada, Vera was very serious, and despite having lived in the West for the past five years, she didn't look very good. She was dressed in shapeless clothes and wore no makeup. Vera treated me like a child, but I was still grateful.

Vera's aunt organised an interview for me with a Jewish organisation – the CBF (Central British Fund for World Jewish Relief). It was an organisation that started helping Jews in 1933. I told them about my family. I also told them my father was not Jewish and that I was not religious. I did not tell them I was seeking asylum from the oppression by my mother rather than by that of the communist state, as I didn't think they'd like it. When people felt sorry for me, and asked me if I was homesick, I told them, "No, not at all, I am pleased to be here."

They said I was brave, but I felt free. It was a wonderful feeling. I could do whatever I wanted. The Jewish organisation found me a temporary accommodation in a shelter in Kilburn. It was a Jewish orthodox place, and I learnt rules about not having coffee with milk after a meaty dish, dairy products mustn't be eaten within three hours of any meat, shellfish was prohibited, and even crisps or biscuits had to be bought in a special kosher store. I noticed they had three separate sets of all dishes and cutlery, pots and pans in the kitchen, to separate meat, dairy and neutral food utensils. I celebrated Sabbath with them for the first time in my life with a small cup of sweet dessert wine. There was praying in Hebrew before every meal. *Pretty exotic*, I thought.

I was not alone anymore. One day at the British Museum, I met Jose, a young boy from Mexico City, travelling around Europe. He had long hair, dark, large, flirty eyes and sexy, accented English. We started meeting for galleries or walks. Then one day we ended up in his room. It had been a long time since I had sex, and it was easy; we both knew we wanted it and that this was temporary. Jose would be leaving Europe soon. He was passionate and I liked his hands on my body. He told me he loved me, but neither of us believed it. He just thought he was expected to say it.

I liked spending time with Jose. We were both foreigners in this wonderful city and we explored parts of London other tourists did not get to. I had my first Indian meal in Brick Lane. The area looked like something from another continent: waiters talking to each other in Bengali, and all those unusual meals and spices.

Jose was obsessed with British music. I was never that interested, but Jose was raving about some groups I knew, like Deep Purple, Pink Floyd, Genesis, Black Sabbath and some groups I had never heard about with weird names: Wishbone Ash, Van der Graaf Generator, King Crimson, Caravan and Camel. If it was not too loud, I let him play their records for me. When he got too enthusiastic talking about music, I shut him up with a long kiss. That was my best trick. When I found men attractive but boring, I initiated sex. When they were boring sexually, too, they were dropped fast. Jose was good in bed, but soon it was time for him to go home. We promised to write, but never did.

It had been four years since the Soviet invasion of Czechoslovakia but the British were still eager to help Czech political refugees. When I got my papers as an asylum seeker, it was time to phone home. I was dreading it. I was at the post office, shaking all over. Mum picked up the phone.

"Oh, hello, darling, how are you? When are you coming home?" She was nice – that made it worse.

"I am not coming home, Mum. I will stay in England. I am all right, it's all arranged, I had help. Don't worry."

There was silence, and she began to cry. I almost changed my mind, but she started screaming, "You are so selfish. How can you do this to me? I would never abandon my mother like that!"

She carried on like this for ages, and the polite English post office worker looked worried. I pulled the receiver away from my ear and waited for a pause. "I am sorry, Mum, but I am an adult, and this is my life. You are married; Tomas will look after you. And one day, we will see each other again. I will phone again tomorrow, Mum, bye!"

When I got back to the shelter, I wrote her a long letter, explaining things. Her letters were angry at first, and then she wrote about Tomas, the weekend house, the weather. Her later letters were short but no longer nasty. I wrote long notes about London, the weather, nothing personal. When she commented on that, I started making things up. I had no English friends yet, but in the letters to my mum, I told her I made many and had fun describing those imaginary friends, and what we did together. I was writing what my mother wanted to hear.

In my letters, I was safe, studying English in the evenings instead of going to clubs and discos; I made friends from wealthy, educated families, and I was looking for a place at university. Only the last thing was true. My mother liked the imaginary Zuzana much better than me. *Maybe if we never met again, our relationship would get better*, I thought.

My father did not write to me. For career reasons he was a member of the communist party, and probably felt he couldn't communicate with his criminal daughter. Like most emigres, I was sentenced to five years in prison in absence for my flight to the West. I understood his reasons, but it still hurt.

I missed my friends, the Czech food, especially bread. I missed being able to communicate well; learning English wasn't easy. I didn't make any friends until university. I spent my free time wandering around London and reading.

CHAPTER FOURTEEN

Zuzana 1973

ENGLISH BEGINNINGS

It was easier for Milada's sister Vera, who emigrated in 1968, The Russian invasion made the British government very sympathetic. They gave Czechs open work permits without the need to apply for a formal political asylum. They even recognised the Czech secondary school results.

Even when I arrived in 1972, I still got my work permit and a grant to go to university. I didn't start until 1973 and enrolled on a sociology course.

"You will have no problem finding a job as a researcher or maybe a social worker," said Vera's aunt. I felt free.

Then Vera and her family started to interfere a little too much. They wanted me to attend the synagogue and celebrate Shabbat with them every Friday. *No chance*, I thought. Mrs Blumenthal kept asking me about my mother, and how she was coping on her own.

"My mother is not alone; she is married to Tomas."

"Yes, but you are her only daughter, and her husband is not Jewish." *As if that matters!* The Jewish people I met in London were, I suppose, more Jewish. They spoke about 'marrying out', which was apparently a problem. *In my family, there were mixed marriages from well before the First World War!* I thought. *Which century are these people living in?*

I regretted telling the Blumenthals about my family. Yes, they meant well, but sometimes I felt like screaming. I wasn't ungrateful, but I wanted to use my freedom. I was thinking about going to Manchester, a big enough city, far enough from Paris and London, but in the end, I stayed in London to study at Middlesex Polytechnic. Vera's aunt made a face. "Polytechnics aren't proper universities. You went to Charles University in Prague, didn't you? One of the oldest in Europe." *But who cares how old a university is?*

For me, a polytechnic was just fine. I had a grant and the accommodation in a tower block was cheap. I was living on my own for the first time. I still saw Vera and her family, but not as often. One day, I bought Vera's aunt a bouquet of flowers and thanked her for everything. I bought Vera a box of chocolates. "I will be busy at the university," I said. We all knew it was goodbye.

Freedom was important. I was free from my mother. I was free from the beautiful old furniture and paintings, free from the remnants of my family's wealthy past. My Prague room, furnished in an elegant, decorative style, was large and beautiful. But I always envied my friends who lived in tiny rooms that were truly theirs, rooms where they could hang posters on the walls and have a mess.

My student accommodation was small, and the wardrobe was cheap pine. There were common showers, toilets and a kitchen. But I put posters on the wall, and I could do whatever I wanted. Another outsider had the room next door – a black girl, as tall as she was beautiful. Roxanne was older than me, and she was British, having moved from Jamaica as a little girl. Roxanne had already worked in social services, and when somebody discovered how smart she was, they arranged for her to study. She told me that her father left when she and her brother were little, and her mother Debara worked first as an auxiliary nurse but later studied to get a proper qualification. Eventually, she got her nursing degree and now worked as a district nurse, visiting patients. She must have been super smart to be able to do that. She still managed to bring up two children, both of whom ended up going to university.

I liked Roxanne's family, but particularly her brother, Bob. Tall and slim, he was darker than Roxanne and very muscular. I found him sexy and attractive. In fact, I was hoping he might find me attractive, too; he was easy to talk to and seemed to like my company. I was still changing boyfriends like shoes, but I could imagine giving Bob exclusive rights. I asked Roxanne if she thought he would be all right with me asking him out. "I know women are not supposed to do that, but I can't see why not. We should be equal."

Roxanne looked at me and smiled. "If you are hoping to date him, that is never going to happen. Bob is gay. He likes you, but not in that way."

I was surprised. But I suppose I shouldn't have been. Bob, who had just finished his art degree, was so well dressed, and interested in cooking, culture and fashion – for some people, he would fit the stereotype. That is, of course, a silly stereotype. I think I had a different silly prejudice. I always heard homosexuality was not tolerated in Afro-Caribbean society, so I somehow thought gay black men were rare. Of course, that was as stupid as people thinking that me being Jewish made me good with money, or that all black people could sing. Roxanne and Bob were both completely tone-deaf.

"Is your mother alright with that?"

"Of course, my mother is fine, and she adores Bob's boyfriend. She says why can't I find a nice boyfriend like Angus."

I told Roxanne about my family, the war. She was interested, and she could relate.

"You see, my black skin was like the yellow star your mother had to wear. An invitation for idiots to abuse me."

"Did you experience a lot of racism, Roxanne?" I asked.

I had no experience with antisemitism, but I remembered the discussion with Milada and Daniel about it. It was complicated.

"As a girl, I wasn't bothered much. We had several black and Asian kids in our school. Some of the boys were being picked on by other boys. I remember Bob once fought with three white boys who attacked him on the street. He came back with a black eye, but he told Mother that she should see the other boys. Bob was always good at fighting; he went to judo and ju-jitsu classes."

She told me the racism was much more of a problem for her mum's generation.

"Soon after my mother came, she would sit on a bus, and people would say nasty things, like, 'Monkey, go home.' You know, Zuzana, my mother's sister, Aunt Gabrielle, came to England, too, but she couldn't cope with the racism and job rejections. She went back home to Jamaica. She had a British passport, she loved the Queen and thought she would be treated like any other citizen. Their family had money, a nice house; they had land with cattle, horses and a sugar mill. They also sold cocoa to the government. In England she was poor."

"Why did your parents stay, if they were wealthy in Jamaica?"

"I think it was because of us – my mother felt we would have a better education and opportunity here. She came to England looking for adventure and a better life. My grandparents were not happy about it. She didn't want to admit defeat, come home poor, without a husband. Aunt Gabrielle had to promise my mum that she would not tell anybody back home in Jamaica about the fact that my dad ran away. I think Gabrielle kept her promise. Mum has done well, but she told me that she always felt she had to work doubly hard if she wanted to keep up with her white colleagues."

Roxanne was beautiful, but she didn't have a boyfriend. In fact, I suspected she might still be a virgin. You would not think so from the low tops and short skirts. She was amused by my promiscuity, but not shocked.

"You are funny, Zuzana, because you do not seem to fall in love; you use the men the way men usually use women. I am waiting till I fall in love for sex. I will need some tips from you then." I laughed, but when I looked at her, she seemed serious.

Her mother was religious, some weird Evangelical sect, but I doubt Roxanne believed in God. She believed in her mother, though. I envied her. Her mother was tough but very loving. When she came to visit Roxanne, they took me out for lunch, because I had no relatives close by. There was lots of laughter.

In the student hall, friends – usually from Roxanne's basketball team, but some of mine, too – came in the evening; we talked about politics, listened to music, ate bits of cheese and those weird salt and vinegar-flavoured crisps. We drank cheap German white wine and smoked. Everybody seemed to smoke at that time. I smoked, too, and so did my boyfriends. I never had a problem finding a boyfriend. It was women I found difficult to get close to. I didn't trust other women. They reminded me of those bullying girls in the language school, or my mother. Roxanne was an exception.

After the parties, the smoke made everything look hazy. My long black hair smelled of cigarettes and so did the bedding. I didn't always have time in the morning to wash my hair, so I smelt of smoke the next day... It didn't really matter, as most of the other students smoked, too. Unlike in Prague, they also smoked dope. I never did. As my future husband later would say, I was crazy enough without drugs.

Roxanne did not smoke anything. She didn't drink, either. Sometimes, she complained about the smoke and she was right.

I enjoyed sociology, despite finding out that it was not a straightforward training for a job as a social worker.

CHAPTER FIFTEEN

Zuzana 1973

I GET TOLD OFF BY UNCLE OTTO AND MY FATHER DIES

"You have a visitor," called the woman in the student hall office. "The gentleman is waiting for you here."

Gentleman? My boyfriends never went through the office.

When I came to the office, I saw a short, elegant bald man. He turned, and it was Uncle Otto. Uncharacteristically, he was not smiling. "Let's go for lunch," he said.

I did not know how Uncle Otto always found the most expensive places. The restaurant in the Hotel Savoy looked like something from a movie. The art deco furnishings, even the toilets were beautiful. I went to the loo to calm down, but I was still nervous.

He ordered for me, wine, too. For a chatty man, he was unusually quiet. I was scared. *What can he do to you, stupid? He just came because your mother sent him, and he was worried.* I tried to look cool.

Otto wasn't fooled. "You are shaking – good, you have a reason to be scared." He was still not smiling.

His tirade lasted for at least ten minutes. Cold, sarcastic, scathing. Telling me off for leaving my mother, and for being deceitful, not telling anybody. I was desperately trying not to cry, but I did.

He let me sob into my plate and then passed me his handkerchief.

Otto was a dandy; he had a handkerchief in his front pocket but passed me another one so as not to spoil his look.

I blew my nose and said, "Let's finish eating, and then I will say what I want to say."

I think that impressed him. The food was probably delicious, but I do not remember it. I asked for another glass of red wine and then I told him. I told him about the difficult relationship I had with my mother. I told him that I knew the family history, and how whenever they decided *not* to emigrate, it was wrong. I reminded him of the war, and of his own emigration in 1948.

He interrupted me. "I never saw my darling mother alive again, and I couldn't even go to her funeral." This time it was him who was crying.

"But she urged you to go; my grandmother told me that. And my Grandma Franzi wanted my mother and me to emigrate in 1968. We didn't, and she died. She would have been happier if we left. You are still upset about not being able to go to your mother's funeral. I was there when my grandma died, and Mother lied to me and let me miss her funeral!"

Otto took my hand. "I know, and believe me, Zuzana, I tried to make Magda tell you."

He seemed to be listening to me, so I carried on. "If I ever have children, I want them to grow up in a free society, Otto. But I also don't want my future adult children to feel responsible for my happiness once they grow up. I will set them free."

Otto was quiet again, but his eyes were no longer angry. "Okay, I will go to Prague and tell your mother not to worry. You are a grown-up, and you can look after yourself."

I did not say what I thought: that my mother worried about herself, not me. I was glad I did not say it. I thought, *who knows? My mother probably does love me and worry about me. She just has a strange way of showing it.*

Otto insisted he was going to open a bank account in my name and deposit an amount every month. That felt awkward, but his generosity and care made my life in England much easier.

Before he left, we embraced. "Come to Paris in the holidays. I'll pay for your ticket," he said. "Aunt Marie wants to see you, too."

Next time, about three months later, he came with Marie and I introduced them to Roxanne. I was worried, so I warned them she was black. "We are Jewish," said Marie.

"But you are not, Aunt Marie!" I protested.

"I am, by choice."

Aunt Marie never converted to Judaism and still wore her cross, but I knew what she meant. That was in stark contrast to what my mother wrote when I wrote to her about Roxanne.

Her reply to my long letter talking about Roxanne and her family, and what fun we had, was short.

Dear Zuzana,

I hope you are healthy and doing well.

Uncle Otto said you look well. I wish I could see you. I have been applying for permission, but so far, no luck.

I was a bit worried that you are spending time with a negro. Is she clean enough?

I was furious and did not tell Roxanne. I wrote back to my mother saying that Roxanne was cleaner, smarter and more beautiful than me, and that a Jew who had survived the Holocaust should know better than to be racist.

My mother wrote back matching my angry tone, but after a few letters we both dropped it. When my mother finally met Roxanne, she was charmed by her like everyone else.

I never saw my father again. He died of a heart attack a year after my emigration. We used to be close, but my emigration stopped that. I felt slightly guilty but also angry. I was his only daughter; he could have kept in touch. Even though they'd been divorced for a long time, my mother still cried at the news that he had died. She told me on the phone, and she was sobbing. She loved him, probably more than he'd ever loved her. I was surprised. I was always surprised finding out my mother cared about anybody apart from herself. I wrote a short letter of condolences to Dagmar, my father's widow, but I had no intention to keep in touch with her. *There are enough stupid people in England – no need to keep in touch with Dagmar.* I didn't think Dagmar would mind.

CHAPTER SIXTEEN

Zuzana 1974–1976

I HELP ROXANNE GET OVER THE PAST AND I FALL IN LOVE

After my degree, a tutor said I should do an MA in social work if I wanted to be a social worker, so I carried on. In Czechoslovakia, all university courses were full master's degrees, so studying for five years didn't seem unusual. And I still had a grant.

Roxanne and I moved into digs and, although the landlord's family was strange, we enjoyed the freedom. The house in Enfield was cold and dirty, and the landlady never shut up. Whenever she met me in the corridor, she started complaining about her husband. We tried to avoid her when we could. Neither Roxanne nor I were interested in her awful marriage or her alcoholic husband. He never helped her with anything in the house and kept porn magazines behind the downstairs toilet.

The bathroom didn't have a shower, and we had to share it with the landlords, but it was very cheap, and we had fun.

After a while, we had had enough and moved. Roxanne graduated and re-started her work full time. She was promoted and could afford better accommodation, but she preferred to live with me. The flat we rented was above a Greek Cypriot restaurant in Turnpike Lane. It was tiny, but we had it all to ourselves. Sometimes, I earned a little extra waitressing in the restaurant. The money was not great, but we also both got a free dinner. I was getting closer to Roxanne; it was like having a sister.

Roxanne still didn't have a boyfriend. I often wondered why; I didn't want to ask her, but it was bothering me. Was she gay, too? By then, I'd met Bob's partner, Angus Scott: freckled, red hair, tall and very white. They made a good-looking couple. Angus always wore some tartan – a tie, handkerchief, once even a kilt. I had to concentrate to understand him, but even the accent was sexy.

"Damn," I said to Roxanne. "Why are all the handsome, nice men gay – it's not fair!"

Roxanne and I often went out with Bob and Angus, and other women threw us envious looks. "Where did they get such gorgeous-looking men?" they probably thought.

One day I asked Bob: "Your sister is so great and so beautiful – why doesn't she have a boyfriend?"

"I cannot tell you much without asking her permission – let's have dinner tomorrow. Just you and me. But Sue, she might not want me to tell you." Bob and Angus called me Sue; Zuzana was too complicated. In fact, I was thinking of anglicising my name anyway. I had problems with my surname already, even though I thought Novotna was easy. The British pronounced it with a Russian accent, and of course, I didn't like that.

I didn't see Roxanne until next morning, as I was out till late. At breakfast, she said, "I gave Bob permission to tell you, because I'd like you to know, and I don't know how to tell you myself."

Bob looked nervous. The story he told me was shocking. Roxanne apparently had a boyfriend called Tom. They both knew each other vaguely as children; his mother was also from Jamaica. Roxanne was only 17, and she was in love. She did not talk about anybody else, just Tom.

"I never liked the bloke – even as a child he seemed too bossy, a spoiled brat. He was also jealous of her friends, and even of me. When he found out I was gay, he told me he felt sorry for me for not being a proper man. I should have punched him, but I told him to concentrate on my sister's happiness, not mine.

"Then, one day, Roxanne came home, and cried and cried. My

mother tried to get it out of her, but she couldn't. I came to her room and asked her what was going on. She was still sobbing. Then she told me what the bastard Tom did to her."

Listening to Bob was painful. Roxanne was a virgin, but she loved Tom and he was pestering her for sex. His parents were away; Roxanne and Tom were alone in his house.

"She agreed to have sex, but then she heard some other voices – two of his bloody friends."

I was shocked. "Wow, did he want to have a foursome? With his virgin girlfriend who loved him? What an idiot. Did she run away?"

Bob started to shake. "Those bastards told her they would like to start her off in style. They started taking her clothes off. She protested, but Tom was kissing her, telling her how beautiful she was, and how she was special and deserved special treatment; he said they would all be gentle. My idiotic sister was so in love with that bastard that she agreed. They all had sex with her, one by one. They didn't even use condoms. She told me that the two not fucking her were touching her breasts. When she told me, she cried throughout. You know, Sue, I think some women might enjoy this, but you are right, not when they are 17-year-old virgins. Roxanne claimed they didn't rape her, only that Tom manipulated her. But of course, what those bastards did was rape. The other men left, and Tom told her to get dressed."

Bob stopped talking and punched the wall. I could see tears in his eyes.

Apparently, Tom told her he had some things to do, and he would call her the next day. He did not. Roxanne went to see him.

Bob took a deep breath and told me the rest. "Tom said to her, 'You were too easy. I don't believe you were a virgin; you are a slut! And it was not that great. You were a bit boring, Roxanne, not a very good slut, you have lots to learn. Let's stop.' She tried to call him; he put the phone down on her. He'd had his fun. Then she found out he was dating someone else."

"That fucking arsehole! Oh, Bob! Did she report it to the police?"

"She couldn't even tell Mum; you know how religious she is. And Mum has double standards, too – she thinks girls should stay virgins before marriage. Yet it is OK that I am gay and have a partner. I am fucking glad I am a man, Sue."

Roxanne had told Bob she felt unattractive, that she never wanted to risk being rejected like this again. That she felt sick thinking about a man touching her. Bob tried to make her go to the police, but she wouldn't; he made her have an STD test and a pregnancy test. Fortunately, the tests were negative.

"Did you talk to Tom?"

"No, I let my fists do the talking. I broke his nose. Gave him some bruises, too. He didn't go to the police because I told him I would tell the police and his parents what he had done to Roxanne. I only hit him five times, and I gave him a tissue to wipe the blood."

"How generous of you, Bob." I smirked, but I still thought they should have reported Tom to the police. I promised Bob I would try to help.

Roxanne was sitting in the dark when I came home. "Bob told me about Tom. I had no idea. Why didn't you tell me? That bastard. You need to go and talk to someone, a psychologist."

She didn't want to, but I learnt from my mum that if you persist, people often give in and do what you ask them to do.

"If you don't deal with it, you will still be upset about an idiotic arsehole for years from now. Don't give him the power to change your life. You need help to get over this."

The fact that she agreed changed our lives in different ways. My then-boyfriend Hugo was a medical student, and his sister was a psychiatric nurse in the hospital. I told him a friend had some psychological problems. I didn't tell him any details. His sister Olivia arranged for us to see a young doctor in the psychiatry department, just to get some advice. She said he was very nice. Hugo had a feeling that Olivia was dating him. Olivia met us in the hospital entrance and said Dr Williams would see us, but he would need to refer me back to the polytechnic GP if it was something important. I think she misunderstood, and thought I was the patient. She was probably curious what problem her brother's girlfriend had and she was hoping to find out. Olivia didn't like me much, and she liked me even less two weeks later when she found out Dr Harry Williams started dating me.

It was lust at first sight. Harry Williams was tall and as good-looking as Bob. He was black, too. Roxanne let me do the talking. I was brief. I said she was raped.

"No, I let them," whispered Roxanne.

"It was still rape," I insisted.

The young doctor agreed. He was appalled by Tom's behaviour. Then he asked me to leave. They talked for almost an hour. He said he could arrange some counselling for her. There was a nice female psychologist. Dr Williams told Roxanne how to get a formal referral from the polytechnic doctor. He gave her a note for the GP.

He asked her to go to the office to fill in some forms, and he quickly asked me for my phone number. I gave him my name and the Cypriot restaurant number; they would call me to the phone. I only realised later that Harry did something very unorthodox, breaking several rules. He was a GP trainee; six months of psychiatry was part of his rotation. Normally, nobody would see Roxanne without a referral. Harry not only did this, but it was also not part of his role. Harry originally just agreed to see us because of Olivia, telling her that we would need to go through the normal channels and that he would just give us advice on how to do it.

In the end, he did much more than that. I think that was because of me. He kept phoning me. Spiros from the restaurant started teasing me about it. Harry asked me for a date, and he immediately started kissing me.

"I wanted to show you right away what my intentions were," he told me later, laughing.

"Yes, you wanted to fuck me as soon as you could." But of course, he knew that we both wanted that.

Roxanne had therapy, and Bob, Angus and I tried to supplement this by trying to boost her self-esteem. Bob and Angus had a plan. We kept taking her out to make her realise how attractive other men found her. That was not difficult: Roxanne could have been a model; she was beautiful. I still gave her intensive theoretical sex education just in case. I knew what I was talking about. She listened with eyes wide open. It was difficult to see if she was blushing. Eventually, Roxanne was ready to try to date.

"Maybe you will have sex with someone who is not an arsehole. Believe me, it is fun!"

Roxanne made a face. She thought my attitude to sex was outrageous, but then she smiled. She didn't think she would like sex, but I was hoping she would meet someone who would change her mind.

Roxanne was carrying on with her counselling, while I was carrying on with Dr Harry Williams, and surprisingly, it was not just lust. The lust was there, of course. I would have a phone call: "Zuzana, I'd like to fuck you. I don't have many patients' visits today – how about that?" I missed a lot of lectures that spring.

Then Olivia came to our student hall and made a scene. I told her I was sorry, that I didn't know Harry and she were dating.

Hugo came, too. "How could you do that? You met the black bastard through my sister! Nobody ever treated me that way. You slut!"

Embarrassed, I shot back, "You're so dramatic! Go join an amateur theatre company and find yourself a new slut." I refused to let myself feel much guilt. I liked Harry too much and would not let Hugo taint my new relationship. Still, what I said was not very nice. Hugo tried to hit me but stopped just an inch from my face. My stare stopped him; I can be scary when I want to be.

I fell in love with Harry. I'd had sex with many people before him, but he was my first love. He was funny, kind, smart and, of course, almost as gorgeous as Roxanne's brother Bob. We both felt we'd found the right person. I used to keep my private life to myself, but now I was telling my new boyfriend everything: about my childhood, my mother, the 'Jewish thing'. Harry was a good listener. I wondered if it was because he was a doctor, but I had known plenty of doctors who did not listen. I liked how tactile he was, kissing me and holding my hand in public. He was kind, but not a pushover. He teased me about my habit of constantly comparing life situations to novels.

"You always find some literary quote or comparison; you are like some crazy librarian." He teased me even more when I told him I wanted to write novels.

"It is true, Harry, life is like novels. And when I write mine, I will take situations and dialogues from real life."

"God help me." He chuckled. "You mean our conversations will end up in a book? I'd better be careful what I say!"

Harry took me to meet his parents, Angela and Richard. They were reserved and watched me with suspicion, a white girlfriend. Harry knew just the right thing to say. "Zuzana is Jewish," he said. "Her mother is a Holocaust survivor."

We spoke about racism and antisemitism. We spoke about the 'black experience'. I could choose if I told people that I am Jewish or not. Harry didn't have that choice. The colour of his skin didn't let him hide anything. Unlike me, he wasn't a foreigner, but people still asked him, "Where are you from?"

"Enfield, London," he usually said.

Harry's mum Angela asked me a lot of questions about my mother and the Holocaust, but she didn't tell me much about herself. When I asked Harry later, he told me about some of the experiences of his parents when they first came to Britain.

"My father was seasick through the whole journey. He told me he didn't think there was anything left in him to vomit. My mother was fine, apparently – she's tough."

Harry told me the ship landed in Tilbury dock. It was cold, and the sky was grey.

"Where are the colours?" said Angela. "Everything is grey or black." She told Harry that even the people with their pale faces and dull, dark clothing were colourless, almost like a black-and-white movie. Angela liked colours, and they suited her. Somehow, I associated her Roman Catholic religion with dark, shapeless outfits, but Harry's mother looked sexy.

Harry laughed when I told him. "Sexy? My mum? She would give you a look if she heard you."

He stopped laughing when he told me about the racism. Finding a job was not a problem; the British recruited them for the transport system, the NHS and as labourers. Some of them got a job the day they arrived.

Accommodation was supposed to be supported by local councils, but this didn't happen, so they would go door to door, with money in their pockets, to pay the rent. However, almost every sign they saw said, *No blacks, no Irish.*

His parents looked for landlords letting rooms, but the notices were everywhere.

"Some of those said, *No dogs, no blacks, no Irish.* My father told me that as they were in the same situation, the Irish and black people often became friends. You know, Zuzana, my parents were British, from a British colony and they had great respect for the Queen. They were excited to travel to the mother country and looked forward to the adventure. The English didn't feel the newcomers belonged. The racism was everywhere. People crossed the road when they saw a black person. My father queued for a black cab at Paddington, but when it was his turn, the white cabbie told him to go to the other queue for cabs with black drivers. 'We don't take niggers,' he said."

I embraced Harry and told him more about what I knew about my mum: how she couldn't go to school, travel by tram, go to the cinema. I asked him if he had any experience with racism.

He smiled. "Just with some bullies at school, but I was strong, so I beat them up."

His eyes were not smiling; I knew he was not telling me everything. I wanted to ask, but his long fingers were touching my legs, going higher and higher, and I felt warm, and when I looked at him, his eyes were smiling now, and he had the face he gets just before he makes love to me. Sex stopped our discussion, but I was still curious, so when we were sitting, fully dressed again, I asked him more questions.

He told me that when finding accommodation was so hard for the black newcomers, the council found a solution. Empty houses. They were large crumbling houses in all parts of London waiting to be repaired and furnished. Harry's parents rented a big crumbling town house with eight rooms, and they shared it with ten other black families; the men did the repairs to make the house inhabitable, while the women made bedding and looked for blankets and kitchen equipment in junk shops. One of the women would look after the children while the other women went to work.

"That is like a commune," I said. It was fascinating.

"Don't repeat that in front of my mum; the word commune would give her an image of the hippies and free love. It was nothing like that. I don't remember that first house, I was a baby, but later, we were sharing a house with five different families with children. It was crowded but also fun."

It made me think about the cramped Theresienstadt ghetto, but of course, Harry's family were not imprisoned in Britain.

Harry told me that people gradually earned more money and moved to separate houses. Some went back to Grenada.

"Father said that some people who came with them on the ship were so shocked by the racism and the cold British weather that they went straight back. My mother doesn't feel British. She used to, before she came. She says their lucky friends made some money and then returned home to build a house or buy land. She said the unlucky ones like my dad and her were 'trapped' here. My mother has rheumatoid arthritis, and the NHS British treatment was better than what she would get at home. And I was born in London. I often wondered if my parents would have moved back to Grenada if it wasn't for me."

Harry stopped talking; he looked sad, so I stopped asking questions and kissed him.

At first, I didn't tell Roxanne about me dating Harry. I was worried she might feel uneasy about meeting him again. But after three months of thinking about how to tell her, she saw us holding hands in the street. Roxanne was shy with Harry to start with, but Harry sorted it out.

"Roxanne, I never think about you the way you were when you and Zuzana first came to see me in the hospital. If you don't stop treating me like a doctor, I am going to start boring you with medical stories till you beg me to stop!"

Bob and Angus hit it off with Harry, too. They were now extremely busy after opening their own interior design company.

"Angus has that uncanny Scottish business brain – I just draw stuff." Bob grinned when he told me. In fact, I think Bob just disliked the business part of the job and was happy to leave it to Angus.

In a year, they moved to a lovely small flat in St John's Wood, one of London's expensive areas. I asked how much they paid for it, but Angus told me I would faint if I knew. That year, Bob paid for his mother to go on a Caribbean cruise and then stay in Jamaica for a month.

"I can't take a holiday!" she protested.

In the end, Bob and Roxanne made her take unpaid leave.

"I hope the Lord will forgive me this indulgence," she apparently said. I heard Bob and Roxanne joking about it. Their mother had two good but totally godless children. *It is interesting,* I thought. *Harry has a religious mother, too.*

Harry and I were happy. I was no longer interested in other men. I loved his company. He was now a GP and he enjoyed his job. For Easter 1976, I took him to Paris to meet Otto and Marie. They liked him.

I took Otto aside. "Uncle Otto, I think I would like to marry him. Will you help me with Mother?"

I hadn't seen my mother for more than two years. We spoke on the phone, but we both suspected the police were eavesdropping.

"I miss you so much, Zuzana. You are all alone in England – are you all right? Otto says you are, but you have nobody there."

When my mum spoke like that, I forgot all those nasty things she used to tell me.

"I love you too, Mum, and eventually we'll meet again."

I didn't tell her I missed her, too – that would be a lie. Even the 'I love you' was not completely sincere.

Otto and Marie went to Prague a lot. They were no longer in danger of being arrested.

They did not stay with my mother but always booked a room in the expensive Hotel Pariz. "We are going from Paris to Pariz," joked Otto.

He promised to talk to my mother about Harry. I was worried.

My mother might not be the easiest mother-in-law, especially to a black man.

When I saw Otto after his next trip to Prague, he looked uneasy.

"Zuzana, your mother seems to be happy with Tomas, but you might find some things hard to cope with. Marie had a big argument with him about racism." Otto looked at Marie with a humorous smile.

"Your aunt doesn't tolerate racism, and good for her!"

I asked, and after some hesitation, Marie told me.

They'd spoken about Roxanne. Tomas said a stupid joke about black people and gorillas. *What do you get when you mix a gorilla with a black man? A dumb gorilla.* Marie told him off. "Do you realise your wife is Jewish and that most of our relatives were killed by the Nazis? Magda, how can you listen to this?" she'd said, and left, banging the door.

"I had to leave, Zuzana," she said, slightly embarrassed about her behaviour with my mum. Marie was not the door-banging type. "I had lunch with your mother next day, just the two of us. At lunch, your mother seemed uneasy. She told me she found a book Tomas was reading, something about *The Elders of Zion*, and it was all about the Jewish conspiracy to rule the world. She told me she looked, and it was awful. Like something the Nazis would write. I was surprised that Magda has never heard about that awful book."

"My mother doesn't read, and she had her education on a fast track, remember?" I reminded them.

Marie continued: "Magda told me she asked Tomas about it, and he said, 'Well, you are more competent, and look at all those clever and rich Jews. I am lucky to be married to one. The Jews do rule the world!' I was not completely surprised, but how could Magda have married him?"

"Did you tell Mum about Harry? If she won't be nice to him, I will stop speaking to her. I love him." I was anxious; I imagined my mother saying nasty things to Harry or Roxanne.

"I told her you might want to get married but that I told you to wait till you finish your studies. By then she might be able to get a permission to visit," said Otto.

"She probably said that by then, I might have started dating some nice white man. My mother is a racist, too."

Otto gave me yet another lecture about being nicer to my mother and giving her a chance. But he knew I was right. I was getting anxious about the time my mother would meet Roxanne or Harry.

CHAPTER SEVENTEEN

Zuzana 1977–1978

In 1977, the dissidents in Czechoslovakia signed a document, Charter 77, asking the government to keep to the 1975 Helsinki agreement signed by 35 European states. There was a big backlash. Some of my friends I knew from the Jewish centre in Prague were involved, but I only found out about that much later, when the regime ended in the Velvet Revolution of 1989. I regret not having been able to play my part, but I would have probably been arrested; I was safer in the West. Charter 77 did not change much inside Czechoslovakia, and many dissidents, including the future president, Vaclav Havel, were arrested. The Helsinki agreement was a big deal for me though, because people who had relatives abroad were now allowed to visit them. My mother obtained a permission to visit me in England. Tomas didn't get the permission, but I was looking forward to seeing Mum.

She took some unpaid leave and was planning to stay for six weeks. Otto paid for her accommodation. I was now sharing a different small flat with Roxanne. I was thinking about moving in with Harry, but I decided to wait until after my graduation. Roxanne, who was now dating a nice, sporty mountain climber, Derek, offered to go and stay with her boyfriend so that my mother could stay with me. I declined. I was dreading my mother's visit already and I didn't want to be with her for 24 hours a day.

I drove to pick her up at the airport; I had just passed my driving test and had an old second-hand car. I was nervous. Would her poisonous words re-appear after four years? Harry could not understand it. "It's your mother. Aren't you pleased that she is coming?"

I wasn't. I got used to a life where nobody criticised me and told me how selfish I was.

I tried to explain it to Harry. "I've thought about it a lot lately. When I emigrated, it was because of the regime, of course, and because of the times my family should have emigrated and didn't. But maybe I was running away from my mother. The Iron Curtain was a good shield." I didn't want Harry to come with me to the airport.

The first ten minutes were great. She kissed me, hugged me, told me how she missed me, how much she loved me. I was getting less anxious. But it didn't last long. In the car, the nagging came back.

"You cannot imagine how awful it was for me when you left. I would never do this to my mother; you spoiled my life…"

She only stopped when I almost crashed the car. I dropped her at the hotel and told her that Harry and I would pick her up at seven for dinner. Fortunately, my mother's English was not particularly good, so they were mostly just smiling at each other. I remembered my father talking about the son of a friend who married a Chinese girl. "He cannot understand his mother-in-law – what a blessing!" It was only the three of us at dinner. I translated and they grinned at each other.

I told Mum that Harry and I had changed our minds. I originally wanted to get married after graduation, but we'd decided to have the wedding while she was still in England. A small wedding, just our parents and close friends. Otto and Marie, too. In Czechoslovakia, most people weren't getting engaged; people usually just planned a wedding, and it was not always a big affair. Harry at first wanted to get me an engagement ring, but I told him we could use the money for a holiday instead. I loved Harry, but weddings, even mine, left me cold. I could never understand why women bought expensive white wedding gowns, never to wear them again, and wasted money on entertaining people who were not close to them.

"Romantic you ain't," was Harry's remark.

"Do you mind?" I asked.

He just kissed me, smiling.

"There will be more black than white people – blacks have lots of children," said Mother. I was glad Harry did not understand Czech. He was sitting there relaxed, but I had various embarrassing scenarios in my head, imagining my mother at our wedding. I was getting cold feet. But then my dear friend Roxanne changed everything. Roxanne is good at languages; she spoke French and German, so she could speak German with my mum.

"You told me so many bad things about your mother, but she is lovely." And yes, my mother was charming.

We had a small wedding and no honeymoon. Harry couldn't get the time off. Otto offered to buy me a wedding gown, but I didn't want a white dress. I wore a navy and red Moroccan-style kaftan with golden tassels. Rather hippie looking. My mother didn't like it; she said I looked like an Arab. Harry liked the kaftan, though. "Rather African." He spoke slowly and clearly, and my mother could understand some of what he said. Surprisingly, Mother continued with her charm offensive at my wedding, too, and all those people talked about how I must have missed her. My mouth hurt from translating the conversations.

Otto paid for the reception in the same hotel my mother was staying at. Just a small party: Harry's parents, some of their relatives I did not know, my mother, Otto and Marie, Roxanne, Derek, Bob, Angus, and Harry's best man Jack, an Aussie doctor who was soon moving back to Australia. Harry's father Richard, a pharmacist like my mother, tried to have a conversation with her, but it was too much for me to translate. "I will start learning English properly," my mother said.

We danced and had dinner. I spoke to a small, thin, very dark woman with white hair, sitting next to Harry's mother across the table. Dressed in a colourful suit with a flared skirt and a jacket with a pattern of large peonies, she looked like some tropical bird with her long nose.

"I am Harry's Auntie Sybil," she said. Then the interrogation started. It was funny; she wanted to know everything, but she also started to tell me about the family, how they got there. Sybil was my mother-in-law's cousin. "We were not high and mighty enough for Harry's family in Grenada; his father used to be a real bossy-boots, but he's all right now. I came to England five years after Angie, and she helped me. I stayed with them for the first year. I helped look after Harry."

"What was he like? Naughty?"

Sybil chuckled and told me a story about her telling little Harry off for leaving half of his dinner on the plate when children in Africa were starving. "That little rascal told me to wrap the food from his plate and send it to the starving children!"

Just when it started to be interesting, Harry stopped everybody's conversation. That was after we'd all had a cake and people were drinking coffee. Harry, who was caressing my thigh under the table while I was trying to keep a straight face, suddenly got up, pulled me up too and said, "Sorry, I need to make love to my wife now. Enjoy the party!"

"Harry!" gasped his mother Angela, who was already upset by us not having a wedding in her Catholic church. But Harry was already pulling me away, laughing. I looked at his father Richard, and he was laughing, too. Sybil was making a loud cackling sound, but my mother looked as disapproving as Harry's mum. I didn't think our wedding night was going to be special, but it was. Harry made love to me all night, whispering how happy he was and how beautiful I was. I was happy, too.

My happiness disappeared the next day, when Harry went back to work and Mother and I were alone. She did not like my wedding; she would have wanted me to have a proper big white wedding, not a small one where I was wearing that ugly kaftan. She didn't want me to be a social worker and work with 'the riff-raff'. She was talking about me abandoning her, that she was scared about the future, what would happen to her when she gets old. Eventually we argued, and it ended the same as always: I cried. Two days later, I was happy driving her to the airport. Six weeks was too long.

I was free again, a married woman, Zuzana Williams. I was going to be able to apply for British citizenship soon. *I must stop crying because of something my mother said. I am too old for that,* I thought.

Soon after the wedding, I graduated from the polytechnic. I now had a BA in sociology and an MA in social work.

Graduation from university has always been a big thing in Czechoslovakia, maybe more than a wedding. Yet, I didn't think Mother would come. She did, as a surprise for me, coming by a taxi straight from Heathrow. She said Tomas sent his regards. Her 'congratulations' was insincere; she really didn't think it was a big deal.

"I wish you did something different. Social worker – what sort of job is that? You are just going to be working with losers! Pity you didn't become a medical doctor like your husband, or a lawyer."

In Prague, graduation meant a big family celebration, but we didn't have any relatives apart from Otto and Marie anyway. Suddenly I remembered there were all these cousins in the USA, and Hana in Israel, that I'd never met. The only people at my graduation ceremony were Harry and his parents, my mother, and Otto with Marie. I wore a square hat, like they did in films, and after the ceremony, I introduced Harry to some friends he didn't know yet. We all had a nice lunch.

CHAPTER EIGHTEEN

Zuzana 1978-1986

MARRIED LIFE SUITS ME

We moved to Harrow, closer to Harry's parents, who lived in Ealing. I worked for the social services; Harry was working in a general practice close to our house. A lot of his colleagues and patients were Indian, first- or second-generation. Harrow was very mixed, full of Indian shops and restaurants. I liked it. It was also nice not to be the only person with a foreign accent.

St John's Wood, where Bob and Angus lived, was not far – just a couple of stops on the tube. We saw them and Roxanne a lot.

I liked my job. It was interesting to hear about people's problems. A lot of my clients were refugees, new to the country. They were surprised and pleased when I told them I was a refugee, too. After spending most of my life purely with white people, meeting all those people from Uganda, India, Pakistan, Bangladesh and many other countries was fascinating. Many of my clients were Indian from Uganda who spoke Gujarati, and I was taking lessons in the language.

Mrs Janet McBride, a freckled, red-haired, small woman with a strong Irish accent, told me I had a lawyer's brain. Maybe Mother was right; I would have enjoyed being a lawyer, but it was too late for that. I didn't want to go back to university. The people I met in my job were fascinating. I would go and visit single parents, Ugandan Indian refugees, Irish travellers in caravans, old English people living in terrace houses without heating and with steep staircases like ladders – my work was mostly with people with no money and their lives were hard. It felt good to be able to help them, make their life easier. It was incredible how many of those people coped with the hardships with a sense of humour. Again, it made me judge my mother. Ever since the war, her life was stable compared to the lives of my clients.

Harry disagreed. "Yes," he said sarcastically, "all her relatives died or emigrated, her husband left her, and her only child emigrated. An easy life indeed!"

This situation of Harry being on my mother's side was irritating. I ignored him and told him that in my job, I was collecting material for the novels I would eventually write. I had no doubt that I was going to be a writer – it was no question of if, just when.

Apart from being occasionally annoyed by a feeling that Harry and my mum were ganging up on me, I was blissfully happy.

My day started with a cup of tea in bed. Both Harry's parents came from Grenada, but Harry was so British that I wondered if he was just pretending to tease me. The umpteen 'nice cups of tea'; the love of baked beans, custard, rice pudding and other – in my opinion – disgusting English delicacies; the obsession with football and cricket; the polite, circumspect manner. Of course, cricket was as popular in the Caribbean as in England. But I found Harry's devotion to his football club, Arsenal, even more bizarre. He wore an Arsenal scarf, had a sticker on his car, and one Saturday he insisted on me going to a game with him, until he caught me reading a book during the match on the day. I only had a seat behind him, not next to him.

"I turned to see what she thought about Frank Stapleton's stunning goal – right in the top corner, it was – and saw that she'd missed it because she was reading a book!" he told his father, who shook his head in disbelief.

"What was so stunning about it?" I said. "He almost missed!"

I couldn't understand why they were laughing. But at least I was excused from football after that.

At first, Harry found my directness shocking. "You do call a spade a spade, Zuzana, don't you?"

"I don't call a spade anything, I hate gardening."

Fortunately for our house, Harry loved gardening. He stopped talking to me about weather and gardening only after I teased him mercilessly. "It's raining, isn't it? Yes, it is, isn't it? What sort of conversation is that?"

It was the same at the dinner parties. They all avoided anything controversial like politics, religion or money. It was safe, but often boring. I sometimes had fun intentionally putting my foot in it. I could do that, being an alien had advantages. They probably thought it was 'part of my culture'.

There was nothing boring about my husband. When he abandoned his traditional English airs, he was great fun. He seemed so interested in anything I said: the family stories, life in a communist country, my opinions. Yet I was interested in his stories, too. He told me about Grenada, where his grandparents still lived, the history of the slaves' uprising in 1795, the beautiful island, full of colours. He now talked more about being black in England, the surprise of encountering racism when he did not expect it and being sometimes taken aback by the surprise of the friendliness of people whom he thought might be racist. He told me how often he was stopped by the police when he was younger. Even when he was already a doctor, a policeman stopped him to check if the car was stolen. He told me that when he was a teenager, his parents often worried about him. If a group of a few black teenagers were just standing on the street chatting, police would arrest them, search them for drugs and charge them if they found cannabis.

"White teenagers smoked cannabis as often as the black ones did, but they didn't get arrested."

"Oh, Harry, did it happen to you?"

"No, I never smoked dope, and I was a swot, so I didn't go anywhere. I stayed at home. My parents do not feel British, and from what I can gather from my other relatives of that generation, I think that is a universal feeling. I feel British and Grenadian. Just like someone might feel Welsh and British or Cornish and British. You feel British, Czech and Jewish, don't you?"

He was right.

"How about at school?" I asked.

"I did not experience much racism at school, but I was quite confident and maybe they just didn't pick on me. Weirdly, I had no concept of being a second-class citizen and naturally assumed I had the same opportunities as anyone else. With that attitude, most of the white teachers were helpful and keen to assist me. I really enjoyed school, especially science, and I did not go anywhere apart from school and home."

"I hated school," I said.

He kissed me. "But Zuzana, that was different – your school was full of communist propaganda."

"Nope, I hated school purely because it was a school. I usually didn't pay much attention and read novels hidden on my lap instead of listening to the teachers. School was boring."

Harry asked me why the teachers didn't confiscate my novels. I often asked myself the same question. I think the teachers knew that if I wasn't reading, I would be disruptive. They let me read for peace and quiet. When I was reading, I didn't talk.

"Did you have any white friends, Harry?"

"Yes, several. Thinking about it, I was weirdly colour-blind as a child, and remain so. I just pick people with whom I get along. I can honestly say the thought had not even crossed my mind until you started asking me, Zuzana. You are doing research for your future novels, aren't you?"

That was typical of Harry: his sunny attitude and optimism meant he couldn't see the bad parts of life. And he was right. None of his white patients minded having a black GP. But Harry was a fabulous GP, so they would be mad to mind it.

My mother-in-law had a strong Grenadian accent, but funnily enough, my father-in-law Richard hardly had any accent at all. I always wondered why. I asked Harry if he thought that his ethnic background didn't really matter.

"No, I think my ethnic background is important in my life. Having been around older Grenadians growing up, seeing and hearing their experiences has given me a perspective on life and sympathy for differences that I do not think I would otherwise have.

It is great to be able to draw on the culture not of one country but two. It has made me a better doctor, too, I think."

All this talk made me feel homesick. *Will I ever see Prague again? I cannot go back like Harry can go to Grenada; I would be arrested.* I told him about the war history of my family, how they kept trying to cover the yellow star.

"I told Roxanne about that once, and she told me that being black cannot be covered," I said.

"Yes. Well, I suppose I could have just socialised with blind people pretending to be white." That was also typical Harry: he always turned to jokes when the discussions became too serious.

It was the same when we were making love. In the middle of passion, Harry would crack some outrageous joke that made the bed shake with our laughter. I was experienced in sex, after all those boyfriends, but sex with Harry was surprising. I asked him if he was good at sex because he was a doctor.

He laughed. "No, I just like sex. Just don't tell my mother. The way she is, I probably came about by immaculate conception."

Harry had a point. Mrs Williams (I still found it hard to call her Angela), despite her curvy figure and colourful dresses, was so prim and proper, you would think she was a nun. I wondered what Harry's father felt. It was not that I did not get on with my mother-in-law; I did. I'd had training; no mother-in-law could be as difficult as my mother. Angela was a nice woman, a traditional church-going Roman Catholic, active in the community, a marvellous cook. She occasionally revealed a dry sense of humour, but we mostly had nothing to talk about, so we talked about the weather, food or travel. I was careful not to offend her. I didn't like small talk, but it came in handy with her.

"It is really hot today, isn't it? I love the heat."

"You should feel the heat in the Caribbean, this is nothing."

Richard, my father-in-law, was usually quiet. I never knew what he thought. He usually left us after lunch and watched TV. I hoped that when my mother's English got better, they could talk shop.

I wanted to find out more about Harry's family history; I wanted to understand my husband better, and their grandchildren, if we had some, would want to know.

Harry told me his father used to play ball games with him, take him to the zoo and watch cartoons with him on TV. "I think he enjoyed the children's TV as much as I did; he didn't have TV growing up. We both liked *Thunderbirds*. My mother thought he was being silly."

Many years later, Harry showed me a programme he used to love when he was small. It was called *Bill and Ben*. They talked in an incomprehensible language. I agreed with my mother-in-law. Silly, indeed. I thought the Czech cartoons when I was growing up were better. There was no censorship on TV and books for little children, so a lot of artists who would normally aim their work at adults wrote and illustrated children's books.

Angela didn't like animals. In fact, she used to panic when Harry befriended a neighbour's cat and let it inside the house. "Cats transport diseases, and it could scratch you. It walked on the kitchen counter – who knows where it has been before?"

Harry tried to explain to her that cats are exceptionally clean, but Angela apparently said, "Cleaner than you, son, maybe, but that's no achievement!"

Harry was remarkably relaxed around my mother. "She can't help it; she is damaged. Anybody would be. She is alright. Imagine what she went through – be a bit more tolerant around your mum, Zuzana, you seem to be so judgemental. Relax, she loves you and you love her, you just don't want to admit it."

He told me about post-traumatic stress disorder, and yes, my mother probably had it. But then I remembered my wonderful, always positive Grandma Franzi. I told Harry about her.

"Yes, Zuzana, but your grandma was an adult; your mum was a teenager. That makes a big difference to how people cope."

I changed the subject. Maybe Harry was right, but I was not going to admit it.

Mother came twice a year, and once or twice, Tomas came with her. Tomas spoke remarkably good English, much better than my mum, although she was taking lessons and improving rapidly.

"My mum is so determined; she will probably speak better English than I do soon," I told Harry.

I was worried about Tomas. I remembered his jokes about gypsies and black people. But with Harry, Tomas seems to be colour-blind. He really liked Harry. He helped him in the garden, which left me in the company of my mother. That was tough.

We were both having fun, meeting friends, going to galleries and the theatre. Many of my friends were getting pregnant, but we were not in a hurry. In fact, I wasn't even sure if either of us wanted children. I didn't think I did. What if I became a horrible parent, like my mum? Not even my dad was good at parenting. After four years, both Angela and my mother started hinting, asking questions. Harry told Angela that we might have children eventually, but not yet. My mother loved babies; she couldn't wait to have a grandchild, but whenever she asked, I changed the subject, she asked a lot, though.

"You are getting old, Zuzana, don't wait too long, it might never happen!" Hearing my mother talking about my age, it was as if I was ancient.

About seven years after our wedding, I started thinking that maybe I would like a baby. Maybe – I wasn't sure. Then one day, when we were making love, I asked Harry if it was all right for me to stop taking the pill. He stopped, moved next to me in bed and asked if I was sure.

"I think so," I said.

Harry picked me up from the bed and started dancing with me. He changed the lyrics to 'I Do Like to Be Beside the Seaside' and sang in his deep voice:

"Oh, I do like to be trying for a baby
I do like to be inside of you,
Oh, I do like it even better when a baby
Is made by me and you."

The rhyming was corny, but his enthusiasm was contagious. I thought about my marriage and how Harry waited patiently for such a long time until I said something about having children, although he obviously wanted them so badly. Oh, I loved Harry so much; I felt safe knowing how considerate he was, always thinking about my feelings. *If he wants children, we will have several*, I thought.

It was not that easy; it took me several years to get pregnant. We started to have some tests, but just after we were referred to an infertility clinic, it happened. I was 34. Nine years after our wedding, we were going to have a baby.

Suddenly I wasn't sure having a baby was a good idea. Did I really want to stop working, be a mum? No, I didn't want to quit my job and talk with other women about breastfeeding and nappies. I wished the baby would just stay there in my body and look after itself.

I didn't share my doubts with Harry, but he somehow guessed and came up with a brilliant way to make me feel better. One day, almost three months into my pregnancy, Harry came home with a surprise. A trip to New York. "Let's do this before we have the baby. Neither of us has been to America before."

"Can we afford it, Harry?"

"Sure," he said.

CHAPTER NINETEEN

Zuzana 1986

TRIP TO NEW YORK, MEETING MY MOTHER'S COUSIN IRMA

The trip was wonderful – the museums, Central Park, the walks by Hudson River – but there was another thing I wanted to do. Mum's cousin Irma lived in New York and I wanted to see her. My mother spoke of Irma as if she was stupid, but I also knew the amazing story of her escape from a death march. I remembered my mother telling me, on one of the rare occasions she spoke about the war, about Irma's mother Helena kissing the SS officer's boots when he told her she could go with a transport east to join her family... She, like her husband and son, was killed, probably gassed – nobody knows. Irma, the only one who survived, apparently saw her brother Gerd once at distance in Auschwitz. But she couldn't talk to him.

Irma was pleased when I wrote to her about our trip. She invited us for dinner. Irma looked old. She had grey hair with a perm, out of fashion for the past 20 years, a wide grey skirt, not flattering her wide hips, and a grey blouse. She looked like a mouse. She behaved like a mouse, too: fidgety, shy and quiet. Irma's husband Petr, a tall bald man with metal-rimmed glasses, was chatty and rather domineering; he had strong opinions on everything. He explained Czech politics to me even though he hadn't been there since 1948 and told me that my occupation was useless.

"Social worker? What for? To help those lazy spongers who never do any work and want to be looked after by the state? That's a waste of your brain, Zuzana. Irma's Uncle Otto said you are smart. You live in a capitalist society now – why don't you open a business, or help your husband open a private medical practice?"

"Harry works for the NHS, he doesn't want a private practice, and I have my own job." We spent a useless hour discussing healthcare and social services, which he knew nothing about.

They had a teenage daughter called Joan, but she was not at home. Irma had her daughter late, aged 37. I remember my mother talking about it. Irma probably needed to recover from the war first. I asked about Joan, but Petr mumbled something incomprehensible, and Irma was quiet. She looked like that shy, frightened cousin in my mother's descriptions. I went to talk to her in her kitchen, leaving poor Harry talking to the annoying Petr. Irma and I started speaking in Czech. In my company, she changed: she smiled and talked more. She stopped smiling when I asked her about the war. I already knew about her escape, and the Austrian girl, Rosa. But no details. I thought she might not want to talk about it, but surprisingly, she told me a lot. It was as if those words needed to come out.

"Oh, Zuzana, Rosa was lovely. When I met her, she was singing – nobody sang in Auschwitz. Did your mother teach you the silly German song about the fox and goose?"

"Yes." I started singing and she joined me.

"Fuchs, du hast die Gans gestohlen,
Gib sie wieder her!
Gib sie wieder her!
Sonst wird dich der Jäger holen
Mit dem Schießgewehr,
Sonst wird dich der Jäger holen
Mit dem Schießgewehr."

(Fox, you've stolen the goose
Give it back!
Give it back!

Or the hunter will get you
With his gun,
Or the hunter will get you
With his gun.)

Both Irma and I started laughing. She hugged me and kissed me. But then she started telling me more. I thought that one of the reasons was the fact she'd rather be in the kitchen with me than in the living room with her husband.

"Rosa, with her Viennese singsong accent, asked me to sing with her; she said that life's more fun with singing. Rosa was right: singing helped. She was lucky to be working in the kitchen. She did not know where her parents and sister were. Rosa was an optimist, one of those happy people. Sometimes I wondered if she was simple – couldn't she see we were doomed? She couldn't, and being with her made me almost happy, too. We laughed together. Laughter was rare in that place. On my birthday, Rosa made me a cake. It was a piece of bread cut round, with some jam spread on it. She put a piece of wood in the middle and pretended it was a candle. I pretended to blow, like a child. I was 18 and I still remember that birthday; Rosa made it memorable."

"Oh, Irma, Rosa sounds wonderful, tell me more." It was exciting to find out about Irma's war and compare it with my mum's memories.

"She saved my life. It was only after the war that people called it a 'death march'. It was July 1944, and they were marching us from Auschwitz to Loslau. It was hot, and I felt faint. I was walking slowly with the others, trying to ignore the shouting, people being beaten, sometimes shot when they fell to the ground. I was stumbling, too, and then I tripped and fell. A young male guard approached me and kicked me, hard. His boots were dusty. Then I saw the gun. I was staring at the gun, waiting for it to go off, but I did not have the strength to get up."

I looked at Irma; she was alive, so something must have saved her! "What happened? Did he shoot and miss you?"

"No, a miracle happened. A female guard, Anneliese Schmidt who had enjoyed beating us, came closer. I expected a blow, but instead, she hit the man's arm so that he dropped the gun, and shouted, 'You idiot, you are too wet behind the ears to decide who lives and who dies!' Then she pulled me up by my hand, kicked me, but only slightly, and pushed me forward. I didn't dare look at her."

"Aunt Irma, why do you think she did it? Was she just showing the young man she was the boss? Did she feel sorry for you?"

"I really don't know. After the war, we were looking for family, not the Nazis."

Irma told me that Rosa saw what happened and grabbed her hand. She was shaking, and told Irma, "Walk with me, Irma. I'll look after you."

"So, the SS woman saved your life?" I asked.

"Yes. Maybe she knew the war was ending and wanted to have a story that showed her in a good light."

Irma told me they were marching all day and most of the night, holding hands. The march was a mess; even the Germans were tired, so they did not pay much attention.

"Mum told me that you escaped, burnt your number and pretended to be German. How did it happen? Weren't you scared?"

Irma doesn't look like somebody capable of such heroism – it must have been the other girl, Rosa, I thought. I was right.

"We were marching through a thick wood, and suddenly, Rosa took my hand and pulled me behind a bush. Oh, Zuzana, my heart was beating so fast. 'We will be shot,' I whispered. But nobody seemed to have noticed. That night, we stayed in the woods. Rosa had matches; we made a small fire. I had the bold idea to get rid of our tattooed numbers, so nobody would be able to tell we were Jewish."

"Burning the numbers must have been so painful! How did you do it?"

"We did it to each other. We used sticks from the fire. I cried, but Rosa didn't even wince."

"That was so brave, Irma, you are an amazing woman. I am so pleased we finally met!" I was thinking about my mother's description of Irma: her timid and not very bright cousin. I liked Irma, and she didn't seem stupid to me. Her Czech was also still good, although, unlike my mother, she had German schools and used to speak mostly German with her parents.

"So, what happened in the morning?" I asked.

"We covered our very sore forearms with long sleeves and went and knocked on the door of a nearby cottage. We were hoping the people would be Polish and hide us, but it was a German family. My brain was buzzing, and then I blurted out the first thing I thought of. I told them the Russians were coming and had burned our home, that we had just managed to escape."

"Did they believe you?" It was fascinating. I completely forgot about Harry having to talk to Irma's husband; I wanted to find out more. I sat on the kitchen table and stopped drying the dishes. Irma talked while preparing the dessert.

"Yes. They took us in and gave us soup. Zuzana, I don't know how we managed to hold the conversation and agree with them that the Führer had a secret weapon and that everything was going to turn around. Lying convincingly is a useful skill. Rosa was a very convincing liar. You know, Zuzana, my parents told me not to lie, but lying saved our lives. The German family gave us food and money for train tickets. On the long journey, we kept repeating the story. All those Germans felt sorry for us, refugees from the east. Once, somebody asked Rosa why she had an Austrian accent. "My mum was Austrian," she said. For once, she was telling the truth, and I smiled at her. When we were together, we had fun, despite the fear of being discovered. Being with Rosa was almost like being in another world, a world where the Nazis were gone, and we were just two friends, girls giggling about silly jokes, happy people. She made me happy. We sang children's songs, and she taught me some silly ones. One was: *Du bist Verrückt, my Kind... You're crazy, my child, you have to go to Vienna, where the crazy people are – that's where you belong!* We sang it on the train, laughing, and the German woman sitting close to us smiled. Was she a Nazi? Who knows? She probably thought we were."

"I know that song from my grandma, too," I said.

"Rosa was funny. She embellished our story with details just to amuse herself. My lies were always clumsy, so I kept quiet. I told her that she should become a writer after the Nazis lose the war. We both believed the Nazis were going to lose. The hope kept us alive. Well, it kept me alive, Zuzana."

Irma started crying, and I embraced her. I was crying, too. I didn't want Rosa to die, but if she did not die, why was Irma crying? In the end, they split up. Rosa wanted to go to Austria. She thought she might find some friends who would hide her. She wanted Irma to go with her, but Irma stayed in Liberec – or Reichenberg, as the Germans called it – a town in Sudetenland and worked as a maid for a local German family. The husband worked on the railways. They had two children: a little girl and an older son. Horst, a 12-year-old boy in a Hitlerjugend uniform, kept talking about joining the army. The father kept saying the same thing a lot of Germans were saying: "Führer has a secret weapon; we will win the war." His wife, a blonde, plump woman who always dressed in an apron, looked scared. He was local and spoke Czech. She didn't.

"She seemed lonely, Zuzana, and always wanted me to talk to her. But I am not good at lying or making up stories, so I kept quiet most of the time. I never told them that I spoke or understood Czech – I was a German refugee from Eastern Poland."

"Did they find out the truth?" I asked.

"No, but I was so frightened! He was transferred to Prague and they took me with them."

"Yes, Mum told me you ended up in Prague. Did you go to Otto and Marie?"

"No, I was scared. I was worried someone would recognise me, so I bleached my hair and avoided busy streets. I didn't dare look for my friends or family."

Irma told me the German family lived in a large apartment on the top floor in an old 19th-century house in Vinohrady, a nice part of Prague. She told me she was not a very good servant, but she must have been good enough, because at the end of April 1945, when the German family was escaping west, they wanted to take her with them.

"Oh, Zuzana, I panicked. Where could I hide? The only Czech woman in the building was the concierge, Tonka, a grumpy woman who never smiled even if I smiled at her. Tonka never spoke to me, although she spoke German. I heard her telling off Horst, the son of my employers, for stepping on wet, newly washed stairs. She was my only chance. She lived in a small flat in the basement. I thought she might report me, but she didn't. That was the first time in a year I spoke Czech.

"Please, please, hide me, I'm Jewish, a Czech, I pretended to be German, and now they want to take me with them to Germany. Please help me!" The woman was cagey, so I showed her the scar on my forearm and told her how I got it. Then she pulled me into her flat."

This was so fascinating; I couldn't wait to tell Harry.

Petr and Harry came into the kitchen. "What are you talking about in the kitchen? Is it some sort of female conspiracy? Are you planning to run away to circus, or murder us for our money?" Petr joked.

It was not a particularly good joke, but I doubted Petr had a sense of humour. Harry looked bored; it was time Irma and I joined them. I quickly told Harry Irma's story.

Petr looked proud. "She was a brave girl, wasn't she?" he said.

"So did the concierge hide you?" Harry wanted to know more.

"Yes, I spent the last days of the war hiding in a wardrobe in the basement. Tonka didn't give me much food, but she didn't have much herself. Still, it was ten times more than in the camps."

"Were the Germans not looking for you? What happened at the end of the war?"

" 9 May, Tonka opened the door and shouted, 'Irma, come out, the Russians are here!'"

Irma told us that the German family managed to escape. They were not real Nazis – apart from Horst, who didn't know any better. At the end of the war, even boys like him from the Hitlerjugend were drafted to fight. Irma said she hoped he wasn't killed; he was only a child.

"Yes, I know, Zuzana, the Germans killed so many Jewish children. But that doesn't make killing a German child right."

I really liked Irma. *What a contrast to my mother – Irma is kind and friendly*, I thought.

Irma was free. That day, she rang the bell on the door of the apartment of her uncle Otto. His wife Marie opened the door. The nightmare was over.

Slowly, some of the family returned. Most of them never did. Irma found out later that Rosa was recognised in Vienna and shot by the Gestapo. We cried when she told me. Harry cried, too. Petr looked bored; he had heard it all before. I imagined the brave, lovely Rosa, with her songs. Was it a friend who'd betrayed her? Irma never found out – she just had the information from the Red Cross about Rosa being shot in March 1945. It was a month before Vienna fell to the Soviet army.

Unlike my mother, Irma never finished secondary school. She lived with Otto and Marie and worked in a shop.

Then she met Petr. He was a distant American cousin whose parents had sent him to the USA in the summer of 1938. He came to Europe with the American army, looking for his family. Most of them were dead.

"I brought her to America from that European nightmare!"

I remembered that Mum told me that Petr wanted to date her first. He could have been my father! I didn't like Petr at all. He didn't deserve a nice woman like Irma. In my opinion, Irma was a much better wife than my egocentric mother would be. Almost every woman would, although my mother was an attractive girl and a flirt, and there was never anything flirty about Irma.

Later in our hotel room, I told Harry that my mother wouldn't let Petr be so bossy if she was his wife.

"Yes, he doesn't deserve Irma, she is sweet."

I didn't tell him the shocking thing Irma told me when we were still alone in the kitchen. "I will never forgive Grandma Olga for killing my parents and my brother!" she said with dry eyes. I didn't know what to say. I just got up and embraced her. We both started crying. I only understood it years later, when Irma told me more about the past and introduced me to Miriam. That was when I found out why, in the eyes of Irma, Great-Grandmother Olga was a murderer.

CHAPTER TWENTY

Zuzana 1987

When we came back from New York, I told my mother about my pregnancy. She was ecstatic.

"A baby, a baby," she repeated. She seemed to be happier than I was. She got angry, however, when she found out I was already more than four months pregnant.

"Why didn't you tell me right away? You knew how I wanted to be a grandmother. And how could you travel to America? What if you had a miscarriage? And not telling me? Other daughters tell their mothers even before their husband." Blah, blah, blah. I stopped listening.

Both Angela and my mother couldn't wait for the baby to be born. Mum would phone me, asking not how I was, but how the baby was. "I don't know," I said. "It can't talk to me yet."

On the phone, Harry asked my mother if she wanted to be there at the delivery. I gave him a nasty look. He should have asked me before.

I didn't want her there.

"Mum, I don't need anybody – you would just make me nervous."

She asked if Angela was going to be there. She was jealous. I told her that I didn't want grannies interfering. Angela didn't make scenes like my mum, but I didn't want her there either.

It happened the way I wanted it. Adam was born in the hospital. The delivery was long and hard, as if he didn't want to come out. The pain was worse than I imagined, and in the end, they needed forceps to get him out. I bled a lot and needed a blood transfusion, but when Harry wanted to sit with me all night, I told the midwife, "Chuck my husband out – he needs sleep."

He did what I said. When Angela wanted to change the nappies and help, I chucked her out, too. It was my baby, and I wanted everybody to leave me alone.

Mother came when Adam was three months old. She thought her grandson was beautiful.

"He has such nice brown skin, your eyes and nose, and his hair is curly but not like his father. He doesn't really look like a negro."

I'd told my mother many times never to use the word negro, but she didn't get it. She thought Adam looked more Mediterranean than black.

I thought he looked like any other baby: wrinkly, big head, chubby body. I never found babies particularly attractive. And he screamed a lot. *It'll be much more fun when he grows older and can talk*, I thought. Still, holding him, singing silly songs to him, that tiny body – it felt special. I loved him, and I wanted to be a good mother. I had no doubt Harry would be a good father, and he was.

My mother liked Harry, and he liked her. They talked and joked together. The tension that was always present between my mother and me was never there between them.

I never thought my mother had a sense of humour, but around Harry, she did. She told him that she worried about racism, and the effect it might have on her darling little grandson.

"What if people are nasty to him because he's not white? Zuzana always says it is fine. How does she know? I didn't experience any antisemitism before I had to wear the yellow star. My family considered themselves Czechs, but then we were told we were Jewish, only Jewish. Zuzana tells people she is Jewish – it is stupid, why? Nobody needs to know. Adam will be seen as half Jewish, half black; the poor child is marked from the start. I worry about him! What about you? Do people do racist things to you, Harry?"

Harry, instead of being offended, told her he understood. "Of course, there are people who are antisemitic or racist, but most people are not. And sometimes people change. Magda, look at Tomas – he changed. I knew he didn't like black people, but we get on and like each other. He might have me as the token black man who is different, but it is a start. People love your daughter, so when Zuzana tells them she is Jewish, their opinion about Jews gets more favourable."

My mother didn't say anything. Harry claimed it was because she was thinking about it. I thought she just didn't know what to say.

I had everything under control. That didn't necessarily mean I liked being a stay-at-home mum. My mother was trying to help. She wanted to take the baby out, but I asked her to cook instead; I was going out anyway. "I don't feel like cooking!" Mother said.

"Okay, I thought you wanted to help me. That's all right, I don't need your help anyway." I left, not giving her space to talk to me. I felt guilty. I knew she meant well, and that she loved me and Adam. Still, that didn't make her less annoying.

Maybe I am a bad daughter. Maybe I don't love her enough. Grandma loved both of us with unconditional love. My love, like my mother's, comes with conditions. I have spent most of my life trying not to be like my mother, but recently, I'd wondered if I was like her. That was a scary thought.

CHAPTER TWENTY-ONE

Zuzana 1987–1994

ADAM IS A GOOD CHILD, DESPITE HIS TENDENCY TO CLIMB TREES

My concern that it was a bad idea to have a baby disappeared very quickly. I liked being a mother, and Adam was a good child. As a baby he smiled a lot, slept most of the night and liked his food. The only problem was, he constantly climbed trees. It started before he could walk. I was visiting a friend, and her husband had a ladder leaning on a tree. I let Adam crawl in the grass, while I talked to my friend and drank coffee. Suddenly, my friend screamed. My ten-month-old baby was high up on the ladder. I took him down, but he climbed everything after that: furniture, walls, trees. My son was growing. I had to watch him all the time. I turned, and the triumphant voice of the three-year-old shouted from two metres high, "Mummy! Look where I am!" I can't climb trees; if he'd said he couldn't get down, I would have needed to call the fire brigade.

"We should send him to a rock-climbing club, or put him in the zoo, like a monkey."

Harry thought it was funny. His mother didn't. "He will fall and get killed! I am praying for him every day."

Neither Harry nor I believed in God or prayers, but we kept our mouths shut.

Adam learnt how to read long before he went to school. He

didn't stop the tree climbing, but now he climbed with a book. The neighbours got used to our son sitting high above them, reading *Winnie the Pooh*. I wondered if he was going to be naughty at school like I used to be, but either he was alright, or the British teachers were more lenient than the Czech ones. Adam seemed happy in the local school, but my mother-in-law kept trying to persuade us to put him in a Roman Catholic school.

"Catholic state schools are the best, as good as the public schools. Why don't you try?"

It's one of British idiosyncrasies that expensive private schools are called 'public'.

I said I didn't want to move him, thinking, *Religious school? No way! I don't want my son indoctrinated by any ideology.*

However, Angela won in the end. That was when Mireille, our French au pair, left after an argument with my mother. Mireille was very good with Adam, but terribly untidy. Our house was a mess. Mireille did not stay long. It was the old story, like with my cleaners. Whenever my mother came to visit, I had to look for a new cleaner. They all gave me their notice soon after being left with my mother alone.

"You can't tell her anything!" my mother said.

She said that a lot about people. These people experienced my mother's tongue and unlike me, they did not have to put up with it. They voted with their feet.

My mother told Mireille that she was paid to clean the house, too, not just for looking after Adam. There were limits to what an au pair was supposed to do, and Mireille never did much housework, but she was a good cook and Adam liked her. I wondered if Mother was jealous of her.

Losing Mireille was a problem. I couldn't get anybody to look after Adam after school. So when Angela, who was now only working part time in the pharmacy, suggested that we put Adam in the Roman Catholic school close to her house and that she would pick him up from school, it sounded like a good idea.

"So, you finally got what you wanted, Mum – your grandson in a Catholic school!" Harry teased Angela.

Having Angela picking Adam from school was great. The school seemed tolerant enough. Adam was not forced to go to mass. He did start talking about God and angels, but I told him it was just fairy tales, like *Cinderella*. The other children in the school were mainly Irish or Polish, and they were all real Catholics. Nobody was black. I asked Harry if it mattered, and he said hopefully not; Adam had to learn how to live in mainly white society.

Then in class, Adam told the teacher that I said there was no God. That was probably not a clever thing to say. The next day, the teacher phoned me and asked me to come to school. That should have warned me that maybe this was not the right school for a non-Catholic child. The teacher was pleasant enough. She told me most children at the school are religious, and that I should maybe let Adam make up his mind. I told her my family is Jewish, but not religious, that I thought religion divided people and often lead to discrimination, but I also acknowledged that this was a Catholic school, and that I was going to speak to Adam and ask him to respect other children's views by not questioning their beliefs.

I felt uncomfortable and remembered the indoctrination of my school – the belief in Lenin and communism – and how my quasi-religious belief in communism vanished thanks to coloured plastic drinking straws in Bavaria.

The school was like all English schools: in the breaks, the children were all let out to the school courtyard, running, kicking a ball, screaming. When I passed the school at break times, they sounded like a jungle full of screeching birds and monkeys. We never had this in Prague when I was a child; we had to walk in an orderly way around the corridors and not talk. Thinking about it, my school was like a prison.

I imagined Adam as being one of the monkeys. Unfortunately, I later found out the football-playing boys never asked him to join. Adam sat on a wall, reading a book. He would have never told me if it wasn't for the evil redhead.

She wasn't from his class, and Adam didn't know her name. Every break, she came to him, stuck her tongue out at him and slapped him. Then she turned and walked away. Adam didn't know what to do. We always told him not to fight.

"Physical violence is stupid," I told him. "The people who do it are usually not smart enough to find the proper words. Only stupid people fight."

My heart bleeds for my son even now. Adam, at the age of six, didn't have any friends in this new school. He was black, the new pupil, whose mother talked to him in Czech. He did not believe in God. The Polish children laughed at him, saying Czech was a funny, lisping language like baby talk. I always thought Polish was like that. The boys mocked everything he did, and now the redhead. She was the last straw.

He should have told us about it, but whenever we asked about school, he told us it was alright. I never used to tell my mother anything; I thought I was a better mother than she was, but my son still kept secrets from me.

In the end, Adam fought. And yes, it was because he could not find the right words.

It was a sunny, hot day, and the redhead was approaching, but he was ready. He slapped her back. However, she was not like Adam. She started crying very loudly and complained to the teacher.

"He hit me, he hit me!"

Adam told me later she was sobbing loudly, but he noticed her eyes were dry. The teacher didn't. "You should *never* fight with girls; I will give you a note for your parents." She looked angry.

When he brought the note, I was angry, too.

"Are you stupid? Why are you hitting girls?" Adam did not say anything, but he could not help crying. No sobbing, unlike the redhead, just tears. I knew this was not right. "What's going on? Please tell me!" I wanted Adam to know that talking to me or Harry was safe.

He told me. I hugged him and kissed his wet eyes. I wanted to tell the teacher, but Adam didn't want that.

"Nobody likes a tell-tale, Mum."

I listened. I thought about my mother, how she would have gone to school and made things even harder. Maybe having a difficult mother did make me a better parent.

"Show me the girl, and I will sort her out."

It took me a couple of days to rearrange my work. Adam told me the redhead resumed her daily slapping routine. But the week after, when the children were out in the schoolyard, I was standing at the gate. I walked in and asked Adam to show me the girl. She was not far. She was already approaching when she spotted me.

"Hello, what a lovely hair colour," I said.

The girl stared at me towering over her, and she looked scared.

"I wanted to tell you something important. I know what you have been doing to my son. I have a lesson for you, a lesson in fair play. That is very important in this country, so I hope you will listen. Adam was taught good manners, but he had only two choices as a response to your slapping. Let you do it, or fight. Fighting got him into trouble. But you cannot even imagine what sort of trouble I can make for you if you don't stop doing it. I will not talk to your teacher about it yet. But if you *ever* slap my son again, you will be very sorry. You can go now, but not before you tell me you understand."

I spoke quietly and slowly. That was always a sign that I was angry. Talking quietly, slowly, often with a rather deadly sarcasm. It is effective, especially as it is in such contrast with my loud, chatty personality. My mother was the one who shouted and made scenes. I didn't, but I could be formidable when I tried.

The redhead whispered something.

"You understand?" I asked again.

"Yes," whispered the girl.

When the girl ran away, I smiled at Adam, who was standing there, staring.

"That's it – tell me if she ever slaps you again."

"What would you do?" he asked.

"I don't have a clue – I was bluffing." I smiled and went away without embarrassing him with a kiss.

The redhead girl never hit Adam again. We still didn't know what her name was.

Adam and Angela got on well. Harry remembered his mum as being quite strict, insisting on Harry keeping his room tidy, doing chores, coming home straight from school instead of playing with other boys in the park.

"You didn't mess with my mum. When she told me to do something, she wanted it to be done then and there. She is so much more laid back with Adam!"

Harry was right: seeing Angela with her grandson, they looked relaxed, happy; they joked, teased each other.

"If I teased my mother like this when I was a child, she would give me a scary look. Adam can be quite cheeky, and my mother laughs!"

"Harry, you tease Angela all the time! Sometimes you are quite outrageous, so stop making Angela into a monstrous dragon!"

He smiled, knowing I was right.

CHAPTER TWENTY-TWO

Zuzana 1989-1995

THE COMMUNIST SYSTEM CRUMBLES AND WE CAN GO TO PRAGUE

In spring 1989, I had an official letter from the Czechoslovak Ministry of Justice saying there was amnesty, and my sentence to be imprisoned for five years for defecting illegally was no longer valid. What was scary was that they had my address. They even knew my married name. It gave me hope that maybe I would be able to go to Prague again. In spring 1989, it didn't look like the communist system would ever go, but eight months later, in November 1989, the change happened. The Czechoslovakian communist government was one of the last to fall. They called it the Velvet Revolution because there was no violence. I felt the battles were won by the other nations – mainly the Poles, with their long-term dissident movement – but I was careful not to mention this to my Czech friends.

Travelling was now easy, and apart from my mother, we had many friends visiting us from Prague. Mother didn't like it.

"They are just using you – are you stupid, Zuzana? Do you think they come because they love you? They come because it's a free holiday."

I wanted to say something, but Harry looked at me, slightly shaking his head. I swallowed my answer.

"Your mum doesn't trust anybody. Are you surprised, after

what she's been through? I know it is hard, Zuzana, but just give her a break."

I realised he might be right, but it didn't make mother less irritating.

Going back to Prague was not much fun the first time. Harry, Adam and I first went in summer 1992. Adam was five. We stayed with Mother and Tomas, and it was a nightmare.

When she asked us what we wanted to drink, and I said sparkling water, she gave it to me, saying, "Don't think it is easy to carry all this shopping and to cook for you."

My mother kept telling me how hard it was to have us visiting her, how complicated the shopping and cooking for us was, that she was not so young, and yet, she was jealous when we didn't spend all the time with her.

You visit me all the time, and I never say it's too much bother, although I hate it. I didn't say it.

I wanted to see my friends. I hadn't seen them for 20 years, but they still remembered me.

After several similar scenes, we moved to stay with an old skiing friend. My mother phoned and shouted, and I hung up. From that point forward, we always stayed with friends, seeing my mother and Tomas every other day. Even that was too much for me.

People started asking me when I would move back, but I didn't want to. My life was in England. Czechoslovakia is a very white country, and I had a black husband and son. Harry didn't speak Czech, and even Adam's Czech was not very good yet. And I liked having the Canal La Manche – I still didn't call it the English Channel – between me and my mother.

The other problem was the politics. I understood my friends' opinions; I used to think the same. I detested anything the communist government praised. Now my Czech friends thought I was too 'left-wing', and they didn't like it. "You changed, Zuzana!" Yes, I had.

I couldn't wait to show Prague to Harry, Adam and Roxanne. She was now a teacher, instead of going back to the social services. She married her boyfriend Derek, and they were now also living in

Harrow, not far from us. I liked Derek, a PE teacher and a fanatical rock-climber. My tree-climbing son hung on to Derek's words when he talked about climbing and mountaineering. "You cannot start till you are about 12," Derek said.

"No, Derek, he will never do it, it is too dangerous. I am worried, I do not want my only child killed."

Derek was interested in the rock formations in Czechoslovakia – Prachovske Skaly and Adrschbach – which are good for climbing.

In 1995, our family visited Prague with Derek and Roxanne. Derek left for a few days of rock-climbing, which Roxanne didn't mind. She was heavily pregnant at the time. I enjoyed showing my best friend my country.

We now visited several times a year. Adam's Czech was getting better. Uncle Otto and Aunt Marie bought a flat in Prague. It was a large apartment on the same embankment where my mother lived – walking distance from her. The apartment was overlooking the river and the castle. It had high stucco ceilings and large rooms. My mother gave them some of her furniture and they bought some antique furniture, paintings, chandeliers and Persian rugs. Otto and Marie only came once a year and told me we could use the apartment. I wondered if the always-generous Otto bought it for me. Otto was like a fairy godmother: always there to help. He and Marie were both getting old, but Otto didn't look 85. They both seemed to be in good shape.

We developed a travelling pattern. We kept visiting each other. England, Paris, Prague. It was nice. Adam was only little, but he was learning Czech and French. He made friends easily and soon became close to some of my friends' children. We invited them to England; Adam sometimes went to Prague on his own and stayed with them. His Czech and the other children's English improved – it was a win-win situation. My mother didn't like it: "He can learn Czech from me!", but I told her I wanted him to become friends with some Czech children.

"You would have to look after Adam, Mum, it is tiring," I tried to reassure her.

CHAPTER TWENTY-THREE

Zuzana 1994–2002

ADAM IS GROWING UP

Angela looked after Adam after school for a long time, but then we moved. Harry became a partner in a general practice in a town in Hertfordshire. It was rather rural – parks, the Grand Union canal – and it looked as if we were living in the country, but we were still on the London underground. The houses were still expensive, although cheaper than Harrow. We took on a big mortgage, but Harry was earning good money and my salary was not bad either. The house was relatively small for the area but had a nice garden with bushes and a little fishpond.

In the new school, Adam went to an after-school club. It was not a religious school, and the children seemed to like him there. Adam told me he didn't know why he was more popular at his new school. "I haven't changed," he said.

I remembered my school and that skiing trip and told him about it. Sometimes I remembered that nasty redheaded girl in the Roman Catholic school, and I wondered what the girl was like now, older. I imagined she was as evil as before.

Much later, when Adam started to write short sci-fi stories, the evil aliens always had red hair. In his writing, boys and men were not always tougher than girls and women.

He spoke to me about it. "When I hear that men need to protect women, I think, *Yes, and women need to protect men*."

Adam's stories were good. My favourite one had yet another tall red-haired alien woman cruelly torturing a human prisoner. The prisoner was saved by a doctor, who distracted the alien by talking about books, while suddenly injecting her with a shrinking drug. Now only the size of a mouse, the alien runs away. The funny thing was the description – that doctor sounded like me. I asked my son and he smiled. "It's fiction, Mum," he said.

Still, he made me happy.

The boy growing up in my house was smart and thoughtful. The reason he believed men and women were equal was not my influence but Harry's. I was lucky; I married a man who didn't have a sexist bone in his body. His mother Angela was a strong woman. Maybe I should thank her. It would compensate for her disappointment at us taking Adam out of the Roman Catholic school.

Adam joined Derek's climbing club when he was 14. I was not thrilled.

"You will fall and get killed!"

Both my mother and Angela agreed with me, but Harry was on Adam's side. "Climbing with ropes and mountaineering equipment is safer than what he has been doing since he was a little boy. He is always somewhere in the trees above you! Let Derek teach him how to do it properly."

Harry and Derek always ganged up on me and Roxanne.

"Men need to hold together," Harry said.

Angela didn't like the idea of a climbing club either. But Adam and Harry just laughed.

"Maybe I should tell Grandma that I would be safe from dogs when I climb."

We all laughed, remembering the day when Angela was walking with me and Adam in the park, and she saw Adam stroke a dog. She screamed and scared both Adam and the dog. It was safe, but Angela still didn't like it. I remember that the owner of the dog, a very British grey-haired old lady, was offended. "But he is so friendly, he wouldn't hurt a fly!" she repeated.

I apologised. "Sorry, my mother-in-law is scared of animals."

"Yes, Grandma, come and stroke the dog – he is lovely."

Angela said, "Sorry, I am sure your dog is perfectly friendly!" and started walking away. She told us both off when we were out of the dog owner's hearing.

"I am *not* afraid of stupid dogs. I just don't think it is safe to stroke them unless you know them well."

Adam wanted to say something, but he didn't when I gave him a look. I smiled at my mother-in-law and told her she was right, and we would be more careful.

When we came home Adam told Harry about it, exaggerating dramatically, so that it looked as if Angela and the dog owner had a fight. Harry then pretended to be a tiny little dog yapping and chasing Adam, who pretended to be Angela. If my mother-in-law had seen Adam pretending to be her, screaming and jumping on chairs, petrified of a dog, she would probably have killed them both and I would be a widow without a child. But maybe not – Harry and Angela had a habit of starting to laugh in the middle of an argument. I envied Harry the easy relationship he had with his mother.

Roxanne and Derek now had a little girl, Susan, the anglicised version of my name. There was no danger that Susan was going to be a climber; she was afraid even to slide on a children's slide in the park. Roxanne had to hold her hand.

Adam liked Derek, and he thought the club was brilliant; it had a special wall with all the equipment. Derek said Adam was doing well.

"One day, I will climb real mountains, maybe in the Himalayas."

When Adam said it at dinner, I told him, "Over my dead body!" But I saw that Harry winked at him.

Adam liked his new school, especially history and the history teacher Mr Thompson. He told us about the lessons. I did not know if Mr Thompson followed the curriculum – Adam told me the lessons were more like television or a good book.

He gave them a new project. At first, he said he would like them to write a family tree. The children were supposed to ask their grandparents where their families came from. Living in Greater

London, the class photographs looked like those United Colours of Benetton posters. Adam was not the only black boy nor the only Jewish one. He had English, Irish, Chinese, Sri Lankan, Pakistani, Polish and Nigerian classmates. It was like my clients or Harry's patients – so many cultures. I loved it.

My mother didn't like it at all. "There are so many black people!" I reminded her that she had a black son-in-law.

"Yes Zuzana, but he is different – he is from a good family. His father is a pharmacist like me."

It wasn't just the black people she commented on. "Why are there so many cripples in the streets? In Prague, you never see them – do people get more ill here?"

"No, but in communist Czechoslovakia, there were no arrangements for the disabled – they had to stay at home or in an institution – and don't say cripple, please."

Adam's school was tough on any sort of name-calling or racial prejudice. Adam told me that one boy got suspended for two weeks because he called somebody a 'Paki'.

When Adam presented his family tree, saying he was a Black Jewish Czech Briton, the boys started sniggering. There were some other ones with mixed heritage, but not as mixed as Adam. In the break, the boys started making fun of Adam.

"So, what are you precisely?" his friend Tom asked. Tom was half Irish, half Polish, so white, of course.

"I have a black father and a Czech Jewish mother," Adam said.

"You are like a bag of Smarties, all colours, a right mongrel!"

"Mum, I always thought Tom was my friend. The nickname caught on. Everybody calls me 'Mongrel'. They shortened it to 'Mongie'. Even the girls started calling me that."

Adam told me he almost got into a fight, but thinking of me saying, "Only stupid people fight," made him stop.

I didn't know what to say, but fortunately, the teacher helped.

Mr Thompson told the class to pick an interesting heritage and write about it. Adam stayed behind in class; he did not want to hear that stupid teasing about mongrels. Mr Thompson asked him what he was going to pick.

"I thought I'd write about slavery; my dad's family is from Grenada," Adam said.

"Yes, that is a possibility, but you are the only one who could write something about the Holocaust. I once spoke to your mum and she told me your grandma is a Holocaust survivor. You could ask her."

When Adam told me, we both chuckled. My mother hated it when Adam mentioned that he was Jewish. "What kind of Jew are you – only a quarter!" But we know the rules. Having a Jewish mother makes a Jew. When Adam was younger, he wrote this little silly poem, put some drawings of animals around it and gave it to the teacher:

"My mum is Jewish, but she's also Czech.
She is beautiful, with a long neck.
My father's parents are from a tropical island.
My dad is tall, almost like a giant.
Nobody wants to go back to those places.
We like England, and our faces
Have different colours, but we are home.
Life is not bad on this island called Britain.
Read this poem, now it is written."

The teacher liked it and put it on the board with the best pictures. When the holiday started, Adam brought it home. I loved his poem and I hung it on the fridge, but my mother didn't like it. "Why do you tell him he is Jewish – isn't it bad enough he is partly black? It's a mistake. He will have problems; people are antisemitic and racist."

"Yes, like you and Tomas – you are both racist!" I said. I kept Adam's poem on my fridge door.

My mother will be cross when she finds out about Adam's project, I thought. *But since when have I worried about what she thinks anyway?*

Adam was enthusiastic. "If I write about that, my stupid classmates will forget about me being a mongrel; I will be a Jew. Well, a black Jew."

I took out some family photos and showed him the ones that were killed by the Nazis.

"This is horrible – some of them were children."

After half an hour, Adam cried. He hated crying, so he was angry, too. "Why were they so fucking stupid, all of them? Why didn't they leave? They could have survived! Why? They were all idiots!"

Adam was 15 with a temper. He often shouted, threw things, stomped out of the room. But right now, he was just shouting; he stayed.

Adam's voice was shaking. "Hitler had been in Germany since 1933, so they must have known about the antisemitism – were they stupid? They had money; they could have emigrated."

I agreed, but Adam was missing the point. "Their life was good, and they didn't want to change it, Adam. They couldn't imagine what would happen to Jews. Our family was not religious, and they felt more Czech than Jewish. You know how I always say I am a Jewish Czech, not a Czech Jew? There is a difference. I still feel that way."

Adam was listening. He kept quiet.

Harry thought it was more complicated. "Identity doesn't only depend on what you think; it depends on what other people think. I could decide I am not black, but other people would still see my black skin. It was the same with the Jews in the war. Your family felt Czech, but did the other Czechs and Germans agree with them?"

"This is a horrible week – the 'Mongie' and now this. They were all idiots! Why did they not emigrate? And what am I? Jewish, Czech, Grenadian, British? I don't belong anywhere." Adam kicked a chair and it fell over.

Harry hugged him. "Look at me, Adam. You belong in all those boxes, and that is wonderful. It is a privilege; you are white and black, Czech and Jewish, and British, because you were born here. You are a mixture of interesting, brave, smart people. My parents came from the other side of the world – you need guts to do that. Their ancestors survived slavery. They coped with racism when they first came to England. Your mum escaped communism when she was only 19. You have got good genes. And you are at home in many places. You are lucky."

And then he said that maybe Adam would be the first complete mongrel mish-mash person to climb Mount Everest.

I pretended to try to strangle him; I really didn't want Adam becoming a mountain climber. Still, Harry made even Adam laugh.

Adam got an A* for his essay. I gave him some old family photographs and he copied them and wrote about my mother. Mr Thompson asked Adam if his grandma could come and talk to the class about her Holocaust experiences when she came to visit.

"I doubt it; her English is not very good," said Adam. Of course, he lied – my mother's English was pretty good now, but she didn't like people to know that any of us were Jewish. Adam had overheard that argument when she was angry that I told him we were Jewish and when I told her she was racist. It was funny, because when we were alone, he told me: "But Grandma is not racist, she gets on better with Dad than with you, and he is black and you are white."

After Adam's presentation, the 'Mongie' business stopped. Now Adam was a Jew, and his classmates were not antisemitic.

Much later, Adam thought that to become more Jewish, he could start going to a synagogue. "Mum, there is one not too far away. What would I need to do – go to a religious Sunday school?" He even brought some leaflets.

I had a long discussion with him about why I didn't think God was real. I told him that if he wants to go to the synagogue, he can, but fortunately, that phase didn't last long. None of us believed in God. *Well, there might be a God, but not one that is interested in humans*, I thought.

CHAPTER TWENTY-FOUR

Zuzana 2000-2002

AM I STILL CZECH?

I loved going back to Prague meeting my friends from school and university, and I tried to follow Czech politics. Harry liked to come, too; most of my friends spoke English, and their surprise at him being so English despite being black didn't last long. He had already done all the touristy things, saw Mozart's *Don Giovanni* in the theatre where it premiered and walked through the old parts of the city. Now he joined the locals in complaining about the tourist crowds on the Charles Bridge. Adam often stayed with his new Czech friends. People in Prague talked about all those subjects that were taboo in polite British conversation.

When I started going back to Prague, I looked forward to those long, passionate conversations I used to have with my friends before I emigrated.

"People in Prague talk about real things: politics, art, relationships. Nobody talks about the weather – just wait, those parties will be such fun."

I probably annoyed Harry with that, but he was polite; he didn't tell me to stop being a Czech bore.

In the beginning, it was alright. My friends told me about the exciting time in 1989. Most of them were part of the demonstrations that started in 1988; some were beaten by the police, but none of them were arrested. Some told me about their involvement in Charter 77 and other dissident activities. I loved hearing about the demonstrations, and I regretted that I was not part of it.

I thought about the 'survivors' guilt' of people who emigrated before the war and did not suffer under the Nazis. Uncle Otto had a Jewish friend who was in London on business in March 1939 when the Nazis invaded Czechoslovakia. He stayed in London; his family went to concentration camps. I met this man in Paris when he visited Otto and Marie.

"In the bombing of London, I never went to the air raid shelter; I hid in my room and ignored the wardens. I didn't deserve the safety when my parents and brother and sisters were in such danger."

"But that couldn't help them, even if you were killed," I said.

"It's not always about the logic; it's about the feeling, Zuzana," said my great-aunt Marie.

Marie instinctively always knew what was important. She never had a job, but she would have made a wonderful teacher or psychotherapist.

I did not have survivors' guilt; I had survivors' envy. I was jealous of my friends who helped to get rid of the communists. When I came back, I discovered that some of my friends had been members of the communist party. I didn't blame them; it was difficult not to join if your job depended on it. Pavel, one of my good friends, told me that his way of avoiding party membership was sport. He became a ski instructor, a lifesaver in water sports and worked for the Red Cross. He would tell them that he was so engaged with all those activities in the community that he didn't have time for anything else. I could imagine the conversation as he described it.

"You know, comrades, I would love to engage politically, but the work for young people and the Red Cross fills all my free time, so I could not give my political engagement the proper attention it needs."

'The comrades' knew it was an excuse, but it was acceptable. They didn't believe in communism either. Friends told me about lists of secret police informers. They said I could go and see my police file, but I didn't want to. I didn't want to find out some of my close friends used to be police informers. I also didn't trust the records.

Harry understood. "Even if you read there about somebody being an informer, you wouldn't know how it happened, and if that person was really informing on you or just pretending to. Your friends seem like good people."

"Yes, and there is a Czech saying, something like 'If you ask too many questions, you get too many answers. My mother always said that."

My friends told me about the demonstrations throughout 1989: first brutally suppressed, then the system crumbled. One of my friends showed me photos of his bloodied face. The police broke his nose in January 1989. He told me about being swept away by the water cannons. I remembered one of the later demonstrations shown on BBC News. Everybody in the crowd was holding and shaking their house keys. "It's time to go!" they shouted to the communist government. Even my mother, always so careful, was on this demonstration. For me, the best part of the change was the borders. When I emigrated, crossing the border to Austria or West Germany, there were high electric fences with barbed wire, no man's land, watchtowers, soldiers with guns and Alsatians. This time when my Czech friends took me skiing to Austria, we just drove through. There was no border. We could only tell that we were in another country by the notices in German. That gave me an incredible feeling of freedom.

But gradually, something changed. The parties in Prague were less fun than I was hoping them to be. Most of my Czech friends had no doubts that they were not racist or homophobic; they were living in one the most tolerant, liberal, civilised countries. There was a certain arrogance I didn't remember from the old times. Was it always there? I didn't know. At first, I had discussions about the political correctness that they all used as a pejorative term. Suddenly, I didn't understand where they were coming from, and they didn't understand me either. They called me left-wing, or a 'sunshine person', a pejorative term meaning naïve, and again, I felt like an alien – painful in my native country.

They considered themselves civilised even in their Velvet Revolution. My sarcastic brain thought, *Yes, but you only rebelled when those nations you despise like the Poles fought those battles before you.*

I was having lunch with my friend Milada and her husband David. They were both now attending synagogues regularly, but Milada was not any more religious than when she'd first introduced me to the Jewish community so many years ago. She seemed to be even more Jewish, though. We talked about infidelity, after watching *Unfaithful*, a film with Diane Lane and Richard Gere. Harry and I both liked that film.

"It would be so easy to slip, but what a mess it can turn a marriage into," I said. I told them about my friend in London whose mother left her father for another woman recently.

"I could probably forgive David an affair with another woman, but I would never talk to him again if he had sex with a man. I couldn't let him touch me either," said Milada.

"I would have thought the jealousy would be less; you couldn't compete with a man."

But Milada didn't agree. "I could never touch David again; it's disgusting."

"What's disgusting?"

"Two men having sex – yuck, and it is not natural. They are not real men either."

"That is a bit homophobic, Milada!" I thought about Bob and Angus: so tolerant, nice, and most definitely real men. I also remembered the talk Milada and I had years ago about antisemitism.

But Milada disagreed. "I am not homophobic; I have nothing against homosexuals. I have a colleague at work who is gay, and another friend of a friend. They are both nice." But then she started mocking one of them for looking at himself in the mirror at work 'adjusting his clothes like a woman'.

David joined the conversation. "What I don't like is putting homosexuals on a pedestal; they are only four per cent of the population. And it is not normal."

I changed the subject. Tolerant, liberal society? I didn't think so. I was torn. When I was in London, I felt Czech; when I was in Prague, I felt British. I felt Jewish when I was with non-Jews, but not so much with other Jewish people. I felt a bit like Adam. *Who am I?*

CHAPTER TWENTY-FIVE

Zuzana 2002

I TRY TO FIND OUT SOMETHING ABOUT HARRY'S FAMILY HISTORY

I never talked to Harry's father Richard much. He was quiet and often went to watch TV when we were visiting. He made it difficult for people to get to know him. I often wondered if he talked to his customers in the pharmacy. The pharmacists I knew were chatty, full of small talk. Richard had even less small talk than I did. Even when he sat with us, most of the talking was done by Angela, Harry, Adam and me. Maybe we just didn't let Richard speak. Harry was more like his mum; they had the same sense of humour. The Roman Catholic Angela cracked surprising jokes. Harry told me that when he was learning to play the guitar, she came to the room and said, "Quick! Go and catch your rhythm, it's running away!"

I was never sure when she or Harry were joking. Once, when I didn't get one of her jokes, I said, "Sorry I am so gullible!"

"Zuzana, do you realise that there is no such English word, gullible?" said Angela with a straight face.

"Really?" I answered, without thinking. Then I looked at Harry and he was laughing.

Richard sometimes seemed to be the only serious member of the family.

One Sunday, when we were visiting Harry's parents, I went to sit with Richard. He was watching tennis.

"Richard," I said, "I know Angela doesn't want to tell me anything, but I think Adam should know about his father's side of the family – would you tell me what it was like when you came here, if I promise I won't put it into a novel? Your wife doesn't trust me. Harry told me maybe you would; shall we have lunch?"

Richard looked at me with serious eyes, but then he winked at me. "Angie is probably right. You want to be a writer – what if you are planning to write a novel about a family from the West Indies? Writers are vultures, stealing stories and dialogues. I even caught Adam writing down something Angela said the other day. When I asked him why, he said it'll be a sentence for one of the aliens in his short stories. Angela told him that he is not too old to be spanked, but we both thought it was funny. You and Harry make smart children; you should have more."

I ignored it the way I always did. I didn't want any more children – too much responsibility. I didn't say this either. I let people wonder if Harry or I had infertility problems.

"Adam writes about me in his alien stories, too." I didn't mind; his portrait of me was always rather flattering.

"OK, Zuzana, let's have lunch tomorrow, but you must protect me from Angela's wrath!"

The next day, in an Indian restaurant close to Richard's pharmacy, I found out Richard had a sense of humour, and that, like me, he had run away from his parents.

The lunch was long, and he described those first hard years in England as if they were scenes from a slapstick comedy. The humour reminded me of great-uncle Otto.

"I was 20. My parents didn't know I was leaving. My father was a pharmacist, and we had money. He also owned land and had people working on it. I remember sometimes spending the holiday in the house on the farm. We had servants, a cook and a maid. I became a lab technician and was later going to study pharmacy, not because I wanted to but because my father told me to. I was going to study in the USA or Britain. My pa was strict; you didn't argue with him. No back chat, as he used to say. He wanted me to join him in the family business and marry a daughter of his friend, Joshua Campbell.

"I did become a pharmacist, although much later, but I was most definitely not planning to marry Tonya Campbell, a girl with legs like a stick insect and shy eyes. She never looked at people; her eyes were constantly looking at the ground, as if she was a bird looking for worms. Besides, I was dating a beautiful and clever girl with a big round bottom, nice curves and a loud laugh. Your mother-in-law used to be a real hot cake, Zuzana. Angie and I used to go dancing, and we always kissed in the dark on the way back. She never let me go any further, with her religious ways; the only way to make Angie make love to me was to marry her."

Wow, he is talking about sex – my mother-in-law would kill him if she knew, I thought.

Richard asked me what I was grinning about.

"Nothing, just carry on, please!"

He told me that Angela came from a very poor family. Her mother did people's laundry and her father was a farm labourer.

"Is this why Angela's Grenadian accent is so much stronger than yours?"

"Yes, my pa was proud of his received pronunciation BBC English. He made me listen to the BBC World Service radio to pick up the accent. I remember he always told me off for saying, 'Wah say?', or 'ax' instead of ask."

"What does 'Wah say' mean?" I asked.

"It is just 'How are you?' Angela always used Grenadian slang words, and if you think she has a strong accent now, you should have heard her then. Not good enough for my snobbish family. My father saw us in the street, and he almost had a heart attack. 'Come home right now,' he said. Zuzana, I used to do what he told me to do, but I was getting fed up with being the good boy."

"What did he tell you?"

"He said he forbade me going out with that ordinary girl, that he didn't care how beautiful she was; she was common. Arguing with my father was hopeless. That was when I started thinking about going to the UK."

Richard told me that the British government was recruiting. He described it as 'army recruitment'. You wrote your name and details, and they paid for passage, which was by ship and took two to three weeks. People travelling later had to pay for themselves, but Richard and Angela didn't. They all had British passports, and at that time immigration from the Commonwealth was easy. Richard asked Angie to go with him to London. He told her that they could marry and start a family there. When she asked about money, Richard explained to her that the journey was free, and they would get a job allocated to them. Richard was relaxed telling me things; I was surprised how open he was.

"Angie didn't want to go, but she also didn't want me to go alone. Her family was poor, and she asked if she could send them money from London. 'Definitely,' I said. Anything to make her come with me. That evening, our kisses got less church-like." Richard chuckled. "It took all Angie's faith to marry me as a virgin; she didn't let me do anything but kiss her, but I could tell when a woman was on fire. We married two weeks after we arrived in London."

I almost asked him how the sex was, but I didn't. Even I wasn't bold enough to ask that.

"Harry told me that you were seasick on the ship."

Richard chuckled. "My son talks too much!"

I already knew how tough Richard and Angela's beginning in England was; it must have been hard especially for Richard. He was used to a comfortable life, servants and being treated with respect as the son of a wealthy, distinguished father. Angela was probably tougher; she was used to being poor and looked down upon. When I said to Richard I knew from Harry about the hardship in the beginning, he said, "But we had some fun, too, making friends, all of them black, listening to blues, cooking home dishes. At one point we lived with eight other families; some of them are still our friends. And Angie and I had each other. Life is all right when you're in love."

It was obvious that Angela and Richard still loved each other. I hoped it was going to be the same for Harry and me as we grew older. I always admired my mother-in-law, but now I liked her, too. It was Angela, with her determination, who'd pulled them through. She started working in Sainsbury's and soon progressed from night shelf filler to cashier, and later worked her way up to become a manager. She was also working as a cleaner.

She had three jobs and insisted Richard went to evening classes. He passed some more British lab technician exams, but Angela insisted he went to university. It was Angela who supported him so that he could study to become a pharmacist like his father.

He did, and when he was able to buy his own pharmacy, Angela quit her job in Sainsbury's and started to work with Richard in the shop, taking stock, selling cosmetics and vitamins, doing bookkeeping.

Richard told me about the time much later when Harry was 12, and the whole family went back to Grenada on holiday. He wrote to his father and stressed that he only became a pharmacist thanks to Angela. He was still worried how his family would accept his wife.

"There was no need, Zuzana," he said. "My hard, snobbish father had tears in his eyes when he embraced Angie and thanked her for being a wonderful wife for me. Then we were all crying, even Angie."

I tried to ask about his family's past – were they slaves? Did they take part in the 1795 uprising? I did my homework.

Richard didn't know anything. "Does your brain ever hurt, being stuffed with useless knowledge? Uprising in 1795? Never heard of it."

"Harry told me about it."

"You all read too many books." Richard chuckled, but I knew how proud he was of Harry.

I thought about Harry as a child: with his parents working so hard, who looked after him? I asked Harry later. "We had neighbours with kids; we all visited each other, and sometimes it was as if I had several parents. Black people had to help each other, and they did. Sybil helped, remember? She was at our wedding."

Richard told me he used to think about taking over the family pharmacy in Grenada, but he didn't want to move Harry. "Harry is British, not Grenadian."

"Yes, Adam is British, too. I would not move back to Prague either," I said.

Richard and I became closer that day, and from then on, we sometimes had lunch or coffee and talked. I told him about my family, the war, about my mother, and how similar racism and antisemitism are.

I also told him what I read about America. Apparently black people use a strange term, 'passing'. It is for people who look white enough despite being black. Pass for white.

"Jewish people have that; they can hide their Jewishness. My family didn't think being Jewish was important. The Nazis thought otherwise. I could pass, but I tell everybody I am Jewish. If they are surprised, they might realise that the Jews are no different to other people."

I sometimes worried about Adam. It was still not easy to be a young black man in a mostly white country. I remember how Harry told me how often he was stopped by police while driving, as if they thought he stole the car.

Will this happen to Adam? He is quite light; maybe he could pass for white. I told myself off for having such ridiculous thoughts.

CHAPTER TWENTY-SIX

Zuzana, 1997–2002

DID I LOVE MY MOTHER?

I tried to call my mother several times a week. We also wrote emails. I bought her a laptop. At first, she found using her computer difficult; she was never good with technology. She kept complaining that: "They did something to Yahoo, and I can't log in. They did something to my computer and emails." She didn't specify who 'they' were. She got annoyed when I said she must have done something wrong. I didn't dare say what Harry used to tell me or his mum when we had computer problems: "The problem is between the monitor and the chair!"

"Maybe we could go back to letters; you don't have to use emails if you find it hard." That was probably the worst thing I could say, or maybe the best thing. My doubts about my mother's technological ability spurred her to show me that she could learn. She asked a son of a friend to help her and soon was using the laptop almost without a problem. If she did have a problem, it was the 'people running the computers' who were responsible. Still, she could use the new technology better and better, and she even began to look up things on the internet.

I found the phone conversations hard and it was difficult to end them. If I tried, she would get upset. "You never find enough time for me, and I am your mother!" Ten minutes would have felt like a whole afternoon; an hour felt like a lifetime. I tried to look at websites and emails while talking to her, but as if she could see me, she noticed. "You are doing something on your computer instead of listening to me, Zuzana!"

"Other people see their daughters every week," she said.

"I live in another country – what's your point?"

"You should never have left me."

Once, she told me that she would move to us if she was too frail to live alone.

"No," I said, "you wouldn't like it any better than I would. If you needed care, I would visit you often and pay for somebody to look after you."

She got very upset and angry. Several years later, she would say things like, "People are shocked that you wouldn't look after me. You would let me die alone."

I wondered who those people were. She was trying to make me feel ashamed, and she succeeded. I also knew that Harry would most likely want me to take her in.

Am I some sort of monster? Or is it just honesty? I could have told her that of course I'd look after her and then not do it.

I always used to keep lots of secrets from my mother. It was easy. She never asked about my life; the conversations were about her life or about me being selfish for emigrating and leaving her. She complained about having to look after Tomas, and that nobody helped her. She went to hospital to have a hip operation. I called her mobile every day only to hear that other people had daughters who visited them in hospital.

"Well, I work, and I don't have a private plane to take me to Prague every day!" It was always the same conversation.

All my friends seemed to have a special bond with their parents, and that made me feel even more ashamed. I used to joke that it was a pity I could not divorce my mother. My friends would laugh, not imagining I was serious, that I would never see her again if I could. As an only child, I didn't have that option. I was the one with the burden of responsibility.

When my mother retired, she came to see us more often.

She no longer stayed in a hotel paid for by Uncle Otto; now we had a house, she stayed in our spare bedroom. She was still feisty, determined and completely self-centred. The only person she was nice to was Harry. Even Adam felt her poisonous tongue. She usually came alone; Tomas was older than my mother, and he was getting frail. With poor eyesight and hearing, he did not feel like travelling anymore. When my mother was in England, he stayed with his younger married sister in a little town close to Prague.

One day, when my mother was much older, Roxanne's brother Bob met me and my mum in the Royal Academy. He is an RA Friend. Later, when we had lunch in the members' restaurant and my mother went to the bathroom, he said something interesting.

"Your mother is like a little Darth Vader, a petite bulldozer walking in a straight line, as if she could walk through people that are in her way. She is only little, but so powerful."

Maybe she could, but they always moved out of her way. Funny, I never noticed that. In the gallery, they asked us if my mother wanted a wheelchair. She was sitting in a chair, waiting for our time to start the exhibition.

"I wouldn't ask her if I was you," Bob told the man. He chuckled. "Imagine, Zuzana, how annoyed your mum would be."

Everyone liked my mother, but our relationship deteriorated as time went on. She criticised everything. "You put too many herbs and spices on the meat – why don't you cook normal meals? And who boils potatoes in their skins?"

"Why don't you wear your hair longer? You have nice hair, and nobody can see it when it is short."

That was typical. She didn't let me grow my hair long when I desperately wanted to as a teenager. Not giving me what I wanted, but giving me what I did not want instead, was how she kept her power over me.

I remember once, years ago, I think 1968, we were in Paris, and I wanted to see a film that was not shown in Prague. It was *Doctor Zhivago*. Not even the book was available in Czechoslovakia, although I read it – a friend had it at home in German. Pasternak was a blacklisted author.

"No, you can't have everything you like. The tickets are a waste of money," said Mother, and then spent much more money on buying me a dress I didn't want or need. It was all about power.

In the days leading up to her visit, I was always nervous. I was snappy and slept badly.

Even Adam noticed. I tried to hide my criticism of my mother from Adam, but he was smart. He was also the only family member apart from me she criticised and tried to manipulate.

"Adam, your essays for school are too long – do you think the teacher will read it?"

He showed her his short stories about aliens, but she just shrugged and told him that he should do some sport or improve his French and German.

"This scribbling is pointless – a waste of time!"

"Mum writes stories, too; she is going to write novels."

My mother dismissed it. "Waste of time."

Yet my mother loved Adam and kept telling her friends and Tomas how clever he was.

When she was with him, though, she couldn't help herself: she criticised him almost as much as she criticised me. His appearance, his choice of friends: "You have all those foreigners, black people, the Indians, the Polish – why don't you make friends with some nice English boys?"

It was easy for Harry and my in-laws; she was always nice to them.

I must do something to make this easier!

Then I read a book by an American psychologist who compared relationships to dance.

She wrote something like: "*Nobody can change other people's behaviour, but we can change ours. It is like a dance. When you change your steps, or stop dancing, the dancing partner needs to change or stop, too.*"

So I changed the dance. When my mother said something that included a sharp sting of a hornet straight to my most sensitive spot, I stopped the conversation.

On the phone, I said, "Sorry, there is someone at the door, I have to go, bye, talk to you next week."

In my house, when she visited and the sting came, I went upstairs to the loo.

In the past, I used to cry in the loo. Now I picked up one of those funny books I kept there. I read a couple of pages, then I came down, with a well-rehearsed smile, and said something pleasant. If she stung me again, I left the room again. No argument, no tears. One evening, I left the room nine times.

My mother was not a stupid woman; she learnt. I still had to remind her by stopping the conversations sometimes, but it became less often. Victory was sweet.

She still said things like, "I am scared to tell you anything."

Good, I thought.

Once, when I drove her to the airport, she told me how great her visit was and how nice I was to her and thanked me. I was surprised and touched. Not for long.

"I know I get on your nerves," she said, "but everybody gets on your nerves, because you are the most intolerant person I know."

"Have a good flight," I said, giving her a kiss and driving off. On the way home, I did not cry; I smiled. Victory was indeed sweet.

CHAPTER TWENTY-SEVEN

Zuzana, 2002

HANA IN LONDON

The next time my mother came, everything was different, because we had another visitor. Mother's older cousin Hana found out about my emigration and came to visit. She was well over 80 and lived in Israel. She flew to Paris, spent some time with Otto and Marie, and took the Eurostar to London.

When Mum found out that Hana was going to come to London, she was excited. My mother loved Hana – that was different to her relationship with her other cousin, Irma. She told me about the lessons Hana gave her and her brother Oskar in the beginning of the war.

"You'll like Hana, she is clever and nice – not like Irma, who is nice but not clever. Irma was always slow."

"Mum, Irma is also wonderful. I met her in New York, and she was lovely, and so brave in the war. How can you say she is not clever?"

"You must always contradict everything I say, Zuzana!"

I didn't argue; I changed the subject.

I looked forward to meeting Hana; I'd heard so much about her not only from my mother, but also from Otto and Marie. I had a feeling I would like her. I did. I invited her to stay in our house, but she said she would just stay for the first night and booked a hotel for the rest of her stay. I was glad, we didn't have enough space. Harry was away at a conference and Adam was staying with a friend for one night.

I knew from my mother that Hana escaped with her boyfriend Vladimir in 1942, but Hana's Czech friend Pavla, who told Hana's parents that Hana and Vladimir got safely to the Soviet Union, was wrong. Maybe that was a good thing. I couldn't imagine how Hana would have coped living in Stalinist Russia. Hana had strong opinions on everything, and without a filter between her brain and her mouth, people found her difficult to cope with. She was bold, brave, not afraid of anything. Although she was a member of the communist party, she found the party discipline difficult. That was not a problem before the war, but it would have been a problem in a communist country.

Hana was still stunning: thick white short hair, dark almond-shaped eyes, tanned skin, high cheekbones and her wrinkles added to her beauty. I had never seen her photographs apart from before the war; she did not look that good in them. I think it was because she couldn't care less. I knew she didn't come back with her boyfriend Vladimir, but I didn't know anything else. I asked her why she never married after the war.

"I always thought lovers treat a woman better than husbands." She had a wicked smile.

"Hana!" said my mother.

"Don't play so innocent, Magda – you always knew what you wanted, and you usually got it!"

Instead of taking offence, my mum chuckled.

However, when Hana started telling me about what she had to go through during the war, my mother left the room; she didn't like to hear it.

"My family believed I was safe, but Vladimir and I never got further than Ukraine, already occupied by the Nazis. Occupied is not the right word. The Ukrainians seemed to prefer the Nazis to the Russians. I suppose they had a reason. We had to hide."

"Did you try to go east to the unoccupied Soviet Union?" I knew Hana ended up in a concentration camp, so I knew this was not going to be a happy story.

Hana suddenly looked old. "Vladimir was caught. It was stupid. He was pissing next to a Ukrainian man outside a pub where we were finally having something to eat, and the man noticed Vladimir was circumcised. That was something nobody in our family did, but of course, Vladimir was from a Jewish orthodox family. That man, not a German, a local Ukrainian, smiled and said, 'Yid,' and left. Five minutes later, Vladimir was arrested by the SS and shot. I saw it, hiding behind a fence."

Hana's eyes were dark, deep and sad; she spoke in a quiet, monotonous voice, in Czech similar to Uncle Otto and Marie, an elegant, old-fashioned Czech, without the slang my generation used.

"Zuzana, I saw so many people killed! Whole little Jewish towns – the shtetls. I still don't know how I survived. Luck, probably. When I was caught, they didn't shoot me; maybe it was because I spoke such good German, maybe because even the SS officers were sick of that much killing. They sent me to Treblinka. After what I saw and heard, I considered myself lucky. We were hungry, dirty, tired. We had to work; sometimes they beat us. Everybody knows about that. In the summer of 1943, there was an uprising in the camp. Some people escaped, but I couldn't. Most of them were caught again and killed. I was sent to another small camp, just for women. But Zuzana, maybe Magda is right, I should not talk about it. It just makes everybody upset."

I didn't know Hana, but I felt close to her. I hugged her and felt her tight body relax.

"I will tell you a different story. It's about the time when the women's camp was liberated by the Russian army. I still think about that sometimes. The Germans ran away, leaving the camp empty. We broke into the storage rooms with food. We were starving, and getting the food felt so good! We were all sick the next couple of days, after eating so much."

"Irma in America said the same, that she got sick when she started eating normal food after the war."

"Oh, you met Irma. How is she? I haven't seen her since 1949. She was such a sweet girl."

Hana smiled. She no longer looked sad. And then she told me her story of the liberation of the camp. Hana told me that in the corner of the storage room, there was a small door to a cellar. She thought there might be more food, but when she opened the door, she saw him. A small balding man with metal glasses. He was not wearing a uniform.

"I did not remember ever seeing him. He was probably one of the clerks. I was scared. *He will pull a gun and shoot me*, I thought."

"Wow, I know he didn't shoot you, Hana, so what happened?"

"He looked as scared as I was. He got up when he saw me, and he said something which shocked me. 'You are beautiful. The Russians will find me here and shoot me. Please, would you have sex with me, the last sex of my life?' Of course, Zuzana, there was nothing beautiful about me. I weighed 40 kilos when the Red Cross later weighed me, my head was shaven, I was anaemic and covered in scratches – the lice. The first time I saw myself in a mirror two weeks later, I still looked awful."

I was quiet, but my brain was buzzing. *Did she have sex with him? Will she tell me?*

Hana did not have sex with the German. But she also did not call the Russian soldiers. She said, "No," very quietly and left the room, closing the door behind her.

Still, the German clerk was right: the Russians found him. She heard the shot.

"Wow," I said. And then I asked Hana a completely unacceptable question. "Hana, did you ever regret that you didn't grant him his last wish? Did you ever think that you should have fucked him?"

I felt like pushing the words back to my mouth, but this was Hana, a former captain in Israeli army: she didn't shock easily. She smiled. She was not offended by my language either.

"You're sharp, Zuzana," she said. I didn't ask any more.

In my mind, I often imagined Hana giving that frightened little German the ultimate mercy fuck; somehow it would finish her war on a gentler, forgiving tone. But that is naïve of me. He was a Nazi, working in an extermination camp. Most people would say he deserved no mercy. But I was glad Hana did not call the Russian soldiers to kill him. Mercy and civilisation must start somewhere.

In my vivid imagination, I thought about the man: what was he like? Was he married? What made him ask that question? What was his story?

I still wanted to know more, but my mother came into the room and said dinner was ready. She cooked it, spoiling that by telling me before that Hana wouldn't like my weird cooking.

We didn't talk about the war anymore, but two days later when Harry and Adam were back, Hana came for breakfast. It was early, my mother was still asleep, but Hana, who was still on Israeli time, came at 7am on Sunday. We were up but still in our pyjamas. Hana apologised; so did we. When the apologies took too long, I reminded them of the joke about the British twins who never got born, because they both kept saying, 'after you!'

"She has no manners, my wife!" said Harry, holding my shoulder.

At breakfast, Hana told us more about herself.

"When I came back and found out that my parents had been killed, I moved to Brno for a while. I met a new friend, a Zionist. She told me that she would never live in Europe again, that Jews need a country of their own where they would be safe, that they need to be prepared to fight for it. She made sense."

"Yes, but how did you manage to get to Palestine? It couldn't have been easy," asked Harry.

"Why?" asked Adam.

"You know, Adam," Harry explained. "The British were not letting the Holocaust survivors go to Palestine, they were turning the ships back. In Palestine, the Jewish organisation Irgun was fighting the British. In 1947, the ship *Exodus*, full of Holocaust survivors, was returned to Germany by the British, but slowly, the international opinion turned against the British. In 1947 and 1948, the British withdrew. Israel was founded in 1948, but it was immediately attacked by various Arab countries."

Adam was listening. He liked history. It was funny that Harry used 'The British' not 'us'.

"I read a book called *Exodus* about it, but I thought it was full of Israeli propaganda!" I said.

"Did you now?" Hana looked as if she wanted to say something more, but she didn't.

Hana told us that when the communists took over Czechoslovakia, she thought she would stay. But she didn't like what she heard at the communist party meetings. Hana found it difficult to keep her mouth shut when she thought something was wrong, and she was disciplined by the party committee. That was in May 1948, when emigration was already quite difficult, as the borders were closed.

"You know, your Great-Grandmother Olga was telling all of us to leave. We all remembered what happened in 1938. But it was difficult until I got permission to travel to a meeting in the newly formed communist East Germany. There was no Berlin wall yet; I could cross to West Berlin easily."

Hana started chuckling and told us how my Grandma Franzi told her before the war that going to Palestine was crazy, living among Bedouins and camels!

So, after all, Hana eventually did end up living with the camels.

Mother got up and came to the kitchen. She was dressed, whereas apart from Hana, we were all in our pyjamas.

"Is that the way we welcome a visitor now? Adam, Zuzana, go dress." My mother frowned, embarrassed in front of her older cousin.

"What about me, Magda?" said Harry. "I can stay in my pyjamas?" In the end none of us changed. We didn't want to miss any of the conversation.

"Did you and Grandma used to write letters, Aunt Hana?" Adam asked. I smiled. I imagine Hana's letters as being long and eloquent, while my mother's were short and strained.

They wrote at first. Even after the communists took over, Israel was a friendly country for a while. Czechoslovakia even sent them weapons. But that changed in 1950 with the political trials with Communist party bosses singled out as 'enemies of the people'. Several were executed. They were all Jewish. The 'International Zionists' were suddenly the enemy.

"We didn't write for long; it was dangerous," said my mother. "I was afraid I would get into trouble with the police. I already had my bourgeois background. Relatives in the West or in Israel were bad news. I didn't write to Uncle Otto and Aunt Marie either. The 1950s were dreadful; everybody had to fill in various political family questionnaires.

"*What did your parents do in the war?*'

"*Have you got any relatives abroad?*'

"*Are you a member of any political party or organisation?*'

"When I was asked if I had any relatives abroad, I always said no."

Hana embraced my mother. "Of course, I understand why you couldn't write. It is great that the communist system is gone, isn't it?"

"You used to be a communist, Hana, remember? Grandma Olga kept talking about your father letting you do that; I heard the grown-ups talking about you." They both laughed.

"You were always eavesdropping as a little girl, Magda. Does Adam know how naughty his grandmother used to be?"

Adam was listening.

Mum was nicer when she was around her relatives: Otto, Marie, now Hana. She probably missed her family, most of them long dead.

Maybe it is my fault that Mum is so nasty to me but to nobody else. That was an uncomfortable thought.

Harry said he was confused. "I wonder how come that the secret police did not know the facts? They must have known you had relatives abroad, Magda."

"You never talked about it, Grandma – what was it like, living under the communists?" Adam was curious. To him, it must have sounded like it was from a *James Bond* movie.

"They probably did know, but there was no reason for them to use the information. Or maybe the secret police followed the same pattern as most of the country. 'They pretend to pay us; we pretend to work.' Nobody used to work very hard. Everything was owned and run by the state, and people didn't feel the state was treating them well. There were other cynical quotes: 'He who doesn't steal from the state steals from his family!' After the money reform in 1953, when the state took most of people's savings, not many people still believed in communism. They were just trying to get by."

"Dad was in the communist party, wasn't he?" I asked.

"Yes, but it was me who made him join. I thought it would be safer for us all; he didn't want to do it," replied my mother. I'd never heard that before; I thought joining the communist party was my father's decision.

"People were careful, pretending to believe in communism, but in close company, the political jokes told another story. Parodies on the official songs of the building of a communist society: Instead of *Let's roll our sleeves up and start the machines* people sang *Let's roll our sleeves up and let the bosses do the work!*" Mum started to sing, and we all laughed.

I remembered how it was before I emigrated.

"It was like a sick game, Adam. Even the censors let things be published if they were given a false blurb about the socialist message of the books. The dustcovers turned Hemingway, Steinbeck, Kerouac into communist sympathisers so that their books could be published. One day, I'd like to collect those blurbs. The censors didn't believe in communism any more than our teachers, who still gave us history from the Marxist-Leninist perspective. It was a country where everybody lied."

I shouldn't have said that. Mother stopped smiling. "It was not that bad – not bad enough for you to leave me and emigrate. There was never any harm to you, just the communist propaganda, and it made you leave your mother. I would never do such a thing to my darling mother, Zuzana!"

Hana looked at us all with her big dark eyes and changed the subject. "You have many relatives abroad, Magda. Otto and Marie in France, me in Israel, Irma in New York, Judita and Simon in California… You are retired; you should visit us all. Come to Tel Aviv, it's lovely."

"It's too far; I am glad Zuzana stayed in Europe. I only see Otto and Marie. But in the 1950s I only wrote to them once, in 1953, when Grandmother Olga died."

Breakfast changed to lunch, with us just nibbling on cold food I kept bringing from the fridge. We only showered and changed when Hana and Mother left for the Victoria and Albert Museum. They didn't come back until dinnertime. Mother was in a good mood, and she even praised my cooking. "Zuzana is great at cooking, and at many other things." I almost fell off my chair when she said it! Hana was a good influence.

That week in London, Hana told me about Israel: the beginning, the British, the Arabs. She spent ten years in the army. I was curious to know if she ever killed anybody, but she said she was never in combat. She became a doctor, a gynaecologist. She told me about her life in Tel Aviv, a beautiful, modern city built in the Bauhaus style by German-Jewish architects. She wanted me to visit, and I planned to visit her in Israel soon. Hana only spent one week with us. But eight months later, she died of ovarian cancer. It was quick. I regret not getting to know her better. If I had a daughter, she would have been called Hana. But I wasn't going to have any more children. One was enough. I liked my work; I felt useful, much more useful than when I was changing my baby's nappies. I was not good with babies; children are easier when they can talk. I asked Harry if he was all right with my decision not to have any more children.

"Yes, Zuzana, we are lucky – we have each other and Adam," Harry said.

At least the beautiful, intelligent Hana survived the war. And maybe she had fun in life with those lovers.

PART THREE
Life without Magda

CHAPTER ONE

Zuzana, 2003

MY MOTHER DIES

My mother was a terrible driver. She didn't think so. In fact, she thought she was incredibly good. She was often caught speeding but never paid a fine. She had her way with policemen. I remember the day when she was caught twice. She was driving over the speed limit when a police car made her stop. She took her papers out and gave them to the police officer.

"Oh, I am sorry, was I driving too fast? I was in a hurry – I left my windows open and it is going to rain. Please, Officer, don't fine me, be nice."

The police officer didn't have the heart to charge this sweet little old woman. He let her go. "Was I nice?" he asked, grinning, returning her papers.

In the afternoon, returning from a short trip to the weekend house, she was speeding again, overtaking other cars, until she heard a police siren. She stopped, getting the papers out, prepared to negotiate again.

"I don't need your papers; I have already seen them." The officer found it hard not to laugh. "You wanted me to be nice, so I will, but please, drive slower – you don't want to have an accident."

"Oh, you are so lovely," my mother said, and drove off.

"Did you drive slower, Grandma?" Adam asked when she was telling us the story.

"I drive like a racing driver, Adam, and I drive very well."

Even Adam knew that was not true; my mother was fast and impatient, overtaking other cars, so she had many accidents, and they were always her fault. Her parking was worse than mine, and I am pretty useless. She didn't pay attention and drove in a jerky way. Adam used to be carsick when she was driving, but never in other people's cars.

The way she died was rather typical. We spoke on the phone, and she told me that she was going to the weekend house to mow the lawn. Despite her recent hip operation, she was determined to do it herself. "Why don't you pay someone to do that? You have the money. The weekend house is too much now Tomas can't help you. Why don't you sell it?"

"You always try to spoil all the joy I have. I like gardening and lawn mowing. I hold on to the lawn mower and do not need my stick," my mother said.

I still didn't think she should go. "It's also a long drive. One day, you are going to die in a car crash with your driving!"

Those words came to haunt me. She died later that day in a head-on collision with a lorry, going 30km over the speed limit. She was only 75.

I was in the supermarket when the call came. I left the trolley full of shopping and drove home, trembling. I phoned Otto and Marie; Otto cried, "My beautiful, brave niece. I will miss her. Now I only have you and your family; the others in America are too far."

CHAPTER TWO

Zuzana 2003

THE FUNERAL

The man at the Jewish community centre was extremely helpful. He arranged transport of my mother's body from the town in North Bohemia where they did her post-mortem after the accident and advised me about all the practicalities. The funeral seemed strange, like something from a film. Most Czech people get cremated and, as faith in any God is rare, the ceremonies are secular and simple.

My family had a tomb in Prague's New Jewish cemetery. The first person buried in the tomb was Olga's husband Ruben, my great-grandfather who died in 1922. There would have had to be a Jewish ceremony with her urn anyway, so if I got Mother cremated, we would need to have two funerals. I didn't have time or energy to do that. My completely secular mum was buried with Jewish orthodox rites. Would she mind? When one of my Czech friends asked, I said, "She is dead." That probably sounded callous.

Not many people came to her funeral. My mother did not have many friends. Some of my Czech friends who hardly knew my mother came to support me. Uncle Otto and Aunt Marie, who flew in from Paris, were the only relatives. They looked frail.

In a small ceremonial room with poor acoustics, we were asked to talk about my mother.

Tomas's speech was one sentence: "She was my wife; I'll miss her." Tomas was frail, too; he looked older than he was.

I prepared a speech, too. I spoke about my mother's difficult life, the war, her incredible achievements in graduating from secondary school in 1946 with her class and becoming a pharmacist after her divorce. But I didn't finish my speech. I cried and couldn't stop. Harry squeezed my hand and started talking. He asked me if it was OK to talk in English. He spoke about his admiration for his feisty mother-in-law, a woman who was a proof that 'everything is possible if you try'. He talked about her determination to learn English to be able to talk to people in her daughter's adopted country. His speech was funny, and kind.

Otto and Marie spoke, too, in their perfect, old-fashioned Czech. They sounded like people from a long time ago.

Adam was the last to speak. His Czech was good, but he had a strong English accent. I kept his draft of the speech. He made me so proud of him.

"My grandma never wanted to be treated as an old person. She said she didn't like old people. When she went to the spa, her biggest fear was always that the doctor would only give her procedures for the old people, not the gym and swimming, which was what she really wanted. Recently at every gym she went to she became a celebrity, being 80 – she always made herself older to impress people. She was only 75. They kept taking her pictures. Grandma would always exercise on every machine. She was not very technical, so she asked the young people in the gym to show her how to use the machines. I think the other people must have found it both very funny and very inspiring. One of the last pictures of Grandma we have is when she is exercising on a stomach cruncher."

Everybody laughed. He showed the photo from the gym. Adam was well prepared.

"My grandma hated wasting anything, something which was clear from the amount of stuff she had in her flat. Whenever she went to a hotel, she would keep the fruit and bread that she received and bring it home so that her bags were heavier on the way coming back than going out. She used the bread to prepare breadcrumbs.

She was also a dedicated farmer, and she would grow fruit and vegetables in vast quantities at her cottage: gooseberries, all types of currants, apples, strawberries, raspberries and potatoes. She made this beverage out of raspberries that she would call wine, and she had to add a lot of sugar to make it drinkable, but Mum said it was disgusting. Grandma always complained about that. Another thing was her potatoes which she would grow in a small field near the back of her garden. With the trips to and from Prague these were quite possibly the most expensive potatoes in the Czech Republic."

Harry chuckled. He remembered how whenever we had potatoes in my mother's apartment, she never forgot to ask him if he liked them, telling him they were much better than the potatoes you could buy in shops in Prague or in London. "They are just potatoes," he whispered when she was not in the room.

"My grandma always claimed she was a great driver, but I remember being terrified when I was sitting in her car." Adam choked, and couldn't continue. Everybody was crying. Harry got up and embraced him, but Adam wanted to finish his speech.

"My grandma always wanted to be the best at everything; everything was a competition for her, and she wouldn't let anything defeat her. Once she found out I used to play cards with my other grandma in England, she was determined that we should also play cards together.

"When I kept winning, she stopped playing with me, though. She told me it was because she couldn't see the cards properly or that her neck hurt. She could see her book perfectly well, and I never heard about her neck pain otherwise. My mum once told me she used to let Grandma win in cards when she was little. Maybe I should have also let her win, but perhaps I am competitive, too; maybe I take after her.

In her old age she also learned how to use the computer, being able to email and surf the internet. She frequently had problems. Then she would call my mum or me to fix it. I don't know why she called my mum, who is not very technical either.

My grandma had a terrible sense of direction; once when trying to take her car to the garage, a journey which normally takes 20 minutes, she ended up driving for three hours before she managed, with some assistance, to find it. Near our home in England, she would always get lost between the town centre and our house despite taking the route hundreds of times. She was very stubborn with this and would usually continue walking, frequently in completely the wrong direction, and only asked for help when she was well and truly lost.

I guess the most important thing to take from her life was that she was a fighter. She would persevere at everything no matter what. We should all try to be a little bit like she was. Not completely, just a little bit."

I was happy that Adam had had the opportunity to say goodbye to his grandmother. My mother stole my chance to say goodbye to my beloved Grandmother Franzi by only telling me about her death after the funeral. That day, I forgave her.

Later, I had emails from people telling me how wonderful my son was. Yes, I was immensely proud of Adam. He was not 17 yet. That speech, so mature for his age, was the best of all the speeches.

Adam and Harry both held my hand when we walked behind the coffin.

The New Jewish cemetery in Prague is a solemn place: long alleys of tall trees and old, neglected graves. Not many people tend to them. They have all died or emigrated. But even the tended graves look abandoned. Jews put stones on graves, not flowers.

We followed the coffin carried by four men with yarmulkes and listened to the singsong words being recited that we didn't understand. They were dressed in long black coats and white shirts, with tassels from praying shawls showing; the rabbi was wearing a big hat. I'd seen people dressed like this in London but never in Prague.

Mr Stern, the kind man who organised the funeral, wanted my son Adam to say kaddish. Only men can say it. Adam didn't want to do it. "I won't recite some verses I don't understand!"

We didn't have enough Jewish men to form the required group of ten anyway. In the office, I read the kaddish written phonetically.

"Oh, I have never heard anybody read it so well!" Mr Stern said.

"Pity I am a woman, ha?" I replied.

He smiled.

The grave by the large family tomb was already dug, and after they lowered the coffin, we all threw soil on it. I was the one to start, but I made a mistake; I should have done it with my left hand, as one of my friends later told me. My mother was not religious, so she wouldn't have minded. She wouldn't have been keen on a Jewish funeral in the first place, but it was simpler when we wanted to bury her in the family tomb.

The men who carried the coffin started covering the grave immediately, the sounds of the shovels scraping, the soil landing in the grave with a dull thump made me shiver.

When I walked from the cemetery with Harry and Adam, I started sobbing and couldn't stop.

We went out to eat a typical Czech meal – roast pork with cabbage and dumplings.

I was thinking about the day. A traditional Jewish funeral with Aramaic verses, and then instead of a kosher meal we had a dinner with pork. I had a coffee with milk – also forbidden in Jewish religion, as no dairy was allowed after eating meat.

Thinking about this, imagining our large Jewish family, including the long-dead ones, sitting at the table, eating non-kosher food, and talking about my mother, made me sad again.

Adam looked alarmed; he was not used to seeing me cry.

"Don't worry, Adam, Mum will get better. Her mother died; it's normal to be upset."

CHAPTER THREE

Zuzana 2003

WATCHING THE FAMILY FILM FROM 1936 IS UPSETTING

Adam and Harry first saw the film soon after my mother's funeral. I found the VHS tape in her flat. My grandfather filmed it in 1936. When I was a child, my mother used the same old 8mm Kodak camera for filming when we were on holiday, and then we would watch the films on a pre-war film projector. It never worked properly, and the films often ended up tangled on the floor. When that happened, my mother screamed. My mother screamed a lot.

"Zuzana, you keep talking, interrupting and look what you made me do – the films are all entangled now. It's all your fault! You distracted me!"

Arguing and defending myself was pointless. Now I didn't have to try anymore. I should have been pleased, but I couldn't stop crying. I thought I hated my mother, so why was I so upset?

Mother never told me that she had the old films transferred to VHS. I always liked watching the oldest films from before the war. This one was my favourite. I'd last seen it as a child. The film showed my mother and her brother running about in a garden, fishing in a stream, my grandfather riding a horse, the family picnics. Happy life.

But today, I was crying. "Shall we stop watching it, Zuzana?" Harry kissed my wet eyes.

It tickled, and I stopped crying. "No, let's watch to the end. Adam has never seen this."

On the screen, they were having a picnic. All those uncles, aunts and cousins in the garden, the maid bringing tea on a tray, the adults talking, the children playing with a ball. Then the ball hits the maid, who drops the tray with the china teapot and cups. I can see my grandmother talking to the children with a strict face, and then the film stops. My grandfather presumably stopped filming and told the children off, too. Of course, those films are silent; we can't hear what they are saying. I remember my mother telling me about that. She said Grandfather confiscated the ball.

There were lots of relatives in this picnic film. I had asked my mother who they were. Now my son Adam was asking me the same question. I was not sure if I remembered all their names. Most of them were killed by the Nazis. We saw some of their names on our family tomb. My mother's name would now be on that tomb, too. We know the date of her death. It is different with her father and brother, and some others, when the tomb shows their exact date of birth, but the second date, the time of death, is just a year: 1943, 1944, sometimes 1945. Some names have a place of death added – Majdanek, Treblinka, Auschwitz, Theresienstadt – but next to several names, even that information is missing. Most of the members of my family who came back from the concentration camps didn't stay in Czechoslovakia; they spread all around the world. The USA, France, Israel… only my mother and grandmother remained in Prague.

I started telling Harry and Adam what I remembered my mother had told me. We were all crying now.

That was when I realised that I would like to know more, to be able to answer my son's questions. My mother was not the only survivor in our family – the answers were out there. This was my family's history. I wanted to meet the relatives that were still alive. We all went to sleep early.

At breakfast, as if he could read my thoughts from last night, Harry said, "Zuzana, you should write to all those American relatives. They are getting old; maybe you should travel to America to meet them all before it is too late. Adam needs to know where he comes from; it is important for him. He needs to understand. Maybe he could even go with you."

It was tempting, but I declined. I had to work and be there for Adam's A levels. Travelling could wait, but I would write to some of them and try to get the missing addresses for a start. Maybe we could phone, too.

CHAPTER FOUR

Zuzana, 2003

WHY AM I SO SAD?

I felt relieved when we flew back to London. The most difficult relationship in my life had just ended. I would never see my mother again. I would never dial her telephone number and pretend to listen to her self-centred monologues, waiting for those pointed remarks. I was never going to hear those accusing sentences, telling me that I wasn't good enough. I felt free. But relief also brought guilt.

Daughters are supposed to grieve for their mothers. I remembered my mother telling me that the worst thing that ever happened to her was her mother dying. I did not feel that way. So why was I bursting into tears, especially in those pre-dawn hours when I couldn't sleep? I was happy that she died, wasn't I?

It was getting worse. I listened to a song. The singer sang about mother lighting the room and that it is darker when she leaves. I did not feel that way, so why did that song bring uncontrolled sobbing?

I went back to Prague to sort out the formalities. Under Czech inheritance laws, Tomas inherited three quarters of all their belongings, while I got the last quarter, including their weekend cottage. I hadn't seen it since before I emigrated. I preferred staying in Prague and seeing my friends when I visited. *Why couldn't I do this for her? She was always asking me; it was important to her. She was right: she was unlucky to have a daughter like me.*

Tomas was generous. He didn't want any of the furniture, paintings or the things my mother inherited from her parents. Tomas took his share of the bank accounts, nothing more. I went to see the weekend house with him. I wanted him to have it, but he said he was too old, and we should sell it. *My mother was killed driving to the cottage.* I started to cry and couldn't stop. I never thought I loved my mother, but I probably did. I never thought she loved me, but Tomas gave me a box with all my letters from the time I was a little child to the letters from England. *Why would she keep them if she didn't love me?* Now I remembered the good things: how she worried about me, how protective she got if she thought somebody was nasty to me. I remembered how she always asked for my opinion and advice. I remembered how unhappy she was when I emigrated. *Oh, Mother, I wish I had been nicer to you. I wish we had been nicer to each other...*

CHAPTER FIVE

Zuzana 2003

THE INHERITANCE – THINGS FROM THE PAST

I was sorting through the old family things: the silver, crystal, Rosenthal china, furniture, paintings. Not practical, but beautiful. I put most of it into the flat Otto bought in Prague, but I took some to England. It felt strange, knowing that all these things survived the war, being hidden with friends of my grandparents. Messengers from the past, from the time before the Nazis changed everything.

There was one thing I treasured the most, although I would probably never wear it: my grandmother's black evening gown. My mother didn't want to give it to me when I first found it, aged 16. Now I could have it. It still fitted me.

That dress was made in 1922 in an expensive salon called Rosenbaum in Prague for my grandmother Franzi. It was made of thin, see-through black chiffon silk – crepe de chine, my mother called it. It was long and elegant in the beautiful fashion of that time. I could imagine cocktail parties, dances, conversations about the Great war that recently finished and how war would never happen again. A happy, frivolous time – at least, for people with money. I imagined introductions of men in tuxedos to women in stylish dresses and diamond and gold jewellery. I imagined my grandmother, young, just after getting married, trying to please her formidable mother-in-law Olga. She never managed to do that.

When Grandma got the dress back in 1945, she had lost so much weight that it was too loose for her. Then she put on weight and could not wear it. But there were few opportunities to wear it in communist Czechoslovakia anyway. I didn't have any occasions to wear an evening gown either, as my world was more casual, but I was pleased I had it now.

I inherited many paintings; some were beautiful. The portraits of my mother and her brother Oskar painted before the war were not beautiful, but they told a story. My grandparents wanted to have portraits of the children, not just photographs. My mum told me about those portraits a long time ago. She told me she didn't want to sit for the painting. I sympathised. Just letting a dressmaker pin a new dress on me used to drive me crazy. When I imagined my mother – an eight-year-old girl sitting for hours while the painter was working on the portrait – I couldn't blame her. But crying didn't help this time. Grandma apparently promised my mother a spanking if she didn't sit still. Mum told me she still covered her face with her hands whenever her mum was not in the room. The painter didn't tell on her and still finished the portraits, but he had his revenge. Oskar looked alright on his, but in my mother's portrait, she had red eyes and nose. It was obvious from the picture that she was crying. Mum told me she was always cross when anybody asked her why the tears.

My mother had her brother's portrait hanging in her apartment, but hers was hidden behind a wardrobe. I found it once when the apartment was being decorated, and that was when she told me the story. Mum also told me that one day, soon after the portraits were finished, she had tried to get rid of the painting. She took a chair from the dining room, climbed on it and threw the painting on the floor. The glass broke, but the picture wasn't damaged. Her father, who'd heard the crash, came to the hall, and when he saw his daughter, he knew immediately what had happened. Still, she quickly told him she'd heard a crash and the chair was there to help her hang the picture back. Mum told me she didn't think Grandfather believed her, but he pretended to. Grandfather always tried his utmost not to have to discipline his beloved daughter. I changed the positions of those portraits. My mum's brother Oskar was now behind one of my wardrobes, but the portrait of my crying, irrepressible mother now hung on the wall of my bedroom.

CHAPTER SIX

Zuzana, 2005

Even after more than a year following the funeral, I wasn't much better. Harry and Adam were getting worried.

"Zuzana, you should get some therapy."

"But I am OK – this is probably normal bereavement."

I argued every time it was brought up by Roxanne or my in-laws, but mainly Harry. He held me when I cried, and despite his busy job as a GP, he took over the household. My GP started me on antidepressants, but he also organised therapy. I didn't want to go, but Harry forced me.

"Give me two good reasons to have the therapy!" I texted him when he was at work.

"Because it's the right thing to do; because it's the right thing to do," he typed. He probably copied and pasted it.

"That's not two reasons! Do you want me to kill you?"

I gave in. Funnily enough, I saw the same therapist, Dr O'Hare, whom Roxanne saw all those years ago. A small, slim woman with cropped grey hair, always dressed the same. Navy trouser suit, white blouse, brogues. Like a uniform. She looked like a strict schoolteacher, but she had lovely, smiling blue eyes. Dr O'Hare asked good questions. I told her about my lifelong wish not to be like my mother and about that sentence that haunted me: "If I could divorce my mother, I would!"

"But you did not divorce her; you behaved well. You should not feel guilty about your thoughts, only your actions."

Cognitive behavioural therapy was interesting. There were templates.

What is the evidence? What would other people think in your place? What were you doing when you got upset, and why do you think it was?

I copied the templates to my computer and filled in the questionnaires every week before my session. Psychotherapy was painful. It was hard work, but it was helping.

The therapist wanted me to write a letter to my mother. I thought it was silly. You can't write a letter to a dead person.

"You always wanted to be a writer – why don't you do it like a writing exercise? I challenge you!" Harry was pushing me, and deep down, I knew he was right.

I wrote the letter:

Dear Mummy (my mother didn't like me calling her Mother, but I usually did. I did a lot of things she didn't want me to do),

You are dead, and there are so many things I wish I had told you when you were still alive. I didn't understand how deeply the war must have affected you. The diagnosis of post-traumatic stress disorder didn't exist then, but I should have listened to Harry, who kept telling me about the damage which made you the way you were.

I have been thinking about our relationship. We probably loved each other, but maybe we didn't like each other enough. At least I didn't. I spent most of my life trying not to be like you. The most painful thing about your death was that at first, I felt relieved. A daughter is supposed to mourn the death of her mother. I cry a lot, and people think it is because I miss you.

Today I realised they are right: I do miss you.

To start with, my mourning was for what could have been. The yearning for the unconditional love of a mother for a daughter like you got from Grandma. But now I think that you did love me. I was blind not to see it.

You are dead, and it is too late, but I would like you to know how I admired your achievements, skipping five years and graduating with your year from secondary school in 1946, a year after you came back from Theresienstadt. That was an amazing achievement. How you went to university and studied pharmacy when Dad left you. The love you had for your mother, Grandma Franzi.

I admired your photographic memory, your mantra of, "Everything is possible if you try!" You achieved everything you set your mind to. You were so brave – why did I not see that? I saw it with your cousins Irma and Hana, but you were younger, and yet, you were as brave as they were.

You missed your teenage years, and maybe you were not ready to be a mother. It was hard to be your daughter, but maybe it was hard to be my mother, too. I should have known, and I am so sorry.

I wish I'd asked you more about the family. I don't want the stories to be lost; that would make the Nazis win. I will try to get in touch with all those relatives in the USA for Adam and for myself.

My emigration was painful for you, and I am sorry that you felt abandoned. It was hard for you, after losing all those other members of the family in the war, and after Grandma died.

I want you to know I loved you. I didn't know, but perhaps you knew. I found signs of your love by clearing your flat in Prague after you died. You kept all my letters from when I was a child! Did you feel my love from my actions? I didn't feel yours from your words. But from your actions? Oh yes, often. How you were always trying to protect me from being hurt by other people. I remember how you worried about me and wanted to help me. I remember how you used to embarrass me by telling other people how brilliant, beautiful and accomplished I was. I somehow didn't notice the love, because of your poisonous words, but even those words were often meant to protect me. You craved my company, and I tried to avoid yours. You were jealous of my friends. When I started to come back to Prague, you wanted me to go to see the weekend house; I didn't.

Oh, Mother, I should have been nicer.

Maybe, after years trying not to, I am becoming more like you: determined, tough, persistent. Everything is possible if you try. I believe that, too. You were special: brave, smart, competent. And those angry words were a shield, to protect you from hurt. You were hurt so badly at such a young age.

I probably hurt you, too. How could I not have known that I loved you?

I cannot tell you anything anymore. But you were such a smart woman, you probably don't need to be told.

Love, Zuzana

Harry asked if he could read the letter. After reading it, he hugged me, and I didn't want him to let go.

The letter helped me to express my feelings, but I had a nasty little voice in my head telling me I didn't really love my mother, that I just wrote the letter to impress the therapist.

Hearing that little voice was very painful. I felt worthless, a bad person. *Nobody likes you, and if they do, they wouldn't like you if they knew what you are really like.* I was thinking about death. I wouldn't kill myself, as it would hurt Harry and Adam, but the idea of dying was always on my mind; I didn't tell anybody. After six months of weekly therapy sessions, I started to feel slightly better. The guilt was still there. I didn't want to feel the joy of my mother's death; it was not right.

"It's a feeling. Feeling guilty about it would be like feeling guilty about being thirsty or hungry. You can't help it," said Dr O'Hare.

I told her about that Yiddish song, about the mother who lights up the room. My life got lighter, sunnier when my mother died. Was that weird and wrong?

"Maybe. But it is what it is." Dr O'Hare knew what she was doing. She was really very helpful.

It was hard to do my work properly. A social worker needs to be calm and optimistic when sorting out other people's problems. Now I often had to hide my tears when I was with clients.

There were some better moments. That was when I started to recall the good things, happy occasions, fun ones. I opened the box where mother kept all my letters. I read them. These were replies to my mother's letters – letters that, unlike her, I didn't keep. Suddenly I saw love where I'd never noticed it before.

One day, Harry said, "Zuzana, you need a break. We spoke about it almost two years ago, on the day of Magda's funeral, when you were showing us the films, remember? You were going to write to your relatives in America, but you didn't. Adam is going to university soon – why don't you take some unpaid leave and go to America for a couple of months? Adam and I will be OK. He will be at uni most of the time anyway. We will enjoy having a whole male household for a while."

"I can imagine the mess when I come back!" I said, but I was grateful.

I spoke to my supervisor, who agreed to give me unpaid leave. I think she was relieved; she saw I was struggling.

The only American relatives I had met were mother's meek cousin Irma and her annoying husband Petr. Irma gave me the address of her cousin Miriam; I'd never heard of her before. Miriam was a daughter of Samuel, brother of Irma's father Hans. So Miriam and my mother were both Irma's cousins, but they were not blood related to each other. Those family connections were complicated. When I tried to explain it to Harry, he said his simple doctor's brain couldn't cope with it. Unlike Irma's family, her cousin Miriam's family emigrated to the USA before the war.

"Miriam will tell you a fascinating story," Irma wrote.

I was curious. Later, when I found out the almost unbelievable story of Miriam's father and the German spies, it made me like my great-grandmother Olga even less.

Irma also gave me the address of her aunt Judita, the one who emigrated to California in 1938. I was too late for her husband Simon; he'd died about five years previously. I wrote to Judita, but it was Nathan, her son, who replied. He was born in California in

1939. He told me his mother was ill and frail, recovering from a chest infection.

There were so many people I wanted to see. Of course, I wanted to see those romantic heroes, Hilda and her German knight in shining armour Jürgen. There were not many happy endings in my family, but that was one. I was planning to meet them as soon as possible because they were so old. My mother lost contact with them when my grandma Franzi died. I didn't know how many children or grandchildren they had. I only found their address recently, in a book in my mother's flat. Grandma Franzi was using it as a bookmark.

I wrote to them first, but in the end, they were the ones I saw last.

I waited till Adam started university and then I left.

CHAPTER SEVEN

Zuzana 2005

AMERICA – I MEET MOTHER'S COUSIN IRMA AGAIN

The first person I visited was Irma. I was looking forward to seeing her again, but not Petr. I didn't meet their daughter Joan last time; I was hoping to meet her now. Irma invited me to stay in their large brownstone house in New York. Petr was not at home much; he was away on business.

"Is he not going to retire?" I asked.

"No, he doesn't think anybody would do the work as well as he does," replied Irma. She sounded different from before – bitter. She used to think her husband was wonderful. I wondered what happened.

"How is Joan? She must be a young woman now," I asked.

Irma frowned. "Petr drove Joan out. She did have some problems, and she dropped out of high school, but she is a good girl. But he was shouting at her, and…" Irma began to sob.

"What happened?" I embraced her; she was shaking. Her body was petite, like my mother's. Now I was crying, too. *Why was I not nicer to my mum?*

Irma told me about the argument. When Petr was shouting at Joan that she was a useless, lazy, stupid girl, not finishing high school, she said, "But Mom didn't finish high school either."

"Petr said, 'And look what happened to her: an uneducated

woman who can't even run a household properly.' It was awful to see how little Petr thought of me!"

I kept holding her. I got furious with Petr. "Oh, Irma, how could he say something like that? You were so brave in the war, and you are such a lovely woman. Petr doesn't deserve you. Where is Joan?"

"She has gone to California. She probably takes drugs. She doesn't write, but I know she had a baby. I have a grandchild and I don't even know if it is a boy or a girl. I cannot see them. Oh, Zuzana, it took me such a long time to get pregnant with Joan. I thought I would never have a baby; she was a miracle. My darling daughter, and now she is gone, and I might never see her again!"

How could have Irma been so brave in the war and then allow my mother or her husband treat her like that? I wasn't looking forward to meeting Petr again.

CHAPTER EIGHT

Zuzana 2005

AMERICA – MIRIAM AND THE SPIES

I rma had given me the email address of her cousin Miriam when I was still at home. Miriam replied to my email from London with a long, friendly and witty reply. We spoke on the phone. She spoke perfect Czech.

"I must tell you about my father and the spies," she said. Spies? I was curious. I liked her dry sense of humour. I phoned her from Irma's, and she suggested that I should stay with her. I was glad; I'd had enough of Petr, even though he wasn't at home a lot, and when he was, he was watching TV.

I moved from Irma and Petr's house to Miriam's. I liked her immediately. A petite old woman, straight back, thick white hair, smiling brownish green eyes. Her house was full of books. All the walls were full; there was hardly any space between the posters, shelves and artwork. Miriam was wearing several beautiful rings: diamonds and rubies. She wore elegant dresses, even at home, and makeup. What a difference to the mouse-like Irma. Yet Miriam was a year older than Irma. She was fun to talk to, but then she came up with a story that changed my perception of the rest of the family forever.

We were both sipping red wine when she started; it was 4pm. She was still talking at 7pm. I took her out for dinner in a little Italian place, and the story continued. I wanted to call a taxi, but she said, "No, I need the exercise – let's walk." She walked fast, without a stick. She reminded me of a colourful little bird – a kingfisher, maybe. She also reminded me of my mum with her exercise. I was entranced. Miriam was a good storyteller; she should have been a writer. But she became an architect like her father Samuel, the brother of my mother's uncle Hans.

It was strange that my mother never mentioned Miriam, so I wondered if Miriam was in touch with anybody else. "Did you know Hana Stein, my mother's and Irma's cousin?" I asked.

"Yes, of course, I visited Hana in Tel Aviv several times. I first started going there because of the Bauhaus architecture, but then I just went to see her; she was an interesting woman. Men loved her – there was always a different one whenever I came. She was very beautiful, wasn't she?"

So my image of Hana having many lovers was right. I didn't think it shocked Miriam; she looked rather mischievous.

Miriam got serious again. She looked at the portrait of her father on the wall, a handsome man with large eyes and heavy eyelids, looking like some medieval king, "My father was an architect in the Bauhaus style. He was extremely successful. Have you heard of Adolf Loos, Zuzana? He was a colleague and a friend of my father's."

"Of course – wow, Loos is famous."

"That name, Adolf, nobody is called that anymore... My mother didn't like his buildings; she preferred the romantic turn-of-the-century houses with their curves, gargoyles, decorative doors and windows, like the type of house we lived in, in Parizska Street in Prague. My father used to say that my mother had typical bourgeois taste."

I knew Parizska Street; I thought it was much more beautiful than the simple white Bauhaus buildings, but I didn't say anything.

"My father used to draw me pictures and taught me how to draw. I knew I was going to be an architect when I grew up. I remember him telling me stories and drawing pictures, illustrations to go with the stories he made up. They were about dragons, but when I was older, I found out the pictures were dinosaurs. For me, dinosaurs and dragons are the same thing." Miriam showed me her father's dinosaur drawings. She brought them to America, and she kept them. She must have loved her father very much.

"My father always had tracing papers and pencils with him. That is important in what happened later and how we got to America. It was useful in travelling, too. We were in Rome and Father couldn't find a toilet. Nobody spoke Czech, German, French or English, the languages he knew. He saw an Italian policeman and went to ask him. When he came back, my mother asked, 'How in the world did you make him understand what you wanted, Samuel?' My father showed her a little drawing of a urinal."

"Did you keep that drawing as well?"

"No, but what a pity I didn't!" Miriam was fun.

"I told my parents that I wouldn't have to learn foreign languages if I learnt how to draw, but Mummy didn't agree." Miriam's laugh was loud. It reminded me of my grandma Franzi.

"Of course, I already spoke German – the entire family was bilingual. I didn't know at that time that I would soon have to learn another language, English, in a hurry."

"Did you speak German at home, like Irma's family?" I asked. My mother's family spoke Czech.

"No, Czech, of course." Miriam seemed a bit offended.

"My father was proud of the fact that our ancestors were Sephardic Jews who came from Spain in 1492, the same year Columbus sailed to America."

"Did they go to the Spanish synagogue like my family?" The Spanish synagogue in Prague is decorated in Moorish style.

"Yes they did. Father liked history and told me about the Crusaders, about the Moors in Spain and how the Jews were expelled with the Moors. He drew me pictures of the Moors in turbans, peacocks, and showed me a book about Alhambra in Spain. But he also told me we were Czechs now as much as we were Jewish. Father loved Czechoslovakia, and the first president, Tomas Garrigue Masaryk."

"My mother used to talk about President Masaryk as 'Daddy Masaryk', but in the communist schools, we didn't learn about him at all."

"We worshiped him. I remember how once we went for a walk in the park in Lany, the president's residence, and we saw an old man on a horse. It was the president, our hero! I never forgot that day."

Miriam told me she was the only Jewish girl in her Czech school. I remember my mother told me that there were only three in her class, so most Jewish children must have gone to German schools. Miriam often used to play with Gerd and Irma, children of my grandfather's sister Helena and her husband Hans, who was Miriam's father's brother.

Harry was right, these family relations were complicated.

"You know, Zuzana, my father once told me that Aunt Helena could have been my mother. Apparently, Helena's father Ruben, who knew my grandparents, came to my father once and told him he would like him to marry his daughter Helena. Helena was getting older and did not have any suitors. He used that word – old-fashioned now, of course. He told my father that if he married his daughter, Ruben would pay for a large office with many employees, that Father would be able to design more buildings and he would never lack money. Imagine, Zuzana, the cheek."

"Was that the husband of my Great-Grandma Olga?" I asked. I'd never liked Olga, and her husband, my great-grandfather, sounded like an arrogant rich man!

"Yes, I call her the Evil Witch." Miriam looked at me, and when I chuckled, she said it was not funny. But she smiled.

"Daddy was not going to do it – he wanted to make his own fortune. But Ruben would not give up. He asked my father if he knew about some other nice Jewish boy who would be interested. Daddy told him he could ask his younger brother Hans. Hans was a gynaecologist and never had enough money. You know how quiet, gentle and shy Irma is? He was the same."

"And he married my great-aunt Helena?"

"Yes, Ruben paid for Hans's private gynaecological office and Helena had a big dowry. When I was a child, we used to have lunch with them every other Sunday. Cousin Gerd was my age, but I never liked him."

"Why?" My mother never said anything about Gerd, just about Irma.

"He was a spoiled brat. I remember how he kept saying, 'I want this; I want that.' My parents wouldn't let me be like that! His grandmother Olga wanted to pay for him to learn a musical instrument. Aunt Helena was a pianist, and Irma played, too. She thought about the piano or violin, but Gerd picked a tuba. My daddy said Gerd did it out of spite so that he could disturb his father's patients. The tuba is so noisy! He was right. Listening to Gerd playing the tuba was like listening to a demented elephant."

Miriam got up and I followed her to one of the bedrooms where she started making my bed. She also took out a large album and showed me pictures of Gerd, Irma, herself as a child and her parents. Miriam's mother was beautiful. She was an artist and a dressmaker. Miriam's house walls were hung with tapestries made by her mother.

"Did your grandma tell you about the Freemasons?" Miriam asked. "Your grandfather was one."

I wasn't sure what Freemasons were. *Some weird religious sect?*

Miriam read my face. "No, Zuzana, at that time, before the war, the Freemasons were a very liberal organisation. A lot of famous Czech artists and scientists belonged to it; my father was proud to be among them."

"Really?" I was not convinced.

"I loved the Masonic ring my father wore, decorated with the compass, square and the letter G. I thought the letter G was for our surname, Goldman. I told him that, and he didn't correct me that it was G for God. My father didn't believe in God. In fact, I remember him arguing with a friend, also a Freemason, that the G was for geometry. I thought my explanation, that it was G for my father's and my surname, was better. Being a Freemason is significant in my story, so, Zuzana, listen carefully."

Miriam, an old lady living alone, finally had someone to talk to. The conversation branched and branched, and she didn't get to the importance of the Freemasons that evening. I didn't mind; it was all fascinating, and it was my family she was talking about. It was 2 am when we went to bed.

The next morning, drinking rather weak coffee and eating a plum cake Miriam had baked, she was going to tell me about the Freemasons.

"The Freemasons met every two weeks," Miriam began. "My father Samuel, his brother Hans, your grandfather Bruno and his brother Otto were all members of the same lodge. I never knew why our families, your mother's and mine, didn't meet. I suspect your great-grandmother Olga was behind it. She never trusted my father. She probably did not forget that he refused to marry Helena when Ruben came with his 'oh-so-generous offer'. I remember that stupid Gerd telling me once: 'My grandma Olga told my mummy that your father is a bad influence on Daddy; I heard that.' That made me angry. I loved my father; nobody was going to speak badly of him! 'And you are a bad influence on everybody, you stupid tuba-playing monkey!' I said. I thought Irma was going to defend her younger brother, but she pretended she didn't hear us."

"She probably agreed with you, Miriam."

"You know, when Irma and Petr came to America after the war, my father gave them money to open their business. Daddy told me about her bravery in the war. Now she looks like a quiet mouse again."

"Her husband Petr is annoying, isn't he? Was he always like that?" I asked.

"Yes, he is a *schmendrick*," she said.

That didn't exactly help. "What's a *schmendrick*? I've never heard that."

Miriam was a New Yorker; they all use Yiddish. "*Schmendrick* is just another word for a schmuck," she said, and laughed, a loud, cackling sound.

I didn't know what a schmuck was either. Miriam found it funny.

Then she suddenly became sad again. "I don't see Gerd as an annoying, tuba-playing spoilt brat anymore, Zuzana. It is hard to detest someone who was gassed in Auschwitz."

"But Miriam, you were going to tell me something about the Freemasons."

She made a funny face, like a child, almost as if she were going to stick her tongue out at me. "All right, all right, you are impatient. It was summer 1938; after the Anschluss of Austria, my parents wanted to emigrate. I heard them talking about it. I had always been nosey, listening behind doors. You find out things!" Miriam really was mischievous. I liked it.

"In July, my father travelled to America. Before he left, he tried to get an American settlement visa, but there were quotas and it looked hopeless. He wanted to visit some places, especially to see Frank Lloyd Wright's buildings in Chicago, but of course, he was looking for a job opportunity. He travelled on an ocean liner from Holland. He flew to Holland instead of going via Germany; he didn't think he would be safe. He was a very active Freemason and a Jew; he knew that he was blacklisted by the Nazis."

"Flying must have been quite unusual in 1938."

Of course, Miriam's father was right not to go through Germany. He sounded like a smart man.

"He sent us postcards from Chicago and New York, but they only arrived after he came back home. I remember asking him if he would see any Indian chiefs. I loved reading Karl May's books about the Wild West. We had the books at home in German."

"Oh, I read Karl May's books about Indians, too, in Czech, but nobody knows Karl May in England. Still, I read them to Adam as well. He can speak Czech but doesn't read in it. I loved those books, I was in love with Vinetou, the Apache chief."

"Weren't we all?" Miriam smiled.

"So what happened in America?" I nudged her.

"My father loved America. But now I will finally come to the Freemasons and the spies."

"Spies? Already, so soon?" I joked. I was sitting at the edge of my seat, but I didn't expect the story to be that unbelievable.

Miriam smiled. "I do talk too much, always have done – the worst chatterbox in the family."

"I talk a lot, too, Aunt Miriam. But my husband said once that I do not talk too much, although I talk a lot. And that it doesn't matter because I am intelligent, articulate and never boring. Nice, ha?" Miriam wasn't really my aunt, but by now, I felt really close to her.

"He must love you – that is nice."

"Yes, Harry and I love each other." Suddenly I missed Harry terribly. "Let's go back to your story, Aunt Miriam – I can't bear the suspense anymore."

"Let me open another bottle of red wine first." For an old woman, she drank rather a lot. But her hands were not shaking, and she talked fast and without hesitation.

"Did your father find a job in the USA? Is that how you came over?"

"No, they didn't want refugees from Europe."

I was getting impatient. I knew they got to America, so I wanted to know how.

"On the ship on the way back, he saw an older man with a group of students in the dining room. They were conspicuous, sitting only in their shirtsleeves, no jackets! My father and the other European passengers all wore jackets to dinner. The Americans just didn't have any manners!" Miriam laughed her loud, contagious laugh. "My father would have probably never joined the Americans at their table if it wasn't for one of the students spilling a drink over him. The sea was rough, and when the student got up to pronounce a toast, he lost his balance."

"Red wine?" I asked.

"No, fortunately, it was white, not red wine. The student was very apologetic and tried to use his napkin to reduce the damage. Then the professor got up and called a waiter to sort it out. He apologised to my father and asked him to join them. Daddy said the professor spoke slowly; he wasn't sure how good my father's English was. It was not particularly good, but fortunately it was better than the English of the two German spies. Zuzana, you probably think: *What German spies? Will Miriam ever get to the point?* But I will, don't worry."

At that point, the professor noticed the masonic ring. He apparently stopped talking and put his hand out. He was wearing a similar ring. Miriam told me they shook hands in that strange Masonic handshake.

"What is that?" I wondered if she knew. But she showed me. That is how I learnt the Masonic handshake. Of course, we were both women, and the Freemasons haven't heard about feminism and equality.

Miriam told me that her father Samuel joined the Americans at their table and not to look different, he left his jacket in his cabin. The next evening, he was early. The Americans were not in the dining room yet, but he noticed two other men whispering in the corner and transferring some drawings onto thin tracing paper. They were talking in German. He almost went to talk to them, thinking maybe they were fellow architects, but then he noticed a small swastika on one of the men's lapel.

"Daddy sat down with his back towards them, but he tried to listen to their conversation. He was quite close to them and they did not whisper; they thought an American – no jacket, see, Zuzana? – would not understand German. They looked serious and one of them, the one who was not drawing, was obviously the superior. The other, a tall slim man, treated him with a polite, deferential manner. My father noticed they were talking about factories, bridges and some weapons. It was suspicious."

"So what were they doing?" I asked. It was like a thriller. It got better.

"Daddy always claimed some of their drawings were of weapons, but he didn't really know what they were drawing. Still, he immediately suspected they were Nazi spies. And that was exactly what they were. They took the papers and left without having dinner. That was suspicious, too," said Miriam.

Now I understood why the tracing paper, always in Samuel Goldman's pocket, was important. Miriam told me that her father noticed there were imprints from the German's drawings on the white tablecloth. Without hesitation, he quickly took out his own tracing papers and pencil and copied those imprints. When the Americans came, he told them he was drawing ideas for a new building. I was impressed – quick thinking!

This was fascinating, but we were still sitting at her breakfast table. I didn't have my makeup on, and I was going to have a shower.

"God, it is midday. Zuzana, you do bring out the talker in me!"

I didn't think she needed my help; she was as chatty as I was. I suggested we went out for lunch – my treat – and we ended up in a nice Jewish deli. Miriam ordered me something called a Reuben sandwich; I had never tasted one before – it had beef, sauerkraut and cheese on rye bread. Delicious.

"But a proper Jewish sandwich would not have the cheese and beef, right?" I asked.

"Kosher mosher – we never kept it." Miriam had a veal wiener schnitzel in a bun. At home, we always had a pork wiener schnitzel, but this was a Jewish deli.

"We are a good couple of Jewish women!"

Miriam winked. It was hard to believe she was 80. When we finished eating, she carried on with her story. The voyage to Europe lasted seven days, and Miriam's father always moved to the Germans' table when they left. Most of the time, there were some traces for him to copy.

"The Germans still thought he was just another American. Talking about it later, my father always said that those spies were careless and stupid. Why did they not suspect somebody might understand what they were talking about? Why were they not more careful with the drawings? The Germans were supposed to be efficient and organised! At the end of the journey, my father's cabin was full of drawings. He didn't tell us about them when he came back, so I never saw them. Oh, Zuzana, we were so excited when he came home. I thought he looked different: tanned and slimmer, almost American. He had a leather jacket he'd bought in America. I remember him talking about his trip, but he told me about those spies only much later. He brought me a doll from America. Didn't he know that I no longer played with dolls? My father did not notice I was growing up."

"What did he do with the drawings?" I asked. I started to suspect what had happened.

The day after he arrived from America, Samuel Goldman went to the American embassy in Prague. He asked for an audience with the attaché, telling the secretary he had some important papers to show him.

"I remember he talked about the same secretary when he was at the embassy before to arrange his American visa. He asked about settlement visas for us, but the secretary, a tall woman with a blonde bob, high cheekbones and long red nails, told him they had quotas and a very long waiting list for settlement visas. At that time, she was rather unpleasant. This time, she was still cold but polite. She took the drawings and told Daddy she would phone him within a week."

Miriam told me that two days later, her father got a phone call to come for an audience with the ambassador himself. The ambassador and Samuel Goldman talked for a long time. The blonde secretary was called in and asked to get them some tea and sandwiches. She was much friendlier after that.

"The ambassador asked my father if he could eat the sandwiches, thinking about kosher. 'I am a Jew, but not observant. I eat pork,' said my father. And Zuzana then the miracle happened. The ambassador said: 'I would like to thank you on behalf of the government of United States of America for those drawings. They were of great use to us. We identified and arrested the spy network responsible. As a reward, I am authorised to offer you, and up to 25 of your relatives, passage to the USA and settlement visas. This is a letter to the application department.' My father was stunned. 'But what about the quotas? I tried to apply before,' he said."

"The ambassador told my father not to worry, that our family had been put to the front of the line. Oh, Zuzana, I remember how excited my parents were, and all those hectic phone calls and discussions with relatives. My grandparents were no longer alive, but my parents asked Cousin Emma, and Uncle Hans and Helena. They also planned to ask your grandparents and other relatives. Cousin Emma was Jewish, but, like many others, she was a Jewish antisemite. She refused to come. 'I will not be at the mercy and charity of those New York Jews,' she told Daddy."

Miriam was red in the face and talked louder. She almost shouted.

"Stupid woman, her Jewish antisemitism cost her her life. Instead of emigrating to America, Cousin Emma was sent to Poland and vanished like most of the family members who stayed."

"It was at the time when the Germans stole Sudety." Miriam was referring to October 1938, at the time of the Munich agreement, which saw parts of Czechoslovakia given to Nazi Germany by the British, French and Italians. She called the part of Czechoslovakia by the Czech name Sudety, not the German name Sudetenland. I remembered it well from history lessons. It all started on 22 September when Hitler threatened the Czechoslovak border region of Sudeten with annexation. There was a strong German minority living there. Hitler wanted all the Czechs out of the area by the end of the month. The Czechoslovak government started mobilising troops to defend Sudeten against the Nazi invasion, and Miriam's father, like my grandfather and Uncle Otto, joined the army. I told her that.

"Yes, Daddy was mobilised, too. 'We are going to fight for our freedom,' he said, but they didn't fight. The mobilisation was called off by President Benes. He was under pressure from the British and French, so he signed the Munich agreement and left for exile in England."

"Oh, I remember my mother's uncle Otto telling me a joke about it," I said. "The joke was that Benes said he had a plan, but in fact he took a plane."

"Yes, my daddy told me the same joke," said Miriam. "In two days, Daddy was back home in his uniform. He was very angry. My mother was glad when he came back unharmed. I remember she said that the British and the French betrayed Czechoslovakia, but that without them it would have been suicide to fight the Nazis alone."

I remembered what I heard from my grandmother. "Miriam, my grandfather Bruno apparently cried when he came back without fighting. There was a saying about the Munich agreement: *about us, without us*. We learnt this at school."

I wanted to hear more.

"My mother told me that my Great-Grandmother Olga didn't want anybody to emigrate," I said. "I asked my mother why they listened to her, but they all thought Olga was wonderful. I often wondered why? Did my Great-Grandmother Olga know about the American ambassador's offer? Did your parents ask her?"

"Your Great-Grandmother Olga was an evil witch," said Miriam. She continued. "Soon after Daddy's audience with the ambassador, Hans and Helena came to lunch. After lunch, our parents sent Gerd, Irma and me out so that they could talk. I wanted to listen, but my father opened the door, catching me. 'Miriam, go and play with Irma and Gerd – stop snooping!' After coffee, they left. Aunt Helena had red eyes. Was she crying? Next day, that monster, your Great-Grandmother Olga, came unannounced. 'How dare you try to break up my family?!' she shouted at my father. 'I am not letting them move to America among those barbarians. How dare you?'

"'It's my family, too,' my father said. He wasn't shouting, but I could see he was furious. Then she noticed me. 'Go away, child. Stop listening to adult conversations. And Samuel, aren't you going to invite me in?' Olga changed her tone. My mother appeared, sent me away and invited Olga in. She asked the cook to bring them coffee and cake. 'Miriam can have the cake, too, but let her eat it in the kitchen.' So, the fate of Irma's family was decided while we were all eating cake." Miriam started to cry.

"Let's go," I said. The waiters were staring at us.

At home, she opened another bottle of red wine and started talking again. She looked serious and detached, almost unfriendly.

"Hans and Helena listened to that evil witch Olga and did not join us on the ship. In the end, none of the other relatives came with us. The visa application, despite us being first in line, took a long time. When Kristallnacht happened 9 November, and Jews in Germany and Austria were beaten and their property looted, we were still waiting for the visas. There was no doubt that staying in Czechoslovakia was not safe."

Miriam said that her father had several meetings with his brother Hans. He always came back furious. She told me that he once kicked the door and stubbed his toe. "At that time, I thought it was funny, Daddy swearing and jumping on one foot. We got the visas and left in December, just before Christmas."

"Do you remember the journey?" I asked. "What was it like? Did you fly to Holland like your father, to avoid Germany?"

This is like a thriller, I thought, but they had got to the USA; it ended up well.

"Yes, we flew. My mother was scared, but Daddy told her that it was safer than going by land through Nazi Germany. I was excited. Being on the plane at that time was special. The ship was worse. The sea was rough, and I was cold. My father started to teach me English. He drew pictures with English underneath. I remember the word 'dog' was underneath a drawing of a funny little dog with a bow. I thought maybe we could have a dog in America. I was sitting on the deck looking at the grey sea, feeling cold and lonely. But I was also trying to be the first to see the shores of America. I thought it was going to be an adventure. We never found out what was in those drawings Daddy copied from the tablecloth. Those drawings saved our lives."

Miriam's eyes teared up and her voice sounded strangled when she told me about the others. "Most of the ones who stayed died. What a waste of life – what a waste."

I remembered what Irma told me in her kitchen two years before: "I will never forgive Grandma Olga for killing my parents and my brother!" Now I understood.

At least Miriam's family was safe. When the war ended, Samuel looked for his brother Hans and other members of his family: he put advertisements into newspapers in Holland, Germany and England; he asked the Red Cross. He only found Irma, who was in Prague. She was already married to Petr, who was in the American army. Miriam only met him after the war.

"I never liked Petr; he was always self-centred and domineering. But Irma kept telling everybody how happy she was. She probably kept repeating it so that she believed it herself. Irma always puts other people first. Being too selfless is not good, Zuzana." Miriam's father helped Petr and Irma open a shop, and they did very well. Petr was a competent businessman.

"What about Irma's daughter Joan? Irma told me she lives in California, but they lost contact," I asked.

"She became some sort of hippie, lives in California in a commune. I think she had a baby. But she had a massive argument with Petr when she dropped out of high school, and she never sees her parents. Takes drugs, probably."

That made me sad. I didn't think there were still hippies in California; that was Miriam's age showing. I thought about Irma, who didn't have anybody apart from her domineering husband. But maybe they were happy, as she claimed. I hoped so.

CHAPTER NINE

Adam 2005

WHILE I AM IN AMERICA, ADAM MEETS THE EVIL REDHEAD AT UNIVERSITY

I talked with Harry and Adam on the phone every week. Adam was enjoying university. He wrote me an email:

Dear Mum,

The creative writing course is brilliant, and I am writing more, not just sci-fi stories. One day, I hope I will become a full-time writer. Grandma Angela and Grandad Richard are sceptical. They keep telling me stuff like, "Writing is not a job; it is a hobby. You need to earn a living, and your chance of earning a living by writing is almost zero." You always wanted to be a writer; you'd understand. Dad tried to pacify them by telling them not to worry, that the course is a combined course – creative writing with English, so I could always teach.

He also said, "If we are going to have two writers in the family, God help us!" But we both know he doesn't mean it. LOL. My writing teacher would faint if she saw me writing LOL; she is always moaning about stuff like that – OMG, etc., but she doesn't mind when we use, etc., and it is the same thing! LOL LOL LOL.

In freshers' week, they showed us around the campus, but mostly we just got drunk. Don't worry, Mum, it won't happen

often. Being drunk is stupid. I didn't count how many beers I had, and somebody gave me dope, too. I still don't smoke cigarettes, and don't worry, I won't become a dope head.

I joined a skiing team. Are you pleased that I ski like you did? It's funny; I am now the age you were when you emigrated. Wow, escaping to another country, that was kind of brave of you.

I wanted to write for the student paper or work for the student radio, but they don't take first-year students. Maybe next year.

Must go, meeting friends in a pub.

Love you, Adam.

Adam was sharing a house with three other boys: John, Chris and Tom, also skiers. He told me that they teased him that English and writing is not science; everybody can speak English and write. They all studied maths. Adam wrote that he replied to the teasing by correcting two spelling mistakes on a shopping list note in John's handwriting that was pinned with a magnet to the fridge.

On the phone later, Adam told me something really strange. "Mum, do you remember the evil redhead? I met her on campus today; she is really beautiful: long red hair, long legs, good figure."

"Did you talk to her?" I was curious.

"No, I almost said hello, but she looked right through me with really cold, evil, grey-blue eyes. We stared at each other for a while, but I blinked first. I turned and walked fast in the opposite direction. She's probably as evil as before. She is on the same course as John and Tom. Mathematics. Her name is Siobhan. Tom said she is a genius at maths but that she is a freak. A beautiful freak."

"Are you going to talk to her, Adam?" I asked again.

"I don't know, she's probably nuts." He changed the subject so quickly that I was sure this was not the last we would hear about Siobhan. "How is America, Mum? I'm so envious; I would love to go there. I should also meet all those relatives! What are they like? They are all old – are they not all senile?"

I told him not to be stupid; they probably had a better memory than he did. When I told him about the spy story, and what fun it was, he got excited.

"Maybe you could take me next time! Dad says hello; we're going to Grandma's for dinner. Write me the spy story properly in an email! Bye!"

Adam always finished phone calls fast. No 'Have a good time', just 'Bye'. I didn't mind. He was of a different generation.

I had an email from Harry, too. He said Adam was happy and that he was a good cook. I thought he couldn't even boil an egg. I missed them, but I had far to go – all those other relatives.

CHAPTER TEN

Zuzana 2005

Being with Miriam was great, but I had to go. My next stop was the west coast. I had never been. My depression was gone; I was too busy writing things down, emailing Harry and Adam. I spoke to Harry on the phone only once a week; it was difficult with the time difference. I missed him, but now I was in America, I was going to see all my relatives. I told everybody I was going to visit Judita, but I was secretly thinking about seeing Joan, the cousin I had never met. Cousin twice removed, as they call it. But I had a several times removed mother — maybe Joan was going to be a nice surprise, however related we were. After all, she was the only one close to my age.

When I arrived at San Francisco International Airport, Nathan was waiting to pick me up. I recognised him from the photos. My great-aunt Judita was pregnant when she and her husband Simon emigrated; Nathan was born in California in spring 1939. They were lucky.

Nathan looked well, much younger than his age, 66. Tall, thick grey hair, bright blue eyes. He didn't look Jewish like I did. But then Kirk and Michael Douglas are Jewish, and Paul Newman – none of them were dark like I was. I remembered that great-uncle Otto once told me, like her father told Miriam, that we were Sephardic Jews, originally from Spain. The family had lived in Prague for more than 400 years. That must have made it harder for them to emigrate. I wondered if that was the reason for the evil witch Olga's – I'd started calling her that since my visit with Miriam – stubborn refusal to let anybody go. Nathan surprised me because he hugged me. We had never met before, but I suppose we were close relatives, as he was my mother's cousin. Nathan's father Simon had died five years ago. Irma told me that she used to correspond with Judita – first letters, then emails. "But she was not a very good correspondent. Pity."

They were different generations, but there was not that much of an age difference between Judita and her niece Irma, only seven years.

Irma told me that Judita had recently become frail. Of course, she was 85. I remembered her photographs: a slim, serious-looking woman with beautiful almond-shaped brown eyes, straight black hair in a bun, a narrow long nose and arched eyebrows. She looked gentle and almost scared, like some animal caught in the headlights. My mother never told me much about her; she was a child when Judita and Simon emigrated. Mum told me she vaguely remembered there was a family dinner and a big argument. Judita was already pregnant with Nathan. Funnily enough, Great-Grandmother Olga did not stop Simon and Judita going. I wondered why. Maybe they told her she was pregnant. Mum told me they used to get letters and pictures; she remembered photos of the palm trees and Nathan as a baby. The letters stopped when America entered the war.

I was going to book a hotel, but Nathan insisted that I stayed with him and his wife. They lived in one of those crazy San Francisco steep streets with steps instead of pavement. The house was small but stylish.

"We don't drive much; usually we take the tram. It is simpler."

Nathan's wife Jiu, a beautiful, much younger Chinese woman, welcomed me. She spoke with a Californian accent; I already knew she was second-generation Chinese. Nathan, a French teacher, apparently learnt Mandarin anyway.

"He speaks better Mandarin than I do," joked Jiu.

They gave me coffee, and then Nathan noticed I was shaking. I felt cold.

"This is supposed to be hot, sunny California, but it was warmer on the east coast," I said. "Shouldn't it be hot here in May?"

"It's always chilly in SanFran. Mark Twain claimed that the worst winter he ever lived through was the summer in San Francisco," Jiu said in her deep, slightly rasping voice.

"Everybody in this country quotes Mark Twain and Benjamin Franklin," I said, getting a sweater from my luggage.

"It's just the literary types like my father or Jiu," explained Nathan. "When my dad was still alive, he and Jiu bored me and Mother stiff with their highbrow discussions."

I didn't tell him I also talked about books all the time. I smiled at Jiu and asked if she liked Amy Tan, and if her books reflected the way of life of second-generation Chinese women in San Francisco. Nathan made a face and left the room as his wife eagerly answered.

I shivered with the cold all afternoon and I was wondering if I was getting ill. I wore thermal underwear, long shirts, jumpers and a quilted jacket, but I was still freezing. Maybe I was tired. The locals wore shorts, men and women.

Jiu and Nathan were very hospitable but busy. They both worked: Jiu as a violin teacher and a part-time violin player in an orchestra, Nathan as a French and piano teacher. I heard him practising; he was good. They both were.

I wanted to see Judita in hospital, but Nathan told me to wait until mid-week. I went sight-seeing, but something wasn't right. Nathan seemed secretive. I asked Jiu how Judita was, but she changed the subject. It was peculiar. In his email, Nathan wrote about Judita's frailty and a chest infection, but when I asked if she was still coughing Nathan said she didn't have a cough. Then he blushed and changed the subject. What was he hiding?

I decided to challenge them. I didn't want to do it in their house, so one evening, I took them out to a restaurant in the Castro District. It was recommended to me by Roxanne's brother Bob. It was interesting to see most people in the street being same-sex couples, holding hands, sometimes kissing. Bob told me the restaurants were wonderful. He was right. The food was great. The dressing on the salad, steak, red Zinfandel – my favourite wine. In the middle of dinner, I raised my glass and thanked them for their wonderful hospitality. Then I dropped the bombshell.

"Nathan, Jiu, you are not telling me the truth. What is wrong with Great-Aunt Judita? Why can't I see her?"

Nathan stared at me. Jiu reached out and took his hand. At last, he sighed. "My mother doesn't have a chest infection. She is in a psychiatric hospital."

I nodded. I thought about what Harry told me about post-traumatic stress disorder. I thought about my mother and her dreams, and how she chased them away by screaming and waving her arms. When I suggested a psychologist or psychiatric help, my mother got offended. "I am not crazy," she said.

But Judita emigrated before the war; she should have been better! I thought. Then I remembered Miriam, crying about the relatives who didn't emigrate and were killed.

"She has been in the psychiatric hospital on and off ever since my father died four years ago. She tried to kill herself several times after he died. The last time she broke her hip and foot. It took her months to learn to walk again – she has no will to live. She doesn't want to see her granddaughter or great-granddaughter. They have to inject her with meds because she refuses to take them." He hung his head.

"Is she getting better? The medication should help, and therapy. Depression is treatable."

Nathan looked so sad; I was trying to cheer him up. Surely it couldn't be that bad.

"She's still talking about suicide. Oh, Zuzana, it is so hard. She asked the doctors to kill her. She stopped the medication for her blood pressure, but physically, she is healthy. She hates it. She keeps repeating, 'Why can't I have a bad heart and die? I am already 86. I don't want to live without Simon!'"

Jiu told me that she tried to bring over their daughter Becky and her baby Amy. "Becky married a Kiwi. Her husband Ben studied here; that's how they met. I thought the baby Amy would cheer up Judita – Amy is so cute!" Jiu started showing me pictures.

"My mother refused to see them when they flew over. Becky was quite upset; it's a long journey. You know, Zuzana, maybe I should help her die when that is what she wants. Maybe I'm failing her as a son." Nathan stopped talking. He was not looking at me or Jiu; he was staring into the space between us.

I thought he was going to burst into tears, but he managed not to. I felt like telling him, "Let it out!", but of course, I didn't say anything. I just took his hand and squeezed it. Jiu took over. She told me her mother asked Judita if the reason she wanted to die was to join her husband Simon and her relatives in heaven. Jiu explained to me that her mother Ann Mei was a devout Christian. Judita told her not to be an idiot, that there was no afterlife; when you were dead, you were dead. But then the pain stops. Ann Mei was shocked.

"My mother prays for everybody; she thinks it helps. I don't believe in God."

So, we were sitting there in the restaurant – three atheists, two Czech Jews, one Chinese Christian – and talked about faith, and how we are 'faith-blind', that none of us could imagine afterlife, or God, or another supernatural being.

The conversation calmed Nathan down and he told me more about his parents.

CHAPTER ELEVEN

Zuzana 2005

FINDING OUT ABOUT JUDITA AND SIMON, 1939–2000

I already knew about their emigration. My mother told me how she'd listened to the adults at lunch with her grandma Olga when Judita and Simon decided to emigrate.

"Were they happy in America? Or did they spend the war worrying about the relatives?"

"I remember a happy house: my parents played with me, read to me, told me stories. Father even kicked a ball with me, although he was terribly clumsy; his natural habitat was a library. You are a bit like that, Zuzana, aren't you?" Nathan had seen me trying to throw a paper into the wastepaper basket and missing twice. I was offended and told him about my skiing and figure skating. But he had a point: my hand to eye coordination was non-existent. Harry always said that if I threw a pebble into the sea, I would probably miss.

"Nathan is not that good with ball games either; I always beat him in tennis!" I thought the main reason for Jiu saying this was to cheer Nathan up by distraction. It worked: they bickered about their tennis skills for at least five minutes.

Then, eyes dry, he carried on telling me about his parents. "After the war, my parents both searched for their relatives. Father lost everybody. Searching through Red Cross and newspaper adverts was painful."

"Miriam told me the same thing," I said, but Nathan had never met Miriam.

"My mother started writing letters to the ones who came back alive, to her mother Olga. her nieces Hana and Irma, her brother Otto, your grandma Franzi, and your mother Magda, her niece. My parents didn't have much money, but they were planning to visit Prague as soon as possible. They were planning to fly via New York, to see Irma and Petr. But then in 1948, the communists took over Czechoslovakia, and my parents didn't want to go there. My father said he escaped one evil regime; he was not going to get stuck in another one. My mother never saw her mother Olga again. I don't remember any of it; I was only five when the war finished. But I do remember my mother crying a lot. My father had a job at the university, teaching philosophy. When he was at home, he did a lot of housework."

"That must have been unusual, in their generation," I said. "Even my father never did anything at home, and he was younger."

"Yes, none of my friends' fathers did that. My image of my mother when I was little was of a sickly person. She hugged me a lot, and she looked so sad! I felt so desperate to help her, but I didn't know how. I used to offer her my toy animals to play with."

"What was your dad like?"

"My father was fantastic. He played with me, cooked when Mum was in bed and played me music. He tried to speak Czech to me, but when I started going to school, I didn't like that. I didn't want to be different." Nathan only knew five words in Czech; four of those were names of animals: elephant, tortoise, horse and rabbit. The last word was potty.

"Very useful, Nathan, if you ever go to Prague!" I said.

Of course, Nathan was different even when he insisted to only speak English. Unlike other mothers, when Judita picked him up from school, she never spoke to the parents or other children. She often asked a neighbour who had a daughter in the same school to pick Nathan up.

"She must have been depressed; didn't they discover that?" I asked.

"Of course she was depressed. But in the '50s and '60s, the treatment of depression was not well advanced. It consisted of sedatives, which were addictive, and ECT. I remember mother had her first ECT when I was about ten. When she came home, she told my father, 'They gave me electric shocks, it was terrible. Please, please, don't let them do it to me again!' I had nightmares of my mother sitting in an electric chair!"

Jiu had a strange, expressionless face, as if she were trying not to hear him.

Nathan carried on, in a low, monotonous voice. "I was about 15 when she tried to kill herself, again and again, so she had to be admitted to hospital and I think they gave her electric shocks again. After that, she got better, though. Sometimes she smiled, and she started reading novels and taking me to museums and galleries. I had my mother back. Zuzana, she often talked about your mother Magda, how smart and naughty she was as a child. A competent manipulator. She was telling me about her, and all the other relatives I'd never met. Oh, Zuzana, I am so glad you finally came!"

I was glad, too – why had it taken me so long?

"So she was cured?" I asked.

"It seemed so, and it was wonderful; we went on trips, all three of us, and vacations. When I was 17, my parents took me to Italy and France: Paris, Florence, Venice, Rome. In Paris, we stayed with my mother's brother Otto and his wife Marie. They were lovely, but of course you know them well, too."

"Otto is the family fairy godmother." I told them about our visits to Paris and about the Prague flat Otto bought.

"I thought about studying French and art history, and Uncle Otto suggested I could come to Paris.

'We cannot afford that,' said my father. 'But we can,' said Aunt Marie.

Later, I overheard them talking about it; Otto said that I needed to get out of the family. He was right: Mother was getting depressed again; I couldn't wait to go away."

"How come you could study in France? Did you speak French?" I was good at languages – maybe it runs in the family.

"I told you he speaks better Mandarin than I do!" Jiu came back to the conversation.

Then Nathan told me something surprising. "Studying in France was great. To my father's annoyance, I joined the communist party. This was the McCarthy era; the police came to interview my parents."

Jiu had heard it all before; she was tapping out a text on her phone.

"Uncle Otto was furious. The communists had taken everything we had, and they were the reason we emigrated and why I could not go to my beloved mother's funeral – how could I do that?! That was almost as bad as joining the Nazi party!'

"We argued a lot. He still paid for my studies, but I visited them less often."

"Otto was right," I said. "You don't understand this – you didn't grow up in a totalitarian country!"

"I didn't stay a communist for long." Nathan was quick to point that out; he didn't want a lecture. "I fell in love with a Hungarian girl, Klarisza, who came with her parents in 1956. She was beautiful, and I was smitten. After she told me about the Soviet invasion of 1956, and what happened in Budapest, I returned my communist party card. She made my parents and Uncle Otto very happy. However, Klarisza's father was less than happy when he met me. 'You are a Jew, aren't you?' he asked. Me telling him that I was not religious did not make any difference. I later found out he was in the Arrow Cross Party – the Hungarian fascists during the war."

"Wow, what did you do?"

"I loved Klarisza and would have stayed with her if she said that it was not OK to be a fascist. But she didn't. She said, 'I don't care that you are Jewish. You are not typical: you have a small nose, blue eyes and you are not money-grabbing. You are different from those other, nasty Jews.'"

How well I knew this from Harry. People also told him he wasn't typical.

"That was the end. I told her that her father probably killed some of my distant relatives and he would kill my parents. I said that I could cope with that if she was not an idiotic antisemite, too. She was beautiful, but stupid!"

"Did you tell her she was stupid?"

"Yes, I did."

"What did she do?"

Jiu stopped tapping her phone and started listening again. She'd never heard about Klarisza before.

"She slapped my cheek and I slapped her back."

Jiu was even more surprised than I was. "You really slapped her back?" She was amazed.

"Yes, and she deserved it!"

Nathan then told me about his studies and how when he came back from France, he returned to a happy home. Judita had started new antidepressants, and she was better. Simon and Judita started meeting friends, playing tennis, and Nathan discovered for the first time that his mother could be funny.

"There was laughter in our house. My mother sang funny songs, baked cakes, and my father could concentrate on his academic career. It was wonderful.

"In October 1968, they were going to Prague to visit you. Of course, 21 August 1968, the Russians invaded. My father never went back to Prague, and I doubt my mother ever will.

"I'd like to go. I wasn't going to go with them in 1968, though, because I fell in love with Jiu.

"Her parents were not crazy about her marrying a white person, and a Jew. But when I met Ann Mei, my future mother-in-law, we hit it off immediately."

"Yes, he and my mum keep ganging up on me!" Jiu smiled. "They agree on so many things. Mainly that I am untidy, read and shop too much, and never looked after Becky properly. Well, she survived."

"Maybe she moved to New Zealand to put some distance between you and her." But Nathan was joking.

Jiu slapped him playfully and kissed him. "You are an awful husband, Nathan!"

"And now she is beating me – Zuzana, have you seen it?"

"You deserved it." I liked Jiu very much.

She was also obviously a good mother; Becky and Jiu spent an hour on the phone three times a week. The time zones were not bad: 21 hours – that made it easy, as they just had to remember that the date was different.

I remembered those painful conversations I used to have with my mother. This was different.

We all kept away from talking about Judita; it was too painful for Nathan. But the next day, he started talking about it on his own, while Jiu was at work.

He told me they had about ten happy years. Jiu and Nathan were temporarily in North Carolina, and one year, when they came back for Thanksgiving, Simon was ill, skeletal and pale.

"Did your parents celebrate Thanksgiving? I never thought they would – not a European thing."

"They no longer felt European. My parents were always telling me that we were American." Nathan looked slightly offended.

I told him that in England, despite living there for the past 25 years, I was always going to be a foreigner. "They keep asking me where my lovely accent comes from, which is annoying. Sometimes I wish I emigrated to the USA. What was wrong with your dad?" I asked.

"He wasn't looking good so I told him to go and see a doctor. Father said, 'Don't worry, I'm all right.' He was not. It only took about a week to diagnose his pancreatic cancer. Mother looked after him like a professional nurse and held it in till his funeral. We had a funeral reception; she prepared all the food and invited many guests. Everybody said how brave she was."

Nathan spoke so quietly I had to lean forward to hear. He told me that the next day was her first suicide attempt. The first of about ten. She was put on new, stronger antidepressants, but nothing helped. The psychiatrists kept changing her medication; they even put her on lithium. She wasn't eating and spent most of her day in bed. Nathan worried she might have cancer, too, but physically, she was healthy.

"She is slowly dying, Zuzana." Nathan had tears in his eyes again.

CHAPTER TWELVE

Zuzana 2005

VISITING JUDITA IN HOSPITAL

Next day, he took me to see her. He said that I might cheer her up.

It was awkward to start with. The thin old woman in the hospital room had her eyes closed. When she heard us, she whispered, "Nathan, I told you not to come; it upsets you, and you cannot help."

Then I had an idea. A brilliant idea, I thought. "Aunt Judita, but you can help me; in fact, you could help me a lot. I am Zuzana, Magda's daughter, and I came to the USA to meet all my relatives."

She didn't seem interested, but I noticed her eyes opening and closing again. She saw me. So, I told her about my life, my mother, my emigration. It's hard to stop me once I get going. She didn't move, but she was listening. Nathan was quiet, too. He was staring at me. Then I got even bolder. What did I have to lose?

"Aunt Judita, I know you want to die, but nobody can help you do that. Why don't you try to help me? It must be more interesting than lying in bed with your eyes closed!"

Nathan's jaw dropped, but he didn't say anything.

And then, astonishingly, Judita smiled. "You know, you are like your mother. Even as a child, she never took no for an answer."

I didn't like to be compared to my mother, but I supposed it was worth it.

I started visiting Judita daily with my laptop. I always brought some food, allegedly for my packed lunch, but she didn't refuse when I offered her half, saying working people needed food. Judita started talking in a quiet, monotonous voice, but it was getting stronger. She told me about her life before the war, her mother Olga and falling in love with Simon.

She talked slowly, and sometimes it was too quiet for me to hear.

"You know, Zuzana, the guilt will never leave me."

Guilt? I thought. *What guilt? I am sure your terrible mother Olga never felt guilty.*

Judita told me about her marrying Simon in summer 1938. "Simon and I were so in love. You have never met a man like Simon; he was gentle and so smart. Simon used to tell me about books he'd read; he was far more educated than I was, but he never let me feel that my brain was inferior to his. The day he asked me to marry him, he said, 'Judita, you are not only beautiful and kind but also a very smart, articulate woman – I love you. Will you marry me?'"

"That is so romantic, but I am sure he was right: of course you are smart, Aunt Judita."

She told me that her family, especially Hana's father – Judita's brother Karel – always treated her like some retarded pupil.

"But I met Hana in London, and she was lovely." I wanted to say some more, but I was glad Judita was talking to me, so I shut up.

"I loved Simon. Living with him was like living with a walking encyclopaedia. He knew everything. It was always the same: he seemed always right. Once when I told him that, he smiled. 'I am always right because I only talk about things I know. There are many things I don't know.'"

Hmmm, that was smart, I thought.

Judita told me that she could never understand how this good-looking, kind and so intelligent man could have married her. "My mother sometimes used to say I was slow. I often felt stupid."

Judita seemed to be still hurt by that. I remembered my mother and her critical comments. There was nothing stupid about Judita.

I got angry. "So if your mother made you feel that way, it was good that you emigrated, Aunt Judita!"

She didn't like that. "Zuzana, it was so hard. I worried when he decided we should emigrate. I feared my mother. She didn't want us to leave."

Judita was tired and upset. "You should go, Zuzana," she said.

However, Judita let me come back the next day. She told me that like many other Jewish people at that time, they used to talk about emigration constantly. They all knew somebody in Austria. Some refugees from Vienna managed to come to Prague just after Hitler marched to Austria in March 1938.

Judita suddenly seemed young and gossipy. "I remember Emilia, the sleek blonde from Vienna, an elegant girl with pearl earrings and a necklace, always dressed in black. When she was around, we all spoke German, especially the men. Zuzana, she was flirting with all of them, and the men were all flocking around her, bringing her drinks, undressing her with their eyes. I even worried about Simon. I was testing waters and said how beautiful Emilia was. But Simon surprised me. 'She is a flirt; she doesn't have your beautiful eyes, and you are much more intelligent than she is. Besides, I never liked dyed blonde hair.' That felt good."

Simon really knew exactly what to say. I was amused.

"Emilia didn't want to stay in Prague; she wanted to leave Europe, go to America. She said that Prague was too close to Vienna. We all thought Emilia was being too dramatic, pretending to feel faint when nobody paid her enough attention or complaining of 'dreadful migraines'. It always worked, with the men offering her a glass of water or an arm to lean on. She cried easily and talked about nightmares. But we were foolish not to take her seriously."

"Did you meet other Austrian refugees?" I'd read about many famous people who came scientists, writers, artists.

"I met the painter Kokoschka, at your grandparents' – Franzi and Bruno's – house. He and Bruno were in the cavalry together in 1915 in the war. He was a strange man, but nice, although I did not like his paintings. Simon did. Kokoschka was not Jewish, but the Nazis didn't like his paintings either. This was one thing I agreed with them on, but his art did not do any harm. Why didn't the Nazis leave him alone?' 'Why don't they leave the Jews alone, Judita?' said Simon. Mr Kokoschka was nervous about staying in Prague, too. It was still too close."

Judita carried on in her monotonous voice.

"I remember talking to Otto and Marie; Otto wanted to emigrate, too. Marie told him Czechs were different, not antisemitic. Still Simon, Otto and my sister Helena's husband Hans kept talking about leaving. I didn't really want to leave, but when Kristallnacht came in November, it was obvious that Emilia was right. There were more Jews coming now, from Sudetenland, from Slovakia; some of them were those Polish Jews with their hats and long coats, speaking Yiddish. We didn't like them. They endangered our assimilation. Some of the Czech press didn't like them either. They kept writing about Czechoslovakia being filled with foreign Jews."

"What made you leave?" I asked Judita, but there was a knock on the door; the nurses brought her medication.

"I have to go, but I'll be back tomorrow, then you can tell me," I said.

"A bad penny always turns up," Judita mumbled, but when I looked at her, she was smiling.

I told Nathan about Judita telling me about the time before the war, and the next day, he insisted he would come with me. He was curious. "I am so amazed that you got Mother talking! What's your secret, Zuzana?"

"Pure chutzpah," I said. Funny, I was learning all those Yiddish expressions here in America. I'd heard this one from Petr.

Next day, Nathan and I asked Judita to tell us why they didn't obey my Great-Grandma Olga like the others.

"It was hard. Everybody was arguing. The worst was my sister Helena and her husband Hans. 'It is all your brother's influence. Let him move to America if he wants to; I want to stay here, by my family!' shouted Helena. My mother gave Hans a nasty look. 'Are you and your brother still thinking about that crazy plan?' Hans just shrugged. In the end, Samuel, my sister Helena's brother-in-law, left, with his wife and daughter. Samuel wanted his brother Hans and his family to go, too, but Helena had her way and they stayed."

"Yes, Miriam told me."

Judita was still jealous of the pretty Austrian girl, Emilia. "Emilia left for America," she said. "None of my female friends missed Emilia, but the men probably did. Simon was getting restless. He wanted us to leave, too. It made me so nervous. I felt sick and I couldn't eat. But it was not just nerves that made me sick: I was pregnant. Simon and I talked all night, and the next day, when we were all having another lunch with my mother, we told them all that we'd decided to emigrate.

"Everybody was talking at once, shouting; only Hana, the niece I didn't really like, was with us. She was thinking about emigration, too. 'We all go, or nobody leaves; the family belongs together,' said my mother. My heart sank. *This is it. We will never leave*, I thought. Part of me was upset, but also relieved. Simon wanted to go to America – he had some distant relatives in California – but I did not speak English and travelling that far was frightening. But then Simon squeezed my hand and said quietly, 'Go, tell your mother that you are pregnant. Ask her if she really thinks this is a good place for having a baby. Tell her we don't.' I told her, Nathan. I don't know what gave me the courage – your grandmother Olga was the strongest woman I met."

Judita told us that she whispered in her mother's ear that she was pregnant, and that Olga surprisingly straightened her back, looked at Judita, and said,

"Oh, go then, if you must! But I don't like it."

"Zuzana, I still didn't feel like I could do it, but Simon was adamant. 'Our baby will be born in a safe country, Judita – that is important. You know it is the right decision.'"

"That probably saved our lives," said Nathan. He'd never heard this story before.

Judita continued: "On the liner to America, I was very seasick. My pregnancy didn't help. Not very attractive – a vomiting woman. But Simon held my head when I was sick and kept bringing me tea and some food which would surely make it better. The food didn't help but his kindness did."

"He sounds like a wonderful husband. My husband is like that: kind, reliable, loving," I said. *And great in bed*, I thought but didn't say. I missed Harry.

"Oh, Simon was so wonderful. In America, when I couldn't speak English, he arranged for a teacher, and he gave me lessons, too. He was so kind and such a wonderful father. It was not common for fathers to change nappies or help their wives. He always did.

"He got a job as a clerk in a bank, although he was a doctor of philosophy. He never complained. And Nathan, you were such a wonderful baby. There was a war, but we were happy. California was full of Jewish people, and they were trying to help us."

"Did they find Simon work?" I asked.

"Yes, one of them arranged an interview for Simon at the university and he got the job." Judita told us that Simon loved his job, teaching philosophy, and the American students, who he said were bright and enthusiastic.

He used to invite them home on Sunday evening. Judita told me she was shy to start with, but they were all so polite!

"They called me Ma'am. I gave them dinner, but they always insisted on doing the washing up. Zuzana, we had such a wonderful life that I felt it couldn't last. Of course, we were worried about our families, but somehow, I thought: *No news is good news. They will be alright. Hitler is losing the war.* I was naïve."

Judita looked different; her eyes had a sparkle, but then she started talking about 1945. The time the news came. Those films of the liberated camps, the skeletal survivors.

"In California, throughout the war, hearing the news, I was so glad we left, but I also felt guilty, as if the fact that I abandoned my family made things worse for them. I was safe; they were not. After the war, we found out the details of all the horrors. It was awful. We wrote, put adverts into newspapers; we hoped. Then we got a letter from Prague from my brother Otto with all the news."

Judita started to cry. "Oh, Zuzana, I couldn't bear the thought of my nieces and nephews, all those other relatives, their suffering, their despair. I couldn't bear the thought of my old mother, sick in Prague, feeling guilty, as if it was all her fault."

But it was her fault, I thought.

"I couldn't bear the guilt, the guilt of a survivor. I cried a lot. Simon was brave, Zuzana. 'Life has to go on and we have little Nathan to think about,' he said. But he had nightmares, too, waking up sweating. I worried, but he told me he was all right. My brave Simon. His parents, sister, grandparents – they all vanished in Auschwitz. We never talked about it in detail. I couldn't stop crying; I did not manage to get up, look after my child. I didn't wash; I was getting smelly."

Nathan looked worried. "Let's stop," he said. "This is making you worse, Mom."

"There is not much more. Your father suggested I go to a psychiatrist. I didn't want to go. 'You think I am crazy?' I screamed at him. He kissed me and told me that I was not crazy, just too sad. In the end, I did see the psychiatrist and had various treatments, even ECT. Nothing helped. And as you can see, I am back with the shrinks, those wretched creatures."

The strange thing was, Judita smiled when she said that. She then told me about all the treatments, the relapses – I knew about that from her son Nathan already. She told us about the despair but also about the good times. She told me how she felt she could beat the depression when Simon was on her side.

"But Judita, you have Nathan and his family, and now me. You must meet my husband Harry; the way I feel about him is the same way you felt about your Simon. We are so lucky to get married to such wonderful men."

I ended up changing my ticket. I decided to stay in California longer. I took more unpaid leave from work. I felt like we were helping each other. Judita was getting better, but so was I.

I told her about my mother and about my depression after she died.

One day, the psychiatrist told Judita she could go home if she would agree to come for consultation three times a week.

"You just want more money," Judita said, but again, her smile, so rare, appeared.

When I told Nathan on the phone, he gasped. He didn't say anything. When I got to their house and went to the guest bedroom to change, there was a big bouquet of roses on the bedside table with a card. *Thank you for bringing my mother back!*

CHAPTER THIRTEEN

Zuzana 2005

When I was not talking to Judita or spending time with Nathan and Jiu, I was looking for Joan, Irma's daughter. Nathan and Jiu said they'd last seen her a year ago and gave me her address, but when I went there, I was told that she no longer lived there. I thought the girl who lived in the apartment looked a bit shifty, so I gave her a note: "Just in case Joan pops by." The girl did not say anything, but she took the note.

Our whole family is curious – maybe Joan is, too, I thought. She was. In a week, a tall dark-haired woman in dreadlocks, holding the hand of a little boy, rang the bell of Nathan's house. She didn't have to say anything; she looked exactly like Irma from the old photographs I'd seen. Apart from the dreadlocks, of course.

I immediately said, "Joan?"

The boy was almost black; his father must have been a dark African American. "Yes," Joan said. "You were looking for me? Why?"

I seemed to be lucky; with my family, I somehow always said the right things. "We are the same age, and I had such a difficult mother that I illegally emigrated from Prague aged 19 just to get away. Your dad is not easy either."

Joan chuckled and followed me in. The boy's name was Aaron.

He was four. He spoke Spanish to me, but when I didn't understand, he switched to English.

"My husband's family is from Grenada; my son is black, too. I think gene pool mixing is good, don't you? I took unpaid leave to find out about all those relatives I never met. My mother never talked about the past; she didn't even tell me I was Jewish. I met your mum; she is so lovely. I visited years ago, when you were a teenager, but you weren't at home."

I was going to tell Joan about Miriam and Judita, but she was more curious about my mother. I told her about my mother's ability to hurt me with words.

"Unfortunately, you can't divorce your mother."

"Can't you? I divorced my father," said Joan.

We spent a pleasant hour moaning about our parents.

I told her that my mother had died, and how the bereavement was harder for the sorrow that our relationship was not better. I told her that having a difficult mother made me hopefully a better parent. Joan was easy to talk to, but I noticed she did not tell me much about herself.

I told her about Miriam and what she'd told me about our great-grandmother Olga.

"What a bitch!" she said. I agreed.

Joan had a sarcastic sense of humour. I liked the way she talked to her son, who was very well behaved. We went for dinner; she took me to a small Dominican restaurant. The food was amazing; I had goat curry.

"They should get a Michelin star," I said.

"Whoa, Juan, come here, my cousin says you should get a Michelin star!" Juan, the cook, a handsome, tall black man chuckled, and came to our table.

"Daddy, Daddy!" shouted Aaron jumping and laughing. Juan kissed Aaron and Joan, and said, "Hello, Joan's cousin from Europe. Nice to meet you, Zuzana!" He pronounced my name in a strange way. It sounded like 'Huhanna'.

We talked long after the restaurant closed. Aaron was sleeping on his father's lap, and Joan and I talked and talked. Juan was dozing off, too. My mobile rang. Nathan was worried, but when I told him where I was, he asked me to invite Joan and her family for lunch on Sunday.

Joan and I saw each other almost every day. I invited her and her family to England. "I don't have the money," she said. I remembered the generosity of Uncle Otto. "If we can find some cheap flights, I will pay for your tickets."

"Juan wouldn't allow you to pay for his ticket, but maybe I could come with Aaron."

"Yes, our Adam is good with kids; the only thing is he might teach Aaron how to climb trees. He used to be like a monkey, always somewhere high." I showed Joan a picture of Adam the same age Aaron is now, sitting on the top of a tree in the garden.

When I got back to Nathan and Jiu's house, I had an email from the sister of my stepfather Tomas, telling me that Tomas died. I felt guilty; I didn't keep in touch with him. I was no better stepdaughter than I was a daughter. I couldn't go to his funeral because I was in the USA, but I arranged to send flowers. I was pleased to have a good excuse for not going; I didn't want to talk about my mother and Tomas with his sister. I never had much in common with Tomas. He was probably nicer than I thought, but I couldn't respect him, with his ignorant opinions. I suppose I should have been grateful that he took my mother off my hands for a while.

I stayed in California for another two weeks and then I flew to New Jersey. It was time to meet the other part of my family – Grandma Franzi's sister Hilda, her German husband and their family.

I also planned to see Irma again and talk to her about Joan.

I asked for Joan's permission. "It won't be any good – my father won't forgive me for leaving."

I hugged her; she looked sad. *We'll see*, I thought. *Maybe I can help to patch things up before it is too late. Then Joan won't have regrets when Petr dies.* I didn't want Joan to go through what I'd been through.

CHAPTER FOURTEEN

Zuzana 2005

It was nice to see that some good people lived as long as Jürgen and Hilda. My grandmother Franzi's sister Hilda was now 94. Her German husband Jürgen was almost 96. Even their daughter Lucy, born after the war, was 57. Time was running out, so I flew to visit them in New Jersey from California. I had another ten days before flying home to London.

I was picked up at Newark Airport by Lucy, a rather fat woman wearing trainers and a long skirt with elasticated waist. I remembered Grandma Franzi telling me how elegant Lucy's mother used to be. I wondered what she thought about her daughter's appearance. Lucy looked awful, but she was jolly, in a loud, friendly way. We had never met before, but she behaved as if she'd known me since childhood.

In the car, she offered me chocolate and had a large piece, too. It was nice, Hershey's. I only had a small piece, as I'd put on weight in America, and I didn't want to end up looking like Lucy.

It was a long drive to the seaside resort Sea Girt where they all lived.

"Ma and Pa moved here when they sold their shop in New York – my mother loves the ocean. She used to collect sea glass."

I didn't know what sea glass was, so she explained it was ordinary glass shaped and smoothed by the sea. Sea Girt was picturesque, with wooden bungalows – the Americans call them 'ranches' – and some large houses. Lucy parked in front of an enormous wooden house, close to the beach, with three floors and a wide, large garden.

"Is this a hotel?" I asked.

"A hotel? Are you shitting me? This is where we all live. We moved in when my parents became too frail."

The good-looking old man who opened the door did not look frail: tall, very straight back, blue eyes, face full of wrinkles but thick white hair. Jürgen didn't look 96. He had a wide smile, and I remembered the family gossip that he used to work as a gigolo. He was still handsome and charming.

Hilda was frail, bent with osteoporosis and walking with two sticks; she was a tiny woman. Her face looked confused. "Who are you?" she asked. I told her. "Who are you?" she asked again. She was in a loop.

"Dementia," Lucy whispered in my ear.

Jürgen took Hilda's hand and said, "She is a niece, a very nice girl." He repeated it patiently five times.

Hilda's eyes brightened when she looked at him. They were not the dull eyes of a confused old woman; they were sparkling with love. It didn't last long, she got quickly tired and went to sleep. Jürgen went with her to tuck her in, like a child.

"It started with the hoarding," said Lucy. "My mother never threw anything out – you should have seen this house when I moved in. All the furniture was covered in stuff. Books, journals, programmes of concerts, but also packaging from things, just in case she could use it in the future. Dad tried to tidy things up, but it was impossible, wasn't it?"

"Lucy, stop it, it wasn't so bad." Jürgen seemed embarrassed.

"Jesus, it was! The house started to get smelly, too. It took forever before we realised that Mum was losing it. She did a good job trying to hide it. I think the doctors call it a good social front. But in the end, the confusion got bad quickly. That was when I decided to move in with my boys."

"You wouldn't think three boys moving in would make the house tidier, but they all helped." Jürgen smiled at his daughter.

"I just chucked a lot of things out." Lucy laughed. "I am going to make some dinner and let you two talk about the past, Zuzana. You are writing it down for your son, right? Can't wait to read it!"

Jürgen told me about their beginning in America after the war. People treated him with suspicion because of his German accent.

"My darling Hilda kept telling everybody I was a hero who saved her from the Nazis. It was embarrassing, but it helped." I didn't detect any German accent remaining.

The house was full of beautiful ceramic sculptures and unusual vases. All Hilda's work.

Lucy brought us a coffee. "Yes, we always had an American flag on the house, and my father kept telling me 20 times a day how this is the best country in the world. It made me want to move to another continent. You were embarrassing, Daddy!" But she smiled.

I asked about Lucy's three sons.

"Jack and Tony are with my ex, Sean, in LA. The guy is a real douchebag, but the kids are beach bums, and the sea is warmer there, so what d'ya do?" Lucy shrugged. "Honestly, though. I appreciate the quiet – teenagers are a god-awful menace. Ross lives in New York."

When we were alone, I asked Lucy about her ex and why he was an asshole.

Lucy just waved her arm. "He was a nebbish. A schmuck. But he loves the boys, spoils them rotten."

Here is the Yiddish again; my mother told me they never spoke it, but here in America, all of them use those Yiddish expressions. I wonder why? I thought. I asked Lucy.

"All New Yorkers use Yiddish expressions, even non-Jews." She smiled. "We also swear more than Europeans." Yes, I had noticed that, too.

I stayed for five days. Sea Girt was beautiful. I walked by the ocean and swam; it was surprisingly warmer than in California.

I admired the way Lucy looked after Hilda. She helped her do some simple drawings and pottery, talked to her, read her poems – simple, childish ones. She patiently answered Hilda's questions again and again. She treated her like a small child, but with respect.

I tried to talk to Jürgen more about the past, but he didn't want to. "We left Europe behind, as well as us being German or Jewish. We are Americans. The past is not relevant," said Jürgen. So I didn't find out anything more. I wanted to ask him about his imprisonment in the war, about his other German daughter, but he wouldn't talk to me about it. Like any true hero, Jürgen didn't feel heroic.

After that, there was nothing much to talk about. I told him how I found out about being Jewish. He thought it was wise of Grandma and Mum not telling me. I used to be so angry about Mother lying to me like that, but I started to understand the reasons. It seemed that by getting to know the relatives, I was getting to know Mother better, too.

I went for walks, pushing Hilda in a wheelchair, but she still didn't recognise me and asked me who I was every morning.

I thought about the other older ones: my mother, Miriam, Hana, Judita, those women with sharp brains. Yet Hilda seemed happy.

It was time to go back home. I hadn't seen Harry for almost two months. Suddenly, I wanted to hold him, kiss him, talk to him. And yes, make love to him. It had been too long dealing with the past. I was going back to the present and future.

CHAPTER FIFTEEN

Zuzana 2005

I AM BACK HOME, BUT I LOSE MY JOB

I was back home. I wondered if I was a bad mother because I was glad just being with Harry. I loved it when Adam came back from university for a weekend, but I also loved it when he left again. Being alone with Harry was wonderful, especially after my long American trip. We talked, and he wanted to know everything about my relatives. We didn't even see much of our friends; we were both hungry for each other. People talked about the 'empty nest syndrome' when their children went to university. I liked having an empty nest and an adult son who was independent but enjoyed our company enough to see us often.

I wanted to go back to work, but when I called my supervisor Mrs McBride to tell her I could start next week, she said,

"I have arranged for you to have an appointment with the head of the department. We need to talk." I was nervous. *Don't they want me back?*

The interview was strange. "We have Adrianne Price, a young social worker who did your work when you were away. She was inexperienced to start with, but she is very good. We were thinking about putting you in the office, to deal with the paper reports of other social workers and to organise their work. You would be an assistant to Janet McBride, who would have more time to deal with problems and complaints." The director sounded as if he was reading a speech.

"You mean I wouldn't be dealing with clients anymore? I love working with people; that was the reason I became a social worker!"

I was speaking slowly and quietly, but I was furious. "I only took the unpaid leave on Janet's suggestion and I thought the agreement was that I was coming back to my job, that it would be protected!"

"You were crying with clients and you couldn't do your job – you should have gone off sick for longer! But you were so stubborn about it that the unpaid leave was the only solution. It was your husband's idea!"

I had to admit that she was right, but I was all right now, and I wanted my job back. We had another half an hour with Janet and the director trying to sell me the idea of office work, and I got more and more cross. I didn't want to work in an office.

In the end, we agreed to another meeting. The director and Janet tried to pretend that this job was a promotion; they told me the salary would be the same but would go up after six months.

"How long will the young social worker stay? Her name is Adrianne, right? I am happy to wait for two to three months until she goes."

That was me being manipulative. It was obvious they wanted to keep things as they were.

"Oh, Adrianne is staying; she now has a permanent contract," Janet said.

After arranging the next meeting, I left quickly to avoid them seeing me crying. That would not have helped my case. I had to be rational.

Harry helped. He listened and asked questions.

"Are you sure you don't want to do what they are suggesting, Zuzana? If you are, don't do it. You always wanted to be a writer. Maybe this is a sign. We have savings, I earn good money and I could do some extra nights or weekends. And when I come home from work, you can read to me what you wrote, but not before we fuck each other senseless."

I just stared at him. Was he serious? Was he teasing me? What would my in-laws say? That I was a kept woman? Angela always worked. But then I started dreaming; stories, sentences, plots just got to my head, trying to get out. *Harry is right: I am a writer. If not now, when?* I thought.

Adam came for the weekend. "Oh, Mum, I am so jealous. I have to finish my course, otherwise Grandma Angie will kill me. And I need to live a bit more so that I have stuff to write about. But then, I will write, too."

At first, I was going to write down all those family stories for Adam and maybe future grandchildren, not to publish, just for us. After that, I was thinking seriously about writing fiction. Harry was convinced I could do it. Of course, Harry loved me, he was deluded.

I kept worrying about my literary English not being good enough.

"Rubbish," said Adam. "Your English is fine, Mum. Let's see which one of us becomes a more successful writer."

Harry had enough of being a family saint and started to tease us.

"Yes, you can both support me in my old age with those bestsellers. Will you buy me a house in the south of France? I will let you use it as your writing base while I am swimming in the sea or eating all that marvellous food."

"Nope," I said. "You don't deserve it because you are being sarcastic. We will have an authors' nest there, but you can stay in a hotel. Unless you are really nice to us and act as our secretary. Chasing journalists away, dealing with publishers, running the house. Right, Adam, shouldn't that be Dad's role?"

"I think I'd rather stay a doctor. Running your business would be like trying to herd cats."

"Miaow." Adam made a cat face.

But my wonderful husband made a serious face and told us we were both talented, and he couldn't wait to read our books.

At the next meeting at work, I told them I was not coming back. It hurt to see the relief on their faces.

Writing was not as easy as I thought. I would write three pages, then rewrite them, again and again. *Tolstoy rewrote Anna Karenina nine times and it's a masterpiece*, I thought. But I was not Tolstoy. I was full of doubts. But like any skill, writing improves with practice. Apart from poetry and short stories, I started writing a novel about a woman emigrating from Czechoslovakia, like I did. I made her a doctor; Harry could help me with the practical details. I suppose all first novels are partly autobiographical. The main character, whom I named after Hana, but with a different spelling – Hannah – would have a wonderful relationship with her parents, and she would take them with her when she emigrates. Hannah would be a mirror image of me. She would be nicer, happier, more loving to her family. Her mother would be a lucky woman. *That book might help me, like that letter I wrote to my mother on advice of the psychotherapist*, I thought.

I liked having a go at being a full-time writer, but I was probably going to need another job, if our money ran out.

CHAPTER SIXTEEN

Zuzana 2005

I TURN INTO A SNOOPING MOTHER

I was worried about Adam. When I was in America, he'd told me he had met that redhead from school. He'd told me she was weird but stunningly beautiful. They'd started dating while I was still away. It didn't last. Harry told me that they'd split up but now were together again.

"Adam told me she was being nasty in front of his friends, but he was unhappy when they split up. Now they are together again. It's probably lust rather than love," said Harry. Did he think I would find that reassuring?

"Adam is dating the evil redhead! She is going to hurt him!" I said to Harry.

He laughed and accused me of being a typical protective Jewish mama. Bang, I threw the apple I was eating at him.

Adam told me about her, too. "Siobhan is a bit strange but very smart; I think you'll like her. May I invite her for dinner?" I said yes, of course – I was curious.

That was when I started snooping. I was in Adam's room and looked for a book I couldn't find. In his drawer, there was a typed story called *The Evil Redhead*.

I should have left it, but I read it. *It's literature*, I tried to reassure myself. But no, I was a horrible, snooping mother.

What he wrote was not a sci-fi story. It all started with him describing the situation at the playground. I skipped through this; I already knew that. I wanted to read about them at uni.

... The Evil Redhead was at the party.

"Remember me?" I asked.

She wasn't embarrassed. "Yes, and your mother," she said. She is beautiful, but cold, withdrawn. Her name is Siobhan; she studies mathematics. I should hate her, but something pulls me to her. I wonder what my mum would say if I told her: "I am dating the Evil Redhead."

Siobhan never smiles. Is she autistic? No, autistic people are not manipulative.

I ask her out.

"Do you want to fall in love or just want to fuck?" she asks.

That was different to other girls, but I found the right answer. "Let's fuck. If we like it, let's go further."

She smiled, just with her mouth; her eyes were still cold.

We fucked.

In fact, we hardly did anything else for a week. She kissed me, sucked my cock, moved like a beautiful snake. When she came, she made a strange, choked, short noise, then she closed her eyes and went quiet. The sex was great, but I did not get any closer to Siobhan. She doesn't talk much, and when she does, she is often hostile. I am never quite sure why. Sometimes I feel like I am being cross-examined in a court by the prosecutor. But I am not sure what crime I am being accused of.

"Do you want to come running in the park, Siobhan?"

"So that you can show off for being faster? Nope."

"That was lovely, I love being so deep inside you."

"You don't get that deep; your cock would need to be bigger." Siobhan smirked.

Then she started a strange game: humiliating me in public. In the canteen she said loudly, "Oh, Adam, you are going to cry again, aren't you, Mummy's boy?"

I never cried in front of Siobhan. I felt like hitting her. I didn't. I got up. "You think you are such a great fuck that it's worth this? You are just a boring iceberg."

I left; I heard my friends clapping. It felt good.

I was snooping on my son's sex life, unforgivable, but I carried on reading.

The writing continued. Now he wrote from her point of view. The writing was good, but I felt he was just making excuses for her.

Siobhan

At home, anything you said could be used against you. My father said that his main role as a parent was to make us tough. I am tough all right. So are my older brothers; I had to learn how to defend myself. My put-downs work well, though, I met the boy with the scary mother again. His name is Adam. It used to be fun to slap him, trying to provoke a reaction. I am sometimes nasty to people because I can be. Maybe it makes them tougher. And that is a good thing, isn't it?

Yet Adam sometimes kissed me gently all over. I will miss that. I like sex. Being touched, and fucked, slow, or hard and fast. Sometimes I like to be in charge, fucking the boys, not them fucking me.

Adam was different. The careful way he touched me, as if I was fragile and could break. Yet he was not shy: his fingers went everywhere. We didn't talk much. Adam is a writer; he might find me boring. I am good at maths. Not a good conversation topic. It is safer to be mysterious.

Adam used his tongue to gently lick me. I used my tongue to inject him with poison.

I'll find someone else. Boys find me attractive. Mainly because I don't care. It is safer.

It was interesting that he imagined her point of view. He wrote well, but was he right? Then it went back to Adam.

I met Siobhan in the canteen today. Normally she just gives me her cold stare. Today, she smiled. "Hello, Adam, how are you?"

Siobhan doesn't smile or do small talk. "Hello to you, too. Who are you? Siobhan's smiling, talking identical twin?" It just fell from my mouth.

Her smile froze. But she looked vulnerable. Must be her twin, I thought. But my arms wanted to embrace her. I embraced her.

"Oh, Adam, I am so sorry!" she said, and then I just started kissing off her tears. The iceberg started to melt. Climate change, maybe?

Ever since then, Siobhan has changed. We talk about our families and films, and of course, we have sex. In mine or her room, in the park and yesterday in the kitchen. The danger of somebody coming made it more exciting.

She doesn't like to be with my friends; she claims they are boring.

Sometimes, she still gets cold and sarcastic. But I discovered a weapon. I look at her and kiss her. She never pushes me away. I asked her to come over and meet my parents.

"Your scary mother? No way!" she said.

"My parents are fun, and you are not the Evil Redhead anymore!"

"Is that what you called me? Adam, maybe that is what I am." She was crying again, pretending something got in her eye. I kissed her. It always worked.

When I asked my mum, she just said, "Does she eat fish?

Yes, I remembered. This was not a short story; this was a diary masking as literature, and I had no right to read it.

Siobhan came the next day. She didn't talk much; Adam and I did all the talking. Harry would say that was normal. She was interesting, stunning, hiding her shyness behind that cold exterior. She brought me a box of chocolates, Cadbury's Roses. I tried to make her talk; I even asked about mathematics, but of course, I didn't have a clue, so she just stared at me and then politely changed the subject. I remembered the time I met her in the schoolyard. I wondered what was behind it all. I asked about her family, but she didn't answer. She was strange but seemed surprisingly vulnerable.

Siobhan started to come on some Saturdays, sometimes staying overnight in Adam's room, sometimes leaving after lunch. Angela joined us occasionally, and they played bridge while I was cooking lunch. Richard worked in the pharmacy on Saturdays, but he didn't play bridge anyway. Siobhan was scarily good at bridge, but she was rather magnanimous when Adam messed something up. Neither Harry nor Adam were particularly competitive, and they talked, not paying proper attention to the cards. Harry's mother was much more critical of his bridge skills, so he now partnered with Adam, and Angela and Siobhan could play together. They always won, but Adam and Harry didn't care; they just wanted to have fun.

I thought Adam was cheating on Siobhan; when I drove to see him at university, I saw him kissing a different girl. I didn't say anything. I had no right to. I changed boyfriends like knickers when I was his age. Beautiful girls often hurt boys, yet his beautiful Evil Redhead seemed vulnerable. I didn't want my son to hurt her. I didn't say anything, but I wondered if Adam still wrote about her, so I did something inexcusable: I went to snoop again. I found it right away. The diary was in his backpack.

This afternoon, Siobhan saw me kissing Claire in the park. She screamed; it sounded like a fox or a cat, an animal. Claire and I both jumped.

"Hang on, Claire, sorry!" I said and pushed her away.

I ran after Siobhan. I run faster than she does, but when I reached for her, she turned and slapped me, hard.

It was as if we'd made a full circle. But this time I deserved it. I caught her hand; she scratched me with her free hand: long, blue varnished nails. I wanted to hug her.

"Don't!" she said. She was talking in a quiet, flat voice, but I knew she meant it. Then she just walked away, slowly, and I think she was crying. Just big tears, no sound.

What have I done?! I turned back to the bench, but Claire was no longer there.

I am worried about Siobhan, but at the same time, I am also a bit relieved – women, who needs them?

So yes, Adam hurt Siobhan.

He seemed low. I asked what the matter was. "Nothing."

"OK," I said. "Is it Siobhan?"

Surprisingly, Adam replied, "Yes. Mum, I hurt her. I am a cheater; I am sorry. I don't deserve a girlfriend. Claire split up with me, too. I feel like such a bastard!"

"You'll learn, and you won't cheat on the one you truly love."

"Really?"

"Yes, before I met your father, I always had several boyfriends at the same time. But not with him; he was the one. You'll know."

He hugged me and left the room, embarrassed.

Adam is all right. One day, he might make some woman happy. I wondered about Siobhan, though – she seemed damaged. I almost phoned her. But I stopped myself just in time. Not everybody was my problem.

But then I did something foolish. I sent her a text. And then I wished I didn't. Was it disloyal?

As you know, we all sometimes hurt people. This time it was Adam who hurt you. I am sorry.

There is nothing I can do, but I just wanted to say: don't get bitter, Siobhan. You are both young, and one day you will be with someone just right for you, and you will protect each other from any hurt. Don't give anybody the power to make you bitter. Not even my son, whom I love. Unsolicited advice, I know.

Zuzana

She didn't reply.

When I was snooping again in Adam's room, I found a little poem. The name was 'Unencumbered':

I loved this woman,
but I was a cheater.
I love chocolate,
And chocolate is sweeter.

Hmmm. 'Men!' some women would say. But I was no better, and now I was spying on Adam. Not even my mother spied on me! I decided never to read anything private by Adam again. I felt ashamed. I didn't tell Harry; he would tell me not to do it. Adam was an adult, and he had a right to privacy. And now I was lying to Harry by omission. That really was a slippery slope.

I was worried when I drove Adam with his things to university two days later, because I'd decided to tell him about my snooping and about my text message to Siobhan. I didn't want to carry on lying to Adam, but I was nervous.

He was surprised, but I made sure he knew that I would never read his diary or letters again. I apologised, again and again, till he stopped me.

"It's all right, Mum. Dad spoke to me about Siobhan, too – he had lunch with her."

"Really? He didn't tell me. So he was worried about her, too." Harry should have told me, but I thought, *I didn't tell him about my snooping or that text to Siobhan either.*

"Dad said she seemed OK, although quiet. But Mum, Siobhan is a bit on the spectrum," Adam said. "Dad told me Siobhan got a scholarship to study at Stanford University in California."

"She must be very bright," I said.

"Yes, that is great news." Adam was obviously chuffed.

"Men! You are glad you won't have to meet her at uni, right, Adam?"

Adam didn't reply, but I was sure I was right. Siobhan was going to have a great time scaring the wits out of those American boys. I dropped him at the house he was sharing with his friends and left immediately. I was relieved. *I am never going to read Adam's private papers again.* I was looking forward to being at home with Harry.

CHAPTER SEVENTEEN

Zuzana and Adam 2005

GOING BACK TO AMERICA

Hilda died and Jürgen, so ancient and frail now, carried on living with Lucy and her sons. Lucy invited me again. They all wanted to meet Harry and Adam, too, but Harry said he couldn't take time off. Petr died before he could be reconciled with Joan, and Irma called me and cried on the phone. I called Joan who flew over to arrange the funeral, and after a very emotional few days, she confessed to me that she was thinking about moving her mother out to California. I was pleased.

"Zuzana, take Adam and go, before more of them die; they are all old." That sounded morbid, but of course, medics are morbid.

"Adam has a long summer holiday, and you two should go together. You can write in between seeing the relatives. I might fly over for a week." I didn't want to leave Harry again, but he insisted.

"Do you want to get rid of me?" I asked, only partially joking. His 'let's make love all night eyes' told me all I needed to know.

We booked the flight, Adam was excited; he had never been to America, and he'd recently started playing computer games with the twins, Lucy's sons. Now he was going to meet them.

When I was saying goodbye to Harry while Adam was having a shower, I got sentimental. I didn't want to leave Harry again, and I hoped Adam was going to get on with all those new relatives. I loved them, and I loved Adam so much, and I worried that something was going to go wrong. I loved having this big new family, but he might hate it!

But Harry kissed me and said, "Stop it, Zuzana. Adam will love it, and they will all love him. They love you, and he is just like you – you two crazy writers. How do I deserve two artists in the family?! God help me!"

That worked. Harry's jokes always made me feel better.

Losing my job and other things made me feel low. In the car, I managed not to cry by telling Harry and Adam about the itinerary. We were going to start with Lucy and the cousins in Sea Girt, but we were also going to see Miriam and Irma.

"We probably won't see Joan, Nathan and Judita," I said. "California is too far."

We talked about border control. Adam was making fun of that ridiculous ESTA questionnaire.

Are you planning to work illegally in the USA?

Have you ever been arrested or committed a crime with serious harm to property or to a person?

Have you ever dealt illegal drugs?

Are you planning to overstay in the USA?

The best was:

Have you ever engaged or seek to engage in any terrorist activity, in espionage, sabotage or genocide? Harry told him not to make any stupid jokes at the airport. "Adam, they will arrest you or not let you in! I know you; you are bound to say something stupid!" He also told Adam not to say black but Afro-American.

"That is as stupid as Afro-Caribbean – why just not say black?" I agreed with Adam, but I kept my mouth shut.

After I repeated all of Harry's advice on the plane, Adam behaved. The fat black immigration officer was very serious. He asked many questions:

"Why are you visiting? Who are the people? Do you know them?"

I wondered what Adam would say, but he turned his charm on. "No, they all emigrated from Czechoslovakia before the war to escape the Nazis. My family is half Jewish and half Afro-Caribbean, and this is my first time meeting them. My mum, who is travelling with me, met them already." He gave the officer his 'Oh, I am such an innocent, charming young man' smile. It always worked. The officer smiled and stamped his passport after taking his photo and fingerprints.

When we were waiting for luggage, Adam was still talking about the passport control. "Wow, I never had my fingerprints taken!"

"Now you'd better not commit any crime!"

CHAPTER EIGHTEEN

Zuzana and Adam 2005

ADAM GETS ON WITH THE AMERICAN RELATIVES JUST FINE

The airport was chaotic; they kept changing the numbers of the baggage conveyor belts and there were lots of people.

When we finally got out, the twins, Jack and Tony, were holding a board with our name, waving. They were identical, and I couldn't tell them apart. Their older brother Ross was driving. I hadn't met Ross before either.

"I couldn't let these lunatics pick you up, Zuzana, they both only just passed their driving tests."

Adam looked envious; he would have liked to learn how to drive, too. I was waiting for him to have more common sense first.

Ross was only 35 but looked older. He told me he worked on Wall Street.

"Yes, earning an insane amount of money!" one of the twins said.

Ross made a face. "My brothers are nuts!" he said.

Ross didn't live in Sea Girt with their grandfather Jürgen and their mother Lucy. He lived in New York, but he came for the weekend. Tony and Jack were home on holiday from university. They both studied at Penn University in Philadelphia and played American football for their college. It showed as they were both huge. Not fat, just muscles. I always thought the American football players just looked big because of the padding, but Tony and Jack were just wearing T-shirts right now and still looked enormous. Adam looked willowy in comparison. They didn't shut up the whole journey; it seemed as if they were constantly arguing, but it was just banter. Adam asked them about the football team, and Jack said, "Don't ask Tony – he only got to the team because we are twins. He can't run without dropping the ball." Jack had got a football scholarship and Tony hadn't, so there might have been something in it.

"Nope, they only picked Jack by mistake; when the coach came to watch us play in high school, he liked my game, but he thought I was Jack. He still can't tell us apart."

"Sometimes I pretend I am Tony. I play badly and then run faster and score just when the other team think I am my brother who sucks at football. Tony is just in the team as a double, a decoy."

They began play-fighting until Ross had had enough and told them to cut it out and sit in the car. "Act your age, not your shoe size!" he said.

I sighed with relief. The twins were fun, but too loud.

Adam started making fun of the questionnaire at the border.

"*Have you ever engaged or seek to engage in any terrorist activity, in espionage, sabotage or genocide?* Really? What a silly question."

I apologised for his behaviour, but Ross told me that we'd get some adult conversation eventually.

Ross explained the questionnaire. "The question allows for easy prosecution in the future. The point of asking these questions is that if you lie, you have obtained a visa by fraud and can be deported if you are found out. Let's say somebody lies about his previous terrorist activity. He can be deported even if he has not done anything illegal while here."

He sounded like a lawyer. Ross didn't look like somebody you could joke with. Dry and dead serious. Life must have been difficult for him in a family of jokers. I still didn't quite understand his point. Adam opened his mouth to say something but didn't when he saw my warning look. The boys started asking me how they were related.

"I think you are third cousins, but really it is like we Czechs say: 'Our cow and your cow drank from the same pond.' Why don't you google it? Mr Google knows everything!"

Ross gave me a look. He probably thought, *Not another crazy relative!*

The house was more beautiful than I remembered. Lucy stood at the door.

I could see Adam didn't like the way she looked. Lucy wore an almost identical outfit to the last time I saw her. She wasn't attractive, but she was fun. Adam was a bit surprised by her swearing. The F-word was never far away. Adam liked it as neither I nor Harry swore a lot.

"Why don't you sit with my father? He will show you some family pictures."

Jürgen looked frail and seemed confused like his wife used to be. Lucy gave him a large album and I went to help her cook dinner, while the twins set the table. Ross talked into his mobile phone.

Jürgen showed the pictures to Adam: his beautiful wife, many others, even my mother.

"Your grandma Magda was very cute, but boy, she knew it!" I was surprised how fond the relatives were of my mother.

Their house felt like home. We stayed for almost two weeks, and Adam had a great time with the boys: sailing, playing basketball, swimming, fishing in the sea. He climbed all the trees in their garden. Lucy didn't like it. "Zuzana, aren't you worried that he could break his neck?"

"No, Adam was always like a monkey – never fell off a tree."

It was nice seeing the three boys together; they were like brothers.

Lucy had an easy relationship with them; her humour was sometimes cutting but always funny. Even when she was telling the twins off, they ended up laughing. I remember they were supposed to do the vacuum cleaning, but the carpet still had some crumbs visible.

Lucy was not amused. "You were supposed to do the vacuum cleaning, Tony. It was your turn or was it Jack?" she said.

"I know, I did it, but maybe you need a new vacuum cleaner."

I looked at Adam; he looked away. It was obvious Tony was not telling the truth.

Lucy's answer was funny. "Don't talk to me. Whenever your mouth is moving, you're lying."

Tony kissed her and said, "Sorry, Mum," and went to get the vacuum cleaner.

I invited them to London. I told them maybe they could try to play rugby with Adam's friends, that it was like American football, but they laughed. "We heard rugby is vicious, and the players don't wear any protection!"

"Don't take her seriously – Mum doesn't know much about sport," said Adam.

"Our mum doesn't either!" said Jack.

Then all three tried to make me and Lucy join them for a ball game, which was only a way to tease us. I have always been useless at ball games, but Lucy wasn't much better. When we had enough of our sons' teasing, Lucy and I went shopping. I'd like to think Lucy was much better dressed when Adam and I left. I tried to change her wardrobe. Those elasticated skirts were awful.

We went to see Miriam; Adam was excited by the spy story. We stayed with her in Brooklyn, and she was as chatty as before. This time, she talked about her first years in America. Adam listened. She talked more to Adam than me. She said she'd hated America when they first arrived.

"We arrived in New York; it was such a big place, all those tall buildings. My parents were staying with a friend in Brooklyn in a tiny room, and they had no place for me. There was no space, and we all remembered our large apartment in Prague."

"Where did you live?" asked Adam.

"In Parizska."

"Wow, that is the most elegant street in Prague – even I know it."

Miriam liked that Adam spoke Czech. "It is so good your mother made you bilingual. My parents wanted me to learn English and spoke only English to me, but my father still wasn't happy. He said that I needed to learn English from native speakers, so they sent me to live with another family, the Abramovics. Adam, I hated it. They were orthodox, originally from Carpathian-Ukraine, the eastern part of Czechoslovakia. The family spoke Yiddish, and although it is like German, I didn't understand a thing! They mostly spoke English to me and sometimes German, only switching to Yiddish when they didn't want me to understand. I overheard them talking about me. 'The bloody refugee girl – why did we agree to take her in? She is not even a proper Jew.' They were speaking in English; I think they wanted me to hear it." Miriam looked upset.

"Why did they not think you were a proper Jew?" asked Adam.

"They ate kosher, and Mrs Abramovic shaved her hair and wore a wig. Her clothes were black or brown. She was the same age as my mummy, but she looked much older. Mr Abramovic was tall and skinny, with big ears and long locks. He was also dressed in black and wore a hat. The hat was big, but his ears still stuck out."

That made Adam chuckle.

"Adam only saw orthodox Jews in films, and as you know, my husband Harry comes from a black Roman Catholic family," I said.

Miriam gave me a look when I said 'black', but she didn't say anything.

"The family had twin daughters the same age as me," said Miriam with a heavy sigh. "I was miserable. They called me a 'lousy refugee' and to this day I hate that word – refugee. School was also terrible. I spent every evening in front of the bathroom mirror trying to learn English so nobody could tell I was different. The 'th' sound was especially difficult. Then I would cry myself to sleep. I was so unhappy, I wanted to die. I thought about killing myself every day. *I don't want to be in this stupid country; they don't want us here*, I thought. But then I realised that they didn't want us in Europe either."

"You would have died in Europe." Adam was starting to think that maybe the emigration question was not that simple.

Miriam told us she decided to kill herself; she leaned from the window, head down, and she was already almost out when one of the girls, Raisa, pulled her back by her legs.

"Was she nicer to you after that?" asked Adam. He took Miriam's small, wrinkled hand and kissed it.

"That evil little girl saved my life, but no, she wasn't any nicer."

Then Miriam told us about the Natural History Museum.

"I want to take Adam there; it is as nice as the one in London," I said.

"No, I hate that place. I will never go there again."

Miriam told us that the girls took her to the Natural History Museum, and they ran away, losing her on purpose. Miriam didn't know how to get out or how to get home. The image of a little girl crying in that large museum, being lost, was painful. She was there for hours when she saw one of the sisters, Ahava, hiding behind a column. Miriam pretended that she thought that they'd lost her by mistake.

"Sorry, Ahava, I got lost. I am so glad I found you. Where is Raisa?" she said.

"Did you tell their parents?" asked Adam, who was furious with those girls and wanted to hear about their punishment.

"No, when we got home, Mrs Abramovic asked me how it was.

'We had a great time,' I said. She was an enemy. One can lie to enemies."

"Did you at least tell your parents how unhappy you were?" I asked.

"No. Never. I saw my parents once a week; my father and my mother now both had jobs. They still lived in that tiny flat in Brooklyn. I used to visit them on Sundays. My mother cooked lunch, often pork, partly to compensate for my kosher eating, partly because pork was cheap. Daddy usually took me to the Brooklyn museum or to the botanical garden. Sometimes, we sat on a bench and drew pictures; his were so much nicer than mine. My parents counted on me being strong. I tried not to show to them how unhappy I was."

"How old were you? Thirteen?" I asked.

"Yes."

"You were very brave, Aunt Miriam," said Adam.

She just smiled and took another sip of red wine. "I didn't really have a choice."

When she went to the loo, he whispered, "Miriam is wonderful, isn't she?"

At dinner, Adam said something unexpected; I thought Miriam was going to be cross. "I propose a trip tomorrow. I will take you to the Natural History Museum, and we will stay together. Just wait – it will be nice, I promise."

Miriam looked uneasy. "But I hate that building, I have never been there since that day with Raisa and Ahava."

Adam persevered. "Mum said it's a nice museum. Tomorrow, we will wipe those memories away. I won't let you out of my sight. If we get lost, we get lost together."

To my amazement, she agreed. I didn't go with them; I went shopping and met them for lunch. It was a miracle: Miriam smiled and told me about all those things they saw; it was as if she was a little girl again, going to the museum with a loving brother.

In the evening, Adam and I went to dinner. Miriam said she was tired.

"Well done, Adam, I am proud of you," I said.

He told me that after a year with the Abramovic family, Miriam moved back to her parents. Samuel got a good job as an architect, while Bertha worked in an office. After the war, Miriam went to study architecture at the university. She became a successful architect – unusual for a woman of her generation – but never married.

I was curious as to why, so later, when Adam went to play on his computer and we were drinking an evening mint tea, I asked her, "Miriam, why did you never marry?"

"I never wanted to; I have seen too many women sacrificing their careers for their marriage," she told me.

I said, "Yes, it is great that it is different now."

Then Miriam surprised me. She said,

"I had a happy life and many lovers. In fact, I have a lover now, but he lives in Montreal. We see each other every month. It's ideal. I'd recommend it." She chuckled.

What was it with those women in my family – Hana, Miriam? They seemed so modern, emancipated, alive. Hana died, of course, but she was more alive than my mother, or other women of her generation I met. I hoped to be like Miriam when I got old.

I spoke to Harry on the phone. I told him the museum story.

"I told you, Zuzana, everybody loves Adam and you – you have a special charm. That's why I married you. People like me, too, as your husband."

He was joking, of course, but he sounded really proud of Adam. I missed Harry, but first I wanted to show Adam more of New York. Ross offered us the chance to stay with him for a couple of weeks before our flight home. He lived in a beautiful flat in Upper Manhattan, close to Central Park. Ross was mostly at work, and I think Adam, like his brothers, got on his nerves a little. Occasionally he took us to dinner to expensive restaurants, and insisted on paying, but we were mostly alone. It was great, spending time with my grown-up son.

Five days before our flight, Ross told us to come home early, as he had a surprise for us.

When we came to his flat at 5pm we heard voices, one of them of a child.

The cold Ross, whom neither of us liked much, did something wonderful. He paid for Irma, her daughter Joan and the little Aaron to fly from California to meet us. Ross booked a hotel for them all. I didn't think we were going to see the Californian relatives. It was such a generous thing to do.

When we went out to dinner, Irma said she would stay in the hotel room to look after Aaron. "Mom is such a wonderful grandmother, but she spoils Aaron rotten," said Joan. Irma and Joan both looked happy.

Adam played with Aaron, and they compared their skin colours. "I could be your brother, Aaron." He offered to babysit instead of Irma, saying they were going to have fun. Adam is good with children, and he wanted to take Aaron to Central Park the next day.

Joan was not sure. "Only if you won't climb trees – Zuzana told me about that!"

"I will try," Adam said.

In the end, we made a compromise. Nobody needed to babysit Aaron; we took him for dinner, too.

Ross took us all to a Harlem restaurant called Red Rooster, a fusion of Swedish and African and Creole food. The chef was an African man adopted by a Swedish family. Apparently, it was famous; even Joan knew it. The food was good, and they had Mexican music.

"I love New York – so much better than London. I wish I could study in America," whispered Adam. "Maybe I could stay with Miriam; I would help her."

"No way," I said. "Finish your course first and then we'll see."

Next day, Adam took Aaron to Central Park and the rest of us – Irma, Joan and I – went shopping to meet them later. They were both filthy when we met them, not just little Aaron. "Mummy, Mummy, Adam showed me how to climb trees – we were playing monkeys!"

"Adam, you promised!" I was cross; Aaron was only five years old. What if something had happened?

"Don't worry, Mum, I was careful, and I also told him stories. He was safe."

Aaron was excited. "Yes, yes, and Adam told me about aliens and spaceships, and strange animals – it was awesome!" Although we were all angry with Adam for breaking his word, we couldn't stay angry for long. The next day, Irma, Joan and Aaron flew back to California, and we went back to England. Ross didn't drive us.

"I don't do airports," he said. "That is what taxis are for."

So he got us a taxi to Newark Airport. I tried to kiss him; he was so kind and generous. But Ross probably didn't do kissing either. He shook my hand and patted Adam's shoulder.

We were both looking forward to telling Harry all about our travelling.

Harry picked us up; we planned to go for a curry. Adam and I were talking nonstop, interrupting each other, while Harry just sat there with an amused smile.

"You are dreadful, I can only say something when you pause for breath!"

CHAPTER NINETEEN

Zuzana 2006

MORE DEATHS

Jürgen died in his sleep; Lucy phoned me. She cried, but then she said, "Oh, I should stop being fucking stupid. He was 98 years old – nobody lives for ever!" I told her what a great daughter she had been, looking after him and Hilda. I loved the way she treated her mother with respect despite her condition.

"That's horseshit; I should have been much more patient with her," she replied. I could hear the twins in the background. "Of course, you couldn't come at short notice. I have plenty of people here – even my ex-husband came."

Lucy must be low if she is talking well about her ex-husband, I thought.

Judita seemed to be keeping well. Jiu told me they were planning to go to New Zealand to visit their daughter Becky, her husband Ben and granddaughter Amy.

"We hope Judita will come with us. She doesn't want to; she says she is too old for the long flight."

"Just pass the phone over to her," I said. "Aunt Judita, you must go to New Zealand – you will have a great time, and you can babysit Amy when the others go out to eat and drink Marlborough County Sauvignon Blanc. I am jealous."

"Are you telling me what to do again, Zuzana? I am 87."

"That's no age; you'll live till you're 100. They can arrange assistance for the flight and you can use a wheelchair – you'll be fine."

"You are really like Magda, never taking no for an answer. And I don't need a wheelchair." She pretended to be cross, but there was a chuckle when she said that.

Funny, that time I didn't mind being compared to my mother. Collecting the family stories made me understand my mother better. I'd forgiven her. I even felt that maybe there was nothing to forgive. I wished our relationship had been better, but maybe being my mother's daughter made me a better parent. I wish she knew that I loved her. I wish I knew. I knew now, and maybe she did… Suddenly I wanted to see Otto and Marie; they were getting frail. They were always the bridge between my mum and myself, and their company made my mother treat me better. I flew to Paris and found Otto was in hospital with pneumonia. He'd stopped Marie from telling me, saying I would fret and that he was all right. He wasn't. He died two days later; we were both there. Otto, the fairy godmother to us all. He was the grandfather I never had. I would have liked Marie to move, live with us in London. I wanted to check it with Harry, but he suggested it before I could say anything.

"After the funeral, we can take her back with us, at least for a month, then we'll see." he said.

CHAPTER TWENTY

Zuzana 2006

The solicitor in a large office on the Champs-Élysées was like somebody from the 19th century. His office had Louis VI furniture and a huge crystal chandelier, with high stuccoed ceilings. He read the will, first in French, then he read a prepared English translation.

At first, there were no surprises: the apartment, various stocks and shares of course went to Marie. But then the list started. I got the Prague apartment. "I cannot accept that," I said, but Marie told me they'd both always wanted me to have it. "It's mostly furnished with your family's furniture and carpets anyway, and I am too old to travel there now." There was a long list of all his living relatives, and many charities. I started to worry Marie would not have enough money to live on. "I am still quite rich," whispered Marie.

"I'll accept on the condition that you come back to London with us."

In the end, nobody contested Otto's generous will. Marie came with us and insisted she was going to cook for us. Harry was pleased. I am a lazy cook, always making shortcuts. Marie couldn't get over the fact that I used powdered garlic instead of fresh. Harry, who often used to be too busy in the surgery to come for dinner and ate sandwiches instead, suddenly came home on time. When I teased him about it, he said, kissing Marie, "Our meals didn't used to be Michelin-star standard." He was right: Marie's cooking was wonderful, but she was old, and I worried that it might be too much for her.

I tried to help – cut the vegetables, wash the dishes, clean the kitchen. Marie claimed she was fine. "You know that I enjoy cooking, Zuzana – go back to your writing."

I wasn't looking for another job; I was writing short stories, poetry. I made lists of agents, publishers. I was determined to become a writer. "I can always self-publish if nobody likes what I write," I told Adam. Maybe I was just fishing for compliments: Adam believed in my writing; so did Harry.

Marie spent two months in our house, but then she wanted to go back to Paris.

Unfortunately, we were back in the French solicitor's office three months later: Marie had a stroke at home and died immediately. I was pleased she spent some time with us before that happened.

Marie's estate was going to be divided between various relatives. One of them was her sister I didn't know she had. Marie never talked about her family. In her will there was a long letter for me.

Dear Zuzana,

If you are reading this, I am dead. You must have been wondering why nobody ever mentioned my family. That is because I haven't seen them since my marriage to Otto. I come from a farming family from South Moravia by the Austrian border. My father had a big farm. You wouldn't think so, knowing me, but as a child, I used to milk cows, pluck chickens and feed the geese. My father was strict, but I loved him, until I brought home Otto, who came to ask for my hand in marriage. That is what we used to do in those times.

My father was nice and seemed pleased about my fiancé being a well-dressed man, obviously wealthy, till Otto told him he was a Jew. Antisemitism was not common in Czechoslovakia, and I never thought it could be a problem. My father completely changed. "I will never, never give my daughter to a dirty Jew!"

Otto got red in the face and wanted to leave. I didn't let him. "I am coming with you, my darling." We eloped; I never saw my family again. I wrote for Christmas, but they never replied. Otto made me so happy, and your family was lovely – even your great-grandmother Olga was nice to me. Nicer than to her other daughters-in-law.

Then when the war finished, I saw my father's picture in a newspaper. "A Nazi collaborator and informer sentenced to ten years' imprisonment." I couldn't believe it. Otto asked me if I wanted to go and see him in prison. I didn't. I wrote to my sister, but she didn't reply. The family farm was confiscated even before the communists took power, as the property of a German collaborator. I don't even know when my parents died. My sister never replied to any of my letters.

I never forgave my family for what they did, but my sister is old and frail. I would like her to inherit at least something. I also have an unusual last wish, and I am counting on you to follow it. I do not want to have a funeral. I want to be cremated, and my ashes destroyed. Not spread with a ceremony. The reason I want to do it is to honour and remember all those Jewish relatives who didn't have a grave either. It is also my penitence for my family. I know their behaviour is not my fault but knowing my wish will be fulfilled will make my dying easier. Please, Zuzana, do it for me. I loved Otto's family and I feel not having a funeral or a grave will bring me closer to them. Who knows? Maybe there is an afterlife.

Love,
Your great-aunt Marie

I thought about all those family stories, and about racism, and antisemitism, and how despite that, the world is full of wonderful people like Marie. I was so proud of her, and I wondered if Otto knew about this plan. He would be proud of her, too.

CHAPTER TWENTY-ONE

Zuzana 2006

I CAN FORGIVE OLGA

I never met that formidable matriarch, my grandfather's mother Olga. Listening to my mother talking about her, I never liked Olga. Yet, my mother and all the others loved her. I often wondered why.

Olga was a widow. Her husband Ruben, my great-grandfather, was an owner of a large, thriving leather goods factory. He had made a lot of money supplying the Austro-Hungarian army in the First World War. He died in 1922.

In the photographs, Ruben was short and had a big moustache. He looked like the Austrian Emperor Franz Joseph. I didn't know much about this great-grandfather, but I never liked him either after hearing about his matchmaking, bribing his son-in-law to marry his daughter Helena. After his death, Olga inherited half of the factory, and his children – my grandfather Bruno and his brothers Karel and Otto and his sisters Helena and Judita – inherited the other half. Otto ran it for all of them, drawing a large salary, dividing the profits for his mother and siblings. My grandfather Bruno preferred his law practice and Karel his university post. Of course, nobody asked the girls if they were interested; that was unthinkable. My great-aunts Helena and Judita got married, and the factory dividends were looked after by their husbands. The factory was confiscated by the

Nazis soon after their invasion in March 1939. Aryanised, as they called it.

Olga ruled her children with an iron fist. She was strict, and although they had a governess when they were little, it was Mama Olga who distributed the punishments she deemed necessary. Her children loved her. Olga was beautiful: large almond-shaped eyes, long thick dark red hair which later turned white. She was very elegant. I remember Great-Uncle Otto telling me about her once when I visited them in France. I was pregnant with Adam.

"Mama was a lady. She was perfect and demanded perfection. Even if she had to use the cane on us to get it."

"Did she really beat you, Otto?"

"Oh, yes, but only if we deserved it," he said.

I was not so sure if they all thought like this. I thought about what my mother told me about her childhood. She was quite naughty, but her father almost never beat her. Maybe Bruno remembered those beatings he got as a child from his mother Olga.

"Grandma Olga used to play chess and cards with us. She played well. Everybody always did what she said. I always wanted to be like her," my mother told me. Perhaps she tried; I was just not as obedient as my grandfather and his siblings. And it was a different time.

The main reason why I never liked my great-grandmother Olga was my beloved grandmother Franzi, one of Olga's daughters-in-law. In my eyes, Grandma Franzi was perfect. The fact that Olga never thought her daughter-in-law Franzi was good enough for her son, and that she never treated Franzi with respect, made me dislike Olga, despite never having met her. Later, speaking to other relatives, I found out that Olga was a nightmarish mother-in-law to everybody. Nobody was quite good enough for her children. I also remembered Irma telling me that she would never forgive her grandmother for killing her parents and her brother. And these was Miriam, who called my great-grandmother Olga the Monster, or the Evil Witch.

In 1945, Great-Grandmother Olga came back from Theresienstadt ill with TB and broken. She cried and talked about her poor children. Before she died, she apparently kept saying, "It was all my fault."

Many people emigrated in 1938 or 1939, but to be fair to Olga, at the time, not even the Nazis knew what was coming. The plan to murder all the Jews only came years later, in 1942.

I was already starting to forgive Olga, and then I found the letter in a box in Marie's flat. It was addressed to Otto and dated 3 March 1953 and it was written in German, with beautiful, elegant handwriting. Olga wrote it before I was born. The letter was long, sad and very moving. Some of the ink was smudged, and I wondered whose tears might have caused that. The letter described the family stories I already knew, but from her perspective.

Dear Otto,

Thank you for your lovely letter, but so full of unnecessary remorse. Stop worrying about me, that you left me behind. It was the only solution, and it was what I wanted. You have always been a good son, and I know that you were worried about leaving me here. I am writing this to tell how glad I am that you and Marie are safe in the West. What I am going to write is painful for you and for me, but I must write this down. I need to try to make sense of my life. It is my fault so many of the family died; they could have left. Do you remember how in 1938, everybody was talking about leaving? You thought that we should sell the factory and leave.

But I told everybody that emigrating was unimaginable, that there had always been antisemitism, and our family had coped, that we would cope this time, too. Remember?

"We should stay together," I told you.

Our family had lived in Prague for almost six centuries. That was where we should stay, not break this wonderfully long tradition. I told you all that we were a well-respected good family. That the Czechs were not antisemitic; neither were the Prague Germans. I remember the pressure I put everybody under.

Do you remember the lunch? The cook made roast goose, the soup was marvellous and so was the cake. But nobody paid any attention to the food. I might have as well served you bread and butter. You were all arguing. Marie didn't want to leave and neither did Helena. Hans kept talking about the possibility we all had because of his brother's influence at the American embassy in Prague. Irma's parents and brother could have been alive. In 1946, when Irma found out they were all dead, she shouted at me that I killed them. She immediately apologised, but Otto, she was right.

You all listened to me and you shouldn't have. You were good, loving and obedient children.

Of course, we lost all our property and half of the family died. I keep thinking it was me, not just the Nazis who were responsible.

I was so glad that Judita and Simon left in 1938, too… I didn't want to let her go either, but she was pregnant, and she asked me if I really thought Europe was a good place for a Jewish baby to be born.

"You are my mother," Judita said. "You always did the best for us. I want to do the best thing for my baby, too. Please, don't make us stay!"

I told her to go. The only good decision I made that year.

I was devastated in Theresienstadt. You and Marie could fortunately stay in Prague, but how did everybody suffer! Your poor brothers and Helena. If it weren't for me, most of us could have been safe in America. I stopped it; it was awful when only Franzi, with Magda, Irma and Hana came back, remember?

I want to die. I am an old woman, and I survived the war while my beloved children and grandchildren died. Outliving your grandchildren is unbearable.

Do you understand why I was pushing you to emigrate in 1948 when the communists came to power? You didn't want to leave, but I am so pleased you did. I didn't want you to make the same mistake again. Staying till it's too late.

Franzi looks after me well; she lives with Magda and her husband, but she visits me daily. I am a burden to her, but I hope I will die soon. We might never see you again; we can't travel, and you would go to jail if you came back.

I hope you will all forgive me, especially the young ones – Hana, Irma, Magda. But I don't deserve to be forgiven.

Otto, enjoy your life with your wonderful wife – you made a good choice in Marie – and stop worrying about me. I will die soon, and whatever happens after death, I am ready. Magda is expecting a baby, a new member of the family. Please don't worry about me. Once more, sorry.

Your mother

The baby was me, of course. There were no more letters after that. There was a photo of her, an old frail woman with thick white hair. She died in that year, 1953, before I was born. Reading the letter was heart-breaking.

I was starting to understand Olga. Reading what she felt made me realise that she wasn't a monster. She loved her family. Yes, she was probably snobby and bossy, but not evil. She told them not to emigrate because she believed that was the right thing to do. She made a bad decision.

It made me realise that a parent needs to know when to let go. Olga's children didn't want to leave her behind; my mother didn't want to leave my grandmother behind either. She felt abandoned when I emigrated. Maybe my mother was a better daughter than I was.

However, I also knew that I would not try to prevent my Adam from following his dreams.

Adam still sometimes struggled with his identity. He met some Jewish orthodox students who were shocked when he didn't know about Yom Kippur and other holidays.

"I am not Jewish enough for the Jews or black enough for the Grenadians, or Czech enough for the Czechs. What am I, Mum?"

I told him what Hilda, my great-aunt, wrote in a hospital questionnaire in America years before anybody realised the extent of her dementia. Under 'RACE' she filled in 'HUMAN'.

Adam smiled and said, "Not so demented after all then."